B
Y

You just might get it. And if the wish has been granted by an elf, the consequences may be far different from anything you could possibly imagine, as you'll soon discover when you read these spell-binding, original tales of encounters with the lords and ladies of enchantment.

"Under the Skin"—Would the chance to escape from her current life let her see her world with different eyes?

"Netted"—A simple fisherman, he'd never had much luck until he caught magic in his net. Only time would tell whether this luck was good or bad. . . .

"Woman of the Elfmounds"—They were the ene-mies of his people but he'd forgotten how to hate them. Had he been caught by love, or a most cun-ning spell of imprisonment?

"A Soul to Be Gained"—He really liked the mortal world and wanted to spend his life there. But his seven years were almost up, and unless he could find a magic loophole he'd never be allowed back again. . . .

ELF MAGIC

More Spellbinding Anthologies
Brought to You by DAW:

ELF FANTASTIC *Edited by Martin H. Greenberg*. They are beings of legend from a realm just beyond our own, a kingdom where time holds little power, where beauty casts its aura over the natural world, and where magic can transform anything—or anyone. So let such spellcasters as Jane Yolen, Andre Norton, Dennis McKiernan, and Elizabeth Ann Scarborough reveal the perils and promises of elfin magic in stories that may lead the unsuspecting into the fairy hills only to emerge into a world far different from the one they left behind.

TAROT FANTASTIC *Edited by Martin H. Greenberg and Lawrence Schimel*. Some of today's most imaginative writers—such as Charles de Lint, Tanya Huff, Rosemary Edghill, Nancy Springer, Kate Elliott, Teresa Edgerton, and Michelle West—cast fortunes for the unsuspecting in sixteen unforgettable tales ranging from chilling to whimsical, from provocative to ominous.

CASTLE FANTASTIC *Edited by John DeChancie and Martin H. Greenberg*. Here are sixteen original stories created especially for this volume, from the final tale set in Roger Zelazny's unforgettable *Amber,* to the adventure of a floating castle in search of a kingdom, to the legendary citadel of King Arthur. Join such master architects of enchantment as Roger Zelazny, George Zebrowski, Jane Yolen, David Bischoff, and Nancy Springer on a series of castle adventures that will have fantasy lovers and D&D players begging for the keys to the next keep on the tour.

ELF
MAGIC

edited by Martin H. Greenberg

D A W   B O O K S ,   I N C .

DONALD   A.   WOLLHEIM,   FOUNDER

375 Hudson Street, New York, NY 10014

ELIZABETH R. WOLLHEIM
SHEILA E. GILBERT
PUBLISHERS

First Printing, October 1997

1 2 3 4 5 6 7 8 9

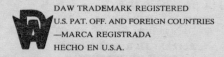

DAW TRADEMARK REGISTERED
U.S. PAT. OFF. AND FOREIGN COUNTRIES
—MARCA REGISTRADA
HECHO EN U.S.A.

PRINTED IN THE U.S.A.

ACKNOWLEDGMENTS

Introduction © 1997 by Martin H. Greenberg.
Under the Skin © 1997 by Michelle West.
Netted © 1997 by Josepha Sherman.
The Phaerie Bride © 1997 by Rosemary Edghill.
Belle Bloody Merciless Dame © 1997 by Jane Yolen.
The Last Warrior © 1997 by Tim Waggoner.
Woman of the Elfmounds © 1997 by Paul Edwin Zimmer.
A Soul to Be Gained © 1997 by Blake Cahoon.
Sleight of Bride © 1997 Brooks Peck.
The Shoemaker and the Elvis © 1997 by Lawrence Schimel.
The Marble King © 1997 by Gary A. Braunbeck.
The Céilidh © 1997 by Connie Hirsch.
Kind Hunter © 1997 by Pati Nagle.
The Gypsies' Curse © 1997 by Elizabeth Ann Scarborough.
Elf Help © 1997 by John DeChancie.
With His Own Wings © 1997 by Bruce Holland Rogers.
The Unbetrayable Reply © 1997 by Peter Crowther.
Mortal Things © 1997 by Esther Friesner.
My Lord Teaser © 1997 by Richard Parks.

CONTENTS

INTRODUCTION

Imagine, just for a moment, that you are not reading this introduction, but are instead walking the gently rolling hills of Ireland. It is a calm spring night, and there is a light mist in the air. You're following a winding road through the grassy meadows when you hear a commotion some distance off, and a faint light catches your eye.

Deciding to get a better look, you creep closer, leaving the road behind. A few more paces and you come upon an event the likes of which you've never seen before.

Dancing gaily around a large fire are creatures whose majestic beauty takes your breath away. Slim, graceful men leap and whirl in the intricate steps of jigs and flings, the traditional dances of Ireland. Lithe, elegant women whose beauty takes your breath away perform the dances faster than the eye can follow, making it appear as easy as walking. Off to one side, a group of the handsome beings plays lively music on flute, bagpipes, and a simple round drum you've learned during your stay is called a *bodhran*.

As if on cue, the music stops and all eyes turn to you. The men and women are not at all shy about being watched; in fact, they motion you to come forward and join in the dance. Their voices are high and musical, and as they come closer, you see the narrow faces with almond-shaped eyes and the slim, pointed ears.

At this point, anyone from the Emerald Isle would be advising you to run away as far and as fast as your legs can carry you. For what you've stumbled upon is a midnight dance of the *Sidhe,* or elves.

Mind you these are not the small, winged faeries of European folklore. The *Sidhe* are the keepers of the faerie kingdom in Celtic folklore, mysterious, immortal, and gifted with powers both wonderful and terrible, depending on how they choose to use them. Do one of them a favor, and you may be rewarded with your heart's delight. Cross them, however insignificantly, and their revenge can be terrible to behold.

So think carefully before you step into that magic circle. You may pass a wonderful time dancing the evening away, only to return to your lodging to find that one, three, perhaps even seven years have passed in your absence. You may be bewitched into going with the *Sidhe,* back to their magic kingdom, where time stands still and the court of the elves reigns forever. No matter what happens, it will be an experience you will never forget.

The stories collected in this book are many different looks at the *Sidhe,* and how they might interact with our mortal world. From a water-elf who grants a remarkable ability to a poor fisherman and teaches him the meaning of compassion in Josepha Sherman's "Netted" to an intrigue-filled adventure in the elfin lands of Richard Parks' "My Lord Teaser," the faerie folk have come forth to put on a regal show like no other. So take that fateful step into the faerie circle, if you dare.

And, as we asked you at the beginning of this introduction, imagine. . . .

UNDER THE SKIN
by Michelle West

Michelle West's latest novel is *The Broken Crown,* the first in the *Sun Sword* series. Other notable novels among her fantasy works include the duology *The Sacred Hunt,* consisting of the books *Hunter's Oath* and *Hunter's Death.* Her extraordinary short fiction also appears in *Tarot Fantastic, Return of the Dinosaurs, Fantastic II,* and *Enchanted Forests.* She lives in Ontario, Canada.

The rain that fell in the city was the color of her eyes, clear and gray where it blanketed the traffic-strewn streets with the persistence of its fall.

The river that ran between roads, set into a valley that nestled between forked branches of highway, was swollen with April movement. She came out of that river, like the first shoots of spring, into air redolent with the speech of cars, strange and terrible and now, to her alone, ordinary—as ordinary as rain, as snow, as the movement of leaves in their season.

She had chosen her form, had slept in it, and now, awakened, she tested the air. And then, at last, she called forth a glimmer of power—power older than even the valley in which she stood—and fashioned for herself a seeming, a glamour, beneath which she might do her work.

For in this diminished time, work was all that was left her; she had no court, no politics, nothing but magic stripped of place, of any context which was not hers.

Hard, to learn the ways of trees. She remembered her youth, and their voices which were now so very muted. Harder, to learn the ways of squirrels, bears, foxes, of stags, for their speech traveled with them, died and was

born again, was perturbed in all things by the short
bursts of their life.

It was easy—she remembered it clearly—to learn the
speech of man. Easy to think that she understood it,
that creatures that barely lived longer than animals could
be understood.

Had she but known.

"Janie, come downstairs now and take the garbage
out! How many times do I have to tell you?"

About as many times, Jane thought, as she shut her
book and rolled off he bed, *as you say everything else.*
"I'm coming!"

"That's what you said fifteen minutes ago, young
lady!"

Jane Thornton was not a stupid girl, so she didn't
correct her mother. Instead, she swung the thin door
wide, ran out into the hall, pivoted on the banister and
practically sailed down the stairs, all in one continuous
motion that ended with the wall in the vestibule. Her
fingers left smudge marks.

Jane's mother was standing, arms folded, beside the
microwave in the kitchen. "I don't know what's gotten
into you lately," she said, as Jane lifted the two twist-
tied garbage bags. "All you do anymore is sit up in your
room doing God knows what."

She mumbled a "Yes, mother" under her breath and
refused to meet her mother's eyes. They were dark,
those eyes, where they'd once been bright. Jane couldn't
remember the last time her mother had smiled, although
a cynical grimace was pretty commonplace these days.
Not much to be happy about, really.

It was probably her father's fault, and her father
was—damn him anyway—quite happy in his new life
with his lovely new wife and his bright new home. No
room there for either Jane or her mother, although he
called Jane regularly and had even sent an idiotic pink
sweater for her last birthday.

On the other hand, it was hard not to understand his
choice when her mother was like this. She dragged the
garbage to the can at the side of the house, and then,
after stuffing the two bags into the can, headed down to

the curb with it. As she trudged back up the walk to the house, it began to rain. Warm drops hit her upturned face as she studied the roiling clouds above without the slightest interest in shelter.

Rain.

Beneath it, a stirring. She finished her work and waited, thinking it odd to have traveled this far.

She had no kin. And perhaps it was time, after all.

It wasn't that Jane didn't have friends; she had them. It was just the only two that she'd ever really given a damn about were now living in Arizona and Quebec. They wrote, and she wrote; after her father left, she wasn't allowed to make long distance calls anymore because it was too expensive. But it didn't matter. The letters had become few and far between, and she knew that Tracy and Corinne had gone on with their lives, meeting new people and learning to fit into the new places that had called them away.

Rain fell, unbroken; the air rumbled as if the skyscape of cloud were the victim of a quake; white light illuminated the sky above, and she tried to catch sight of the heavens in the fading afterimage.

It was hard to believe that at some time in the early 1900s Arundel Avenue and the streets that surrounded it were considered the very outskirts of the city. Now, buried beneath the network of parkettes and parking lots that paralleled the Danforth, the subway trains rumbled like living metal worms, and a mere fifteen minutes took you right to the heart of the city.

The trees that lined the streets here towered over the rooftops; they were huge old maples for the most part, and they had always been huge and old. Their roots were sunk well past people's basements, just as the leaves were well above their bedrooms; they twisted and broke old pipes as they grew, and every so often—in a storm like this—they dropped the heavy burden of their branches on the power lines.

Still, the city hadn't seen fit to cut them down or rid the neighborhood of them, and Jane walked beneath leaves which were lit on the underside by street lamps, and above by lightning's occasional flashes.

Where do you go when you have nowhere to go?

Some people went to cafes, and some to dance clubs; some to bars and some to parks, some to the islands in the harbor and some to bookstores along the Danforth—others with cars went to stretches of empty wilderness where one could be alone by one's own choice and not the choice of everyone else around you. Alone, rather than lonely.

Jane Thornton had no car. She had a license—it was fairly recent—but her dad had taken the car because her mother lived close to a subway. And besides, really, her mother didn't have money for anything that was comfort: alcohol, food.

The city had wild patches, but no wilderness, no wildness.

Except in storms like this. Jane looked down and realized that the streets were empty; even the headlights of cars were gone. She closed her eyes and the rain hit her face. Thunder roared, and she roared back; the roar held no words, but then, words were not needed.

"Where were you?" Her mother's voice, slurred only a little. Later in the evening, it would probably be slurred a whole lot more—Jane gave it fifty-fifty. Her friends wondered why she didn't drink. Well, they had; she didn't see much of them now.

She didn't bother to answer the question, but her mother didn't expect an answer by now; it wasn't so late that she'd been worried. "Your father called."

"So?"

"So call him back or he'll blame me for not delivering his message."

She mounted the stairs two at a time as the rain's momentary clarity was destroyed by her life.

". . . anyway, Pat and I were wondering if you'd like to come over for Sunday dinner this week."

"No."

"Janie, I haven't seen you in almost six months."

"School's been keeping me busy."

"Which is why you're failing."

Mom told you that?

"My grades are none of your business," she said, biting back words, holding them in.

"You're still my daughter, Janie. Your grades are very much my business. Especially if you aren't listening to your mother." He fought the words back, too—his temper and hers were not so different when they were angry. But he was older, better at it. "Janie, we'd really like to see you. *I'd* really like to see you."

She was angry at them both, and her anger was sudden, like the storm had been; the words in her throat were a rumble, and then a roar. "Dad, you just don't get it do you?" He didn't have the chance to reply. "I don't come to dinner because I can't stand the sight of Pat, or you for that matter."

"Janie, don't you—"

"Don't you tell me what to do! You lost that right when you lied to us, cheated on us, and took off on us!"

"If your mother—"

"My mother doesn't have anything to do with this! Do you think I'm too stupid to figure it out on my own? Where do you get off telling me *I'm* selfish or *I'm* spoiled? *I* didn't promise to love and honor Mom until death do us part—*you* did!"

Silence, then. Her hands were shaking as she pressed the receiver to her ear, to her lips. She was waiting for his anger to flood back along the wires that bound them together in this conversation.

But that wasn't what he offered her, smug bastard. He never gave her what she needed. "Janie, try to understand. Life with your mother wasn't ever very easy."

"And living with you was better?"

"No—probably not for her." His words were so calm and so measured; she hated them.

"Is that you speaking, Dad—or is that the fancy therapist you're seeing?"

Silence was better than patience, and he was silent for another thirty seconds. She counted them. Then, "When you fall in love for the first time, you'll understand it better. You've never been in love, Janie."

"You mean I've never been in lust," she snapped back. "And you're wrong. But at least I knew it for what it was."

"That's enough, Janie. You've never been with anyone that's as good for you, as good to you, as Pat is to me."

"Is she? Is she really that good?"

She heard an intake of breath so sharp it made her smile. But then he said, "I'm sorry that we can't talk right now. I never meant to hurt either of you. I didn't do this to hurt you—and I hope one day you'll understand that. But I deserved that chance to be happy, and I won't listen to you cut down my wife."

He hung up before she could.

What about us, you bastard? What about our happiness?

She was strong, was Jane Thornton; she didn't even start to cry.

There was a resonance about anger and grief that had its own feel, stripped of words and expression and humanity. In the valley she had chosen for her awakening, she stirred, stood, lifted her chin. Testing something that was not just air, but the scent of approach. Her own.

The sky's burden was shed by rain's work; sun cast a shadow, long and thin into the straggly grasses. That shadow was unmoving in a way that nothing but the great metal bridge above her was. She waited, as if she were not part of life, of the living.

The next morning, Jane cut school. School was a waste of time, anyway. A bunch of teachers tried to "help" you in your "difficult" situation. Jane wanted nothing from them but to be left alone.

The only way to be left alone was not to be there. So she walked the quiet streets, beneath the towering trees. Followed them, stepping over the cracks in the sidewalk because of the old childhood rhymes. She made a point of hitting all the lines, though.

She even paused in front of her house, thought about going in; her mother was at work at the office. No one

would be there. She made it as far as the front door.
Turned the knob. Walked away.

Home was the last place she wanted to be.

I'd be happy, she thought, *if I never had to see this
place again.*

Done, someone said, and she turned at once. A small
child, trying to escape the grip of his mother's hand for
an excursion into the sparse traffic, was the only thing
in sight that was talking.

Never mind. She shoved her hands into her pockets
and began to walk.

She made her way from Arundel to the Danforth, and
from the Danforth down Broadview and into the Don
Valley, following the bike paths beside the river that
nestled between the two sides of the highway. The trees
here were green, when they were alive, and the weeds
were colorful enough, but the river was a dead one, and
if there was animal life other than the dogs that people
walked, it hid very well.

As Jane maneuvered her way beneath the day branch
of a stunted tree, light caught her eye, flashing like reflected sun over rippling water. It came again as she
lifted her head, and she began to slowly wend her way
toward it, leaving behind the smooth asphalt of the
newly paved bike path. Only when she was halfway there
did Jane wonder what she was doing, but by then she
had no intention of going back until she found the
source of the light itself. She bet that it was probably
the window of some abandoned old wreck.

Good damned thing she didn't have two cents to rub
together. She lost.

The trees seemed to grow darker and rougher as she
approached the light; they were tightly packed and
harder to move around. There were thorny plants that
caught the hem of her pants—tearing it twice; there were
burrs that caught her hair, pulling at it rather than joining it.

*I get it, I'm Prince Charming, and this is the forest
of thorns.* She had no intention of kissing any sleeping
woman—wasn't as if she didn't get abused enough by
moronic idiots passing themselves off as human beings—

but she was damned if she was going to give up before she managed to clear the trees.

And she forgot it all as she managed to peer between the forked trunk of a gnarled old tree whose leaves she wouldn't have recognized had she carried an encyclopedia with her. Because framed by the vee of that split trunk was a woman who was shining with a hazy luminescence.

Her hair was a spill of silver that seemed to catch particles of the sun and reflect them, wayward, back; her eyes were wide and dark and perfect, and her lashes, like her hair, were silver. She wore a sleeveless summer dress that caught the breeze and defined its passage. Her skin was white as ivory, and her arms were long and slender; her fingers were smooth and perfect as she lifted her hands in greeting.

"Welcome," she said. If lightning had a voice, this was it; a flash of brilliance that lingered in the air long after the actual light had passed.

Jane opened her mouth to speak, and nothing came out—although if a toad or a frog had climbed out of her lips, it wouldn't have surprised her much. Compared to the silver-haired woman, Jane was everything ugly and awkward.

"Come, Jane Thornton. You found me for a reason. I am not a danger to you, nor you to me. Come."

Jane scraped her way through the fork of the tree and landed with a clumsy thump on her knees. The woman offered her a hand, and after a moment, Jane took it; she looked down and saw her bleeding and scraped skin against the perfect whiteness of light.

"W-who are you?"

"I am a companion, of sorts. Come, walk a while with me in my forest."

Jane looked over her shoulder, seeing the highway and the bridge that towered overhead.

The woman laughed, and her voice was the brook that trickled in silence. "It has taken me many years to understand it, Jane—it is more difficult than I or my distant kin realized it could be. But wilderness is more than isolated forest, and a forest is more than trees." She turned and started to walk and Jane began to amble awkwardly behind her, stubbing her toes and hurting her knees when she fell. Finally, the woman stopped.

"You are Jane Thornton. I have been waiting, I think, for you. It is our—my—way, to wait; to be sought rather than to seek. I am hidden, always, to those who will not look, who don't know how to look. They are many." Her smile was distant for a moment, cool as the winter white of her hair. Sun caught both.

"You are the first to find me in many years, and it means what it means, Jane Thornton. You could not see me if you did not seek a new life, a new beginning." She held out a hand and pulled Jane up from the ground; her hand was cool and strong. "You do not walk well here, but this is only the first time that you've come. It will get easier, I promise you that. Until then, let me aid you." She reached into the swirling folds of her skirts and from them pulled a glorious silver pelt. "You are too large for this walk. Put this on. You will have to remove your old clothing and set it aside."

What'll get easier, Jane wanted to ask, her suspicion struggling to assert control over the little-girl awe that she knew she was in the grip of, but couldn't quite shake. She even opened her mouth but the pelt seemed so perfectly made, so warm and so soft, that she reached for it as if she had never wanted anything else in her life. And as she picked it up, her hands and feet began to tingle.

"It really is safe," the woman said, smiling.

So Jane put it over her head, matching the tip of her nose with the tip of its nose; she touched the edge of its forepaws with the tips of her fingers, and the edges of its hind paws with the balls of her toes. The light in front of her eyes blurred; she cried out in surprise; there was no pain. And the woman smiled and knelt before her. "Do you see what you've become?" She pulled a silvered glass from the swirl of her skirts, just as she had pulled the pelt.

Jane looked into it and saw the reflection of a beautiful silver fox.

"You see?"

"Yes," Jane said—and found that her voice, too, was changed. She fell silent immediately as she saw that the mouth—with its white sharpness of teeth—that had moved with the words she tried to speak were the fox's.

The woman rose, taking the reflection with her. Jane thought her tall and fair—and stopped to wonder why she, at a good foot taller than Jane herself, could navigate dense branches and burrs without pause.

"I am," the woman said softly, her eyes on some distant spot, "alone, Jane. The last of my kind. I am understanding, slowly, yours. I . . . miss my kin, Jane, but I will not see them again until I face what mortals face. And even then, I do not know—our lives are so different. What happens when the mountains are worn away by sand and sea in the course of time? Are they reborn in their glory in any afterlife of mortal making? I think not. I think perhaps it is merely truth that I will never see them again.

"The fox," she said, turning to the young girl, "is a form that I learned in my youth, but although I understand it well, I do not often wear it." Her smile was quiet. "It is a mortal form. The world is bounded by mortal forms.

"For that reason, the pelt is yours to keep, Jane, if you will but leave the life you so dislike now and explore my world with me in the days and years to come. I have much to teach you, and you have much to learn; you are not happy as you are, and I—I have much to teach, I think. Will you accept this?"

Why not? Jane thought. Any life had to be better than the one she was living. "Where are you going?"

"As I said, to tour my forest. Come."

"But—but that leads to the city."

"Does it indeed?" The woman smiled. "Then you must learn to see your city with the eyes I have lent you."

It was still hard to look at the silver-haired woman, but it was also hard to look away. Jane had never seen anything so close to perfect—no, so perfect—in her life. "Who are you?" Her voice was a tickle that came from a tiny fox's chest as she walked slowly, getting use to four light feet.

The woman smiled almost sadly. "I was called many

things. There are stories that survive that still hold grains of truth, although they change to fit their time and their place, as I have done. I ruled, and I served, in my time; I played my game of iron and steel, I stood in shadow while the bells of man tolled; perhaps I even—" and here, her smile was momentarily sly, "carried away their children to realms that do not age them so." She turned toward the east and stared at the sky as if she could see beyond it. "But that was in a different land, and a different time. They are gone now."

There was a quiet longing in the words that made Jane's throat tighten. "Why—why are you here? I mean, why didn't you stay?"

"We do not always have the choice," she replied gravely. "I gave my word, long before your birth, to travel the wise man's road. I have been learning about human forests, about human people." She smiled. "But I have also been searching the forests of the world for others of my kind."

"Did you ever find them?" Jane asked, cocking her head to one side.

"Come. Let us explore the wilds while we have the time."

Jane thought there would be magic, but there wasn't; there were houses and storefronts and cars and pedestrians.

"Yes, there are those," the woman said softly, as if she could hear every thought. "But there is magic as well. You expect magic to feel a certain way, to look a certain way, to taste a certain way. You expect light and sound, a movement of mountains, some gout of fire. I'm not sure why, but it is the way of your kind. Magic is subtle, Jane, and it takes the context of the form it touches. If you wish fire, you must be fire; if you wish light, you must be light. If you wish the wildness, then you must be the wildness; there is no magic that does not take what is within and use it. Do you understand this?" They walked toward the neighborhood that Jane called home, and it was only once they arrived there that Jane realized that she, and not the woman, was leading. *Show me,* she thought. *Where's the magic here, besides you?*

"You."

"But you gave me that."

"Did I? Very well. Do you see that house? That house was planted in 1916."

"Houses aren't planted."

"Ah, but they are. And they grow as the people who live in them grow, developing a sense for romance and bereavement, for happiness and tragedy—for life. Your house will remember you long after you've passed by it." She began to walk toward Arundel, and Jane followed, until they stood at the foot of her house.

"Look at this house," the woman said, and her tone was completely different. "It is not a well-cared for house at the moment. There is anger and loss and things darker besides."

Jane said nothing.

"And there was no magic at all in it, no belief in magic." She turned then, and looked at Jane with her dark eyes, her light eyes. "Do you understand why you found me, Jane?"

"No."

"Because for you there was no magic, and no life exists in the end without it."

"Most people live without magic," Jane replied, feeling prickles up and down her spine.

"Do they?" She reached down and stroked the top of Jane's head. "Jane, your father left your mother, and you have nothing but pain and anger to give him for it. Why?"

"Because he lied to us. And he hurt us."

"You are hurting him greatly."

"He deserves it."

"Why?"

"Because he lied! Because he cheated on my mother for months before he told her, and because he—he married my mother. He promised to love her forever."

"That," she said gravely, "is magic."

"What?"

"That belief. Your mother believed your father, and

your father believed in himself. That was years ago, but the house remembers."

"Well, if that was magic, then magic isn't worth shit."

"Let it go, Jane. Let it go, if it is worth so little."

Jane's snort came out a growl; it stopped her for a moment. "He can't just get away with it," she said at last.

"No, I suppose he can't. But think: If you will have magic, then you must create it and understand what its value is."

"I had no choice in anything either of them did."

The silver-haired woman did not answer, but instead began to walk away.

"Where are you going?"

"Into your yard."

"Why?"

"Because your mother is there."

"What the hell—my mother is supposed to be at work!" She hesitated at the gate, and the woman opened it. "I don't want to see my mother."

"You may never see her again, Jane; you are being born, and what you will be when you are finished, I cannot say. Will you not at least say your good-byes in some fashion? For your mother has hurt you, but she has been hurt as well, and you will leave her just as your father has done."

"*I* didn't promise her anything."

"No. Of course not."

Jane didn't argue anymore. Instead, she almost meekly crossed the line between the driveway and the patio of the backyard. Her mother sat sprawled in a lawn chair, a magazine over her face and a glass by her side. It was full; not a bad sign. Jane leaped up on the table just as a cat might, gathering her hind muscles and pushing hard against the ground as if she had done it all her life. Then, on impulse, she knocked the glass over.

The magazine fell to the ground in a noisy spill of glossy paper as her mother sat bolt upright. Jane had never seen her mother's mouth open so wide with so little noise coming out of it. The thought made her laugh, but the sound that she made was like a tickle across the air. And then she realized that her mother was staring right at *her,* and she fell silent, returning her mother's regard through a set of silver fox eyes.

"She can see me," she said, to the woman who stood at her side.

"Yes. But she cannot hear you, alas. It has been a long time." And then the woman did the strangest thing; she walked up to Jane's mother and very gently touched her cheek, the way someone might touch a sleeping infant's. "She cannot see me. Remember what you can, Marla. Remember."

But the Marla to whom the woman spoke didn't need the reminder. She stared at the fox for a long time, and then she began to cry. Jane had seen her mother cry several times, but she had never seen tears like this—a mixture of joy and loss that made her angry, cynical mother seem, for a moment, vulnerable.

The older woman reached out and touched the fox's whiskers. Her hands were shaking. "Did you come here just to knock the glass over?" Whiskey dripped down from the table to the cement, and spread into the cracks between the stones. "Are you trying to tell me something?"

Jane started to speak, but the woman gestured her into silence. "Just listen, Jane."

"I should have listened to you years ago. Am I drunk now? Are you real? Do you remember the last time I saw you?"

"What last time?" Jane whispered.

"When she was a girl only a little older than you are," her companion replied.

"She saw me?"

The woman smiled. "She saw *me.*" The smile dimmed. "She had no magic in her life, and a great deal of yearning. I came to her as a little fox for three winter days."

"Then what happened?"

"Do you mean, what did I do next or what did she do next?"

"I mean, why did you stop coming?"

"I? Because she found something else that she thought she could believe in; some other magic, and some other miracle into which to put heart and hope and effort."

"What?"

"Your father."

Jane growled, and her mother drew back, speaking in low, soothing tones.

"It was winter. Don't you remember? I wanted proof that magic existed—that life could get better than what I had. I might've even prayed; I've forgotten. But you came then. And you're here now." Her mother's tears got worse.

"You judge your father harshly, little one. He, too, sought magic and faith. But he could not build that with your mother; they have hurt each other too much."

"And I'm just supposed to forgive him?"

"No; every magic has its price. He knew what that price would be, and he must pay it, whether it hurts him or no. Now come; stop standing in the whiskey and let us continue our walk."

Jane looked at her mother. "Can I—can I come home tonight?"

"You may do as you desire, Jane."

Jane went home after school and found her mother in the kitchen on her knees. Her left hand was bandaged, and her right was covered by a rubber glove; she was scrubbing the floor clean.

"Hi, Mom," she said, awkward although she tried not to be.

"Hi, Janie. I just—I dropped a couple of bottles when I was cleaning the shelves."

"You okay?" Jane said, looking at her mother's hand.

"It's just a sliver. Are you home for dinner tonight?"

"Yeah."

"In a couple of hours, then. Took me longer to clean up the mess than I thought."

Jane went up to her room. And as she crossed the threshold she heard whispers, felt the brush of old cotton and then some stiffer fabric, against her hands. She felt feathers beneath her cheek, and heard a man's voice humming a lullaby. It was not her father's voice.

It was the house speaking.

She walked over to the bed—her bed—and lay down stiffly against it, feeling her arms and legs as if they were far too heavy. And then she listened to the memories of the house, sinking into them enough to almost see her mother.

She'd never done this before. Had never thought to do it, to question what a house might see, might be touched by, might explain in its peculiar, observant way. But now that she knew, she could hear voices that were not her own, see images that were outside of her day-dreams, her hopes, her fears.

Her mother hadn't dropped those bottles—she threw them. And she'd taken them all out, for however long it lasted. Emptied them, rinsed them out so they wouldn't smell, shuffled them under the Pepsi cans in the recycling bin where they might vanish without remark.

Except, of course, Janie took out the recycling boxes. Sometimes her mother could be so stupid.

God, it was *all* so stupid. Her mother set eyes on a little white fox—a stupid white fox—and suddenly she was trying to do all this *cleaning up* that she'd never have done for Jane or her father.

Don't be angry with her, a voice said. *She does it because she remembers what its like to be a girl who can dream. Whether she's strong enough to continue to dream depends on her—but every time you mock her, you strip away her strength.* It was the silver-haired woman. *But come, Jane. Tonight you must leave if you are to continue your journey with me.* She beckoned, and Jane sat up.

The house was empty, the room darkened by sunfall.

She wanted to be angry at her mother.

She wanted to be angry.

"Janie! Dinner!"

Dinner was quiet. Jane was aware of her mother as if for the first time; she was seeing beyond what she looked like to what she was at the moment. It was strange. She always felt stung if her mother laughed at her—but she'd never realized that her mother could be hurt, too. It was odd. She was almost afraid to say anything.

But her mother was quiet as well, very introspective.

It was only when they were gathering up the dishes that she spoke.

"Janie, I know that things have been pretty awful around here lately. I'm sorry. But I was thinking today that maybe I've been looking at things the wrong way. I wasn't—I wasn't always easy to live with. I'm not—"

"You don't have to say this, Mom."

"I do have to say it." Her mother drank air, a heave of chest and lung, a grasp for more than breath. "I'm not easy to live with. I think—I think my mother must've been like me, when I was like you. I don't think you deserve that, I don't deserve it myself. I'm going to do better. I promise."

"I know you will, Mom," Jane said—and for just a moment she allowed herself to believe it.

She came that night, and Janie followed her, sliding out of her room and past her mother's door. On impulse she stopped, peered in between the crack left between open door and frame. Her mother was sleeping on her side, curled around a pillow as if it were her father's back.

She did hate her father, sort of, and that was good. She turned away and crept down the stairs, like a thief or worse. Like that father, meeting the woman of his dreams.

"You are quiet, Jane."

Jane's silver whiskers bobbed in the field of her vision as she shook her head. They traveled the crowded walks of the still-trendy Queen West Village, avoiding the authoritative steps of people who had places to *be* but no time to get there.

"Do you not find the forest night interesting? There are lights here, made by man, and they change constantly over the years. I have always found these lights fascinating for what they reveal and what they conceal. There is a heart to them that is divided."

Jane Thornton said nothing.

"And here, there will be music, and it will be fine and lively; there, there will be poverty, and around it, like broken rivers, riches will pass without stopping."

"Panhandlers," Jane said.

"They have their own stories, Jane. They have a pathos to them that can be both revolting and compelling."

The fox wrinkled its nose.

"Do you not like the gift you've been given?"

"Yes—I do. I like it."

"Do you not desire your freedom?"

"Yes."

"Was it not magic you sought?"

"Yes."

"Ah."

Her mother was up before her alarm went off. Jane knew this because it wasn't the insistent sound of her mother's droning alarm—ignored—that finally pulled her out of bed; it was her mother's voice.

"Janie! Breakfast!"

She went downstairs in a state of shock. "Mom?"

"You aren't dressed yet."

"I'm not even awake," Jane said, and pinched her arm theatrically.

Her mother laughed. "There's too much cholesterol here," she sad apologetically. "But I thought—first breakfast in a while."

Pancakes. Bacon. Scrambled eggs. Butter. Way too much cholesterol.

Jane set the table while her mother finished cooking. Set it for two, remembering when she'd last set it for three in the morning. Then, her dad had done the cooking, and it had been Sunday.

He was gone now. He was free.

She ate with her mother, and even helped her clean up afterward.

What about magic, Jane thought, and school passed by her in a blur of voices and actions and people.

Magic, the woman had said, was a thing that existed in context. If you wanted fire, you had to *be* fire. If you wanted lightning, you had to be a storm.

If you wanted freedom, did you have to be free?

And if you wanted love?

What the hell was magic, anyway?

     *   *   *

Night was dark, but the stars were out. The air was hazy, so they weren't clear, but they were there, and Jane could feel each one as if they were right beside her. She sat on the porch, on an old lawn chair whose plastic strips had almost all fallen off. Waiting.

"Jane."

She looked up to see the silver-haired woman. Her hair, like rays of light, touched the porch railing, illuminating everything. Making it beautiful. It almost hurt to look at her.

"What are you doing?"

"Listening to the house," Jane said softly. "I can hear my mother. I didn't know how young she was."

"And look how she turned out."

"That's not all her fault!"

The woman smiled gently. "No and yes. But come. We have an agreement, I believe." She held out a perfect hand.

Jane reached for it and then let her own hand, calluses and all, drop back to her dirt-stained knee. "I can't come with you."

"No?"

"No. You know why."

"But isn't this what you wanted, Jane? Freedom? Did you not say that you would be happy if you never saw this house again?"

"Yeah, right. And if I leave, my mother forgets about the stupid fox and remembers that everyone deserts her. I bet she even thinks she deserves it. You said yourself that everyone needs magic, and that magic is all context."

She thought the woman would be angry, but the woman only nodded her head. 'Yes. But what will your magic be if you stay?"

"Mine? I don't know. You."

"Not me," she replied with a smile.

"Maybe my mother then. Maybe I can believe in her and she can believe in her, and we can both hold on for long enough that it'll be true."

"Then stay, Jane. But you will not see me again in this life."

"Yeah, I figured," Jane said, but her throat was tight.

"Let me leave you with a gift." And so saying, she drew out of her robe the silver pelt that she had given to Jane once before.

"But—but—I don't understand. Didn't you hear me? I'm not going with you."

"Yes. You will not be able to wear it, Jane. You will not be able to don it without my aid, and I will not be here to grant that to you. Because you have made the hardest decision, you've started a new life. You are not the Jane Thornton that you were. I have enjoyed your company, Jane, and I have learned a little from you. Take the pelt, which is a thing of mortals, and when you need to remember what you are capable of, look at it."

Jane's smile was strained. "You know what'll happen if I try to put it up anywhere in the house, don't you?"

"No," the woman said gravely.

"My mother will think I've gone out and skinned her dreams."

The woman did not laugh; Jane did.

And then she scooped up fur that no longer made her hands and feet tingle, and turned away from the woman. Because she was strong, Jane Thornton, and didn't need to cry.

And then, because she was stronger, and didn't need to hide, she turned and the woman was watching her, as if tears were a salute, some gesture of greatness that only Jane could grant.

She bowed, then, left, then.

This was the hardest thing to understand, and she thought, in the dell of her choosing, that she could see a glimmer of it every time someone made a choice like Jane's—a choice of magic over freedom, a thing of grace and beauty.

What, after all, was this humanity, but a huddled desire for companionship, for love? Who had she loved in her life as they loved in theirs, short and brief? She thought, if she understood it truly, she might find her mortality and lose her fear of it.

Could she but accept it, she knew that she might be free. *The mountains,* she thought, and she turned toward the east, and watched them as the sun rose.

NETTED
by Josepha Sherman

Josepha Sherman is a fantasy writer and folklorist whose latest novels are the historical fantasies *The Shattered Oath* and *Forging the Runes.* Her latest folklore book is entitled *Trickster Tales.*

The door was jammed, trapping him in the close darkness of his one-room home. Ethram, muttering a curse, set his shoulder against the stubborn wood and pushed with muscles made strong by years of hauling in fishing nets. The door gradually creaked open enough to let Ethram slip outside, glaring at the mound of sand that had been blown up against that door. Half the beach seemed to have been washed up here from the shoreline by the waves.

No wonder. That had been a true monster of a storm last night, strong enough to make him wonder, only half in jest, if it hadn't been the result of a quarrel between two angry wizards fighting over earth-power, sky-strength, whatever they called the fabric of their magic.

"Who cares about their quarrels?" Ethram glowered out at the still heavily overcast sky and the still-rough waves—too rough for him to dare launch his boat. Every day away from fishing was another day without the chance for income.

He shrugged. What was, was. At least his boat, *Eliss II,* was still safely berthed under its oilskins. *Eliss I,* no longer seaworthy, hull-side up, as the roof of his house, as was the style here on the Isles: a nice, sturdy roof the old girl made, too, covered with sand from the storm but undamaged. His nets, now—

"Damn. Oh, damn."

Bitterly, Ethram consigned every wizard and every

31

magical squabble and most certainly every one of those
thrice-cursed magic-spawned storms to the darkest corner of Forever. He had stowed the nets away as carefully
as he had berthed his boat, well above high tide; every
fisherman on the Isles took such pains. But the storm
had been supernaturally savage enough to tear off the
oilskin covers, and his precious nets were strewn all over
the beach, with great, gaping holes torn in them by
spears of driftwood—ha, yes, look at that, one of the
nets was tangled about a whole man-sized chunk of stuff!
Now he would have to start the time-consuming, tedious
business of mending all those tears, yes, and miss still
more precious fishing days while—

Ethram stopped short. "Holy Selda. Sweet, holy
Selda."

That wasn't driftwood ensnaring his net. A man lay
tangled in its folds.

A . . . being, anyhow, tall and slender, sleekly muscled
as any sea thing. His long hair was a deep, sea-blue, his
skin (and there was a good deal of skin to be seen since
all the fellow was wearing was the net) a pale blue-white.
His ears . . . were most definitely pointed.

Ethram blinked, shook his head. Old Meggett, back
in the village, had always vowed he'd go mad from solitude some day, and maybe now—

Fish guts. He *liked* living alone, and that didn't make
him crazy. And the man, being, whatever, was still here,
undeniably blue of hair and skin and pointed ears.

And red of blood. Ethram's breath caught in his
throat as he saw how a ragged gash marred the sleekness
of an arm, another wound slashed its way across the
deep chest. The man must have been trapped in the
storm and battered by the sea against the rocks. After
an uneasy moment, Ethram squatted by his side and put
a tentative hand on the pale blue wrist, wondering if
someone so blatantly alien even *had* a pulse.

He had, faint beneath the chilly skin, but steady. He
seemed to be breathing air easily enough, and Ethram
found no sign of gills on his neck, but those long-fin-
gered hands and toes were webbed, and the pointed
ears, seen this close, looked flexible as cloth, as though
they could be tightly furled to keep out water.

"A sea-elf," Ethram realized with a sudden shock. "By all the gods, he's a sea-elf right out of the stories." Had to be. Nothing else could be so perfectly suited to the sea yet be breathing on land.

Going to be a dead sea-elf if something wasn't done to help him.

Like what? Ethram glanced fiercely about, as though he might actually see something more than sea and sand and the upturned ship-curve of his roof. It seemed foolish to bring someone surely used to the cold sea into a warm house, and something deep within Ethram was screaming, *No, alien, he's alien.* But one of the unspoken rules of everyone who fished the Isles was that you didn't deny help to anyone in need, just in case next time it was *you* in need.

So be it. Ethram shouldered the elf—heavier than he looked, that one, dense with swimming muscles—resolutely trying not to shiver at the touch of that too-cool skin, and started back.

Ethram was sitting hunched over by the smoky light of his oil lamp, muttering over his net-mending, when a sudden stillness in the air told him his patient was awake. Heart suddenly racing, he folded the half-mended mass of net, returned the precious bone needle to its case, then looked with forced calm across at the bed.

Eyes dark as the sea at midnight looked back at him, regal as those of any prince, unblinking as the stare of a cat. *A noble,* Ethram thought, *he has to be a noble of his people, or maybe even a ruler.* Or maybe all sea-elves looked so proud.

The silence was growing heavy. Ethram asked, "You . . . uh . . . speak the human tongue?"

The faintest frown creased the sea-elf's elegant brow. He started to raise an arm, then stopped with a hiss of pain as Ethram added hastily, "Don't move! I sewed you up as best I could, same needles as I use on my nets, the good needles."

Damn, he was babbling like an idiot. And all the while, the sea-elf was watching him with inhumanly steady stare. Like a sea-beast watching its prey.

No, Ethram realized with a sudden, unexpected stab of sympathy, like someone trying desperately to hide fear and make sense of the alien place into which he'd been thrown. Ethram watched one long, webbed-fingered hand stroke across the rough woolen blanket as though puzzling over its weave. Then he heard the sea-elf murmuring something that sounded more like the whisper of the sea than actual words. *Sea-magic,* he thought, uneasiness prickling up his spine, sea-magic or whatever they called it.

The sea-elf stopped. "You . . . can . . . understand now?" he asked.

"Y-you magicked the language, didn't you?"

"Not well. I . . . have not enough of . . . of the feel of it. You, human . . . you are . . . ?"

'No one to harm you." Ethram wasn't about to give any elf his name. "A fisherman, that's all."

But the steady blue gaze suddenly shifted to the flickering little flame of the oil lamp. "That. What is that?"

"What?" Ethram echoed. "The lamp—the *flame?* You don't know *fire?*" Ah, no, he wouldn't, would he? No fire in the sea. "That's what we humans use to help us see in the dark. And keep us warm. And cook our food."

The sea-elf was clearly struggling to keep awake. Ethram sighed and picked up his half-mended net. "Enough talking. Get some sleep." Mm, that rip was mended. "And don't worry, you're safe." He drew his knife to cut off the loose end of cord, and straightened in surprise at the sea-elf's sudden gasp. "Now what—ah."

Iron. The sea-elf was clearly terrified of iron, and too weary to hide that fear. Ethram deliberately sheathed the knife, and repeated, "Don't worry, you're safe." After a thoughtful moment, he added a firm, "My word on it," and saw relief flicker in the deep blue eyes.

Eyes that quickly glazed as the sea-elf sank into exhausted sleep.

Weird, having someone sharing his home. Weirder to have that someone be a being who just would not see the point of clothing or cooked food yet retained an eerie grace and elegance even when he was gnawing on dried fish. Outside Ethram's house, the weather remained alarmingly unsettled. Inside, the days passed quietly as he continued to mend his nets and tend his alien patient, who was swiftly picking up the human tongue.

Not that there was much they could discus, other than the obvious matters: no, being out of the sea so long wasn't hurting the elf; yes, the wounded of his people did stay out of the sea till they healed to keep the smell of blood from attracting predators. Yes, Ethram and his guest exchanged names; Ethram couldn't see a way around that. The sea-elf's name turned out to be Sishalah-elek, and apparently (if Ethram understood him correctly) "elek" meant that his guest really was of the nobility.

Difficult to talk about much else, though. How did you get across the idea of villages and selling fish to someone who was having just as much difficulty trying to get across the thought of—what were they? Cities? Cities that didn't have any solid walls or roofs? And nobody sold fish in Sishalah's world, apparently, not in that strange watery place where everyone used the sea's own magic to summon food to them.

Sea-magic.

A sudden sly thought stole into Ethram's mind as he mended his nets and mended his nets and meanwhile watched his store of dried fish grow perilously low. What if . . . ? What if . . . ?

No. He had given his word. Nonhuman or no, this odd guest was safe here.

I wouldn't hurt him. Just . . . well . . . detain him.

It still seemed wrong to even be thinking such things, guilty-wrong. Maybe they weren't really friends, not two such different types of folk, but they had been sort of comrades these past few days, and there was host-honor to consider, and . . . and . . .

Hell, I don't have to worry about it, not yet. He's still too weak to go anywhere.

But Sishalah was healing with inhuman speed, yet had begun looking strangely worn. He needed the sea, no doubt about it. "I am healed," the sea-elf said without warning. "My thanks to you, but now I must go home."

He got smoothly to his feet. *Now,* Ethram thought and, heart racing, jumped to block Sishalah's way.

The sea-elf stopped in surprise. "What?"

"Sorry. But . . ." Ethram whirled, sinking his knife, his iron knife, deeply into the door, hearing Sishalah's startled gasp. "Can't let you go."

The blue eyes narrowed. "Why not? Why betray me now?"

"I'm not betraying you, honest," Ethram said, hearing his voice come out too loud. "It's just . . . well . . . you have magic, and I don't. And I need something."

"What?"

"Look you, there hasn't been a calm day the whole week you've been here. And even if I could have taken out the boat, I haven't got more than one whole net yet, so I couldn't even do any real fishing. But now the weather's finally settled."

"What does that mean to me?"

"Not much. Except you've been eating my stores all the while—not that I'm begrudging you that, understand, you had to eat and so did I. But I haven't got much food left. Today I can take the boat out. And you can help me."

"I am not a slave."

"Well, no, but you're not free, either, not with the iron barring the door. And you're not going anywhere until you help me."

Sishalah's face could have been carved from pale blue stone. "Is this human honor?"

"This is human need. Look, I'm not asking much, just one little spell."

"Are you? What?"

Guilt was flooding him, pounding in his ears. Forgetting all his carefully rehearsed words, Ethram gasped out, "My nets. Give me a net that isn't going to tear."

One thin blue brow raised skeptically. "And is that what you truly want?"

He was missing something. But Ethram was so eager to get the whole business done that he snapped, "Damn right. A net that won't tear, so I can get some fishing done."

The sea-elf sighed. Bending over a net, he murmured

strange, sea-whispery words, eyes half-closed, then straightened. "It is done. The net will not tear, not even at the touch of your ugly iron. Now let me go. Or are you planning to keep me as a pet?"

"Don't be stupid." Ethram pulled the knife free and stood aside to let Sishalah pass, then stood in the doorway, watching. Without a backward look, the sea-elf leaped into the waves and vanished. More shaken than he ever would have admitted, Ethram forced a casual shrug and went to launch his boat.

He caught nothing that day, nothing the next. Wondering if the sea-elf could have put a curse on him, Ethram set out on the morning of the third day, shivering in the chilly air, ignoring the warning the rising wind was giving him. There wasn't a curse, dammit, and he would prove it, hurl his unbreakable net overboard and—

Somehow his foot had gotten tangled in the folds. Before Ethram could cry out, he was overboard, cold water in his eyes, his ears. He fought to swim, to catch hold of the gunwale of his boat, but the net was waterlogged, the weights woven into it pulling him down.

Taking a frantic breath, Ethram dove, trying to untangle his leg. No good. He was snared fast. He struggled back to the surface, gasping in a lungful of air, then dove again, knife drawn, hacking at the net—

The unbreakable net. The net that could not be cut even by iron. And it was damned cold in the water, too cold. The knife slipped from his hand, and he couldn't find the strength to fight back to the surface, to the air . . . he couldn't . . .

A strong arm was suddenly about his waist, pulling him to the surface. Ethram choked, gasped, drew in wonderful air, and only then could turn his head to see who held him:

"Sishalah." It was a croak.

"Sishalah," the sea-elf agreed. "Hold fast to your boat."

As Ethram clung, Sishalah dove. Ethram was too numb to feel much, save that a sudden weight was gone from him; the sea-elf had freed him from the net.

Sishalah surfaced. "Come, into your boat."

He heaved, inhuman strength in him. Ethram collapsed into the boat, convulsively pulling sailcloth abut himself for warmth, gasping out, "Why? Why?"

Sishalah, clearly undisturbed by the cold for all his nakedness, leaned lightly on the gunwale. "Why what? Why save you? It pleased me. How did you enjoy your gift, Ethram? Was it not exactly what you wished?"

"It nearly killed me!"

"And you nearly enslaved me. I would have given you a better gift," the sea-elf said, almost gently. "Had you not betrayed me, I would have taught you how to call the fish to you. Think of that, human. You would never have known hunger. But now I give you the finest of gifts. I give you back your life. Use it well."

With that, Sishalah dove back into the sea and was gone.

THE PHAERIE BRIDE
by Rosemary Edghill

Rosemary Edghill is the author of *The Sword of Maiden's Tears, The Cup of Morning Shadows,* and *The Cloak of Night and Daggers.* Her short fiction has appeared in *Return to Avalon, Chicks in Chainmail,* and *Tarot Fantastic.* She is a full-time author who lives in Poughkeepsie.

April 30, 1800: *County Berwick, Scotland*
With a stifled sigh, Jonet Ellen Bellamy let the worn curtain drop back into place over the library window. It wasn't fair. The gowns had been paid for by Carterhall rents, but the Mistress of Carterhall couldn't go to the ball.

At least her stepmama and her two stepsisters were gone—and not to be expected back before dawn's light, as was the way of country balls. She should make the most of her solitude.

The library was dark, lit only by the grudging fire that burned to keep the rot from the books. Jonet's father had begun the practice when he had come to Carterhall as librarian to his distant cousin the Earl of Greenlaw, and it was one standing order that his cousin's widow hadn't overturned.

Jonet's eyes stung, even though Papa had been in his grave these six months. She missed him—and the comfort of their life together. She even missed Mungo Bellamy, the old Earl. They had been happy before old Mungo died and the Edinburgh lawyers found that it was Ninian Bellamy, Jonet's father, who was heir to Carterhall, the Greenlaw Earldom, and the fortune accumulated by a lifetime's cheeseparing. Before Mrs. Heddersfield had come as Jonet's governess—and then, unaccountably, had married Papa. Jonet began to sigh again, stopped herself, and picked up her book: a French volume of *contes de fées* that Stepmama would consider far too worldly for an innocent young girl.

If only Papa had not died! But he had, and now— under Scots law—Jonet was Countess of Greenlaw and mistress of Carterhall in her own right, a fact that roused her stepmama's not inconsiderable ire. But Jonet, as Avice Heddersfield-Bellamy never tired of reminding her, was not yet seventeen, a minor child, in the care of those older and wiser.

And not let to go the ball.

Oh, she knew it would be tedious—the few country dances she had stood up at before Papa died had taught her that. But tonight would be special: a grand entertainment given by the most interesting arrival in the County in the last seven years.

"Auberon Ste. Vertdubois, Prince de la Cockaigne!"

"I know my own name," the big man growled. "And my titles, too. Is there something else, Maitane?"

"Milord looks very elegant tonight," the valet observed cautiously.

"Milord had better. Milord is getting himself betrothed."

The valet tittered, and covered his painted mouth with gilded nails. "And only one thing mars Milord's perfection."

"No."

"But if Milord would just—"

"Milord, having been recently in England, chooses to follow *le mode Anglais.* And Milord is supposed to be at the very tip of fashion, is Milord not, Maitane?"

"French fashion!" Maitane protested.

"Oh, no," Auberon said softly. "Never that. French fashion, my child, is a red cap signifying the liberty to murder. We will not follow French fashion."

Maitane, not certain what to make of his master's fey mood, stood silent.

"Besides," Auberon went on, "only think how appalled my douce countrymen will be to see me playing the English—as if we had not been marrying English for hundreds of years."

"She is Scots," offered Maitane timidly. "This Countess. A Scots widow."

"It doesn't matter." Auberon turned from the mirror and indicated that he was ready to receive his coat. "So she has been widowed twice. I have been widowed a hundred times."

Avice Bellamy unlaced the coach curtains, braving the April chill, and put her face out the window to regard Broceliande House as they approached. Four months ago Prince de la Cockaigne had descended upon the small Scots village of Miching Malicho, made extensive repairs to the largest available house in the neighborhood, and taken a hundred-year lease. By Equinox it was known that the Prince was seeking a bride. By Easter it was known upon whom his choice had fallen. Tonight the County would be confirmed in its suspicions, and anyone who had not yet seen Broceliande House would see it.

The Prince would propose tonight. He would—he must—the whole County was expecting the announcement, and it was Avice's only hope of continuing to keep her accustomed style once that chit of Ninian's came into her estate.

The coach door swung open in a blaze of light and fire-warmed air. Avice and her two daughters stepped down between two lines of torches and entered Broceliande House.

Curtains of blood-red velvet were drawn back to reveal windowpanes like a mosaic of black ice. Beeswax candles, dyed and perfumed, blazed out across the expanse of gilded and painted Chinese paper that covered what few walls the ballroom windows did not. Music filled the air from the velvet-draped dais where the Prince's own private orchestra bowed and blew like maddened automatons—and for those who did not dance, there were side rooms where cards, or punch, or even more hectic pleasures could be procured.

Auberon was bored.

He gazed out the glass at the far-off sparks of flame

on the hilltops and wished he were anywhere but here.
But it was a seven-year. Auberon had a bride to choose.

Half-hidden in velvet, Auberon watched as his guests
appeared in the entryway to the ballroom. The familiar
form of the Dowager Countess of Greenlaw appeared
in the archway. Her two daughters—whom a charitable
observer would call mouselike—hovered behind her.
Auberon, who was not charitable, thought that they
more closely resembled shrews.

His bride. His stepdaughters-to-be. He wondered if he
could marry them each in turn. With a sigh, the Prince
de la Cockaigne moved forward to do his duty.

Avice hesitated on the steps as her intended moved
toward her.

"My very dear Countess," Auberon rumbled deep in
his chest. He made a leg. The Misses Heddersfield
giggled.

The Prince de La Cockaigne stood six-foot-six in his
stocking feet and tipped the scales at nineteen stone.
When he took Avice's hand in his, it was swallowed up
completely, and the band of the massive gold signet ring
he wore clicked against her gold-and-jet mourning
bracelets.

"I trust I find you well, dear Countess?" Auberon
went on. "It was very brave of you to venture to attend
such a grand crush so soon after your tragedy. We must
make it worth your while. And here are your dear
daughters," he announced firmly, as though the matter
might be in dispute. "How lovely you both look."

Under their mother's raptor gaze Grizel and Elspeth
made their curtsies to the Prince, and the little party
moved down the stairs into the ballroom.

"But come, my dear Countess," Auberon continued
relentlessly. "I am certain my cousin will chaperon your
daughters, and I hope you will honor me with a private word."

Avice looked at the fast and painted woman Auberon
named as his cousin. This was what she had waited for,
but now Avice was strangely reluctant to go with him.
Still, she put her gloved hand in his bare one and allowed herself to be borne away.

*   *   *

Auberon led the Dowager Countess through a gilded door and down a hallway into a room lined with books. A single white wax candle burned in an ornate silver holder in the shape of a salamander. Beside it was a squat decanter of blue glass.

Auberon closed the door firmly behind her.

"Marry me," he said flatly. "It is my most earnest desire."

As he spoke a great weariness came over him. Once again the charade was to be played.

"Your Highness—this is an unlooked-for honor," Avice fluted. Greed shone in her eyes with an almost perceptible light, and Auberon felt a pang of revulsion. "I hardly know how to answer you." She held out her hand to him.

Say "no." Auberon bent over the hand and kissed it. "Say you will make me the happiest of creatures." *Honesty was ever my curse.* "Be mine." *Until I forfeit you in exchange for my life.*

"Oh, Your—*Auberon*," Avice breathed, with a fervor usually found in country theatricals. "You have won me. I am yours."

"Then we will wed on Midsummer's Eve. I beg you will not think me too impetuous, but my ardor for our union is such that I can barely restrain myself even now."

An unbiased observer would have said that what the Prince de la Cockaigne could barely restrain himself from was hibernation—still, the Dowager Countess of Greenlaw did not seem to mind.

"Oh, my *Lord*," she gushed inaccurately.

"Then accept this ring as a symbol of my love, and we will drink a toast to our engagement. Dear Countess, I beg you will let me make the whole world a party to our joy." Auberon rattled the words off as if he were reading from a promptbook. As he spoke, he rummaged in his coat pocket and produced a ring.

The ring was made of iron; the surface was so dull that it was hard to make out the true shape of the band and the style of the engraving on its surface. The gem it held was a perfect sphere of bright crystal, clear as dew.

Avice drew back, greed momentarily balked by unease.

"Perhaps some wine first," Auberon said quickly, dropping the ring back into his pocket. He turned to the side table for two of the blue glass cups that went with the decanter.

Avice looked up, her gaze automatically following his motion. He stood in the corner of the room; she could see him mirrored in the uncurtained windows—

But what she saw was not human.

The reflection in the glass was taller even than the prince—black and hideous, with a curly coat and ram's horns, with hoofed feet and taloned hands and a long tufted tail like a lion's.

Avice made a faint mew of distress. The Prince looked up. He caught the doubled movement out of the corner of his eye and turned to confront his reflection.

"Careless of me," he said, but not as if it mattered.

The black beast in the glass clashed its fangs in time with his words. Its eyes glowed red and gold as the brazen hinges of hell, and two great horns curled backward from his swept and furrowed brow. Auberon touched the glass. Fingertip met talon.

Avice moaned and sank to the floor.

"But my dear bride," Auberon said genially, "whatever is the matter?"

He poured the wine and held it out to her. She did not take it, and he set the cup down beside the decanter.

"You are mine, you know. But do not fear, my blushing bride—you are already promised to another."

"Who— What—"

Auberon smiled coldly. "I told you nothing but the truth: I am a prince, driven from his ancestral holdings by the accursed sans-culottes. But the principality I am lord of is Elphame, and to remain in human lands I must pay the *teind* to Hell every seven years with the mortal bride I wed."

The Dowager regarded him in terror. "I won't marry you."

"Then live as long as you may. You mortgaged Carterhall to me—which was not legal, but you've been paid for it in good phaerie gold. Cheat me now and you'll swing for coining from a silken rope."

He watched her face blanch until the powder stood on it like dirty sand.

"Mercy," she croaked. "Please—"

"Alas," Auberon said. "The Fair Folk have no hearts—having none, I can hardly be merciful, can I? But I will strike one more bargain with you, Countess: Give me one of your daughters to die in your place and you will go free—and keep all the rich gifts I have given you."

She won't do it. She would refuse him, Auberon was certain. The bride must be willing, and she would not be, and it was too late for him to choose and court another.

It would be over. He felt relief well up in him and turned away.

"Give you—one of my daughters—and I may go?" Avice said hoarsely.

"Yes." She would not do it. She loved that brace of weasels with all the passion in her withered heart. She would never—

"Very well. One of my daughters—for your bride." the Dowager's voice was crone-harsh.

"Done." Auberon closed the bargain as he must. "Shall we make the announcement?"

"No. I need—I need a little time." And to his amazement, the Phaerie Lord heard the Countess begin to laugh.

Lying in her cold and narrow nursery bed, Jonet Ellen dreamed that she stood looking down at a ballroom. The black and white of the floor changed and swirled, and a man with eyes like amber and honeyed fire came up the steps toward her. She moved toward him and found she wore black silk and silver gauze the color of tears. . . .

He took her in his arms; they danced. She was happy as she had never been before, and he looked only at her. Then her hand was in his; a black ring burned cold witchfire on her hand and everyone was laughing, cheering; a cup was pressed into her hand—

He curled her fingers about it and raised it to her lips. She drank, and the world spilled slowly away in a jeweled dream where Jonet rode upon winged lions and danced with star-crowned bears. . . .

And then she woke up.

The pale May sunlight was harsh through her swollen lids. She rolled over to hide her face from the light only to encounter, not the thin wool of the nursery mattress, but the billowing softness of an eiderdown that nearly smothered her.

"Lady—Lady—Lady—" The soft anxious voice roused Jonet to troubles other than her own. With an effort rapidly turning to panic she floundered upright in the alien bed.

The speaker had the indefinable look of a lady's maid. The servant's perfect elfin face belonged to no one Jonet recognized. Jonet struggled to make sense of what she saw, but for a frightening moment her mind would not obey her.

"I am Jonet Bellamy," she finally said. "Where am I?"

"Only wait, lady, I will bring tea, Lady. Do not grieve, Lady. Be well, Lady." Still offering advice in that whispering unbroken stream, the servant hurried off, leaving Jonet alone in the room.

Jonet threw back the covers. Even her nightshirt was not her own. She slid from the bed to stand on pale blue French carpets, woven with ribbons and roses—

—that coiled and spun like the chiaroscuro inlay of a midnight ballroom floor.

Suddenly dizzy, Jonet sat back down on the bed.

"Lady, Lady, oh, do not get up, Lady, please, Lady—"

The maid had returned, carrying a broad silver tray that flashed painfully as the morning light caught it.

"Here, Lady, you will sit, Lady, you will drink, Lady, all will be well—"

"Who are you?" Jonet's voice cut through the patter sharply.

"I am Perry, Lady, I will serve you Lady, only drink, Lady, please—"

Mostly to gain silence, Jonet took the delicate china cup. It held, not tea, but bitter black chocolate. She drank it down and—after an uncertain moment—felt altogether better.

"Now, Perry. Where is this?"

The abigail seemed to be reassured by Jonet's briskness. "Here is Broceliande, Lady, which is your home."

"Broceliande!" A jangle of dream-images spilled into Jonet's waking mind—a man in a green coat, a ball—

And a ring. Jonet looked down and stared at the ring on her hand. The crystal blazed with morning sun. If that was here, her dream was no dream—it was true.

In a faint voice Jonet said: "I do no wish to seem intolerably missish, but will someone please tell me what is going on?"

"You are to be married. To me. In seven weeks' time."

Jonet stared at the Prince de la Cockaigne blankly. When Perry finally told her that His Highness wished to see her, Jonet had been more relieved than frightened, hoping that His Highness had answers to the questions that tormented her.

He did. But not any she wanted.

"Married? To you?" She knew she ought to sound calm. Forceful. But instead her voice squeaked and shook. This was utter insanity—even if he was French. And handsome. And *rich,* her mind added, cataloging the things that Grizel and Elspeth would deem necessary in a husband.

But Jonet thought kindness more important, and had seen none—nor sanity, which nearly every bride would account of paramount importance in a groom.

"Married. To me. We announced it at the ball last night, though you may not remember. This Sunday the banns will be read out for the first time—and on Midsummer's Eve we will marry."

His Highness spoke as if there could be no possible doubt of this. Jonet trembled inwardly. Though all the tales of the Prince had mentioned his great size, none of them had mentioned how very small a rather small person could be made to feel when the Prince de la Cockaigne was standing over them.

"And what if I do not wish to marry you?" Jonet asked at last.

"You have been promised," the Prince said flatly.

"But *I* have not promised!" Jonet said indignantly. She turned the peculiar ring—obviously a betrothal ring—round and round on her finger. "And I won't promise! I don't love you—I don't even know you!"

"Then learn to love me," the Prince said. "You have seven weeks."

The last time Jonet had seen Broceliane House—six months before—one tower had been burned entirely and the other unable to boast a single unbroken window or shutter. Now both were miraculously whole. How could His Highness have accomplished all this in only six months? Less than that: The lease had been signed on Twelfth Night, and today was only May fifteenth.

Today the banns had been read out in church for the first time—a legal necessity even though His Highness was of the Old Religion—and the Right Reverend Ishmael Goodbook had announced from the pulpit for all the village to hear the sworn intention of Jonet Ellen Bellamy, the Countess of Greenlaw, and Auberon Ste. Vertdubois, the Prince de la Cockaigne, to wed.

It was intolerable.

Jonet rested her forehead against the cool glass of the tower window and twirled her betrothal ring round and round her finger. Before her the lawns swept velvet-green down to the stand of scrub pine that marked the commencement of Carterhall land. Soon the roses in the formal gardens below her would be in bloom.

And she would be married.

It did her no good at all to protest—as she had at the morning's service—and say she had been kidnapped, ravished away, drugged and betrothed against her will. Her stepmother swore it was a love-match that she had known of for weeks, and his vile and disobliging highness, Auberon Ste. Vertdubois, Prince de la Cockaigne and master of Broceliande, said the same.

But why would a man of such wealth and position want her at all?

"Why?" she muttered to herself. "It makes no sense."

"Why not? Surely you are not one of those who expect meaning out of life? The war news from the Continent should preclude that, surely."

Jonet turned. The Prince de la Cockainge stood in the doorway, correct and civilized from his linen neckcloth to the tips of his slippered toes, not omitting every brass button and golden ring between. It gave Jonet the passionate urge to throttle him.

"*Why* do you want to marry me?" Jonet burst out.

"It is my nature—and beyond my control," Auberon said austerely.

"I cannot believe that. Man is a creature of reason—and a rich man—"

"A creature of license? Now, Countess Prettyheart, would you have me believe that? I am rich in all the world's goods—would you have me behave as a ravening beast?"

Jonet threw back. "I am Jonet Bellamy, the Countess of Greenlaw, and I do not wish you to behave as anything at all, save as a man who will answer my questions. You hold me prisoner in the expectation of our marriage, and it makes no sense. Carterhall is well enough, but it is not half so grand as this—" Jonet said desperately.

"And all this will be yours the moment the marriage ring is on your finger. You will have wealth beyond counting. Is that not enough recompense to marry such a fellow as I?"

"No," said Jonet baldly.

Auberon seemed momentarily nonplussed.

"Then what would you, if not wealth? I tell you plainly, Prettyheart, if you will not have me, do not expect to return to such queenly state as that black-swaddled mushroom and her brace of ferrets have allowed you. Money is involved, Prettyheart, and gold is often dearer than blood."

This last speech puzzled Jonet completely. Auberon laughed, seeing her face.

"But come—let us cry truce. I will not let you go; no more will the darling Dowager Countess of Greenlaw take you back while she can use your inheritance as her own. This is the truth; I speak no other."

"And so you think I will stand up with you and be your bride—and I tell you, I would rather scrub pots at The Horn and Wheel!"

"Well," His Highness de la Coakaigne said with due consideration, "perhaps you would. Very well, my heart, deny me if you will. But I shall not stop asking." Abruptly he swept up her hand and kissed it.

Her bare skin burned against his palm like that of a martyr roasting in the flames of hell, and the touch of his lips was ice and molten gold.

"Pat and practiced," Jonet gasped, snatching her hand away. Auberon smiled and bowed again.

Jonet Bellamy stood at the drawing-room window. The Prince walked with her in the garden every evening at sunset, but this was an evening like no other. Today was Midsummer's Day—and tomorrow they would be wed.

It had become a game, these last few weeks. Each evening he would offer Jonet some new inducement to wed him; each evening she would spurn it. But Jonet had known long since that it was only a game. Tonight when he asked she would answer him true.

Seven weeks, he had said. And seven weeks it had been. She would give her consent. Tomorrow they would be wed.

And afterward—

She had not asked him about afterward. But if the Prince loved her as she loved him, all the world's events would be beside that fact.

She heard the door open and turned toward it.

She would refuse him. The Prince de la Cockaigne, serene in that happy certainty, had proceeded this Midsummer's Eve to drive Monsieur Maitane quite mad for two and three-quarters of an hour.

The ribbons for the walking stick—so.

The buckle of the heeled, pointed shoes—so.

The breeches and stockings, the waistcoat and lace, the voluminous linen shirt and the coat, the glorious coat, the finest creation of the admirable Crichton of London, cut from a bolt of superfine the exact raw shade of the midsummer heather: a ghostly gray-green violet the color of June twilight.

Auberon surveyed himself with satisfaction. Tonight

the ship would land with Father Kuiril, who was to join Auberon to his bride on the morrow. And Auberon would tell the good Father that his hazardous journey had been in vain—the mortal bride refused him.

She would. She had refused him every time these last seven weeks that he had asked—refused him through the reading of the banns, through the sewing of the bride-gown. She would refuse him tonight.

Auberon collected hat, stick, and gloves, and went to walk in the garden with his bride. She would refuse him.

Unless she loved him as he loved her.

But she didn't.

Thank God.

"Oh, look! The roses have bloomed!"

Jonet stopped at the edge of the flowers, enchanted. Yesterday the trees and archways had been a mass of tonsured green starred with small hard buds; today there was hardly any green to be seen for the roses red and white and every color between.

"It is summer; they have no choice. As I have none. I fling my heart enthralled at your feet, heart's queen: marry me or I will die," Auberon recited perfunctorily.

"Of course I will," said Jonet.

"Then, alas, I— *What did you say?*"

"That I'll marry you," Jonet said. "You asked me to. And—and I think we shall suit, Your Highness," she added, flushing.

"You can't marry me," the Prince de la Cockaigne said in a strangled voice.

Jonet looked up quickly at the sound of his voice. She turned as white as she had been red, but managed to reply in a steady voice.

"You asked me a question and I answered it. If you wish to begyke me, Your Highness, there is nothing I may do to prevent you."

Auberon spun away and stared blindly at the hedge covered with perfect blossoms. "I will not cry off, my Heart—I may not. My love, how could you do this to me?"

Jonet stared at him, hearing endearments mixed with ravings.

"Do you wish to marry me or not, Your Highness? You have only to tell me, you know." Her tone was even, but her hands clenched into painful fists in the folds of her half-mourning.

"I love you," Auberon groaned.

"And I, you, Your Highness," Jonet answered steadily. "What could be simpler?"

"Anything," Auberon snapped. "Listen, Prettyheart, there is a thing you do not know of me—"

"Only one? There is everything I do not know of you, sir, but one thing I do: If you had never meant to marry me, you might have left me at Carterhall."

"I do not withdraw my offer," Auberon said, "I may not tell you why, but I tell you this much truly: My wealth is no more than phaerie gold. It is an illusion."

"Then we shall have to live in a cot, sir," said Jonet. "Or perhaps you will come with me to The Horn and Wheel and we shall scrub pots together."

Auberon turned back to her and took her arm. "I am telling you the truth," he said menacingly.

"And what if you are? If you were the Lord of the Hollow Hills himself, I would still marry you."

Auberon reared back as if he had been struck.

"You don't know what you're saying, Prettyheart. The Fair Folk are not kind—they are the angels who fell from Heaven when God opened the gates to cast Lucifer down. Now they are too wicked for Heaven and keep their place in Man's world by paying *teind* to the Prince of Hell. Would you wish to be their sacrifice?"

Jonet regarded him steadily from some seconds. "The entire County is coming for the wedding," she offered when he said nothing.

"Didn't you hear what I said?" roared Auberon. "Why do you think your accursed stepmother cried off and gave you to me in her place?"

"Did she? Then I make no doubt it was because you were a Phaerie Lord who wanted her as his *teind* to Hell!" Jonet shot back.

"Yes," Auberon said. "That is why I wanted her. That is why—" He stopped. "That is not why I want you, my sweet Heart."

Jonet hung her head, twisting her betrothal ring round

and round her finger. The tears that trembled unfalling on her lashes were turned to blood by the sunset light.

"You are trying to frighten me with nursery tales," Jonet said in a trembling voice. "This is the Age of Reason. There are no—"

"There are no kingdoms where the tyrant Revolution has not walked, and her creature Napoleon grows daily in power. Do you think France the only land from which its aristocracy has had to flee in fear of their lives? My people, too, have been dispossessed. If you marry me, Jonet Ellen, you give your life into my hands," said the Prince. "Think, I beg you, of what you do!"

"Do you love me as I love you?" Jonet asked. The tears spilled gleaming down her face.

Slowly Auberon sank to his knees before her, and pressed his cheek against her hand. "I love you more than life, my Heart."

"Then I will marry you," Jonet said.

He tried to kiss her hand, but she tore it from his grasp and fled. Over the sound of her running feet Auberon could hear her sobbing.

The wedding was celebrated with an excess of ceremony possibly more fitting to a coronation, solemnized first by Vicar Goodbook in the village church, and then—once the Parish Register was signed—by Auberon's own priest in Auberon's own chapel.

The second ceremony was for Jonet a blurred memory of incense and and singing. The ring of black and crystal was taken from Jonet's finger and replaced with a massive braided band of hot red gold. Then the kiss of peace was placed upon her trembling lips by the Prince whose Princess she now was, and the wedding cup was poured and passed.

And then it was done.

All through the long and public day Jonet was aware of Auberon's eyes upon her, and when they were at last alone, he gave her no chance to protest or reason or soothe, and the fire in his eyes rose up and consumed her utterly.

"Lady—Lady—Lady—" In her dreams Jonet heard Perry calling her. As she opened her eyes, the voice jumbled into notes of birdsong. She blinked, unable to believe what she saw.

Broceliande—as it had been before Auberon came here. She lay in the West Tower, the one that had burned, and its shattered walls were open to the sky.

Her husband was gone. Slowly Jonet rose to her feet. She picked her way through the tumbledown of ancient fire-charred beams and stepped out through the gap in the ruins that only yesterday had been the french doors of the library.

"I tell you this much truly: My wealth is no more than phaerie gold. It is an illusion."

Jonet Bellamy Vertdubois, Princess de la Cockaigne, stood barefoot on the icy broken paving overlooking a wilderness of thorn. It was the garden, wild with half a century's wilderness.

Auberon had been telling the truth.

"If you were the Lord of the Hollow Hills himself, I would still marry you," she heard herself reply.

At least she was not forsworn.

Jonet pressed her hands to her temples and racked her brain for scraps of phaerie lore, turning over all that she could remember of what Auberon had said. Prince of Elphen whose phaerie glamour vanished with his passing, pledged to deliver up, every seven years, his mortal bride to Hell.

But this wasn't Hell, Jonet thought, shivering. *This was Scotland.*

And if Jonet had not been delivered up, there was only one other person who could have filled the bargain.

Jonet walked through the kitchen garden and up to Carterhall's kitchen door. Her thick woolen night rail was wet to the knees and her feet were bruised and bleeding from the stones she trod upon to reach here. This door, of all the doors in Carterhall, would be off the latch.

Her clothes were in the nursery, just as she had left them, shabby and overlooked in the great events that had transformed her life. She hesitated over her two black dresses, but in the end she lifted from the clothes-press the old blue gown that no amount of hard use and country rambling could spoil further. She dressed quickly, and when she was done, the mistress of Carterhall looked like any country farmwife.

"What are you doing here, girl?"

Jonet turned slowly. The Dowager Countess had obviously been hurriedly roused. Her eyes were flat with fear, but she glared at Jonet with the implacability of a cornered kitchen rat.

"I am dressing, Stepmama. And then I am going to Hell to fetch my husband back."

"He is gone?" The Dowager peered behind Jonet as if she expected to see Auberon lurking there. "Then— Then we can all be comfortable again. He forced me to give you up—he swore to kill all of us if I did not. Jonet, child—"

"He is my husband, and I am going to bring him back." Jonet caught up the red riding-hood that lay upon her bed, picked up her hatbox, and turned to go.

"No!" Avice caught her stepdaughter's arm. "You don't know what you are saying—he is a monster; I have seen him as he truly is—"

"And so have I." Jonet pushed past her stepmother and hurried down the stairs.

Darkness fell as Jonet guided the small pony trap through the hills. She tried to convince herself that she was not lost—she had planned to head south to Gretna, and from there take the Great North Road that led to London, because Auberon had said that he had friends there. But she could not even find the road, let alone London.

Over the thud of the pony's slow steps and the unoiled creak of the flywheel trap, Jonet slowly became aware of hoofbeats heading toward her on the road. She strained her ears and heard the jingling of spurs and tack of an animal at a jog-trot. Wearily Jonet let the lines drop. Shochad stopped, and Jonet waited for the horseman to pass. She pulled the hood of her cloak forward over her face and hoped there would be no trouble.

The hoofbeats stopped.

"Stand and deliver," an English voice drawled out of the darkness.

It isn't fair! was Jonet's first thought.

"If you please, sir, let me pass. I am nothing of any interest to you," she said carefully.

"That's as may be," said the voice, "but as a man with a job to do, it's my business to decide whether you're interesting or not."

There was a creak of leather as the rider urged his horse mincingly forward. Its shape swam disorientingly into focus: a piebald roan, coat blotched red and white, with a great red clown-circle about one eye. The eyes themselves were milk-pale; sightless.

"Her name is Justice," the rider said. He wore high black cavalry boots with silver-handled pistols stuffed into their tops. "She may be blind, but she can find her way in the dark." As if in confirmation, the mare snorted and shook her head.

He doffed his plumed tricorn and bowed low over his horse's withers, and the moonlight struck a golden aureole from his midnight hair. Even in such small illumination Jonet could see that his eyes were blue as the winter sea.

"Stand and deliver," he repeated politely. "Rings, watches, valuables . . ."

"Oh, but I haven't got any of those things!" Jonet said crossly. "I'm lost—well, not lost exactly. I just don't know where I'm going."

The highwayman frowned, appearing to consider Jonet's outburst. He replaced his tricorn on his head and as he did so, Jonet saw the blood staining the backs of his pale gloves.

"Oh, but you're hurt, sir!" she said in spite of herself.

The highwayman's lips curved in a mocking smile. "They are old wounds, and hardly trouble me now."

But Jonet was already scrabbling in the hatbox she had brought for her kerchiefs. "Old wounds indeed—they're still bleeding! You must take these," she said, standing in her cart to reach him. "And for heaven's sake, get to a surgeon! Riding out with your hands so marred; I never heard of such foolishness!"

Meekly the highwayman held out first one hand, then the other. Jonet wrapped and tied the handkerchiefs around them. The blood soaked through almost at once.

"It is all of a piece with being a highwayman, I make no doubt, and very likely you were shot by someone with a perfect right to do it," she scolded fiercely.

The highwayman laughed and tipped his hat to her.

"I never was much for the letter of the Law. Despair of my mother. Someone must ride, Jonet Ellen, and I have been at it these many years."

"Who are you?" Jonet demanded. "How do you know my name? I am looking for my husband—have you seen him?"

"I have, but he's a long way from here now—and since you don't know where you're going, and you haven't a watch, perhaps you need one." He reached into his coat-cuff and pulled out something that gleamed silver in the night.

Automatically Jonet spread her knees to catch it; it fell into her apron with a solid thud, and only when she picked it up, did she see what it was. A watch.

Auberon's watch.

"How did you get this?" she demanded, but the highwayman merely laughed.

"The wages of virtue, my child—and of biffing the ungodly on the beezer a time or two. Use it wisely."

He collected his harlequin mount and turned his horse away. Jonet shouted to stop him, but she might as well have been addressing the wind. At last, even the sound of his horse's hooves had vanished.

Sheer weariness nearly made her drop the watch. With shaking fingers Jonet opened it—and received another shock.

The face was still painted with moons and stars and suns, but now the painted face dipped and bobbed in its case with every movement of her hands. And the hands, instead of wheeling with clockwork progress through the day, slid liquidly about the dial, hour and minute hand together, to point down the road in front of her.

Not a watch, now. A *compass*.

Guided by the pointing hands of Auberon's transfigured watch, Jonet's pony trap rolled through Elphame's shadows. June became July; then August, September; and Jonet realized she did not make this journey alone.

September became October as she neared her goal, and now bodies hung in chains along the sides of the road, reminding Jonet afresh of what she had managed to forget in all the months of her journey—that to ransom back her husband, she was not going to Elphame or even to England, but to Hell.

The markers at the sides of the Great North Road now said High Hellborne, and the road itself turned, beneath Shochad's plodding hooves, from rutted autumn mud to dull pale bricks that glistened yellowly where his iron shoes scarred them. The road to Hell was paved with pure gold.

Jonet swallowed her unease and pressed her hand hard beneath her breastbone. On the horizon ahead she could see the shadow of the gallows.

Tyburn.

In London the Tyburn gallows were long since torn down—Papa had attended the last public execution held there on the very day his wife produced his only daughter, so Jonet knew the date precisely: November 7th, 1783. But here the gallows remained. Jonet closed her eyes tightly, urging the pony to hurry past the ghastly spot.

"Jonet! Jonet Ellen!"

Jonet dragged the pony to a stop again; he danced and shied, impatient to be gone.

"Jonet Ellen Bellamy!"

Jonet turned toward the sound. There was a woman sitting on the edge of one of the gallows platforms. She was dressed quite in the first stare of fashion; the only thing not quite *a la mode* was the lady's hair: it was innocent of wig or powder, and even in the evening light it gleamed redder than blood.

"Had enough with staring y'r fill, girl?" she said, making her way down from her grisly perch. Her fashionable West End drawl made it hard for Jonet to understand her.

"I—I beg your pardon," Jonet said.

"And you might that, for leaving it so late. Howbeit that it took you these four months to make your way down from the Wall?"

Jonet had no idea what wall was meant, but she knew

she must be polite; if there was one thing her journey had taught her, it was that rudeness could have consequences far beyond those set forth in the Good Book.

"I am very sorry, but I had no idea I was expected." The strange woman had reached the side of the pony trap, and Jonet saw that her skin was soft and dark together, like figs in honey.

"And how not—with Florizel leading your precious Auberon about Charlatan House like an ape on a chain?" Dark arching brows proclaimed the artifice of her hair; she looked very exotic, like a drawing in a book. Jonet might have been afraid of her, save that what the strange lady said drove everything else from Jonet's mind.

"Auberon? My husband? You know where he is?"

"All Hell knows where he is, girl—his trial and hanging will be the delight of the Little Season, I make no doubt—unless you've come to save him?"

Jonet stared into the bright black eyes before her.

"And if I have?" she said cautiously.

The woman smiled broadly, showing strong white teeth with a rather canine curve to them.

"Then I can tell you a thing or two that will get him back. You've come in good time—with that beneath your stomacher." She pointed to the thickening curve of Jonet's waist, and climbed without further ceremony into the trap. "Well, make haste, girl—or do you want to be outside the gates when the sun sets?"

Mechanically Jonet lifted the ribbons. "But who are you—and what do you care if I get my husband back?"

"In life I was a queen—and dogs licked up my blood when I fell, girl, so beware the sin of pride. And for the other—" for the first time in their short acquaintance the woman seemed to hesitate. "For the other, even the dead in Hell need the living to pray for them," Queen Jezebel said.

"Now tonight will be your only chance—at the end of the month he goes to the Tower and you'll have no chance of claiming him then," Jonet's hostess said briskly from the rose-red parlor of her modest Palladian townhouse on Dark Moon Street.

Jonet leaped to her feet in agitation, nearly spilling her tea. "Tonight? Claim him? But how?"

Queen Jezebel smiled a slow reptilian smile. "By the child you carry, child—there is no surer way."

The soiree this evening at Charlatan House would see the presentation of nearly a score of Perfidious Albion's likeliest damsels. Prince Florizel's corpulence had long since outstripped all but the most militant corsets, but the Prince Regent still had an eye for a pretty girl.

"You must make him speak to you," Jezebel told her, over and over. "He must speak first, then you can speak—without that, you have no chance."

Jonet nodded, barely hearing. Auberon was here, somewhere in this infernal mirror of London, and soon she would have him back. Or she would have failed, and doomed all three of them to a fate unguessable.

With Queen Jezebel at her side, Jonet entered Charlatan House.

The Prince had taken a fancy to the superheated pagnanisms of the East: The prolix interplay of colors was enough to make Jonet's eyes ache. Everywhere she looked there was a new wonder: painted Chinese paper, carved Indian screens, bowls and tables from Aegypt on jewel-bright rugs from fabled Persia. The whole effect, Jonet thought guiltily, was rather Papist—and it was quite as hot as it was supposed to be.

Queen Jezebel's hand was ice cold on Jonet's arm as they moved through the outer rooms. All around them were splendidly dressed men and women. As she and her companion passed, they turned to stare, and then to murmur behind their fans.

Gowns here cost more than the year's living they did on Earth. Here the cost of a presentation gown was all you had, and Dives and his lady were well represented. Among this gaudy company Jonet walked unadorned, in her plain blue gown and her scarlet mantle with her soft brown hair hanging free. They stopped before a set of carved and gilded doors that bore a horribly precise resemblance to the engravings of Carleton House that Jonet had seen in Ackerman's Fashion Repository on the infrequent occasions she chose to peruse it. Wigged and liveried footmen in scarlet coats embroidered with flames and golden serpents stood on either side of the doors; between them was a gigantic Nubian holding a carved ivory truncheon topped with a small gold representation of a lion devouring a unicorn.

He smiled broadly when he saw Jezebel.

"Well, Mrs. Ahab, it's been some time since we've seen you here."

"I have had little reason to come," said Jonet's companion coolly, "but I still have the entrée. Do let me in, Cerberus."

The gigantic majordomo laughed, and struck the doors with his stave. The footmen swung them open, and Jonet and Jezebel passed through.

The room was paneled in red silk. Each panel was bordered by an effusion of baroque gilded plasterwork. The chandeliers and torchières that lit the scene were all made of colored glass, and the drapes half-drawn over the windows at each end of the room were black velvet. The effect was indescribably lurid.

Her sponsor had left her side—Jezebel's presence would only betray Jonet to the suspicious and vindictive Prince—and Jonet was beginning to feel faint when a commotion at the far end of the room signaled that the Regent had arrived.

Everyone in the room immediately drew back toward the walls, so that His Highness would have the space to pass unimpeded about the room. Jonet, alone now, plied elbows and stout shoes to gain herself a place in the foremost ring of preferment-seekers.

"In the name of Mary Virgin, whose Son died upon Tree, Florizel must grant one wish to any woman great with child who comes before him. Only beware, Jonet, that he does not trick you into asking only what he wants to give."

Jonet would have recognized the Prince Regent at once, even without the jeweled orders and ribbons that decked him like a gaudy tinker's cart, but was surprised to find that he was not alone. Several favorites were with him.

She did not see her husband.

The Regent saw her. He beamed; a look of horror

spread over the face of the man beside him, but before anyone could speak, the Prince had uttered the fatal words:

"How now, little lady, and what brings you to Town?"

"My name is Jonet Bellamy Vertdubois, and I have come to ask for my husband back, in Mary's name."

Jonet threw back the scarlet mantle that had concealed her condition. The Prince Regent drew back with a hiss that momentarily transformed his face into something not remotely human.

"A bride!" he gasped. The wildfire buzz of discovery circled the room before Jonet could draw breath.

"Well," said the Prince unpleasantly. Though Jonet had not thought there was any room to spare, the people who had a moment before pressed in on her fell back, and she and Prince Florizel stood in a charmed circle of emptiness.

"Your husband, was it, Lady? I'd ask for safe passage from this place, were I you."

"He will try to trick you," came Jezebel's voice in her memory.

"Give me my husband, Your Highness, in Mary's name," Jonet said again.

"Well p'raps I shall, and p'raps I shan't. I dare say you don't even know where he is."

Jonet looked up and did not see Auberon anywhere. She reached into the pocket of her apron and pulled out his big silver watch. Its doubled hands pointed unerringly to a man who stood at Florizel's left shoulder, garbed all in winter's brown.

"This is he," Jonet said, placing the watch into his hand. As silver touched flesh the deception vanished, and Auberon appeared. Florizel danced a small furious dance step upon the black glass floor.

"Well! Well! Well!" His florid complexion grew even redder; he paused to take snuff and sneezed several times. Jonet waited.

"So you think you've won," Florizel said at last. "I make no doubt where to lay the blame for this trumpery mummery. But you've failed! Ask for anything I have, mortal bride, and you may have it—but you must leave something behind to remove the guests of my father's kingdom."

The room exploded into mocking laughter, and Jonet felt her cheeks grow hot. But surely Queen Jezebel had known this limitation when she told Jonet how to win back her husband! Jonet stood without speaking.

"Very well," snapped Florizel, "I will be merciful. Give me the child and his father may go free."

"No!" Jonet and Auberon spoke with one voice. Florizel turned on the Phaerie lord.

"She pleads prettily—but does she know for what? If she will not give up the child, then you, my lord, must give up your illusion!"

Florizel waved his quizzing-glass. The watch was struck from Auberon's grasp. It fell to the floor and shattered.

And Auberon began to change.

His skin darkened, as if fire consumed him from within. Horns appeared on his brow; they blossomed into great curving spirals that brushed his shoulders. He had been large before, but now he was monstrous; his hooves rang against the glass and when he flexed his arms, his coat split down the back with a single crack like thunder.

"Will she have you, Phaerie lord—once you are made mortal and stripped of all your power?"

In answer Jonet stepped forward and put her small white hand in Auberon's large leathery black one. She turned to Prince Florizel.

"Many husbands who should wear horns do not," she said, "and so I do not mind that my husband wears them with no cause. And I ask you for the third time, Prince Florizel: Give me my husband, in Mary's name."

Snow was still upon the ground this Lady's Day, and along the lane that led to Carterhall a tall man dark as a gypsy walked, leading a fat white pony. The woman on its back was heavy with child; she clung to the pony's ragged mane with one hand and the folds of her red riding-hood with the other.

"I'm sure they'll let us in," she said in the manner of one who is not saying this for the first time.

"If," said her husband dryly, "there is anyone to let us in. Your country inns are an education, lady wife—your stepsisters married, your stepmother taken up for coining—"

"And transported," Jonet added helpfully. "But surely there will be someone there—Papa swore the fires must never go out in the library, and so there must be someone to tend them. They will know me."

"And you will come into your own again," Auberon said.

"I already have," said the Lady of Carterhall.

BELLE BLOODY
MERCILESS DAME

by Jane Yolen

World Fantasy Award winner Jane Yolen has written well
over 150 books for children and adults, and well over 200
short stories, most of them fantastical. She is a past president of the Science Fiction and Fantasy Writers of America
as well as a 25-year veteran of the Board of Directors of
the Society of Children's Book Writers & Illustrators. She
lives with her husband in Hatfield, Mass., and St. An-
drews, Scotland.

An elf, they say, has no real emotions, cannot love,
cannot cry. Do not believe them, that relative of
the infinite Anon. Get an elf at the right time, on a
Solstice for example, and you will get all the emotions
you want.

Only you may not like what you get.

Sam Herriot, for example, ran into one of the elves
of the Western Ridings on a Sunday in June. He'd forgotten—if he'd ever actually known—it was the Summer
Solstice. He'd had a skinful at the local pub, mostly Ten-
nants, that Bud wannabe, thin and pale amber, and was
making his unsteady way home through the dark alley
of Kirk Wynd.

And there was this girl, tall, skinny, actually quite a
bit anorexic, Sam thought, leaning against the gray stone
wall. Her long ankle-length skirt was rucked up in front
and she was scratching her thin thigh lazily with bright
red nails, making runnels in her skin that looked like
veins, or like track marks. He thought she was some
bloody local junkie, you see, out trolling for a john to
make enough money for another round of the whatever.

And Sam, being drunk but not that drunk, thought
he'd accommodate her, even though he preferred his

65

women plump, two handsful he liked to say, hefting his hands palms upward. He had several unopened safes in his pocket, and enough extra pounds in his wallet because he hadn't had to pay for any of the drinks that night. His Mam didn't expect him home early since it had been his bachelor party. And with Jill gone home to spend the last week before their marriage with her own folks, there was no one to wait up for him. So he thought, "What the hell!" and continued down the alley toward the girl.

She didn't look up, but he was pretty sure she knew he was there; it was the way she got quiet all of a sudden, stopped scratching her leg. A kind of still anticipation.

So he went over to her and said, "Miss?" being polite just in case, and only then did she look up and her eyes were not normal eyes. More like a cat's eyes, with yellow pupils that sat up and down rather than side to side. Only, being drunk, he thought that they were just a junkie's eyes.

She smiled at him, and it was a sudden sweet and ravenous smile, if you can imagine those two things together. He took it for lust, which it was, of a sort. Even had he been sober, he wouldn't have known the difference.

She held out her hand, and he took it, drawing her toward him and she said, "Not here," with a peculiar kind of lilt to her voice. And he asked, "Where?"

Then without quite realizing the how of it, he suddenly found himself sitting on a hillside with her, though the nearest one he knew of was way out of town, about a quarter of a mile, near the Boarside Steadings.

He thought, *I'm really drunk, not remembering walking all this way.* But that didn't stop him from kissing her, putting his tongue up against her teeth until she opened her mouth and sucked him in so quickly, so deeply he nearly passed out. So he drew back for a breath, tasting her saliva like some herbal tea, and watched as she shrugged out of the top of her blouse, some filmy little number, no buttons or anything.

She was naked underneath.

"God!" he said, and he really meant it as a sudden

prayer because she was painfully thin. He could actually count her ribs. And she had this odd third nipple, right on the breastbone between the other two. He'd heard that some girls did, but he'd never actually seen anything like it before.

He wondered, suddenly, about Jill and their wedding in a couple of days, and it sobered him a bit, making his own eyes go a bit dead for a moment.

That's when the girl stood up on those long skinny legs and walked over to him, pressing him backward, whispering in some strange, liquid language. Suddenly it all made sense to him. She was a foreigner, not British at all.

"Aren't you cold, lass?" he asked, thinking that maybe he should just cover her up, here on the hillside, and never mind the other stuff at all. Because Jill would kill him if she knew, the girl so skinny and foreign and odd.

But the girl put her hands on his shoulders and pushed him back till he lay on the cold grass staring up at her. It was past midnight and the sky still pearly, this being Scotland where summer days spin across the twenty-four hours with hardly any dark at all. He could see faint stars around her head, and they looked as if they were moving. Then he realized it wasn't stars at all, but something white and fluttering behind her. *Moths,* he thought. *Or gulls.* Only much too big for either.

She lay down on top of him and kissed him again, hard and soft, sighing and weeping. Her hot tears filled his own eyes till he could not see at all. But all the while the wings, not moths, not gulls, wrapped around him. He did not feel the cold.

He woke hours later on the hillside and thought they must have had sex, or had something at any rate, though he couldn't remember any of it, for his trousers were soaked through, back and front. He felt frantically in his pocket. The safes were still there, untouched. His wallet, too. His mouth felt bruised, his head ached from all the beer, and he could feel the heat of a hickey rising on the left side of his neck.

But the girl was gone.

He stood slowly and looked around. Far off was the sea looking, in the morning light, silvery and strange. He was miles from town, not Boarside Steadings at all, and there was no sign of the thin girl, though how she could have disappeared, or when, he did not know. But leaving him here, alone, on the bloody hillside, drained and tired, feeling older than time itself must have given her some bloody big laugh. Well, he hoped she got sick, hoped she got the clap, hoped she got herself pregnant, little tart. And all he had to show for it was a great white feather, as if from some bloody stupid fairy wing.

And brushing himself off, he started down the cold hillside toward—he hoped—home.

THE LAST WARRIOR
by Tim Waggoner

Tim Waggoner's fiction has appeared in 100 Wicked Little Witch Stories, 100 Vicious Little Vampire Stories, and the forthcoming A Horror Story a Day: 365 Scary Stories. He makes his home in Columbus, Ohio.

"Rise, Alfarnin!"

The voice— a woman's, he thought, an old woman's—seemed to come from a great distance. Alfarnin tried to open his eyes, but he was tired, so very tired. . . .

"There is no time for this, elf! Get up! Skuld commands you!"

He felt a pair of age-weakened hands tugging on his arm. He tried to pull away and roll over so that he might shrug off the old woman and give himself up completely to the darkness she was so determined to drag him away from. But he found himself able to turn only partway. Something was blocking him.

He opened a weary eye and found himself staring into the horrid, twisted face of a troll. With a cry, he sat up, right hand instinctively groping for a weapon.

"Don't bother, elf," said the old woman disdainfully. "It's dead. Everything's dead here. Save you, that is."

Alfarnin saw she spoke the truth. The troll's eyes were wide and staring, its hairy chest a ragged ruin. He lifted his gaze from the fell beast to see he sat in the middle of an endless expanse of corpses, all clad in battle gear. A vast array of weapons protruded from the bodies—spears, pikes, swords, axes—and blood covered the twisted, still forms like a crimson blanket.

He looked down at his own simple tunic. Once it had been the plain gray of an elfin farmer; now it was a stiff, dark red edging toward brown. He touched his long silver hair and found it clumped and matted with dried blood. He ran a hand across his chest and stomach, searching for wounds, but those he discovered were, for the most part, minor, though they hurt like blazes.

"Your weapon, *warrior*." The old woman sneered this last word.

Alfarnin turned to look at the woman for the first time. She wore a black robe, hood drawn forth to cover her head, completely obscuring her features. If it hadn't been for her tremulous voice—and for her wrinkled, age-spotted claw which held forth his hand scythe—he couldn't have guessed at her age.

He took his scythe, noting that the dulled blade was caked with flaking red-brown. "I was working in my fields when I heard Heimdall's horn," he explained. "I had little time to prepare before the battle was joined." The final battle: Ragnarok.

He could remember little after Heimdall's signal had echoed throughout the universe, summoning all creation to the last great war. To Alfarnin, it had been a blur of images—flashing blades, thundering warhorses, razor-sharp claws—and a cacophony of sound—the battle cries of the gods, the answering bellow of giants, steel clanging against steel. And above all, the screams of the dying. So many screams.

But it was over now; the warriors, both those who fought for Light and those for Dark, were still, their voices silenced forever. And somehow, miraculously, impossibly, Alfarnin, a simple tender of crops, was the lone survivor.

And then he remembered what the old woman had named herself. "Skuld, you said. You are one of the Norns, the three Fates."

"I am. She whose province is the future."

Alfarnin looked out across the endless open graveyard that surrounded them. There were no buzzing flies, no feasting gore crows. The air was motionless, flat and dead.

He spoke in a weary, hollow voice. "After this day, I would think there is no future."

Skuld chuckled dryly. "That, my dear elf, is entirely up to you."

Gerald Winnick, all of twenty-four years old, stood at the altar sweating and waiting for the Wedding March to begin. His rented tux was too loose around the waist and too tight around the throat. He was having trouble breathing, and what little air he did get in lay hot and heavy in his lungs.

His groomsmen stood beside him, three of his best friends from high school, but the way he felt, he might as well have been alone. *They* weren't the ones getting married today, *they* weren't the ones gambling their entire future on the next half an hour or so.

It wasn't that he didn't love Laura—he did—but the idea of being married to her, being her Husband with a capital H, freaked him out more than a little. Intellectually, he knew it was just a ceremony, a few words and an exchange of rings, a confirmation of a love that already existed, no big deal.

But emotionally, it felt as if something new was about to happen, something almost magical. His whole world— and Laura's, too, of course—was about to change forever.

The priest smiled at Gerald kindly, then gave a nod for the organist to start playing. As soon as the familiar strains of the Wedding March began (though Gerald had never heard them outside of a movie or TV show before), Laura appeared in the rear of the church, holding on to her father's arm. They stood there a moment, then began slowly walking forward arm in arm. Laura was beaming, and her father looked as if this were the proudest, and perhaps in a way the saddest, day of his life.

Gerald started trembling. He loved Laura, he did, but she was a bit self-centered, tended to think of herself before anyone else, and while she expected him to share every little feeling he had, she was reticent about sharing hers. And a dozen other things, minor complaints, really, mostly tiny quirks and eccentricities which everyone had, Lord knows he had his share, but when you took his weirdness and hers and put them together. . . .

Laura and her father reached the foot of the altar.

Her father kissed her on the cheek, then she kissed him. Then they turned to face the priest.

"Who gives this woman away?" the priest asked in a voice which filled the church. It seemed to Gerald as if God himself were speaking.

"Her mother and I," Laura's father answered clearly. Then he gave Laura a last kiss and sat in a pew next to her mother while Laura mounted the steps to stand next to Gerald. Her maid of honor stepped down to arrange her train, then took her place once more.

The priest began talking, but Gerald wasn't listening. He looked at Laura and she smiled at him, a smile full of love and hope, with not a hint of nervousness. Gerald felt her love for him, and while it didn't wash away his doubts completely, it went a long way toward blunting them.

He realized that he had been waiting for something, for some sort of cosmic guarantee that he was doing the right thing. But it was a guarantee which wasn't forthcoming. He knew now that there were no sure things in life, and that a big part of love, real love, was faith. The question was, did he have that kind of faith in Laura? In himself? In them?

When the time came, Gerald said, "I do," and, even if his voice quavered a bit, he was sure he meant it.

"Wake up, elf!"

Alfarnin opened his eyes and rubbed the sleep out of them. The sky above was the same dull gray it had been when he'd lain down. Skuld had said there was no time anymore, so there would be no sunrise, no sunset, just endless gray.

Alfarnin rose to his feet. Skuld stood a few feet away, hands on her hips, and while the elf still couldn't see into the shadowed depths of her hood, he had the impression she was looking at him disapprovingly.

"You certainly sleep a good deal," the Norn grumbled.

Alfarnin brushed dirt from his tunic. He had had to move several bodies in order to clear a space to sleep. There was no way he could move a giant, even though some of them were hardly larger than man-size. Nor could he move one of the Aesir, not just because he was loath to dishonor the gods even in death, but because despite their normal size, they tended to be made of sterner stuff than men and were far heavier than they looked. The dwarves, while less dense structurally, were still heavy enough, and, being a light elf, Alfarnin couldn't bring himself to touch one of the hated dark elves. So in the end, he had moved some of his own lithesome people and prayed for forgiveness to the spirit of Frey, who among other things was—or rather, had been—god of elves.

"I traveled quite a distance yesterday." Alfarnin realized such concepts as *yesterday* and *tomorrow* had no meaning any longer, but he knew no other way to express himself. "I was weary."

Skuld snorted. "An illusion, nothing more. Your body felt tired because it expected to. But without Time, you cannot tire." She gestured toward the endless expanse of bodies which surrounded him. "Have you not noticed that the corpses do not rot? That rigor has not claimed them? They are as fresh as the moment life fled them. No time is passing here, elf, because Time itself has died."

"If Time has died, then why do I seem to experience it? Why must I still walk one step after the other? Why do I still sleep and dream?

"I told you, it's an illusion!" Skuld said impatiently. "You only think—" She broke off. "Did you say you dreamed?"

Alfarnin nodded and told the Norn of his strange dream, of being a young human on the day of joining to his mate.

Skuld said nothing at first. Finally, she made a dismissive gesture. "We exist in an in-between state here, between Life and Death, Existence and Nothingness. Odd experiences are to be expected in such a place."

Alfarnin shrugged. He was no mage or philosopher, just a simple farmer. Such weighty matters were beyond him. Still, it had been an interesting dream. Alfarnin himself had never been fortunate enough to be allowed to take a wife; the elf lord who ruled the lands he farmed had never seen fit to grant his permission.

Alfarnin put the dream out of his mind. He had work to do. "Are you going to accompany me this day, Skuld? Or are you going to remain behind as you did yesterday?"

"I have no need to travel with you, elf. When you reach your destination, I shall be there."

"Very well." He started walking, picking his way carefully around the bodies of the fallen warriors, stepping over them and, when he had no choice, on them. He walked in no particular direction, for according to Skuld, he didn't have to bother with that. He simply needed to concentrate on his goal and continue forward.

It didn't seem so simple to him. As Skuld had explained to him "yesterday," he was to find the body of the Allfather Himself, Odin, and tear the heart from His chest. And then the elf was to bear the heart to Yggdrasill and use it to renew creation itself.

Alfarnin, as did all who lived, knew the prophecy of Ragnarok and what was to occur afterward. The gods and their allies would perish while bravely standing against the forces of Darkness. For a time, the world would be as ashes, cold and barren, but then a spark of life would return and creation would begin again, new and vital.

But the tales had never said exactly how the world would be restored. But Skuld had known. Being the Future, how could she not?

He remembered how she had explained it to him.

"Think of Existence as a wheel, elf," she had said not long after his first awakening. "A wheel which is constantly in motion, turning slowly from today to tomorrow, one day following the next in stately progression until the end is reached and the wheel grinds to a halt. But the Wheel is circular; it has no true beginning and end. All it needs to resume its turning is a push. A push which you shall give, elf."

"Me?" he had said, incredulous. "Such a task is for a god, or a great hero! I'm not even a proper warrior!"

"True," Skuld had agreed, a little too quickly for Alfarnin. "But you are all that remains. I would do it myself if I could, but I cannot. The Future can make itself known, but it cannot create itself."

Alfarnin hadn't been sure he understood the difference, but Skuld said that was the best explanation she could give, and he had no choice but to accept it.

"What will the new world be like?" he asked.

"Much the same as the old. The wheel has turned many, many times before this. There have been other Ragnaroks; this was merely the latest."

"Have I always been the only one to survive?" Alfarnin asked.

Skuld laughed. "Don't flatter yourself, elf! The cycle of Existence has its variations. There is always at least one survivor of the final battle, sometimes more, and I always guide them so that they might restart the wheel on its endless journey. This is the first time you have survived the battle. Last time it was Loki." She shook her head. "Getting him to start the wheel again took quite some doing."

Alfarnin hadn't particularly wanted this duty, what Skuld called "a great honor." After the horrors he had witnessed—and committed—during Ragnarok, he would rather have lain down and surrendered to the ultimate darkness, so he might forget.

But if he truly was the only one left, he had no choice, did he? Besides, Skuld had assured him that when the wheel began its new cycle, he would eventually be reborn, quite likely in a higher station because of his actions.

"Who knows?" she had said, "you might even end up a lesser god."

So now here Alfarnin was, traipsing through the grisly aftermath of the final battle, searching for the corpse of the Allfather, without any more guidance other than Skuld's assurances that as long as he continued on, the elf would eventually stumble across—

He stopped. There, in the sky. Was that . . . yes, it was. Off in the distance, circling in the air, was a large black raven. It seemed Skuld had been right; he had found what he was looking for.

Alfarnin hurried forward.

Gerald, all of thirty now, stood next to his wife, arm around her shoulders, and tried to radiate calm and strength, despite the fact he was scared to death.

Laura wore a blue housecoat and ugly green slippers, the latter provided by the hospital. Her hair was limp and mussed, her face pale, eyes red from crying. Gerald felt like crying himself, but he wouldn't allow it, not in front of Laura. She needed him to be strong.

Make that *they* needed him to be strong. Gerald turned away from Laura and looked through the window at the tiny being who, along with his wife, made *they*. Nurses bustled around the small (so small) infant, a girl, who didn't have a name yet because she'd come so early. Eight weeks, to be precise.

The nurses checked various tubes and monitors while Gerald's tiny daughter lay motionless within the sterile warmth of her incubator. It was a poor substitute for a mother's womb, but it would have to do.

Their baby looked so frail, so weak, so tired, as if it exhausted her just to breathe and pump blood through her not-quite-finished body. She needed a name, they had to think of a name. But right now Gerald couldn't do anything except hope to God the tiny thing would live a few more hours.

Tears began to flow down well traveled paths on Laura's cheeks. Gerald tore his gaze from his struggling daughter. "It'll be okay, honey," he said. He forced a smile. "She's a fighter, just like her mom." He didn't quite manage to sound as he'd have liked, but Laura smiled at him gratefully and wrapped her arms around his waist. And they stood like that, together, and watched, waited, and prayed.

Alfarnin stopped, disoriented and dizzy. He stood before the shaggy, blood-matted corpse of a great wolf, many times larger than any ordinary canine. This was Fenrir, child of Loki and, according to the prophecy of Ragnarok, the slayer of Odin. And above, circling slowly, was the midnight-black raven.

Alfarnin didn't recall anything from the moment he had first spotted the raven in the sky, didn't remember crossing the intervening distance. No, that wasn't quite true. He had had another of those strange dreams. Only this hadn't been a dream, had it, for he had been awake.

A vision of some kind, then. But a vision of what, exactly, Alfarnin wasn't certain.

"Something wrong, elf?"

Skuld stood beside him, as she had promised. Alfarnin started to tell the Norn of his vision, but then decided against it. It hardly seemed important, not compared to the task which lay before him. He shook his head and examined the body of the huge beast that had been the great wolf Fenrir.

From the tales Alfarnin had heard all his long life, he had expected Fenrir to be quite a terror, but despite the wolf's gigantic size, it made no more impression on him than the thousands of other corpses he had seen in the timeless interval since first awakening. Perhaps the horrors he had witnessed during Ragnarok and after had numbed him. Or perhaps even the dire wolf Fenrir didn't seem so fearsome when compared to the sick, helpless terror of a parent desperately praying for the survival of his ailing child.

"Elf?" the Norn prompted, a measure of concern in her voice.

Alfarnin shook his head once more and did his best to cast the vision from his mind. He was an elf, not a man of Midgard, and work lay before him.

Fenrir's jaws had been torn apart, by Odin's son Vidar, taking vengeance for his father's death. Or so it must have been if the tales held true.

'It strikes me as odd, Skuld."

"What does, elf?"

"That Odin and the other Aesir, knowing how Ragnarok was to turn out, did nothing to try to change it."

Skuld's tone was that of an impatient parent lecturing to a slow-witted child. "It was predestined; there was nothing they could do but play out their assigned roles. The Wheel turns, and both gods and mortals follow, whether they like it or not."

"They hardly seem like gods, then, do they?" the elf mused. "More like dancers stepping out their well-rehearsed movements to someone else's tune?"

"Such is the way of existence," Skuld said.

Alfarnin said nothing. Instead, he pointed his hand scythe at a black form which lay partially buried beneath one of Fenrir's huge front paws. "Another raven." He knelt down and prodded it with the blade of his scythe, but it didn't respond. "Dead."

"Huginn," Skuld said. "The raven of Thought. When Odin perished, so did it likewise, for the Allfather was done with thinking."

Akfarnin gestured to the other raven still circling above. "And that one?"

"Muninn, the raven of Memory. Odin may be gone, but as long as we are here to remember him, Muninn lives on."

Alfarnin nodded, though the Norn's explanation made little sense to him. "What do I do now?"

"I told you—you need to retrieve the Allfather's heart." She pointed to the belly of the great wolf, and Alfarnin remembered: Fenrir was supposed to devour Odin.

He glanced at his scythe's dulled blade. It would hardly do the job. He began to search the fallen warriors, looking for a dagger—a very sharp dagger.

Hours later—or at least what seemed like hours later—Alfarnin stepped back from the wolf's open gut and dragged a gore-smeared forearm across his sweaty brow. His gray farmer's tunic was soaked with blood which refused to dry: another feature of the timelessness of this place, according to Skuld. Alfarnin wished he had possessed the foresight to remove his clothing before beginning his grisly work.

"You are close, elf," Skuld said. "I can feel it!"

Alfarnin took a deep breath, ignored the pain from his unhealing wounds, and stepped back into the beast's carcass. After a bit, he reached what he thought was the creature's stomach, and with a final downward swipe of the elf's borrowed dagger, the leathery organ parted. A flood of foul-smelling liquid gushed forth, splashing onto Alfarnin. His gorge rose instantly, and he turned away, fully expecting to empty the contents of his own stomach, but though he retched violently, nothing came up. He didn't have to ask Skuld; this was no doubt yet another result of the strange nature of this place.

When the urge to vomit subsided, Alfarnin turned

back to the cavity he had created in Fenrir and there, mangled and curled into a ball, reposed the body of Odin, Allfather, Lord of the Aesir and all creation.

Alfarnin had never seen Odin before, though he had heard many, many tales of the god over the centuries. And truth to tell, he was rather disappointed. He had expected to find an imposing, kingly being. But instead Odin was a tall, lean old man with a long scraggly gray beard and a black leather patch over one eye, or rather, where an eye had once been. His golden battle armor seemed too large for the scrawny body, as if its owner were a beggar who had suddenly been pressed into service instead of the all-powerful god of gods.

It was difficult for Alfarnin to understand why such a mighty being, forewarned of such an ignominious end, would not choose to take steps to avoid it. Unless, as Skuld had said, He had had no choice. Well, Odin had played out his part; so, too, would Alfarnin.

"Forgive me, Allfather," he whispered, then raised his dagger and returned to his work. A bit later he held in his hand a blood-smeared orb of polished silver. The Heart of Odin.

Skuld clapped her withered hands in glee. "One more journey, elf, and you are through. You must take the heart to the base of Yggdrasill. As before, keep your destination strongly in your mind as you walk, and you shall eventually reach the World Tree. I shall await you there."

And then she was gone.

Alfarnin wiped the heart off on the cloak of one of the low-ranking Aesir lying not far from Fenrir, tucked his dagger in his belt, and then, even though he really did not need it any longer, he picked up his scythe. He had started his journey as a farmer, and it seemed only right that he finish it as such.

He began to walk, but stopped when he heard a soft thump behind him. He turned to see Odin's second raven, Muninn, lying dead on the ground. Now that the Allfather had surrendered His heart, what need was there to remember Him anymore? Alfarnin looked across the field of corpses. What need to remember any of this?

Reeking of blood and gastric juices, he resumed his journey.

Gerald was thirty-nine, too young to have to worry about words like *tumor* and *chemotherapy*. But his cancer hadn't bothered to ask for his I.D. before inviting itself into his body and settling in. Now, after three surgeries (one major, two minor), he sat in a waiting room of the outpatient wing of Holland Memorial Hospital, wracked with nausea from his latest chemo treatment, trying to choke down a horrid concoction of powdered lemon drink mix and contrast dye that would make his innards more photogenic for the CT scan.

His oncologist said his chances for a cure were good; not great, but good. So Gerald endured the surgeries, the CT scans, the blood tests, x-rays, the chemo, and worst of all, the soul-gnawing fear that in the end none of it would be enough. Because he desperately wanted to live.

Not so much for himself. Given the choice, he wanted to squeeze as many years out of his life as he possibly could, but he'd lived to thirty-nine, and overall, he was satisfied with the time he'd had. And while he wanted to live for Laura, he knew he didn't *need* to. Their marriage hadn't exactly been storybook perfect, but it had, on balance, been a good one. But Laura was still young, at least relatively so, and she was a strong woman. If she had to, she'd get by without him, maybe even find someone and remarry. Knowing this comforted him.

No, he wanted to live primarily for Caitlin. She'd be ten next month, and even though she was getting to be quite a big girl, he couldn't bear the thought of leaving his daughter without a daddy.

And so he sat in the uncomfortable waiting room chair, his gut churning angrily, and concentrated on holding the contrast down.

When this latest vision released Alfarnin, he found himself standing at the base of what appeared to be a craggy gray mountain. He looked up to see, beyond the clouds, a vast canopy of green covering the sky. No, which *was* the sky. He had reached Yggdrasill, and as with Fenrir, he had no memory of traveling here. Perhaps Skuld had been right and there really was no Time in this place.

"Of course I was right."

The Norn stood before him, features still hidden within her hood. Her feet touched the edge of one of the World Tree's three gigantic roots.

"I remember the tales," Alfarnin said. "This is the root beneath which the Well of Fate rests."

Skuld nodded. "And where the gods themselves came to hold council each day. As guardian of the Well, I sometimes listened in as they talked." She chuckled. "Or more often, argued."

Alfarnin frowned. "What of your sisters, Urd and Verdandi? Past and Present?"

"We are One." Skuld opened her robe to reveal not the body of a wrinkled old crone as her voice promised, but rather an empty black space in the middle of which hung the motionless shape of an ancient, crude spinning wheel. At the center of the wheel was a circular depression, just the right size, Alfarnin thought, for the heart of Odin.

"Past, present, future . . ." Skuld snorted. "Merely names. They are one and the same. See the Wheel. Does it have a beginning or end? No, it is a circle, unbroken. We are One, and that One is the Wheel."

"It isn't moving."

"The Wheel has completed its cycle. It's up to the last survivor of Ragnarok—to you—to give it a push and start it turning again."

Alfarnin didn't have to ask what was expected of him. All he had to do to renew creation was to place the holy heart in the center of the Wheel, and all would begin anew. It was his duty, to his gods, to his fallen elfin brothers and sisters, to all who had fought and died in service to the Light. But he hesitated.

"The visions I experienced, Norn—what did they signify?"

'They are nothing, elf," Skuld snapped. "Now fulfill your purpose this cycle and give me the heart!"

"Why here? Why did you not ask for the heart when I first removed it from Odin?"

"Because only here, at the base of Yggdrasill, am I truly one with the Wheel. But forget all that; the time for explanations is past. Give me the heart!"

"Why don't you take it from me?"

"I told you, the Future cannot make itself! *You* must make it, here and now!"

"Tell me about the visions, Norn." Alfarnin smiled. "After all, if there is no Time any longer, then we have no need to hurry, do we?"

Skuld was silent for a while before finally sighing. "Very well. I told you that there is always at least one survivor of Ragnarok, and that it is this survivor's task to renew creation. During the journey to salvage Odin's heart and bring it to the World Tree, the survivor has three visions of what his life in the next cycle will be like, so that he understands why he must restart the Wheel and what his reward will be."

"My visions were of mortal life as a man of Midgard," Alfarnin said. "But a Midgard unlike any I have ever heard tell of."

"Being the Future, I am quite aware of the visions you experienced." She paused. "However, I fear that I cannot explain them."

"Perhaps the next cycle will be different from the last," Alfarnin suggested.

"Impossible. The Wheel is the Wheel. There may be minute variations in its turning, but the path remains ever the same. It begins with creation, then comes the rise and flourishing of the gods, and then Ragnarok, turning after turning, cycle after cycle, without end."

Alfarnin thought for a moment. "What if I do not give you the heart? What of the Wheel then?"

"You have no choice; you must give me the heart. It is the role appointed you by destiny."

"I think you are lying, Norn. You told me before that once the Wheel stopped, Time ceased to be. Before Ragnarok, I was just another of Fate's puppets. But I think many things have ceased to be now, Fate among them. For the first time in my existence, I am truly free to choose."

Skuld said nothing.

"I repeat my question," Alfarnin said. "What happens to the Wheel if I do not give you the heart?"

"Without the heart—which is the heart of Creation itself—the Wheel cannot continue. It shall cease to be, as will Existence itself."

"All existence?" Alfarnin challenged. "Or just this one?"

Skuld didn't respond.

"Your Wheel is a prison, Skuld. Perhaps it's time for creation to be free." Alfarnin held the heart of Odin in his left hand and raised his scythe above it with his right.

"Hold, elf! You don't know what you're saying! Without the Wheel to give shape and form to existence, all will be Chaos! Events will unfold randomly, and no one will ever know what might occur next, for anything might happen, anything at all!"

"Considering the senseless carnage of Ragnarok—of Ragnaroks untold—I think not knowing what tomorrow will bring might be better." Alfarnin raised the scythe higher.

"Think hard before you act, elf," Skuld warned. "This other, lesser Midgard you would create would be naught but a bastardized world where uncertainty and ambiguity rule in place of the gods. There would be no fixed roles, no set future, no clear division between Good and Evil. In that world, you would be but a mortal man, weak, frail, doomed to fret over petty anxieties and frustrations all of your short life. Here, in Asgard, you were—and could be again—an elfin warrior, fighting on the side of Light in the most glorious battle Creation has ever known!"

"Glorious?" Alfarnin thought of the slaughter he had witnessed, and its aftermath. "Meaningless is more like it." He tightened his grip on the scythe. "And the man Gerald will be far more of a warrior in his quiet, unsure way than the elf Alfarnin ever was."

He brought down the scythe and plunged its blade into the silver heart of Odin. Skuld screamed, the Wheel cracked apart like thunder, and the world was no more.

"We're ready for you now, Mr. Winnick," the CT technician, a heavyset blonde woman, said gently.

Gerald nodded, set down his empty cup, and stood too quickly. His vision went gray and he swayed dizzily. He thought for a moment he might fall, but then the technician came forward to take his elbow. His vision cleared, the dizziness passed, and he smiled gratefully at the woman, only a little embarrassed.

With the technician's help, Gerald made his way out of the waiting room and walked slowly down the hall toward the CT room, one unsteady step after another.

WOMAN OF THE ELFMOUNDS

by Paul Edwin Zimmer

Paul Edwin Zimmer is best known for his Dark Border series, but has written fine novels such as *The Survivors,* which was coauthored with his sister, Marion Zimmer Bradley. A cofounder of the Society for Creative Anachronism, he has studied both Japanese and Chinese swordfighting styles, and incorporates that knowledge into his fiction where possible. He lives in Berkeley, California.

Conn Mac Cathla rode over the high moors in the twilight, shivering in the icy-fingered wind. He clutched his cloak about him, wondering if he had yet crossed Clann Domnann's border into the lands of his other foes, the Elves of Caer Liath. Earth and sky were gray; hooves on the frozen sod and wind the only sounds.

He had ridden hard that day, fighting and fleeing the men of Clann Domnann. His hewn shield was cast away, his javelins thrown; his horse tired, and he far from the lands of his people.

The first stars pricked the darkening sky. A distant wolf howled, and Conn's face twisted. He hated wolves. While yet a child, he had seen his brother's torn and mangled body, and since that day had hunted and slain the gray killers whenever he could find them.

He drove his heels into his horse's sides and loosened his sword in his scabbard. The wolf cried again, and, nearer, another answered. His horse shied and snorted, ears pricking, hooves pawing at the ground. Another howl rose in the darkness, and then wolves filled the night with howling, echoing wearily over gray wastelands. The horse reared, hooves lashing air. Conn drew his sword, crouching low against the horse's back as it broke into a mad run.

A glimmer on the horizon warned of the moon. A deep-throated chorus rose as silver light spread across the moor. Conn's hand tightened on his sword hilt. Wolves were all about him, black in the moonlight. His horse screamed and reared as one loped across his path, and Conn was nearly thrown. But the wolves did not attack. They were seeking other prey.

As he wondered, a scream came out of the darkness ahead, and Conn, a snarl of hatred on his lips, turned his horse toward the sound. Before the terror-maddened horse was aware, they were in the midst of the pack, and a wolf cried out as it was trodden beneath driving hooves. Conn leaned to slash at another.

Beyond the pack, a man and a woman had their backs to a great tree, and the man held a slim straight sword that seemed to glow with its own fire.

Conn's broadsword lashed in a terrible arc, cleaving flesh and bone. The horse screamed, rearing in terror, and Conn, leaning overbalanced from the horse's back, fell among the wolves. He was on his feet in a moment, with a shout of derision, heavy blade sweeping about him. There was an answering shout. Conn glanced quickly toward the tree and saw the woman, swift as a squirrel, run up the stem.

Then a great black body hurtled toward his throat; a weight struck against his chest and smashed him from his feet. He dropped his sword; one hand shot to a hairy throat, holding the snapping jaws away, while the other hand tore a dirk from his belt and stabbed.

A sword flashed, someone dragged the body from him, and then a slim figure was standing over him with a blade of flame.

Conn rolled to his feet and snatched up his sword, and the two stood back-to-back, wolves snarling about them. Conn's huge iron broadsword whirled in great, blood-splattering swaths; but the stranger's blade, keen point flashing, darted about like a bird.

From the tree, the woman's voice cried out. Over the snarling of the wolves rang an answering cry, and a sound of hoofbeats. A wolf leaped into the air, snapping at the slender shaft that quivered in his side. The warrior at Conn's back shouted exultantly as two horsemen, with longbows in their hands, rode into view, shooting from the saddle into the ranks of the pack. A shimmering hung about them, and Conn half-turned to see. . . .

A wolf sprang from the side, and teeth crunched sickeningly in his swordarm. His head crashed against a stone, and drove a shower of sparks before his eyes. Dimly, as through a mist, Conn saw the flaming blade slash the wolf's throat. He struggled up, then fell into darkness.

He awoke, a long time after, hearing bagpipes play a merry tune. But what piping! Old Buinne, the best piper of Clann Cormac, could not have matched it, nor the piper of the High King. Conn lay quiet in the darkness behind his eyelids, listening to wild weaving patterns of rising and falling sound.

His eyes opened. He was lying on a bed in an arched room, bark-covered walls rising in a gentle curve. A curtain blew aside to reveal a grass-grown slope. From behind the curtain came the piping. A woman with long night-black hair sat beside him. Her body was slender under green cloth; her eyes gleamed like stars. As she saw his eyes open, a smile came into her face.

"Welcome, and be at peace." Her voice was gentle as a dove's call. "Are you in pain?"

"I am not," Conn answered, and knew that he lied, for the injured arm throbbed angrily. "But who are you, and what is this place? And who is it that plays such music? No piper ever played so!"

Her laughter was part of the music.

"I am Ethbrien, daughter of Alador, and you are on the Elfmound of Caer Liath. It is my brother, Kiaran Mac Alador, whose piping you hear, and he is Lord of the Elfmound."

A cold shock washed over him. For generations, there had been war between Clann Cormac and the Elf-Folk of Caer Liath, ever since his forefather, Art Mac Ainnle, had slain the Lord of Caer Liath, and taken from him the jewel called "Daughter of the Sun." For the Elf-

Folk do not die, save in battle, and the hatred of men lives through the ages, passing from father to son.

"How came I here?" he asked.

"After we drove away the wolves, we found you lying senseless, your arm broken. The healers worked long—but we owe you much, Conn Mac Cathla."

"You know my name!"

"Conn of Clann Cormac, son of Cathla of the Mighty Arm. Yet you saved my life, and that of the Lord of Caer Liath."

"It was for no love of you," he answered gruffly. "Yet . . . now that I see you in the sunlight, I am glad. You are too beautiful for wolf's meat."

The piping stopped.

The tall elf entered the room, the pipes under his arm. A green cloak was about him, over a green tunic and a pale brown kilt. A sword hilt of white bronze jutted from a scabbard decked with gold. His face was beardless as a boy's, yet his eyes were ageless. Conn's eyes fell before the age and wisdom and power in those clear, gleaming eyes that seemed to bore into his heart. . . .

Men said that by looking into a man's eyes an elf could strip his soul and read hidden secrets, and there were other, darker tales. . . .

"An enemy you have been, Conn Mac Cathla." Kiaran's voice was light and high, with a music to it that eased Conn's heart. "Yet you are welcome here. A great debt we owe you, one we cannot repay."

"Is not the mending of my arm a payment?" asked Conn. "And twice you saved my life when the wolves would have torn me."

"When two fight side by side, each defends the other, lest both die. Nor is the life of a mortal a fair payment for that of an elf, for a mortal's is forfeit from birth. As for your arm . . ."

"A warrior needs his arms,' said Conn.

'True. Yet that arm was raised in our defense—" He broke off as another entered the room, shorter than Kiaran, but as like him in face as a mirror. His kilt and tunic were green, and a sword, twin to that Kiaran wore, hung at his side.

"So this is the mortal," he said. "A great man he is,

surely. How can those shoulders ever get through a door?"

"My people put wide doors on their houses," Conn replied. "But here perhaps I must walk sideways."

"Well said!" laughed Kiaran. "This is Sian, my brother. It was he with Cahir Mac Indol, who rode to our aid last night." Sian's face sobered.

"It is a strong man you are, and a great debt we owe you. The lives of my brother and sister are dearer than a mortal can know."

Conn had no answer to that, and, tired, lay back, letting his eyes roam until they came to rest on the girl, Ethbrien. They stayed there for a time.

An elf, old as— his mind shied from that thought, and his gaze drifted up to the arch of he roof. Where the bark-clad walls joined, there was a line of meeting, and he saw that the bark of one wall differed from the other, as oak from ash.

"How was this chamber built?" he asked.

"Two ancient trees stand here," Kiaran answered, "so old that only Indol the Healer can recall when they were saplings. When they had grown so large that they began to crowd one another, we taught them to grow so that they formed this arch. Behind you and overhead for many feet, their bark touches in a kiss, and then they branch apart again. From a distance they seem one tree."

Conn drew a deep breath. The smell of the trees came to him: he had never smelled trees before, not to know them.

"They are the most ancient trees on the Mound," said Kiaran, "I fear that the time is not far, as we reckon time, for them to die."

'They fade and die," came Sian's sad voice, "as all things fade and die. Yet these have stayed with us longer than most." Conn saw their eyes fill with tears.

"Come!" cried Ethbrien. "What way is this to cheer a wounded guest? Your pipes, Kiaran; let them sing of joy!"

Kiaran turned, lifting the pipes as he passed from the room. There was a swift, rushing drone as the bag filled; music rippling like children's laughter; rapid dartings of

sound that danced in joy—joy blended with a sadness
that did not weaken the gaiety, but strengthened it—to
hear that music was to live, to feel the heart beat and
the blood flow, and it seemed to Conn that the music
wove about Ethbrien, shimmering in her beauty. She was
life, deathless and eternal. The music wrapped about her,
blended into her. . . .

Another elf appeared in the doorway, eyes laughing.
His face was a child's face, his slight form youthful, but
his eyes were grave and old. He turned and gestured,
and the music ended.

"This is a merry time!" he laughed. "Our mortal's
eyes have opened now, his ears can hear sweet music.
But what of your arm, warrior? I am Indol the Healer."
He gripped Conn's arm and moved it gingerly. Conn
gave a startled grunt of pain.

"It mends," said the elf, "but time will pass ere you
lift a sword again. A wolf's jaws are strong—that bone
snapped like a twig. But it will heal. Now for your
head . . ." His fingers passed gently over Conn's temples.

"Better than I had dared hope. It heals. But next time
choose a softer stone to fall on! You were dying, your
brain bleeding, when they brought you here. For two
days you have lain mindless. Kiaran and I had no time
to spare for your arm at first, for had your brain not
healed, you would have died, and your arm been no use
to you at all."

"My thanks," said Conn, licking suddenly dry lips.
"But how long before I am healed?"

"A month, perhaps, little more than that. We have
greater skill at healing than your druids. If I bind your
arm tightly, and you do not overtire yourself, you should
be able to rise for a time tomorrow."

"It would be good to be on my feet again."

"Today it were best you were on your back," said
Indol. "But now I must change the bandage on your
arm, and then you must eat, and rest." his hands touched
Conn's eyes. "After you eat, you must sleep, understand? Sleep and rest."

He felt the arm with gentle fingers. What he found
seemed to satisfy him, and smiling, he splinted it anew.

Conn ate the thick stew they brought, and his lids grew heavy.

"Eat hearty, warrior; build your bones anew!" came Indol's voice. Conn finished the stew, and lay back, eyes closing. "Sleep!" Indol's voice said, and then all was peace.

The next day, they helped him to rise and dress, and let him walk about the Mound. The Healer strapped Conn's arm tightly to his side.

"Be content to walk—no running, and no dancing, however sweet the music!"

Conn found that he could walk alone, though he felt weak and dizzy. With the Lord of the Elfmound at his elbow, lest he should stumble or fall, Conn walked into the sunlight, wondering to find himself safe among these elves, foes of his clan since the "Daughter of the Sun" was taken from the body of Alador of Caer Liath.

The sides of the mound were thickly wooded with ash, beech and thorn. The sunlight glowed in emerald leaves. Elves wandered among the trees, and off in a clear space a laughing group raced about in some joyful game.

A day passed, and another. Clouds gathered, and when they walked Conn out on the third morning, a fine rain fell. Elves, in merry mood, seemed not to mind rain. Some sat in small groups, laughing and talking, and others shot at a mark. Conn watched them enviously. His wounds ached with the dampness.

"Your people are in no rush to enter the Mound," he said. Indol laughed.

"There are those who love this wet air better than the sun. But it puts the pipes out of tune. Most will be in later, to join the dancing. But you had best go in quickly. Damp is bad for mortal folk, I am told."

They followed a winding path down and around the hill, to the open doors of beaten bronze. A long, torch-lit corridor led into the depths. Elves thronged the passage, and their laughter echoed about him.

At the end of the corridor a bright silver gleam made the torchlight pale. Ethbrien stood glorious in silver radiance.

"Welcome!" she cried in formal greeting. "The knife

is in the meat and the drink is in the horn, but we have
waited for our honored friend." The joy of her smile was
like wine. "Come, Conn Mac Cathla, take your place at
our board."

He followed her into a vast chamber filled with laughing folk, where silver light gleamed on walls paneled
with beaten gold. In the midst of the room, a tripod held
a great crystal sphere, and from this came the silver light;
but in each corner was another tripod, holding a gem.
A great hearth, hewn from the solid stone, blazed
fiercely, but its light was swallowed in the brightness of
the gems. One flamed green, and one red, another blue,
and the fourth a warm golden light.

Conn stood awestruck, and then the smell of roast
meats brought him to himself, and he walked to the long
table, where Kiaran sat beside the crystal sphere. Indol
and Sian helped him into a chair at the Elf-Lord's right,
and Ethbrien beside him.

A horn of mead was set before him, and a dish of
stewed herbs. Across the room a harp began to play,
and a clear tenor voice sang softly.

Conn could make nothing of the words, yet somehow
the sad and beautiful music got into his head and
brought strange visions of Elf-Folk dwelling in green forests, drifting westward before growing tribes of men. He
saw them settle by the shores of the Great Ocean, to
live at last in peace. And then shiploads of men came
out of the East, to land with fire and sword upon the
shore of Eriu. . . .

The music ceased, and Conn found that he had barely
touched the food before him. Guiltily, he began to eat,
and realized that great hunger was on him.

Music began again as he finished the herbs; a woman
singing, a light and happy song that made him wish to
dance, but did not enchant his mind as had the other.
He drank deeply from the horn. Meat was set before
him, and red wine. Fruits followed, and then uisquebaugh, that the elves had learned to brew because no
other liquor was strong enough to affect them. In the
corner near the green gem, a piper played a swift and
happy tune, and many among the elves leaped to their
feet and danced.

Their dancing was unlike any he had seen. Kiaran and
Ethbrien remained at his side, but both Sian and Indol
joined the rushing, leaping elves who whirled about the
chamber like leaves in wind.

The uisquebaugh played like fire in his veins. The
woman at his side was so beautiful. A beauty truly
deathless, that could never age nor die. . . .

A strange glow went through him as her eyes turned
from the dance to meet his. Boldness came to him, perhaps from the uisquebaugh, and they looked at one another for a long time.

The music and the dancing stopped, and the elves returned to their places. Conn, suddenly reckless, turned
to Indol.

"What say you, Healer? Am I strong enough to
dance?"

The elf laughed; then frowned in thought.

"You are not yet strong," he said. "Yet, if the dance
be not too strenuous—most of ours are. I know some
mortal music, if you would have me play."

Conn heaved himself to his feet. The room spun about
him, but he planted his feet firmly, and in a moment the
whirling stopped.

"Can you play 'The Stag in the Spring'?"

"I can."

"Play, then!" said Conn. "But it is not a dance that
should be danced alone. Will you dance also, Lady?"

She looked up, startled. "I know no mortal dances,"
she said hesitantly, "yet if you can show me—"

"I will, then. Come!" Smiles and laughter spread
among the elves, yet Kiaran's face was grave. Conn felt
his feet waver, and cursed himself for a fool. He had not
an elf's head for drinking! The room swayed about him.

The drones burst out with their deep, solemn roar,
and amidst them, shockingly sweet, rose the melody of
the chanter. Conn cursed his unsteady legs, but took a
deep breath and danced.

Ethbrien watched his feet, studying the complex, formal pattern, and after a moment began to imitate him
with grace and ease.

The room reeled about him; his balance was failing.
At any moment he must stumble— The music stopped.

"You must not tire yourself," said Indol, beside him.
"There is yet much healing for your body to do."

Conn sat drinking, his head spinning, watching elves
leaping and whirling in their wild, beautiful dance; but
his eyes wandered to the beautiful face and slender form
of Ethbrien.

Conn awakened in an earth-walled chamber of the
Mound, with his head breaking from the uisequebaugh.
There was a bed of fresh green rushes beneath him, and
a covering of fur, and Ethbrien was watching him from
a corner.

He sat up, his pulse pounding . . . *a dream he had
been having* . . .

But dream and memory faded into pounding pain, and
he closed his eyes. When he opened them again, he saw
amusement and pity in her eyes, and laughed, and she
with him, the laughter in her eyes spilling over into her
face and voice.

"I am sorry," she said, "I should not laugh—"

"Laugh on!" he cried gaily. "I should know better
than to match drinks with elves. But a hoof from the
horse that kicked me will do much."

They laughed again together, and she gave him uisquebaugh out of a leather bottle. The liquor roared in
his veins, and though the hammers in his head did not
stop, the promise was enough.

"I do not remember leaving the Hall last night," he
said, "but I doubt that I walked."

She laughed. "Indol said it were best not to take you
out in the storm."

"It is not an elf's head I have for drink, nor an elf's
strength for rain," he agreed "yet your people seem so
light and fragile, like children. Your men are beardless
and slender, like young boys that I could break with my
one hand."

"It is not strength," she said, "You are like a great
bull, or a bear, with great muscles on the strong bones
of you, and yet you will pass and be gone as quickly as
they. But our life does not devour itself as yours does,
for the light that is in us does not fail. We are children
indeed, for we grow always—not in size, but our flesh is

always that of a child, that can ever mend itself. But why this should be I do not know. And it saddens me," she said, her eyes on his face, "for you are such a strong and a noble man, and there are so many beautiful things that change and fade and—die, while I live on."

Her eyes filled with aching sadness, and Conn felt a driving need to drive the sorrow from her and make her merry once more. He felt himself helpless—a warrior, a man of the sword, with no knowledge of words to make those sad eyes smile again.

He leaned down and kissed her mouth.

Her great eyes gazed into his, her two arms went about his neck. Then she pulled free, and ran from the room.

Conn sat alone, wondering at his own actions. Her leaving left him shaken with longing.

She was life, imperishable, triumphant over time and change and death. He would grow old, and die, yet *she* would live on forever, and death would never touch her, age never frost her dark hair, and he could live on in her memory of his love.

He felt her eyes upon him from the doorway, and as he turned, she ran laughing into his arms.

"I was afraid," she said. "I thought death breathed on me."

"Hush," he said, and cradled her tightly in his arms, but she would not be stilled.

"I am tired of watching all things pass. I had thought that someday—no matter how soon, for there was no hurry—I would take a lover from among my own people, and we could go down the ages together.

"But now there is need, for you are only a man, and soon you will die, and there is an end to our life and our loving. I shall not go to the Land of the Young."

He did not understand, but she was in his arms, her lips were on his, and that was what mattered. He kissed her, silent and wondering, and rocked her in his arms.

After a time she stirred.

"I must speak to my brothers," she said.

He nodded, but fear was on him. She answered his thought.

"I am the daughter of an Elf-Lord. I wed whom I please."

She kissed him once more, and led him through the corridors of the Mound to an emerald curtain. Here she stopped, her hand on his chest.

"I will speak to them alone. All will be well—wait for me." Her lips brushed his, the curtain swayed, and he was alone.

Faint voices came through the curtain, but he could not hear what was said.

He must leave the Mound, he thought, leave now in silence and return to his people. For an immortal to bring to herself the sorrow of mortals—surely the kin who loved her would not permit this madness!

Ethbrien's eyes glowed on him, and her hand was in his.

The Lord of the Elfmound sat in a carven chair, and his sad eyes met Conn's as the man entered. Sian stood behind, in his eyes sorrow and a raging flame.

"So, Mortal," said Kiaran at last, "Ethbrien told us that she has—chosen." He waited for Conn to speak, but the man had no words. He put his arm about Ethbrien and faced them silently.

A flame leaped in Sian's eyes.

Kiaran held Conn's eyes with his own, and a smile touched his lips, to defy the sadness in his eyes. Conn met his gaze squarely, and the elf nodded gently.

"Courage—honor—strength." A bitter smile twisted his mouth. "It is well that the shrub that mates the oak should have *some* virtue.

"'We are few, we last elves. We wait here, on the Shores of the World, for the ship that will bear us to the Ever-Living Land, and we have little to do with mortal men, or with anything which fades and dies, and thus guard ourselves from sorrow. Yet now there is one among us who will not sail to the Land of the Young. And so you bring sorrow to us.

"Yet I have no power over Love, nor can I deny my sister what is the right of all." He lifted something from the floor—a sword in a leather scabbard, like those that he and his brother wore.

"These swords were made in ancient times, before

Man came to this land. Three Alador had for his children, one for myself, and one for Sian, and the third for the Chosen of Ethbrien." The Elf-Lord rose from his seat and stepping forward, buckled the sword about Conn's waist.

"Welcome, Younger Brother, and may your Love for our Sister never falter; may it prove as keen and bright as the Blade you bear."

"May it never falter, Mortal—" Sian spoke, passion in his voice. "For I swear, should you fail my sister or bring her sorrow, wolves will gnaw your bones!"

Ethbrien gasped. Conn's eyes met Sian's, and they glared at one another in silence.

"What folly is this?" Kiaran's calm voice came between them, sharp as bitter steel. "How can you threaten a mortal with death, Sian, he who is born to it? Let us not mar our sister's joy."

Sian glowered, but his eyes dropped. "I wish you well, Mortal," he said at last. But there was weeping in his voice.

Time is not, among the elves, for it does not touch them; yet time draws unto itself those under its sway.

Four years passed, and on a day, Conn rode out hunting with Adiar, Erlin, and Arivel.

The day was bright and warm, though it was near to winter, and the birds already far away upon their year's journey.

They rode far out onto the moor, the elves laughing or singing by turns, seeking about them with hawk-keen eyes for traces of game. Conn carried hunting javelins, and wore the elvish sword, with a round shield at his saddle; but the elves bore long, powerful bows, and long knives and light axes were in their belts.

They spread out in a long line, riding a little apart. Adiar was ahead of the rest, for his horse was swift. They came to a rise in the land and Adiar, passing over it, was lost to view. As they came over the crest they saw him below, sitting stock-still on his horse and gazing sadly into the distance.

"There has been a battle here," he said, as they came up, "and not long since. I saw the spirit of a mortal,

fresh-slain and still in agony, rush past me on the plain.
I tried to speak to him and comfort him, but he fled
away and vanished.'

"May he find peace, and a swift journey—" said Arivel, but Conn felt their eyes upon him.

Then a sudden shout from Erlin drove all thoughts of
human battles and wandering spirits from their minds.

A deer!" he cried, pointing to a line of low hills in
the north. "There by the stream. A young doe—and a
stag—there, in the trees beyond!"

Conn, farsighted for a man, strained his eyes to
glimpse a tiny dot that moved at the limit of his vision.

Arivel was off, his horse bounding toward the hills,
the other elves a hoofbeat behind. Conn touched his
heels to his horse's side and sped after them.

The deer vanished among thickly wooded slopes.
Adiar gestured toward a ravine on their right. The elves'
keen ears were cocked, listening. Conn thought he heard
a sound of hooves.

They turned their horses, and the ravine opened before them, its steep sides thickly grown with brush. They
rode in silence, seeking the herd with their eyes. Conn
could hear movement in the bushes to either side. It
would be good hunting.

But Erlin seemed suddenly ill at ease, glancing warily
about him, drawing an arrow from the quiver at his back.

"I feel eyes upon us," he whispered, "and not . . ."

A shout cut him off, and a crashing of horses through
the brush. Mounted warriors rode down the sides of the
ravine, surrounding them and cutting off their retreat.

There was no need of parley. The elves' bows were
bent and their arrows already flying. A thrown javelin
struck Erlin in the chest. Conn threw the spear in his
hand at the nearest foe, and tearing his shield from his
saddle, whipped out his sword and drove his heels into
his horse's side. Behind him he heard Arivel cry out;
then his blade was flashing among the horsemen. Men
fell before his blows. Rage and sorrow clouded his eyes,
and he saw only dim, confused shapes of men and horses
until a single face swam out of the chaos beneath his
sword—the face of Culain, his brother. . . .

His arms dropped to his sides: the sword fell from his hand.

*   *   *

Culain pulled his tattered cloak more closely about him.

"And now it is clear!" The firelight flickered on his scarred, bearded face, and the shadow of his angry arms clawed at the earthen wall of the hut.

"We thought you dead these four years, but you have been held enchanted by the Moundfolk!" His voice was bitter and harsh. "This long winter, and the wolves that have come upon us, and the sickness of our cattle—there can be no more doubt that these have all been brought upon us by the Moundpeople!"

"But it is not true!" cried Conn, white-faced and angry. "Elf-Folk—it is not their way, to use magic against mortals who cannot ward themselves."

"You have been long within their spells." Culain's eyes brooded upon him. "Their enchantments have ensnared your mind. Did you not take sword against your own clan, and slay men who had been your friends?"

"I did not know you!" said Conn. "All I knew was that you had attacked our party and slain my friends."

"Your friends! And how is it you came to be hunting with foes of your clan, who have warred with us for hundreds of years, who even now use their magic to strike against us?"

"They have used no magic against you—would I not have known if they had?"

"What would a prisoner of the elves know of his captors' deeds? You think they would tell *you* of the attacks on us?"

"I was no prisoner," said Conn. "I am wed to their chieftain's sister, Ethbrien, the daughter of Alador."

"*Alador!* Alador was slain by Art Mac Ainnle, our ancestor; twice a hundred years ago!"

The sun rose over the squalid huts of Clann Cormac. Cattle were driven out on the moor to graze. The men of the clan gathered, like gaunt wolves, before the Chief's hut. Old men, respected for their wisdom, mingled with young warriors famed for bravery.

It was cold, and a brisk breeze blew across the moor. Conn sat close to the fire, his cloak wrapped tightly about him. He had lain awake much of the night, unable to sleep in the suffocating closeness of the hut, arguing against the doubts Culain had raised in his mind.

Coll, his uncle, Chief of Clann Cormac, older than Conn remembered, palsied hands almost helpless with age, sat facing him, wrapped in a heavy woolen cloak.

Culain—interrupted by many shrewd questions from the old men—told of his unsuccessful foray upon the herds of Clann Domnann. Clann Cormac, its herds and fields depleted, was dependent on raiding for food. Culain told how, outnumbered and driven from the herd, they had fled from their foes, at last taking refuge in the ravine.

"We saw horsemen coming across the moor, and hid among the trees. We thought them scouts of Clann Domnann. When we saw by their gear that they were elves, we held to our purpose, for one foe was as good as another."

"I saw that there was a man among them," Aigidiu, one of the younger warriors, broke in, "and I wondered if our foes had combined against us at last. I did not dream he was of our own people, riding with our foes to hunt us out for Clann Domnann!"

"We were hunting deer!" cried Conn.

"A deer fled up the ravine before them and through our ranks—" said Culain. "We could have taken it easily, had we not been after other game."

"You should have," said one of the old men. "We could at least have eaten that, and you would not have lost so many men."

"Elves followed," said Culain. "One sensed us—I saw him turn to speak to the others—but by then they were well within our trap. And we sprang the trap! The elves died quickly—they are weaklings! But my brother is harder to kill! He slew four men—"

"Kinsmen! Men of his own Clan!" shouted Aigidiu. "Why is he yet alive?"

"He did not know us!" said Culain. "He was under spell of the elves. He has been a prisoner of their enchantments for four years!"

"Oh, aye, the elves, it is always the elves." One of the older men spoke. "How do we know the elves plan evil against us? You say the famine is the work of elves. Yet famine has come before, without elf-magic. You say they caused Fingan's death, yet Fingan was an old man, and wasted with many years. It is so strange that a fever should take him?"

"You still doubt?" cried Culain. "After *this* you still doubt? Four years gone my brother vanished, taken, we now know, by the elves, and in that same year our troubles began. Our crops were blighted and our cattle killed, and a wasting fever sent upon Fingan, that we might have no Druid to protect us! Is there no pattern there? Are you so blind?"

"Let us hear what your brother has to say." said Coll. "Let Conn speak!"

"We were attacked by Clann Domnann, and outnumbered." Conn looked around the circle of faces. Some were uncertain, others, cold and grim, glared with hatred. "We scattered, and I rode west, into the country of the elves, trying to circle back to our lands. I saw a man and a woman—I did not know that they were elves—beset by wolves on the moor, and I hate wolves too well to leave them their kill. I rode to their aid. I was injured in the fight that followed, and the elves bore me to Caer Liath. When I was healed, they gave a feast in my honor—"

"A feast?" asked Culain. "And does that not seem strange to you?"

"Strange? I had saved their Chief and his sister from wolves—"

"A Chief and his sister? That explains it, maybe. Yet were—a man of Clann Domnann, say—to save two of our people, we would thank him, surely, and set our Druid to heal his wounds, but a feast? More like flattery than gratitude. But perhaps not to an elf. But tell us how this Chief, and his sister, came to be wandering on the moor when wolves were hunting?"

"Why—" Conn's brow furrowed as, confused by Culain's question, he tried to reach back across four years of time. "—I do not remember, I do not know that they

ever told me—something about a dream, I—" The voice
of Coll the Chief cut into his thoughts.

"Conn, tell me: Did you not fear the elves, knowing
them inhuman, and foes of your people?"

"Aye, at first, but I soon forgot . . ."

"You *forgot!*" cried Culain. "You were afraid, and
then you were not? And are they not immortal, with
uncanny powers, able to commune with the beasts of the
wild, and with the dead?"

"Aye . . ."

"And you did not fear them? You *forgot* that they
were foes of your Clan? And you doubt that an enchantment was on you? But tell us the rest, Conn! Tell us of
the woman."

"What woman?" asked the old Chief.

"The first thing in the Mound that my eyes rested on,"
said Conn, "was Ethbrien, the daughter of Alador. She
was more fair than Etain of whom legend tells, and I
looked upon her and my heart went to her, and after
the feast . . ."

"And after the feast, you were wed to the daughter
of Alador!" rasped Culain. "*Alador,* who was slain by
our forefather twice a hundred years ago! Alador, who
died at the beginning of the feud between our people
and the elves! His *daughter* marries the descendant of his
slayer! And the Chief of the Elk-Folk permitted this—
Alador's *son* permitted this? And there was nothing
strange in it?"

Conn was silent, and he could feel the eyes of the
clansmen upon him. Culain's voice went on relentlessly.

"Nor was it strange, it seems, that you should desire
a woman whose father died two centuries ago, a woman
old when your father was born! Older than the oldest
crone in the village!"

"She is immortal!" cried Conn. "Age does not touch
her!"

"If that be true," Culain said quietly, "what is it that
she wants of a man who will be dust in forty years?"

Conn was aware that it was no longer hostility in the
eyes upon him.

It was pity.

"And what of the others, I wonder?" said Culain. Conn's head snapped up.

"Others?" he said, his voice cold and dangerous.

"Surely you do not think you were the first, in two centuries?" said Culain.

Conn choked back anger, kept his hands at his sides. "I was."

"After two *centuries*? You cannot believe that, man?" said Culain. "An illusion was on you." Conn shook his head. All seemed very simple. In a moment he would strike Culain to the ground.

"If a woman two centuries old can make you see her as young and beautiful, no wonder if she makes you think her a virgin, too," Culain shrugged. "But no matter. So they never told you why a Lord of the Elfmounds and his virgin sister should be alone on the moor while wolves were hunting. Strange, that folk so wise, and skilled in magic, should be saved by a mortal warrior. Well for them that you came when you did! Or did they, perhaps, know that you were coming?"

Conn started. He saw where Culain's speech led, and doubt came to him. His brother's voice seemed to echo in his own thoughts.

'Were they, perhaps, waiting for you? Waiting to weave their spells about you? Why else put themselves in danger from wolves—if, indeed, they were wolves you fought, and not elves in wolf-form. Injured and in their power, they could put spells on you, bind you to them and hold you hostage—with no wish to escape—while they warred against us.'

Conn was silent. The doubts his brother had raised tore at his breast. How did he know that spells had not been laid on him when he had first been brought into the Mound?

One of the older men spoke across the fire.

"Culain is right. Conn has been bespelled, and cannot be blamed for his deeds. He was hostage against the time when we should know of their magic against us."

"Aye, Conn's tale leaves no doubt," said Coll heavily. "Before, I, too, had questioned, thought that it might be but ill-luck that beset us, and no magic of the elves, but now we see that Culain was right."

Fierce mutters of agreement spread around the circle, and wolfish smiles appeared as men who had despaired found hope—hope, at least, of revenge.

But Conn sat with eyes on the ground, his mind warring within him. Culain reached down and gripped Conn's shoulder.

"Do you see it now, my brother? Are you free of their spells now?" Conn looked up and was startled by tears in his brother's eyes. "Do you see it now, man? Are you returned to us?"

Conn's gaze returned to the ground before him. "It seems you must be right," he said at last, tonelessly.

That night Conn dreamed, and the eyes of Ethbrien came into his dream, bright as stars. And he heard Sian and Kiaran behind her say, *"We thought you dead."* And Ethbrien, joyful, *"He lives!"*

And he knew, somehow, that they had been seeking him, sending their minds searching far from the Mound, to find the ravine where ravens feasted on Erlin, Adiar, and Arivel. Fearful then they had searched, and only Ethbrien had thought to find him living. Her longing drew him like silken nets, and tore at him like hooks.

"Come back to me, my love . . ." He seemed to reach for her; but of a sudden Culain stood between them, and she seemed a hideous crone, bent and withered.

"Come back to me, Conn!" she cried. "Come back . . . there is a shadow between us, and he draws away. He doubts me! In some way he doubts me! Conn, do you not love me?"

"Conn!" The thing that Kiaran had become called to him. "Do not let your doubt put false shapes on us. Brush the veil from your mind and see us as we are!"

For a moment the wolf-shape wavered, and Kiaran's beautiful, proud face peered through. But stubbornly Conn willed the wolf back. They should not trap him again!

"Conn, what is wrong?" Sian's voice, puzzled, came from the second wolf. "Why do you bar your mind from us?"

"No!" Ethbrien's voice wept, "he does not love me!

He does not love me! Conn, I am with child, come back!"

Kiaran's voice, calm and soothing. "Fear not, Sister, we will bring him back to you."

Their voices and their presence faded, but the hideous crone-image of Ethbrien remained. The wolves crept toward him. . . .

He awoke in the darkness and stench of the hut, cold sweat drenching his body. The coals of the fire flared briefly, casting a ruddy light on the dirt floor. He lay back, and after a time fell into a sleep troubled by dreams of Ethbrien's warm body turning to cold bones against his own.

The next day a great cry arose, and young warriors came running from the edge of he village. Culain ran to meet them, Conn at his heels.

"Elves!" said the warrior who met them, gasping from his run. "They say they come in peace. From Caer Liath."

Culain turned to look at his brother, his face hard and cold with rage.

"We will ride to meet them."

Conn and Culain rode out with the others of the village. Each had his shield. Culain wore his great sword of hammered iron, and Conn the long keen blade out of the Elfmound, mate to those Sian and Kiaran bore.

Sian and Kiaran, shields on their arms and swords at their sides, were waiting on a hill which overlooked the village. Behind them were ten mounted elves with longbows in their hands.

Kiaran made the sign of peace and rode forward, Sian at his side. Conn and Culain rode to meet them, while the warriors of the clan waited, weapons ready. Kiaran spoke first.

"We searched long for you, Conn, and feared you dead. Our sister waits for you—she has wept much. It is good that you have seen your people again, but surely you will be coming along with us now."

Before Conn could even think what answer he wished to make, Culain's harsh voice broke in, violently.

"Enough of that! My brother is free of your wiles

now. You will not trap him again! Time now for you to
speak of peace, of an end to spells against us, and repa-
ration for the ill you have done. Else we shall attack
your Mound and destroy all the evil within!"

Kiaran looked at Culain with astonishment.

"What is this—? We have tried to make peace before, but . . ."

"But now you seek to regain my brother and enchant
him once more!" shouted Culain. "Four years he has
been slave to your enchantments, while your spells
wrought famine and disease among our people! Do not
think to enslave him again! You shall not have him. Nor
think we will let your attacks on us go unpunished. We
will destroy you utterly if you do not yield!"

"But this is not true!" cried Kiaran. "We do not use
spells against mortals! Conn, surely you do not believe
this madness?"

Conn wavered, uncertain what to believe. Memory of
his dream—vague, confused—the crone-image rose before him—

"So that was why he barred his thought from us last
night!" Sian muttered.

Conn's head snapped erect, his eyes wary; his fist
knotted on the reins and his eyes closed tightly, the
crone-shape floating before him. If the dream had
been true . . .

"Conn," Sian's voice reached him. "Listen to this
madman no more. Come to us, to Ethbrien . . ."

"To Ethbrien?" said Conn, his voice shaking, "that I
may be enspelled once more? Back to your illusions?
No, I will stay with my clansmen. At least I know that
they are real!"

"What are you saying?" cried Kiaran. "Have you
gone mad with this talk of illusion and enchantments
upon you?"

"He speaks of the spell put on him by your foul sister!" shouted Culain. "The illusion of youth and beauty
to make him love her that you might hold him as hostage!" He spurred his horse nearer.

"You lie!" said Sian, face pale, his anger held no
longer.

Culain's iron sword tore from its sheath, slashing at

Kiaran. The elf's shield leaped to block it. Sian drew his own blade and spurred toward Culain.

"Sian! NO!" shouted Kiaran. The men of Clan Cormac shouted their battle cry, and on the hill above, the elves bent their bows.

As Sian and Culain met with a clash of wood and steel, Conn whipped the elvish blade from its scabbard and rode for Kiaran.

"Conn!" the elf shouted, wheeling his horse to flee, sword still at his side. Conn drove his mount against the other, and his sword flashed down in a screaming arc, to cleave through flesh and bone.

The Lord of the Elfmounds toppled from his horse, his skull split to the chin.

The men of Clann Cormac were fleeing. Elves launched flight after flight of pitiless arrows in their ranks. Culain cried out as Sian drove the elf-blade through his wrist, and the heavy iron sword fell from his grasp. Conn saw his brother turn his horse and flee, blood flowing from his wrist.

Sian made no move to pursue, nor did any elf-bolt streak from the hill. The elves were silent, unmoving. Conn felt Sian's eyes upon him. Kiaran's blood dripped from Conn's sword. There was a crashing of hooves, and Sian's horse drove into his own, and as he reeled, a hand gripped his sword arm, and wrested the blade from his grasp.

The elf-horse sprang away, and in Sian's hand the bright blade from the Elfmound shone in the sun, and trapped Conn's eye.

"This blade was given in token of Brotherhood!" cried Sian. "You have stained the sword with a brother's blood! Do you still wish the sword?"

"Give me back my sword!"

"Yours?" called Sian. "No longer! You must take it back. As with it you brought death, so to you shall it bring death! The wolves shall gnaw your bones!"

He waved the sword above his head. Conn could not take his eyes from its bright gleaming.

'And so—follow!" and the elf-steed whirled and fled away toward the north.

Conn pounded his horse's flanks and sped after the gleaming blade.

On he rode, swift as the wind, yet the other was still before him, gleaming sword held high. But it was no longer Sian who rode there, but Kiaran; and Conn could see blood running out of the great cleft in his skull.

The ground rolled away beneath frantically pounding hooves, but the rider ahead was no nearer. Conn's horse faltered, but he whipped it on without mercy, his eyes fixed on the sword. Still the other fled, and could not be overtaken.

The rider seemed to waver, the light of the blade to flicker and dim. It could not vanish! He would not allow it to elude him that way! He fixed his eyes firmly upon the fading phantom, willing it to remain. He could not gain on it, but it wavered no longer.

After a time he became aware of a dim shape riding beside him in the darkness. Turning, he saw Sian, his horse matching Conn's stride for stride.

"Stop him! Turn him back!" he seemed to hear Ethbrien's voice crying in anguish, could almost see her red lips moving. . . .

"Conn!" shouted the figure at his side, but he did not turn.

"Sian, take it off him!" He heard her voice again, but could not find its source. "Take the spell off him and turn him back!"

"*I have taken it off!*" the elf cried, despair in his voice. "But he won't turn back! It's from his own mind now— Conn! Can't you hear me, man?" Conn did not answer, but slipped one of his daggers from its sheath.

"It's your death, man! Can't you see there's nothing there?"

The thing seemed nearer now. He might catch it if they left him.

"Conn! *The sword isn't there!* It's an illusion I put on you! Leave it! Turn away!" He reached out, and his hand closed on Conn's arm.

Whirling in the saddle, Conn slashed at the other's wrist. The elf drew back barely in time. Conn lashed the horse on, but Sian kept pace.

"Can't your spells turn him back?" Ethbrien cried. A

shape rose up, tall as a tree. Conn drove his horse straight toward it, and it broke and vanished before him. An illusion, to draw him from his chase! They were trying to draw him away from his pursuit of Kiaran, but he would not let them. He must overtake the slain elf, kill him again, and take back the sword. That was all that mattered.

Sian was still at his side, riding knee to knee. Conn slashed at him with his dirk, but he only darted his horse to the side, out of reach, and then closed in again. It was like striking at a bat in the darkness.

"Go!" the man croaked. "Leave me! Go!"

"Conn!" Ethbrien's voice came to him again. "Turn back! Can't you see it's an illusion?" Her face rose into his mind once more, but he fixed his eyes on the glowing sword. Witch! Enchantress! Did she think to trap him again? *Lovely woman from the Elfmound, my heart flies to you like a bird.*

"Conn!" shouted Sian. *"Turn back!"*

He did not reply, did not so much as move his eyes.

"Conn!" her voice came again, but his eyes and mind were fixed on the glittering sword.

The elf-horse whirled, and darted away into the night.

Elf-blade brandished high, the gleaming rider floated before him. Conn's weary horse stumbled, breathing in great gasps, but Conn drove it on. When the whip no longer served to rouse it, he slipped his dirk from his belt and slashed it across the withers.

Conn paid no heed to the flame-eyed shapes that howled on the blood-trail behind him. Unmercifully he drove on the screaming, blood-drenched horse, until it lurched and fell, throwing him to the ground, and neither blows nor curses could bring the dead beast to its feet.

Howling shapes came dripping-jawed over the moor, but Conn staggered north, hands outstretched to grasp the bright blade that floated always just beyond his reach.

A SOUL TO BE GAINED

by Blake Cahoon

Blake Cahoon's work has also appeared in *Catfantastic*, edited by Andre Norton. She lives in Oak Park, Illinois.

He ran his finger down the dictionary page. "Elf," he read. "A small mischievous mythological creature known not to have a soul."

"Mmmph!" he snorted. "Okay, I'm short, I'll admit that. Mischievous?" he shrugged. Okay, he did like to pull pranks on his friends. And mythological—well, he was hardly a myth. But come on, not to have a soul? Come on, maybe he played too hard, partied too much, felt a little lost even in the mortal world, but not have a soul. That hurt.

He closed the dictionary with a thud; what he was looking for wasn't in this book. Nor was it in the three sets of encyclopedias, and many reference books on mythological creatures and other such "imaginary" people, that he had been searching through the past five days.

What he was searching for was obviously not going to be in human books.

Damn that O'Grady, anyway! Why did he have to show up now? Now when he had just met someone who just might become Mrs. Eric Frost.

Claire was dreamy, the girl—human girl—he had been searching for all his life. Brown, thick hair that fell almost halfway down her back, large beautiful blue eyes, as deep as the ocean. Rosy cheeks, a button nose and two large, ample—

"Frost!" His boss, Peter Cole, sneaked up behind him disturbing his thoughts. "Do you have the latest drawings and ad copy on the cookie campaign?"

Eric jumped and scooped up the drawings of the cute cookie elves and their cookie factory. "Right here," he said. The boss snorted, grumbled something about it being good work, and stomped off again, drawings and copy in hand.

Despite Cole's attitude, Eric couldn't help but smile and be proud. It was Eric who was the driving force behind keeping the popular elf theme going when the cookie company had almost scrapped the long-running concept, a few years back.

But that was why Eric had been sent here—to keep elfdom alive among the humans. Being in the advertising game—part of the largest ad company in the world—helped. Humans were constantly reminded of elves—they were used to advertise breakfast cereal, cookies, cellular phones, science-fiction television shows and in children's cartoons. He was especially proud of the latest round of elflike aliens on a popular science-fiction show. His predecessor, who left seven years ago, had let them virtually die out. But Eric had managed to bring the popular aliens back. He had even set up a World Wide Web page on elves in general. That would keep the myth going and allow the gateway between the worlds to remain open.

But seven years had gone by too quickly, and when O'Grady appeared on his doorstep five mornings ago with the news that his seven years were up, Eric lost his cool.

"What do you mean I have to go back? I've still got work here to do. My ad campaigns have been really successful! Didn't you guys like all those new Christmas specials this past year? And what about the TV show?"

"You know the rules, Eric," O'Grady told him. The man was slightly smaller than his own five-seven with graying hair that just covered the elder elf's telltale pointed ears. "Didn't you read the fine print?"

Okay, so he hadn't real all that elf legalese that was on the contract when he had been drafted to come into the human realm. Elf lawyers were worse than human lawyers. Besides, he had been having too much fun in his own elfin world. There was Cynthia, Lois, Margaret and Betsy. He hadn't wanted to come to the human realm. But that was then; this was now. "Well, of course, I did," he had lied to O'Grady. "But time passed so quickly! And I found this girl that might—"

"A human girl?" O'Grady shook his head. "Trouble, there," he said.

O'Grady had always frowned on the two races mixing. But that was because O'Grady's human wife had broken her special vow to him, and died as a result, and so he had gone back to the elfin realm heartbroken and bitter. But Eric's Claire could be trusted, he was sure of that. "Look, O'Grady, I just need more time to win this girl and then—"

"You think simply getting a human girl to love you will allow you to stay here? That and all your advertising? It helps—but that's not the answer."

"Then what is? How do I stay? Others stay—I know they do."

"Of course they do. If these silly humans only knew how many of us were actually—but that doesn't matter," he said, with a sigh. "You have to find the answer yourself. With no help from them. That's the rule."

Eric's philosophy had been that rules were meant to be broken. But that was another thing that got him in trouble. "So, what you're telling me is that I've got a week to find the key to staying here or I get shipped back?"

"That's right. You have seven days," O'Grady told him, checking out his watch. "Now, excuse me, I have others to check on before going home."

"Great," Eric moaned. How was he going to explain this to Claire?

The same way he escaped everything else. He hadn't explained it. Instead, he called some of his friends who had found the key to staying longer.

"Michael, tell me, I beg you!" he pleaded to his actor friend, whose newest TV series seemed to be as popular as his time-travel movies and his last family sitcom show.

"Look, Eric, if I could, I would, you know that, man. But I can't. I'd get sent back. And I have my wife and kids to think about, not to mention my career."

Not to mention the money either, you lousy bum, Eric

thought and tried three more actor friends, two jockey friends and even one politician.

"I can't say," his politician friend said in his heavy Texas drawl. "If it's meant to be, you'll find the answer, my friend."

"Thanks, anyway, Ross," Eric said and hung up. Damn, he had to find the answer and quickly. He was running out of time.

The little white elk stood on top of the scarred mahogany dresser. Claire saw that it was an old Christmas ornament, flocked with glitter that had fallen off over the years. Still, the dark eyes held a sparkle and the painted mouth seemed to smile at her.

She touched a finger to its white antlers. "I wonder why this is just sitting out here?" she asked her friend, Annie, who was inspecting a dismantled antique headboard. It was Annie who had dragged her to the estate sale that late April day. She had planned to spend the day with her new boyfriend, Eric. But he had begged off, saying he had lots of work to do at the office.

"What?" Annie said and rose from her squatting position with the elasticity of a dancer.

Annie was small, blonde and had a cute little figure that men drooled over. Claire envied her more than she liked to realize. Claire had her mother's Irish figure and her father's Spanish height. Short and fat, that was what she always pictured herself as. "You don't want that old thing!" Annie scolded her and snatched the little white elk away, putting it on top of the bureau again. "It's junk!" she declared in her loud Bronx manner. "Now that piece over there, that's worth something!" she announced and marched over to a small antique table.

Claire looked wistfully at the small creature. "But it reminded me of my childhood. My grandfather had something like it," she said. But dutifully she followed Annie, weaving around several pieces of furniture that stood upon the lawn of the old estate. Above her the sun was trying to peek out from threatening storm clouds. She wondered how all the furniture would survive or if the estate planners had planned for rain. "April showers bring May flowers," she said, out loud to no one in particular, since Annie had gone off on another tangent.

But just as she said it, a flash of something white caught her attention. She turned toward the flash and found herself staring into the reflection of an old antique gilt-framed mirror that was propped against a large trunk. She stepped closer to the mirror, which was half hidden among the other pieces of furniture, but whose reflection showed the woods that surrounded the estate.

Claire glanced over at the woods, but there was nothing white to be seen. Perhaps it had been a small creature—a rabbit, she thought, whose image had been caught within the looking glass. Like Alice.

She looked again at the mirror and found that the image in the mirror now took her breath away. For quite clearly reflected was an almost double, but quite real and alive version of the small white elk. Claire stared at it, as it seemed to stare back at her, its eyes not dark, but a most peculiar pinkish-red color that was quite startling.

Claire turned quickly to look at the woods where the stag stood, but found the woods empty. She blinked, a cold shiver running down her spine. She looked at the mirror again and caught just a glimpse of the stag as it bounded away into the reflected woods.

Again she looked into the real woods and saw nothing.

"Annie!" she cried out and stumbled away from the mirror, whose enchantment puzzled her and terrified her all at the same time.

"What?" Annie said. "Are you still over here? Come this way!" She began leading her friend away from the mirror.

"But that mirror! The woods! I saw this white elk!"

"Are you still going on about that damn elk? It's junk, I tell you! Come on, now! I see some real treasures over here!" Annie told her and dragged her off.

Claire looked back, but the elk was gone. She let herself be dragged away, still feeling queasy and unsure.

That night she insisted on telling Eric about the elk, despite the fact that he probably would think she was crazy. But Eric was also into fantasy and science fiction, and maybe he wouldn't treat her as a nut.

"It was just so weird, Eric! I know it sounds crazy," she told him over the phone, as he had begged off again that night, much to her disappointment. Eric had been a godsend to her.

Her editor at the romance publishing house where she worked and cranked out novels under several pseud-onyms had worried over Claire's writing. Her heroes had become two-dimensional and lifeless. They had no soul. Eric had changed that for her. He had become inspiration for her and had renewed her interest not only in her writing, but simply in living day to day.

She had met Eric at a Christmas party that past December. He was a most handsome man, his black hair matched his dark bedroom eyes. His smile was infectious. She looked back now at it as one of those enchanted evening moments, where their eyes met across a crowded room. When he had asked her to dance that night, it was magic, but she thought he was simply being nice to her. Although he considered himself short, she felt he was perfect in height to her five feet two.

When he had asked her out for a New Year's party, she thought she had died and gone to heaven. He had proved himself to be a gentleman, although he kept her going with his practical jokes. He was forever scaring her with plastic insects or embarrassing her with whoopee cushions. But his interests in science fiction and fantasy movies and television matched her own, and their four months together so far had been unbelievably wonderful.

But lately he had become moody and sullen and she worried about him. He had broken two dates with her that week. Usually they were inseparable, even when he was busy with an ad campaign and she with a deadline. But this week, Eric had become distant. She had hoped she might find something to give him from the antique sale, since he seemed to have a fondness for the stuff, but instead her strange experience made her wonder if she wasn't going crazy. "But it's true, I don't know what to think."

Eric had listened to Claire prattle on for close to twenty minutes, his concentration on his dilemma, but at the mention of the strange creature, his pointed ears perked up. "A white elk? A stag, maybe? With pink eyes?" He recognized the creature immediately as one from his own realm. What was it doing showing up now? In front of his girlfriend? Could it be the key he was seeking? "Where was that estate sale? Is it still open?"

Claire thought that was an unusual response, but she said, "Well, it was in Westchester. I think it's still going on through tomorrow. Why? You don't think I'm crazy?"

Eric laughed, "No, sweetheart, I don't. I'm heading to your place now. And tomorrow, we're checking out that estate sale."

She was pleased to hear that he was coming over. But puzzled over his strange reaction. "Eric? Why?"

"Never mind. Or maybe I might tell you tomorrow. I don't know yet. You think that small white elk might still be there?"

"I have no idea," she answered. "Eric, is there something you want to tell me?"

"Maybe. I'll know more tomorrow. Tonight, we celebrate!" he said and hung up.

Claire stared at the receiver, happy and confused all at the same time.

The next morning they headed out to Westchester under threatening skies. "I hope it doesn't rain," Claire said.

"I hope the little elk is there. And the mirror," Eric said, his arm draped around her shoulder, fingering her long hair.

"Is the mirror important, too?" she asked. Last night she had tried to question him further, but it was pointless. He wanted to celebrate, and she was afraid not to let him. It was the first time he hadn't been moody in a week, it seemed.

"It could be. Keep your fingers crossed," he said, with a bright smile. "Why didn't you buy the elk, anyway?"

"Annie dragged me off. Said it was junk. I thought it was pretty. It reminded me of a Christmas ornament my grandfather had."

"A white elk Christmas ornament?" Eric asked.

"Yeah, he loved Christmas. He had all these little

wooden Christmas toys that he'd carve for the neighborhood kids."

"Your grandfather made toys?" Eric said, his mind starting with the possibilities of the implications.

"Yeah, he made me a doll once and some other things. But I remember the little elk because it was so cute. I just wish he hadn't died so soon. I barely got to know him," Claire said. "He died when I was seven."

Eric felt a chill go down his spine. There was that damn seven number again. A well-known magical number, it was the maximum number of years elves could stay in the human world unless they found a key to remain. It was amazing what he had found out about his own people in all those books he had read. He had chastised himself more than once for not being a better student when he had had a chance. Now he was paying the price.

"Was he old?" he said.

"My grandmother once said he was old as the hills," Claire said, and directed him off the highway toward the place of the antique sale. "She died the year before him."

Eric nodded. "Did you go to his funeral?" he asked, following up on a hunch that was itching the back of his mind.

"No. Mother said he didn't like funerals," she said. "He really loved my grandmother. Was heartbroken when she died."

"What happened to the elk?"

Claire shrugged. "I don't know. I just remember that little elk and that he really made me feel special." The way Eric made her feel, but she didn't voice that.

Eric's itch remained, but he couldn't quite put his finger on it. He pulled the car into a gravel driveway with huge iron gates. The estate itself sat on a wide expanse of green lawn surrounded by woods. He parked the car near a dozen or so others; then he took Claire's hand and the two walked toward the small grouping of furniture that was left. "Not much left," he noted.

"The bureau was over there," she said, leading the way. "It's gone now, though."

"Where was the mirror? And in what part of the woods did you see the real elk?" he asked.

"The mirror was over there. It too seems to have disappeared." She looked over to the woods and pointed. "That's where I saw the elk's reflected image."

"Okay, wait here. See if you can't find that mirror," he said. He started toward the woods.

"Eric? Where are you going?" she called after him. But he waved her away and sprinted up the small knoll, toward the forest.

She watched him go and shook her head. Maybe this was one of his pranks. April Fool's Day had been a great day for him. His birthday had been the next day and that was even more hilarious with fake dog poop and rubber snakes. Sometimes she wondered why she put up with it and him. He drove her crazy! But then he was awfully good-looking and she was grateful to have such a man pay attention to her. Usually the men in her life were crass, uncouth jerks. She never thought handsome, nice men like Eric would ever ask her out. So she put up with his shenanigans and she had to admit, she was falling in love with him.

She watched him go and then turned and went searching for the mirror.

Eric searched the ground for any sign of the white elk. First he searched the ground for prints and then in the bushes for broken branches. But he wasn't seeing anything. Not even with his elfin vision. Damn it, there should be some sign! Discouraged, he sat down on the grass and began to think about the possibility that he was going to lose Claire, his career, and his life in the mortal realm.

Claire looked behind several pieces of furniture, finding no mirror. Finally, she went to one of the people in charge of the estate and simply asked about the mirror and the little white elk.

"Excuse me, but I was wondering—there was an old antique mirror over by a large bureau yesterday. And on the bureau was this little figurine of a white elk. Have they been sold?"

The lady, dressed in her spring best, complete with yellow frilly dress and hat, frowned in recall. "A mirror and a figurine of a what?"

"An elk? A small white elk?" Claire asked. "I wanted to see if they were sold."

The lady shook her head. "I don't remember any white elk. Several mirrors have been sold. Let me check my book," she said.

Claire waited as the woman dug out several books and began to go through them. She looked toward the woods and saw Eric sitting on the hill by the edge of the woods. Just sitting and staring out into space. What was he thinking? she wondered, and waved at him. But Eric didn't seem to see her.

What was he going to do? Eric was thinking. He didn't want to go back. He had found that he liked the mortal world. It was new and exciting. Unlike the dreary world of his home. That was the one thing humans hadn't gotten right. They were still under the mistaken belief that fairyland was a paradise instead of simply a place of enchantment. It was the enchantment that kept you going, certainly not the atmosphere, which was as gray as the day was today. In the books, the authors talked of the ointment that elves put in humans' eyes when brought across the realm. It kept the humans from seeing their world as it really was—bleak and desolate. Trees weren't green, they were brown or gray. Skies weren't blue, they looked like Los Angeles on a smog-alert day. Even elves were not handsome creatures—instead they were ugly and misshapen. Without enchantment the women were no treat to the eyes. Not like Claire, who surprisingly thought herself ugly, but was beautiful in his eyes.

No, mortals didn't realize how good they had it. Immortal life wasn't what it was cracked up to be, especially if was in a place as dismal as the place he had once called home.

"I don't want to go back. Don't make me go back!" he declared out loud, a fist to the gray skies. "Please, don't make me go back," he moaned, more softly, trying to hold back the overwhelming sadness he was beginning to feel.

*   *   *

Claire was still watching him when he raised a fist to the skies and shouted something. She was too distant to hear it, but still puzzled over it. She frowned as she saw the bright smile he wore earlier fade away. She was losing him again. She turned to the lady. "Have you found anything yet?" she asked, as if finding a stupid old mirror and a figurine was going to make him happy again. "They were right over there," she pointed to an area where the grass was still flattened.

"Oh, those things. Actually, we moved those things inside. It looked like it was going to rain," the lady said. She pointed to an open door of the huge mansion. "Why don't you go inside?"

She nodded and glanced over at Eric who looked so forlorn, it was beginning to break her heart. Should she go fetch him, she wondered? Or maybe she could find the mirror and figurine and surprise him? After watching him a minute more, she decided on the latter and stepped inside.

Eric found himself staring up into space, daydreaming. The day was overcast and gray, heavy with storm clouds, he noted. Then he brought his gaze back down to the lush green lawn that he hated to lose. But he found with a start that the lawn had disappeared along with the mansion. Instead a bleak black swamp greeted his eyes.

"What the—!" He jumped up and looked around at the horrible surroundings. "NO!" he cried out, recognizing his home world. "No! This can't be! I have one day left!"

"Then what are you doing out in that spot and at that time?" a voice behind him said.

He whirled and found O'Grady. But the mortal world veil had been lifted and he saw the fellow elf in his true misshapen form. He looked down at his own hands and saw the gnarled fingers of his former self. He put a hand to his once handsome face and felt bumps and warts. "No! No! I have one more day! I can't be taken back now!" He was almost in tears.

"You haven't found the key yet," O'Grady told him. "And I knew you were a lazy student, but surely after reading all those books you know what today is and how you got here."

Eric tried to think, but could only think about the fact he was home again. And about Claire. "Claire! My girlfriend! Did you see her? The pretty one I was with?"

"Of course, I saw her. I've been watching you. You should know that," O'Grady said and shook his head. "You don't learn, do you?"

Eric really wasn't listening. "I can't stay here," he was protesting. "You've got to send me back. I still have one day!" He looked around with utter revolt at the scenery around. Never to see green again. Never to see Claire again. "I can't leave Claire," he said. "I love her."

"Love her? Well, maybe you should tell her that," O'Grady said. "And I didn't bring you here. You did."

"I did? How? I would never—"

"Simple: you lay on a knoll, home of a fairy realm underneath, on the first of May at noon. Then daydreamed. The portal was opened and you came through. Silly humans do it all the time. Good thing, too, since we have to keep our population going somehow."

"The portal?" Eric said, then slapped his bony forehead. "Damn! How could I be so stupid?"

"Yes, I was wondering the same thing when you appeared early. But what's done is done." He started to turn away.

"But wait! Can't I go back? The portal should still be open!" Eric glanced at his watch out of habit. But it was gone, along with his designer sports jacket. He was now dressed in rags.

"Remember time flies here," O'Grady said. "It may be too late," he told him and with a nasty chuckle walked away.

Eric watched him go and then screamed at the top of his lungs. "Noooooooooooooo!" Then began to sob.

"Eric?" Claire called out, puzzled that he had disappeared off the hill. In her hand she held the antique mirror and the white elk figurine. She had found them inside and quickly snatched them both up and bought them. But when she came back outside, Eric had disappeared. So, she climbed the hill to see if he hadn't wandered into the woods. "Eric?"

But although she found his footprints, there were no signs of him. "Eric, where the hell did you go?" she wondered. Maybe he had gone into the woods, somehow.

The mirror was getting awkward, it was large and clumsy and so she propped it up by a tree. With a sigh, she stood looking around and found where he had been sitting. "Okay, if this is another one of your pranks," she said out loud. But no one answered her. "Fine, I can sit here and wait," she said and promptly sat down on the grass, where moments ago he had been sitting.

She held up her white elk figurine and gently stroked its soft flocked skin. The small stag seemed to smile at her. "I want to give you to my boyfriend, Eric," she said to the small creature. "He's a very nice fellow. Very handsome. And giving. And although he can be a bit mischievous at times, I love him."

Okay, she had finally admitted it. She loved him. Had fallen in love with him. How could she help herself. He made her feel beautiful. So alive. So wonderful.

"That's right, I love him. And I think he loves me," she told the creature. "I just wish he'd get back here," she said, and glanced around behind her, her eye catching the looking glass.

It was back, she saw in that instant and drew her breath in, afraid to move.

From the reflection, the white elk with the pink eyes stared at her. In her hand, she felt nothing, in the same instant, but she was afraid to look or even blink in case the enchantment disappeared. "You are real," she said, barely above a whisper. "I wish Eric were here so I could show him," she said, staring at the enchanted image.

The white elk's reflection stared back. Then the graceful creature seemed to bow toward her and then look away toward the woods.

Ever so carefully, she followed the gaze and looked back at the woods. Eric was standing there, a look of amazement on his handsome face. Tears stained his cheeks.

"I'm back!" he shouted, sniffling. He looked around wildly to see Claire sitting on the knoll. "No! Don't sit there!" he screamed at her and ran to her, grabbed her hands and pulled her to her feet, taking her quickly away from the hill. Then he hugged her to him. "Oh, God, I love you! I don't ever want to leave you again, and I don't want to ever go back there again!"

"Go back where?" Claire said, puzzled and delighted to see him. "Did you wander into the woods?" she asked. Then remembered the elk. "Oh, careful—the white elk!" She turned but the real elk was gone. So, was the figurine. "They're gone!" she said, seeing only the mirror propped up by the tree. "They were here!" she said.

"I don't care!" he said. "I just know I'm back. Let's get out of here," he said and led her away from the woods.

"But the mirror!" she told him.

Already back on level ground, Eric looked back and saw the mirror. In it was O'Grady's reflection along with that of the white elk's. For a moment, he panicked, but O'Grady's voice came to him, carried on the wind.

"You found the key. With a little help. Good luck to you and your new bride," he said.

"Thank you," Eric said back, now sure that O'Grady was once Claire's toy-making grandfather, teaching him how to be human. He turned toward Claire. "Leave the mirror. It's a prankster's tool and I'm through with that stuff. Please, will you marry me?"

Puzzled beyond belief, she wondered if she was ever going to learn the truth about this day and decided she didn't need to know. "Yes," she answered. "I love you, too," she said and kissed her prince.

He kissed her back, then took her hand in his, wiped the last of the tears from his eyes and began their journey home, feeling wonderfully alive and very happy to be in the mortal world.

Elf, he might still be, but now he was certain not only had he found his soulmate, but his own soul as well.

SLEIGHT OF BRIDE
by Brooks Peck

In addition to being an author, Brooks Peck is the associate publisher of *Science Fiction Weekly,* a review magazine on the World Wide Web. His short fiction also appears in *Future Net,* and he has just completed his first novel.

Before a battle, Prince Gullfoss ate enough for three elves or more. Although his generals complained it would slow him down, in this one area he ignored their advice. This is what he usually ate, in part: the grilled shank of an elk, four or five roasted potatoes, a pitcher of white ale, a loaf of thick-crusted bread, a sparrow or chipmunk pie depending on the season, a few bowls of glimmerberries, and a glass of great-grandfather Holmur's shadow wine.

On the fifth day of the week of Turning Moss, Gullfoss needed every bite. Instead of the anticipated skirmish, the kobolds mounted an all-out attack on the town of Blue Dell on the southeastern border. After two hours the situation looked grim. Outnumbered, Gullfoss' troops had been forced to retreat from the fields to the town walls. All of the grain silos burned, each a roaring tower of black smoke. Gullfoss watched through a glass steadied on the shoulder of an archer as a Steam Man, five stories tall, crashed through the trees. He felt a wave of unease ripple through the elvish troops. "Stay together," he called. Most of the remaining elves stood in a ragged mass before the town gate. "That's it," Gullfoss murmured. "Come and get us." He glanced at the covered pit fifty yards in front of the gate. It looked utterly obvious to him, and he was no great woodsman.

The Steam Man lurched onward. Painted with black-and-red stripes in the likeness of some kobold god, its spiked fists could lash out and break a stone wall. Smoke puffed from its ears, and it eyes, covered with metal foil, shone with an unearthly light. Kobold warriors stood ready on its hips, shoulders, and head. It stepped closer, almost to the pit. The next step should do it. At last it brought its left leg down, but a little short, so it landed just at the edge of the pit. The elves groaned and Gullfoss snarled. Then the ground under the Steam Man's foot collapsed sideways into the pit, and it dropped heavily to its right knee, groaning and hissing.

Gullfoss raised Bitter, his father's great sword. "Now!" he yelled. The elves charged. Archers on the walls stood and released a volley of arrows to rain on the Steam Man, pinning the kobold shooters inside while the elves closed in. In the lead, Gullfoss whirled Bitter in a sweeping arc that carved open a wide gash in the Steam Man's leg. Old magic filled Bitter. No armor or shield could withstand its blow. With Bitter in hand, King Ingolfer had broken the siege of Daleur. Some said that Bitter alone kept the Elf Lands secure.

While the other elves scaled the Steam Man, chanting war songs, Gullfoss attacked the metal again and again. Soon he'd cut an opening big enough to crawl through, and he wormed inside, finding a dim, echoing chamber. Half-blind, he struck out at the tangle of cables and rods around him. After some minutes of furious activity, the Steam Man creaked terribly, shifting. Gullfoss scrambled out yelling, "Away! Away!" The elves ran for the gate. Steam poured from every crack and joint of the Man. It toppled forward, and as it struck the ground, the boiler exploded throwing fire, metal, and hot water in every direction.

Amid the cheering, Gullfoss ran to his rooms and left his armor and Bitter with his sister Eyri, shouting the good news. For the rest of the waning afternoon he helped bring in the wounded and contain the fires, hot but happy work.

Back inside the gates he shouldered through the throng of elves excitedly trading iron trinkets from the battlefield. Many had already incorporated gears and bolts into their clothes, hair, and cheeks. They pressed around their Prince, shouting congratulations and

thanks. Gullfoss laughed, gripping hands and shoulders
as he moved toward the barracks. Finally he shut the
door firmly behind him. His sister Eyri sat at a desk
writing what would be a bold and exaggerated account
of the battle, but never exaggerated enough for him.

"Be sure to say the pitfall was my idea," Gullfoss said.

"That's what you said when you left. Anyway that
idea's older than Holmur."

"But not against Steam—" Gullfoss stared at a peg
on the wall above the washstand. "Where's Bitter?" he
asked.

His sister didn't look up. "How should I know?"

"It was *here*!" he shouted, and Eyri crushed the nib
of her pen as she jumped.

"What—"

"I brought the sword here after the battle and told
you to watch it, remember?"

Eyri looked at the peg now. "Oh. Yes."

Gullfoss' eyes blazed so much that Eyri shrank back.
"Did you leave it alone?" he demanded.

"No, I haven't left."

"Did anyone come in?"

"Of course not."

"Are you *sure*?" he shouted.

"Yes I'm sure!" Eyri shouted back.

"It's Father's sword. The sword of the elfin people.
You were supposed to watch it."

"I was busy figuring out how to feed this town this
winter."

Gullfoss could only manage an enraged shriek in
reply. He burst from the rooms yelling, "Someone has
stolen my sword!"

Soon Blue Dell trembled as searchers thrashed
through the intertwined elfin homes with a racket that
equaled that of the battle. After three hours, Gullfoss'
First Light approached him, accompanied by the town's
chief Weaver. "My Prince," the Light said, dropping to
one knee and staring at the ground between them. "The
sword is not here, and no one saw who took it. I failed
my duty and will now leave the Elf Lands forever, if
that is sufficient punishment."

"Nonsense," Gullfoss said. "That would be a ridiculous waste. You're wiser than I am, and I need your advice. The sword has been stolen. Fine. We shall retrieve it."

The palace-tree of the elfin sovereigns, called Year's Beginning, embraced a sienna peak that reared three arrow flights over the forest. Its ancient trunk branched across the rock and its limbs formed leafy towers, ramparts, and keeps. Normally there would have been a small victory ceremony when Gullfoss and Eyri returned, with Gullfoss holding Bitter high before him. Today they entered quietly through a side gate where a sea of chancellors and aides surrounded them.

"The plans for the Solstice festival must be approved!"

"Sagross' seer has died, and a replacement must be appointed!"

"The bards are threatening to strike!"

Gullfoss raised his voice. "Have you asked the King about these matters?" Tense silence. A few aides glanced at the door that led to the King's rooms, barred from the inside for the last six months. Gullfoss was immediately sorry he'd brought it up. "Fire the bards, hire new ones, and speak to Eyri about the rest of it. I have another problem that needs my attention." He rushed to the stairs. Eyri sprinted after him.

"Good job. Now they think you're going mad, too."

"I'll fix things later. Right now I've got to find Bitter before everyone hears it's gone, or there will be panic."

"And how will you do that?"

"*I don't know!* I'm trying to think of something, but it's not working."

Eyri squeezed his arm reassuringly. "Come on. I have an idea."

She led him outside along a limb wide enough for them to walk side by side, then inside the rock again, upstairs past the nursery to a dim landing where the stairs took a turn. "Auntie Myn's been rearranging the rooms again," she said, placing her hand on the wall and mumbling a High Tongue word. A door-sized stone block turned to liquid and poured away through a grate in the floor. "Wait." Eyri disappeared into a dark cham-

ber and Gullfoss heard wooden drawers being opened
and shut, clutter being shoved about, and curses.

Presently Eyri reemerged, holding a flat amulet on a
chain. She spoke again, and the rock flowed up out of
the grate, becoming solid. Outside on a shaded balcony
she showed him the amulet. It was ivory-colored, as soft
as vellum and very light. "Auntie told me this will only
work two more times, but this is an emergency."

"What does it do?" Gullfoss asked even as Eyri hung
it around his neck. He felt a dizzy sensation as if he
were water being poured from one cup to another, and
suddenly the world turned sharp. The Southern Mountains, almost lost in haze, now appeared before him in
perfect detail. He could see insects crawling on the
ground all the way at the base of the palace. He
squawked, flapping feathered wings with a span as wide
as an adult elf. He raised his foot and saw sharp talons.
"Stupendous!" he cried.

"Now go search," Eyri commanded.

"At once." Without a second thought he leaped from
the balcony, dropping like an arrow until he spread his
new wings to carve the air and soar upward.

Gullfoss flew straight for the Kobold Hegemony,
reaching the border in only half a day. Then he slowed,
drifting over any camps or settlements he saw, scrutiniz-
ing them with his keen eyesight, but always heading for
Chokmek, the capital. The lands surrounding Chokmek
were a cacophony of engines. Half-sized Steam Slaves
pulled dozens of plows yoked together like a comb.
Trains emerged from tunnels like whales breaching,
paused to swallow and disgorge passengers, then dived
underground again. Closer to the iron wall that guarded
the main gate to the city, Gullfoss saw Naust, the kobolds' King, walking in a group of kobolds each uglier
than the last. It looked like a war council, based on the
riot of beads and feathers the others wore. A group of
footmen with muskets followed at a discreet distance.
Soon the generals or whatever they were turned back to
the gate, but Naust walked on alone, watching the
farmers.

Gullfoss landed in a tree above the road just before

Naust, and the branches pitched heavily under his weight. Naust wiped his eyes with warty fingers and stared. "I thought our hunters would have taken any bird like you in this area long ago. So perhaps you're not really a bird. Tell me, bird, how go things with the elves?"

"Not great," Gullfoss answered. "Have your people stolen the sword Bitter?"

Naust laughed. "So direct. Indeed we have."

"Where is it?"

Naust laughed so hard his greasy hair bobbed. "I've put it in Chokmek's deepest vault, eight miles under the earth. No elf will ever see it again."

He seemed to Gullfoss on the verge of saying more. "Unless?"

Naust's expression turned shifty, and he tried to hide it, poorly. "Unless the Princess Eyri consents to marry me and live here at Chokmek as my Queen."

"You're mad!" Gullfoss cried, leaping into the air. He wanted to strike at Naust, but a squad of musketeers jogged double-time down the road to meet their King. Naust's freezing laughter followed him as he climbed away.

Gullfoss returned to the elfin palace when dawn was well advanced, alighting on the terrace outside Eyri's rooms. He tapped the window with his beak, and soon his sister opened the door for him. She drew the amulet from around his neck, and after the weird pouring sensation passed, he said, "Well, then, get your wedding dress my dear, and congratulations."

"Whom am I marrying?"

"Naust, highest among kobolds."

"*What?*"

"That's his ransom for Bitter—your lovely hand." Gullfoss tried to take the hand in question, but Eyri yanked it away and shoved him against a bookcase. She had wrapped herself in a blanket when he woke her, and now she pulled it tight around her neck and stood up tall, looking absolutely regal despite her garb. "Marry a kobold and live in his bottomless damp basements? I wouldn't wish that on any elf, even you, I don't think. What did you say? Did you tell him I would?"

"No!" Gullfoss protested.

"Because there's no way—*no way*—that I'm going near that oaf. Damn the sword anyway." She stopped, shocked at her own words. They looked at each other in silence for a moment.

"We need to get that sword back," Gullfoss said.

"I know!" Eyri shouted. She grabbed a necklace from a table and flung it at him. "Idiot! But he asks *too much.*"

Gullfoss caught the necklace, a strand of rubies set in silver. "Pretty," he observed. Then, "Of course you're not going to marry him. That's insane. But we have to figure something out." Eyri stared, looking him up and down as her smile grew. "What?" he asked.

She walked over and took the necklace. "Let me help you with that," she said, turning him around. She held the blanket together with her teeth while she clasped the necklace around his neck. Then she stood back and looked at him appraisingly. "Very nice."

"What?" her brother demanded again.

"*You* will marry him."

Aunt Myn laughed so hard when she finished her spell that she wept, snorted, and finally collapsed in her chair, startling the daybats that perched on it. She gave them each a chestnut to calm them. "Aren't you darling," she said to Gullfoss, passing him a hand mirror. In the glass he saw his sister Eyri's face scowling. His clothes looked ridiculously loose and rumpled on her small frame.

"These clothes feel like they fit fine—why do I look that way?" He looked at Eyri and jumped. She appeared like he normally did, though her dress looked ready to burst across his muscular shoulders.

"You're still you, dear," Aunt Myn said. "You *appear* to be each other, so of course those clothes don't look like they fit." She tried to suppress another fit of mirth. "Oh, go change before I faint. We'll have to take yours in, Gull, and who knows how we'll manage a wedding dress big enough for you. Are you sure you're ready to make this kind of commitment?"

"Auntie—" Gullfoss warned.

"No one will notice that the dress is actually so big?" Eyri asked with Gullfoss' voice. The daybats spat nutshells onto the floor one after another.

"Oh, no, you'll look perfect. And let's get him some ribbons and nice earrings. It's his special day, you know."

King Naust pounded the table, silencing the outraged gabble that filled the Cabinet. "No, I will not change my mind. Prepare the greatest feast this city has ever seen; invite every Governor and Lieutenant Governor. Also send out a party to kidnap five of the best elfin cooks they can find as well as some musicians."

Messengers ran to relay the orders. Around the great table, Naust's generals looked at him with anger and disbelief. Their maps and strategies sat before him ignored.

"The sword is the icon of elfin strength," General Skard said. "Stealing it was your greatest coup. Without it they are seriously weakened, and in our hands, in the hands of a great kobold warrior leading the battle charge, think of the gains we could make."

Naust smiled, and the generals shifted nervously in their chairs at the sight. "I have land in plenty," he said. "I have land, cattle, orchards, mines, this fortress, wine cellars, and treasuries. But I don't have a wife, and I certainly never thought I'd have a wife as beautiful or brilliant as Eyri. Now we must make ready because she will be here soon."

Gullfoss and Eyri traveled for four days to the border, accompanied by a handful of soldiers who pitched their tent and cooked their meals. Across the border a kobold contingent of equal number joined them, and together they traveled another four days, deeper and deeper into the kobolds' strange territories, until they reached Chokmek in the late afternoon. An honor guard met them at the Gate of Three Wheels and fired a deafening salute that made the Princess wince and the Prince yelp. The Prince insisted they stop to wash and change out of their travel clothes before presenting themselves, and the

Princess scowled deeply at this suggestion. She had said little during the journey, but the soldiers noted that she could be heard to mutter some outstanding swear words.

Finally Gullfoss and Eyri emerged from their tent. Although he knew he looked fine, Gullfoss felt like a mess. His wedding gown, pale green with living snowdrops woven into the fabric, could not be fastened all the way up the back, and Eyri had tied ribbons in painful knots across his scalp so his hair stuck up in tufts like some kind of shaman. He hated the veil worst of all because he could hardly see through it and it scratched his face. "I'm already disguised, why do I have to wear the damn thing?" he demanded.

"Tradition," Eyri said.

"Tradition stinks."

She assured him he looked lovely. For her own part Eyri had to stuff rags into his best boots to make them fit, and she stumbled now and then, clutching his arm suddenly for support. Gullfoss also walked slowly so his bare feet wouldn't show. There had been no time to construct proper shoes in his size, so he was forced to do without.

A captain in a black-and-scarlet uniform greeted them politely but with obvious disdain, and asked that the elfin guards remain outside. He then led them through a tunnel pierced with murder holes, beneath a portcullis to an underground thoroughfare. Soldiers held traffic back from the immediate area, but a good number of other soldiers and citizens could be seen crossing the tunnel at intersections farther down the tunnel. Iron pipes, from a finger's width to a hand's breadth across, lined the ceiling. Strange lamps lit the tunnel, sputtering and throwing off sparks, painful to look at directly.

The captain led them to a single metal rail set in a groove on which perched a sort of small open chariot with little metal wheels. It took a moment for him to make it understood that they were to sit inside the chariot. Once aboard, the captain threw some levers, turned a knob, and the chariot trundled fifteen paces along its track into a small chamber. "Could have walked that far," Gullfoss said. Then the chamber floor suddenly dropped and he grabbed the sides of the chariot, noticing the captain's smirk. Bearing the chariot, the floor moved deeper underground past a succession of tunnels leading away, often full of kobolds crowding to have a look at the visitors. The ceiling became lost in the dark shaft above them. Finally the floor wobbled to a halt and the captain maneuvered the chariot along another tunnel that ended at a huge doorway made of ancient dark wood banded with brass. Voices and rich cooking smells drifted out.

"Here we go," Eyri said as they stepped inside. Instantly the Great Hall fell silent as dozens of kobold officials, leaders, and members of society gaped at them.

The towering hall's ceiling was lost in darkness, but stones or metal glittered up there, looking like stars. Naust stood at the head table under long banners that rippled from warm draughts off a fire in a great pit behind him. He stared, too, and for an instant Gullfoss feared the spell had broken, and everyone saw him for what he was, a male elf in a dress and veil and bare feet.

Naust shook himself, then strode forward. "Welcome. Welcome, elves. This is a great day and I am . . . I'm so flattered that you've come." He offered Gullfoss his arm and Gullfoss looked at it blankly until Eyri nudged him. He allowed himself to be led across the hall under the piercing glares of the kobolds, while Naust proclaimed, "Friends, I present to you the Princess Eyri, my betrothed, and her brother Prince Gullfoss of the elves." A few polite nods. "Let us feast and celebrate this historic occasion."

Platters of food including a good number of elfin dishes were brought to the table, but Gullfoss hardly noticed. He looked out at his lifelong enemies, many of whom made little effort to hide their scorn. Naust moved from group to group, greeting them. The generals and other soldiers, kobolds male and female alike whom he'd met in battle, all watched his sister who wore his form as she ate quietly. Gullfoss could see they found this elf prince who ate so daintily and wiped his mouth with a napkin very amusing. Finally a Commander named Odal sauntered up. "Gullfoss! You've had your claws clipped, but that doesn't mean we can't still fight."

"What do you mean?" Eyri asked, swallowing.

In answer Odal pulled up a bench opposite Eyri and put his elbow on the table, hand up for wrestling.

Eyri looked around. "Now isn't a good time," she said.

"Of course it is. What do you elves do at parties? Play chess?" Waves of laughter from the room.

Eyri looked at Gullfoss. "Wrestle," he whispered, "or you'll be a coward."

Reluctantly she held up her arm and Odal's knuckles cracked as he gripped her hand. "Say when, Princess."

"Go," Gullfoss said. In a blink Odal slammed Eyri's hand down into a plate, splashing sauce on both of them. The assembled kobolds roared, and Odal stood, grinning at his audience, and slapped Eyri on the shoulder. *They are laughing at me,* Gullfoss thought. *They think I'm a weakling.*

Eyri wanted to rub her sore elbow but didn't dare. She couldn't see Gullfoss' expression behind his veil, but his knuckles were white and his fists quivered. "I'll break his arm," he muttered.

"Shut up."

"Couldn't you have even tried?"

"You're going to blow it," she whispered through a smile. Ignoring his scowl, she looked around the Great Hall, again surprised by its grace. A flat metal sculpture covered much of one wall: a great deciduous tree of interlocking brass pipes. Water flowed out the tops of the pipes and trickled down the sculpture into a pool carved in the floor so a steady, rainlike patter filled the room.

Naust reappeared, his cheeks flushed, and sat heavily next to Gullfoss. "You must be uncomfortable in that thing," he said, reaching for the veil. "I would just like to look at my bride." When he lifted the veil his eyes went wide, and he sat back suddenly. "Your—your eyes. What's wrong? Why do you look so fierce?"

Eyri clutched Gullfoss' arm before he could speak. "It's because . . . because she's hardly slept these past eight days, she was so eager for her wedding night," she said.

Gullfoss nodded and began to eat. Apparently oblivious to Naust's watching, he made quick work of two broiled fowls and a bowl of fruit tossed with anonymous chunks of meat under a sweet glaze, as well as a whole basket of rolls, calling twice for more ale. His attempts to avoid his veil were not always successful, and soon brown gravy stained its lower edge. Then he stood and went to a table with a tray of small cakes and popped them into his mouth whole, one by one until they were gone. Back at the head table he asked for even more ale, then pulled over a platter of fish he'd missed.

"Well," Naust said slowly. "She certainly has a good appetite."

"She hardly ate during our entire journey here," Eyri said loudly. "She was so eager for her wedding night." Gullfoss grunted in agreement.

"Then we mustn't wait," Naust cried. "Call the priests, but first bring forward the sword. Bring forward Bitter to hallow my bride and may Korklish the Father hear our marriage oath and give his blessing. You stand off there, Gullfoss, you'll get it back outside the gates."

A soldier carried the sword to the head table, handling it with more reverence than Gullfoss would have expected, and his heart leaped. The kobold King held Bitter up for all to see while Eyri went down to stand a little apart from the crowd that now pressed forward. Naust laid the sword across Gullfoss' knees, and the prince's heart thudded with excitement.

"Eyri," the King said, "I hope you are as happy today as I am."

"Oh, I am," Gullfoss answered, gripping Bitter and tearing off his veil with his other hand. "I'm overjoyed!" He kicked back his chair, swung Bitter overhand and struck Naust on the head with the flat of the blade. The company screamed. "Steal my father's sword, will you, you thieving, lurking kobolds?" He jumped onto the table, upsetting tankards and bowls. "Blackmail my sister into marriage, will you?" An alert guard captain rushed him with a carving knife, but Gullfoss parried the swing and struck the captain's wrist, then shoved him back with his foot. Glancing over, he saw that Eyri now looked like herself, his best trousers and cloak hanging loosely around her. His hands on Bitter were the normal, hairy ones he was used to. Apparently he had over-whelmed the illusion.

On the floor, Naust glared up at him with hate. "Gull-foss!" he screamed. "You! You pig! I'll kill you!" Even as he yelled, the hall filled with armed and armored ko-bolds who shoved in between the guests. Bitter flashed as Gullfoss beat them back. Some carried spears which they thrust at him from a safe distance, but Gullfoss smashed down on the poles, breaking off the heads. Naust hurled cups, bottles, and heavy iron plates. Seeing this, the Governors and officials joined in with whatever was at hand, and Gullfoss suffered a rain of bones, scraps, smoked fruit, and pastries. He concentrated on avoiding the sharp or heavy items and soon became so splattered he could barely see. He wiped jam from his eyes and threw it back at the kobolds. His footing on the greasy table became precarious, and the soldiers moved closer on both sides. A quick youth darted in with a spear and Gullfoss could only partly deflect the blow. The spear opened a gash on his calf and he slipped, falling to one knee. The kobolds cheered, pressed closer.

This was turning ugly. "Can't you take a joke?" he yelled.

Eyri watched the battle in dismay. Why hadn't that idiot Gullfoss waited for a better chance? She had tried to join him, but two soldiers grabbed her arms and held her. Elf Prince or no, the kobolds outnumbered him. She watched him slip a second time, then struggle up again, sending a storm of blows all around him. Hair and ribbons were plastered to his scalp with muck, his dress was torn, but his eyes danced with power.

But he was going to be defeated. It was a matter of time.

Eyri's captors paid more attention to the fight than to her, and she gently dipped her hands into her pockets, hoping to find a knife, an arrowhead, anything. Her fin-gers touched a soft bundle which she drew out, glanc-ing down.

Auntie Myn's amulet.

That instant Eyri jerked her arms free, surprising the soldiers, and yelled "Gullfoss!" Her brother looked up. "Here!" She threw the amulet as the kobolds grabbed her again, twisting her arms back painfully.

Gullfoss snatched the amulet from the air, looked at it for a second, then slipped it around his neck. He became a whirlwind of feathers and the kobold host cried out again. Bitter clanged onto the table, but a second later Gullfoss the eagle lifted the sword in his talons and hauled it into the air. He carried it up to the top of the hall, circled once over the upturned faces, laughing, then streaked over to Eyri. "Catch!" he called, dropping Bitter. She caught the sword by its handle just before it hit the floor. Gullfoss descended, beating the kobolds back with powerful strokes from his wings. "Climb on," he said. Eyri scrambled on to his back, clutching the sword in one hand and grasping him around the neck with her free arm. He leaped up and she gasped as the hall and guests shrank below her. Almost immediately Gullfoss said, "Oh, no."

The doors to the Great Hall were shut.

Gullfoss flapped wildly to slow down and made a running, stumbling landing before the doors. The kobolds surrounded them. "We're not finished yet," Gullfoss hissed. "Get the amulet off me and I'll show them fighting."

Then a voice yelled, "Stop!" The kobolds fell back and Naust walked up to the elves. Sweat covered his brow and face and an ugly welt had come up on his forehead. "You broke your word," he said. "Eyri never intended to marry."

"You stole Bitter," Gullfoss retorted as Eyri slipped off his back.

The King pondered, then nodded. "I supposed it's one deceit traded for another. I hope you'll forgive me," he said to Eyri. "You see, I thought this was history."

"History?"

"We have a prophecy that says someday the elves and kobolds will become one people, and that your beauty will replace our ugliness, but our machines will replace your magic. I thought I—we—were destined to fulfill that prophecy."

Eyri looked around the beautiful Great Hall. These kobolds, especially Naust, were not what she had expected. She thought about the elves at Blue Dell bracing for a difficult winter. Peace would be a very good thing for a great many people. "There are better ways to court a woman," she said to Naust.

His face brightened. "Indeed. I'll think on that."

"Do that."

Naust's face brightened even more and he clapped his hands. "Open the doors," he called. He turned to a captain, "Take them to their escorts and see them all safely to the border. By the way—" he turned back. "May I say, Prince Gullfoss, that you made a beautiful bride."

THE SHOEMAKER AND THE ELVIS

by Lawrence Schimel

Lawrence Schimel is the coeditor of *Tarot Fantastic* and *The Fortune Tellers,* among other projects. His stories appear in *Dragon Fantastic, Cat Fantastic III, Weird Tales from Shakespeare, Phantoms of the Night, Return to Avalon,* the *Sword & Sorceress* series, and many other anthologies. Twenty-five years old, he lives in New York City, where he writes and edits full-time.

We'd heard, of course, about that other shoemaker, the one who'd found, upon waking, a set of shoes already made upon his workbench. But who'd have thought it might be true? Or that it could happen to us? I wasn't even a shoemaker, really! I'm a podiatrist. Sometimes I'll fashion orthopedic shoes, the whole she-bang, but mostly I just make inserts for people to slip into their sneakers. So what I can't figure out is: Why me? But isn't that always the case when someone has an encounter with the supernatural? Why me?

It was Jane who found them. She comes in earliest of everyone, to put on the coffee machine and get the office ready for the day's clients, to call and confirm people's appointments. She's got a seven-year-old son, Eric, and so she has to leave by three to pick him up from school.

"That's so cute, Dr. Katzman," Jane said to me by way of greeting, while I was hanging up my coat. "Who's got the Elvis fetish?"

"What Elvis fetish?" I asked her.

"You know, the blue suede shoes," she said.

"What blue suede shoes?" I asked her. I stuffed my scarf into the sleeve of my jacket.

"The ones in Room 2."

I walked down the hall. I hadn't made any blue suede

shoes. I hadn't had a call for a pair of shoes in weeks—not until Mrs. Parker came in yesterday. And she certainly didn't request blue suede shoes, not that I'd have made them for her even if she had. Her arches have fallen so deeply that inserts wouldn't suffice: she practically needed a special set of shoes with full-scale scaffolding.

"What happened to Mrs. Parker's shoes?" I cried.

There, on the counter, right where I'd left the soles of Mrs. Parker's special full-scale support shoes to set and dry overnight before fashioning them into footwear wide enough for her splayed toes to fit into, was a pair of blue suede shoes.

"Didn't you make those for her?" Jane asked me, coming into the room behind me. She lifted a shoe and felt inside. "Feels just like Mrs. Parker's prescription to me."

I picked up the other shoe and felt inside.

"You're right, it does feel like the right prescription. But I didn't make them."

"Well, it couldn't have been Nancy," Jane said.

Nancy was my other secretary. She wasn't the swiftest of girls, but she did try. She was my wife's niece, so I couldn't fire her. We just tried to keep her away from anything easily damaged, like the computer. Or the filing. Or the vacuum. Or—well, anything remotely mechanical.

"Who else could it have been?" I said. "You know how she's totally gone for Elvis." Another of Nancy's endearing charms. "Although I can't fathom why she'd have done something like this," I continued.

"Well, that's exactly why it must have been her: You can't fathom why. That's Nancy for you." Jane has been nagging me to hire someone else, someone competent that is, to help her with all the work. Preferably getting rid of the dead weight while I was at it.

"I don't understand how it could've been Nancy, though," I said, ignoring the problem of Jane's dissatisfaction for the moment. "We don't even carry blue suede. What could she have made them from? And how would she have made them? Nancy doesn't know how to listen to the answering machine, let alone sew a complicated pair of orthopedic shoes like this."

"What are you proposing it was, then," Jane asked, "elves in the middle of the night?"

"I'd believe elves made this a lot sooner than I would Nancy did. Elves, or maybe Elvis." I almost waffled the joke trying to get the accents over the right syllables.

Jane groaned. "I'll call the *Weekly World News*. 'Elvis Sighted in Podiatrist's Office!' 'Blue Suede Shoes Found to Cause Pigeon Toe!' And I get to keep half the money." She smiled and disappeared back to the front desk to begin calling. Clients, that is, not the *Weekly World News*.

I went to the phones as well. I explained to Mrs. Parker that there might be a slight delay in her shoes, unless she didn't mind blue suede. The wholesaler, I lied, had sent us a shipment of blue suede instead of ordinary brown leather, and it would be weeks before they could send us a replacement shipment.

Mrs. Parker said she didn't care what color they were so long as her feet stopped hurting.

Nonetheless, I felt the tip of my nose when I hung up, just to make sure it hadn't grown any from my white lie. I mean, if elves—or Elvises—were making shoes in the middle of the night, why not the rest of all those old stories? I couldn't believe it was Nancy, and I didn't have any other ideas.

Nancy, when she showed up at one, was totally ignorant. Of the shoes, as well, I mean.

"Dr. Katzman!" Nancy squealed when I showed her the blue suedes in Room 2. "You've made a pair of Elvis shoes!"

"I told you so," Jane and I both sighed together.

I was totally baffled by the shoes. Who had made them? And from what material? They obviously used the soles that I had left to set and dry, they'd been molded off Mrs. Parker's feet. I'd done them myself, I knew the warped shape of those fallen arches. But everything else had been changed. And all the materials I'd used, or left ready to be used, were gone.

At least Mrs. Parker didn't mind about the color, so

I wasn't out the time or anything. And they were well-crafted shoes, it seemed. If a bit . . . unfashionable.

Before Jane left, I laid out a new pair of soles in Room 3. I locked the door, took the key off my keyring and handed it to her. "Don't open it tomorrow until I get here," I told her. "I have no way of getting in there without you, now, and I want to be there tomorrow when we prove that it wasn't elves."

I was late getting to the office, despite my best efforts. I was eager to find out what happened with the soles I'd left out, but the Long Island Expressway was doing its imitation of a parking lot that morning, and I was almost an hour late by the time I got there. The traffic didn't seem to have caught any of the morning's clients, who were thick as fleas in the waiting room, and between them and the phone ringing off the hook, Jane and I didn't get a chance to unlock Room 3 until Nancy had shown up and could cover the phones and the front desk while Jane and I had the unveiling. We both stood hesitantly before the door for a few moments, just staring at it, neither of us saying a word. But our doubt and disbelief was quite apparent in our expressions.

"Everything is going to be exactly as we left it," I said, as Jane handed me the key and I opened the door. Still, I couldn't make myself turn the knob, nervous about what I might find, the possibility that I was wrong.

"Until you open the door," Jane said, "both possibilities will continue to exist. On the other side there are either a pair of soles, like we'd left them, or a pair of finished shoes, fashioned by supernatural or other means. We must open the door and find out which scenario is real." She paused for breath. "You open the door and I'll turn on the lights, okay?"

I nodded, unable to find my voice, and flung open the door. Jane reached around the doorjamb and flicked the light switch. Together, we stared in through the open door.

There, on the counter, was a new pair of blue suede shoes, obviously different than the first pair from yesterday. (These were easily four sizes smaller.)

"Now what?" I asked.

"I don't know which is more preposterous," Jane said,

"the fact that elves are real, or that we've had an Elvis sighting right here in our office."

"Not a confirmed Elvis sighting," I reminded her. We went out into the hallway, closing the door behind us. But out of sight, this mystery was hardly out of mind. "What," I wondered aloud, "are we supposed to do, according to the fairy tale?"

I didn't remember the story too well. But Jane's got a seven-year-old son, so she'd read it more recently than any of the rest of us.

"I think this means the King wants a pair of shoes for himself," Jane said. "That's what happens in the story, the elves are all barefoot and naked."

"Naked! I missed a chance of seeing Elvis naked!" I caught Nancy as she swooned. Jane rushed and got her a paper cup of water. I was pleased to see her coming to Nancy's rescue, despite her dislike for the girl.

"I'm all right, I think," Nancy declared. "But I'm not leaving this office until I get a sight of him tonight!"

Jane looked at me. "I'm kind of curious, myself," she said. "To see this story through to the end. In the fairy tale, the shoemaker and his wife make clothes and tiny shoes for the elves for Christmas. And the elves never come back."

"I guess we can't really call an exterminator, so it may just come to that. If it really is elves. Or Elvis. I admit I am curious myself, to find out for sure."

"It's agreed then," Jane said.

"What fun!" Nancy cried. "An Elvis stakeout!"

Jane and I both sighed, and went back to work.

Jane called around and arranged for Eric to stay at his friend Peter's house that night. I had a bit more trouble convincing my wife.

"You're staying late at work," my wife said with this certain tone in her voice. "With your *secretary*."

"I'm hurt that you even suggest such a thing," I told her. "Besides, Nancy will be here, too."

"You're staying late at work," my wife repeated in that same tone, though her voice had gone up an octave, "with *both* of your secretaries!"

"Someone's been breaking into the office," I explained exasperatedly. "Nancy thinks it's Elvis, so she

wants to stay and see him. Speaking of which, we really
need to talk about Nancy one of these days."

"Don't change the subject," my wife said. "Are you
having an affair with my niece or your secretary or both
of them at once?"

I sighed. "Why don't you come spend a boring night
staking out the office with us, and you'll see that I am
not having an affair with my secretary, who has a seven-
year-old son fercrissake, or," and here I dropped my
voice for the next three words, "your brainless niece!"

Adele showed up promptly at 6:30 when the office
closed. I treated us all to Chinese food. We rushed back
because we didn't know when he'd show up. I'd left a
pair of soles on the counter in Room 1 this time, just to
keep our midnight visitor(s) on his or their toes. And
also because Room 1 had a supply closet big enough to
fit four people.

We hid inside, peeking through the slats every now
and again to see if he'd arrived yet. Well, Jane and I only
occasionally peered through; Nancy was riveted, peeping
through the entire time.

Adele complained that she was bored.

"I *told* you to stay home," I told her.

"I thought you were having an affair. I mean, you
were giving me all the right cues. What was I supposed
to do?"

"An affair?" Jane said, with this certain tone to her
voice. Even with no lights on, I just knew she was
sneering. Adele knew it, too, and I could feel her relax
even further. Seeing Nancy over dinner had been reas-
surance enough to dismiss that worry.

"Hush," Nancy reminded us, "who knows when he'll
show up."

Adele, Jane, and I all sighed. Nancy really thought
she was going to see the King.

I didn't know what I thought we would see. Although
I guess I thought we'd see *something*. Or rather, someone. Otherwise I wouldn't have been spending a night
squatting in a supply closet with my secretary, my wife,
and her brainless, Elvis-sick niece.

Adele sat next to me on the floor and leaned against
my shoulder. Pretty soon she was snoring. I wanted to

take a nap myself, but only my leg fell asleep. I was afraid I'd miss all the action, if there was to be any, and I didn't want to have to go through all this bother and discomfort a second time.

After what seemed like hours, Nancy began to sort of squeal—her attempt to keep from shouting in excitement. I was proud of her for even making an attempt.

There was a humming and some fumbling outside the closet. Something clattered to the floor. Someone cursed. And then the lights went on in the room.

The four of us peeked through the lats.

It was the King all right. He hadn't changed a bit. He looked exactly as young as in the last known photos of him, as if decades had not passed.

Well, one thing was different, or at least I'd never noticed it before.

"Look at that," I whispered. "He's worn clear through the insides of his soles."

"Oh, the poor thing," Nancy said aloud, and she rushed forward from our hiding spot into the room.

If Elvis was surprised to find her there, he didn't show it.

"Ya gotta help me, Mama," he drawled. "I'm caught in a trap, I can't get out. La belle dame sans merci hath me in thrall," he explained.

Nancy, of course, would do anything he asked of her.

"La Belle Dumb is in thrall, too," Jane sighed, and followed Nancy out of our hiding spot to rescue her. Once again, I was proud to see her coming to the aid of my wife's brainless niece, despite her dislike of the girl.

And Jane had hit on something profound, I thought, remembering my Keats from the token English class they made us take in med school. I marveled at the similarity of Elvis to the Queen of Elfland, trapping unsuspecting mortals in his glamour, keeping them oblivious to everything but himself, and leaving them senseless because of him.

But I didn't want to miss out on all the action, so I set aside these musings for later and revealed myself as well. "What seems to be the problem?" I asked.

"My feet," the King moaned.

"Yes, I see," I murmured, soothingly. "Why don't you

sit up there while I take a look," I said. Elvis climbed
onto the padded table and drummed his heels against
the drawers.

"I just can't stop dancing," he continued. "It's all the
Queen's fault. She makes me dance. But I don't got the
same stamina these elves do."

Suddenly, at the same moment, it sank home to Jane
and me what he'd said earlier. La belle dame, the Queen
of Elfland, had *the King* in thrall, not the other way
around as I'd earlier thought Jane had meant. At last,
the mystery of Elvis' disappearance was solved! It was
no wonder he looked as young and unchanged as ever;
I remembered this story, still, and according to the poem
time moved differently between the worlds. Seven years
would pass the real world, and only a day would have
gone by in the fairy kingdom.

"*The Enquirer* will *never* believe this," Jane muttered.
"But maybe Spielberg."

"For seven years, I am her slave," the King was saying, as I knelt down before him and unlaced his worn-
through blue suede shoes.

"You poor thing!" Nancy cried. Adele took her
niece's arm, as much to quiet her and prevent her from
doing anything rash as to catch the girl should she
faint again.

I pulled Elvis' socks off. His feet gave off that particular fungal odor.

"You need to change your shoes more often," I told
him. I was afraid Nancy might do me damage if I said
his feet stank. "Rotate them."

"I can only do what she wants me to. And she always
wants me to sing and shake my hips for her. I'm so tired.
And my feet! Just look at my shoes! You've got to help
me, Doctor."

"Yes, I can see that," I said.

"You've got to help him!" Nancy cried.

"How is it you could come here?" Jane asked. My
ever-practical Jane. I don't know what I'd do without
her. The whole office would fall apart without her. I
didn't think I had to worry until Eric was old enough to
go off to college, but I couldn't help thinking how I
really needed to make sure I'd hired someone else,

someone she'd have trained, before she left me. She was just too smart to stay my secretary for long—she deserved more from life.

"It's because of the stories," Elvis said. "The Queen's cast a spell on me, and it makes me more or less an elf while I'm in her thrall. Making shoes is one of the things Elves do, and in return the mortals will make a pair of shoes for us. Please, Doctor, I'm begging you, make me a pair of shoes that will make my feet stop hurting."

I knelt down before the King's feet again, and began examining his soles. I couldn't help feeling like Mary Magdalene washing the feet of Christ. I'd have to tell Jane the analogy, I thought—but not right then. The mood was wrong, and I wasn't sure either Nancy or my wife would catch the irony of it all. Well, I *knew* Nancy wouldn't. I held my tongue, and instead poked and prodded and measured his feet.

"Yes," I murmured. "Pronating. Hmmm."

"Can you help me?" the King begged, in his love-me-tender voice.

"I think I have a solution," I said, and began assembling supplies to take a casting. A silence settled over the room as I worked. Jane immediately fell into helping me, handing me the things I needed as I needed them. Nancy all but vibrated with anxiety and erotic tension; she looked as though she might, at any moment, leap onto the table and tear Elvis' sequined clothes from him. Adele just watched, holding onto her niece with a quiet but firm grip. Elvis began to hum.

Jane and I worked. I poured the soles. "We're not going to have time for these to set," I warned. "They need a full twenty-four hours before I can make them into shoes. You'll have to come back tomorrow."

Nancy made that not-quite-squealing sound again.

"Let me see them," Elvis said. He hoped down off the table, and stood next to me. He looked at them, holding them in his hands as he hummed along. Then he handed them back to me. "They'll be fine like that," he said.

They had dried already.

I didn't question it. So many strange things were happening already, this seemed like nothing special.

The normalcy of sewing a pair of shoes was the only thing that made sense. The fact that they were for Elvis seemed inconsequential. These were just another pair of tired feet that needed to be supported. They just happened to belong to one of the most famous men in history, a man who was surrounded by a mystery that we'd just unraveled.

Not that anyone would believe us, if we told them. I didn't believe it myself.

But I made the shoes anyway, even not believing what was going on. There had to be some sort of rational explanation, I thought, and one day it would all become clear.

Elvis put his socks back on, and tried the shoes on. "They're perfect," he said, shuffling a step or two.

The King was so happy not to have his feet hurting him, he turned and kissed Nancy, who was standing nearest to him.

Nancy fainted.

No one was there to catch her, and she banged her head against the edge of the counter. I bent over her, and checked to see if she was all right. A streak of red stained the linoleum. Jane ran to fetch bandages. Adele went to call an ambulance.

"Where's Elvis?" Nancy cried, when she opened her eyes as we were holding a gauze bandage to the back of her skull.

"Elvis?" I asked. I looked around me. In the commotion, he'd disappeared. Back to Elfland, or wherever he'd come from. However he'd gotten here. I had to wonder if he'd ever been there, and didn't know which questioned my sanity more. And as I caught Jane's eye, I knew she was wondering how much we should tell Nancy, if we'd ever live down the true story.

"You've hit your head, honey," Jane said. "Elvis has been missing for years. He's probably dead by now."

"He can't be dead!" Nancy cried. "I saw him, I swear I saw him. You were all here. He kissed me!" Her eyelids fluttered again, and she sort of hugged herself.

"It was just a dream," Jane explained, patiently. "From when you hit your head."

Adele came back in. "The ambulance is on its way," she said.

"Just a dream," Nancy whispered. You could see her deflate. "It all seemed so real."

It all seemed so real. That's how I felt, too. It seemed so real, but how could it be true? I'd seen him with my own two eyes, I'd touched his naked soles with my own two hands, I'd made blue suede shoes especially for him, shoes that would stand up to the supernatural pounding of elfin dances.

No one spoke while we waited for the ambulance to show up. Adele went with her niece to the hospital, and I promised to follow her there once Jane and I had had a chance to clean up and close down the office.

"What will we tell people?" I asked.

"I don't know that we *can* tell people. Who'd believe us? I don't believe it, myself, and I was there. But at least we got to the end of the story, brought this all to some sort of conclusion."

"I guess," I said, not quite sure I felt a sense of closure. I would never look at an Elvis on velvet painting the same way again, I knew, and every time I heard one of his songs, I'd always remember the feel of his feet beneath my hands. "I just feel there are so many mysteries left unsolved. Like, are all those other fairy tales true, as well? And especially: Why me? But I guess we'll never find out."

Jane took the casting. "All I know," she said, "is that *this* is going to put Eric through college."

I could hardly argue with that.

THE MARBLE KING
by Gary A. Braunbeck

Gary A. Braunbeck has sold over 65 short stories to various mystery, suspense, science fiction, fantasy, and horror markets. His latest fiction also appears in *Future Net* and *Careless Whispers*. His first story collection, *Things Left Behind*, is scheduled for hardcover release this year. He has been a full-time writer since 1992, and lives in Columbus, Ohio.

Squatting on my chest, the dwarf-thing pointed a bony finger at me and said, "No clapperdogeon, angler, or shivering-jemmy me, I've come this eve to tell ye that your squabby, fancy-bloke shaver named Johnny needs our help; them liver-faced bullyraggers what's been givin' jessie to 'im's well in need of a sound batty fang themselves, and 'tis time for thee and me to knife it."

It was only later, after I'd learned some small part of his language, that I understood exactly what he was saying: that he was not a thief, beggar, or con artist, and had come to tell me, with an honest heart and in an honest voice, it was high time the boys who'd been picking on my best friend got a taste of their own medicine so they'd stop terrorizing Johnny.

He thrust out his other, fisted hand and opened his fingers. In the center of his palm was the most beautiful marble I had ever seen; perfectly rounded and smooth, glimmering white, red- and blue-veined, it seemed to say: Use me and you'll never again lose a game, ever, for I am the most magical of marbles.

"W–who are you?" I whispered.

"I be the Marble King, boy."

That was the fall of my ninth year, and before that season was over, there was going to be a lot of needless suffering—something I've since concluded is part and parcel of childhood.

When we were both eight years old, my best friend Johnny Sawyer and I went Christmas shopping with my mother. We were looking at model car kits in the toy department of one of the countless stores we'd visited that day when we overheard two girls talking an aisle over. The older one had obviously been burdened with watching her little sister while Mom or Dad bought gifts elsewhere in the store. The younger girl was upset because her sister was complaining about how stupid Christmas was.

"You better watch out," said the younger girl, "or Santa'll put coal in your stocking."

"You are *such* a child," snapped her sister. "There's no such thing as Santa Claus!"

"You don't believe in Santa?"

"No!"

The younger girl laughed at her sister who'd lost touch with the Miracle. "Well, that's *your* problem."

I was thinking about her as I got out of my car at 7:00 p.m. and headed for the entrance to the Quiet People's Place, a little diner three blocks north of the Altman Museum in downtown Cedar Hill. The majority of the People's staff is composed of handicapped adults and teenagers; its owner, Dave Boggs (imagine Old King Cole without the beard and you'll have some idea of this marvelous, exuberantly cheerful yet oddly sad-eyed man, now well into his sixties had lost his Down's Syndrome son to pneumonia almost thirty years ago and had sworn he'd dedicate the rest of his life to giving developmentally disabled people the opportunities that had been denied his son.

As I entered, Dave was reprimanding some retro-Grunge teens who'd been loudly making fun of the mentally impaired cook. They grumbled halfhearted apologies and went back to their burgers, casting contemptuous glances in Dave's direction for several minutes afterward.

Sitting at the counter, I greeted Dave and said, "You

know you're gonna find your windows smashed or something worse tomorrow morning?"

"Don't matter, I got insurance. I just won't tolerate folks makin' fun of my employees. Sayin' that I hire folks from *'Tards 'R' Us.* These people got enough to deal with without having to—ah, hell, you know what I mean."

True. I'd lost part of my tongue as a child and had undergone years of speech therapy in order to relearn how to speak clearly. Even now my words come out semi-slurred about half the time, and it makes me sound as if I'm . . . well, *not quite right.* I endured a lot of mockery from my peers as a kid, and still get pitying glances from adults who don't know me very well. I suppose that's why I feel such an affinity for the staff of the People's Place.

"So," he said to me, grinning, "that lovely lady who permits you to be her husband—how's she doing?"

"Cathy's fine. She said to tell you 'hey,' and that all of us will be in for brunch on Sunday."

"I'll make sure to clean the grill, then." He cocked a thumb toward the smiling cook who grinned at us from the other side of the pickup counter. "By the way, he's concocted a new burger. Calls it the 'Gut-Buster.' Loaded with everything you can imagine. Order one for you?"

"Medium-well, with onion rings and a large Coke."

"Ah, a man after my own heart—screw that cholesterol count."

"Amen," I said, waving at the cook, who winked at me and waved back.

As I waited for my "Gut-Buster," I found myself reminiscing about the old neighborhood, about a season filled with wonder and terror and, suddenly, there I was, nine years old and on my way to Johnny's house to play darts. . . .

"My turn!" squealed Johnny, grabbing the darts from my hand. We were in his backyard, our dartboard mounted on the back basement door.

"Don't yell," I said, picking up one of the darts he'd dropped in his excitement and tossing it to him. He didn't catch it; he never caught anything that was thrown to him. The other guys hated it when he came to play ball with us—we always lost when he was on our team.

He threw the darts and got the bull's-eye twice out of three times, and *boy* did that make me mad! I ran over to the board and yanked out the darts.

"How come you can throw so good now, but when you play ball you can't even catch a bunt and hold on to it?"

"Because you guys act like it's for millions of dollars or something. It ain't fun when you play it like that."

"*You're* no fun!" I yelled, and, darts still clutched tightly in my hand, started to leave.

"Don't go!" he whined. "I was only jokin'!" If there was one thing I hated more than his squealing, it was his whining, and I was in a bad mood anyway and even as a kid I never thought things out when I got mad, so I whirled around and threw the darts at him and he reached out to catch them, but I guess I threw them a little too hard because even though he missed two, one of them stuck into his shoulder deep enough to draw blood.

He just stood there looking at me—not the dart in his shoulder—and made a sound; it wasn't a crying noise, it was more like the high bleating a new puppy makes when it comes out of the sac. "You did that because you don't like me!"

"*No, I don't!* You're fat and dirty and you always smell bad! *Nobody* likes you! We just let you come along 'cause we feel sorry for you."

Then he started crying. I ran out the gate and all the way up the hill to my house. I fell three times and scraped my knees so bad the skin started coming off.

As soon as I got home, I was sick with worry for what I said and did to him.

So I built a model car. That always made me feel better. I was a good model builder. When it was done, I took it downstairs and set it on the shelf with all my other models. I did a good job on it. But I still felt ashamed about Johnny and the darts.

That night as I lay in my bed I thought about all the good times I'd had with Johnny over the years: building that treehouse in my backyard; going to every new *Godzilla* movie that opened at the Midland Theater; the way he could beat *anyone* at marbles—sometimes without even looking at the circle when he made his shot; the times he'd gone out of his way to cheer me up whenever I wasn't feeling too good about anything, even when I didn't *want* to feel better . . . all of these memories made my guilt even worse. I couldn't shake the expression on his face when I'd said that nobody liked him and he was fat and dirty. It wasn't his fault that his family was poor and he didn't have any nice clothes, or that because they needed to keep the water bill down they had to alternate bath days for everyone. Johnny was my best friend and I had been real mean to him and I felt so sick about it I just wanted to cry.

Sometime in there I closed my eyes for a moment and was awakened by this sudden, hard weight on my chest. Startled, I opened my eyes and tried to sit up—I figured I was having some kind of bad dream—but he wouldn't let me.

He being the small (but heavy), misshapen dwarf who was squatting on the center of my body, crushing my stomach.

In those days of 1969, before political correctness became the curse of the day, people would have called him a "hunchback;" most of the left side of his back was taken up by a hump that looked to me the size of a basketball. When he moved, he shifted his weight to the right, seeming not so much to scoot or walk but to wobble. His hair was white as freshly bleached sheets hanging on a summer's clothesline; his beard at least ten inches long, bushy and messy, mostly gray except for a few streams of white from the corners of his mouth; great, feathery eyebrows, bushier even than my grandpa's mustache, hid at least half his forehead; his nose was thin and sharp, his eyes a shade of sparkling blue-green I'd never seen before (or since, for that matter), and the wrinkles in his old face looked like cracks in flesh-toned plaster.

"No clapperdogeon, angler, or shivering-jemmy me . . ."

The Marble King introduced himself, then—after

seeing that I was having trouble breathing—wobbled off my body and knelt in the air near my head. Despite the length of his hair, he still couldn't hide the ears whose large size seemed comically out of proportion with the rest of his body. It didn't help that they were *pointed* ears, as well; not like Mr. Spock's ears on *Star Trek,* they weren't mostly normal-looking ears that just came to a point and then stopped, huh-uh: The Marble King's ears curved inward at the top, like that black curl of hair on Superman's forehead in the comics. In their way, his funny ears were kind of pretty in a pretty/different/ strange (but not *bad* strange) kind of way.

He gave me a closer look at the magic marble, then shoved it in one of his vest pockets.

"Time for you to hear the tale, lad," he said, smiling.

And began to tell me a story that, over a period of many nights to come, would take almost two months to finish.

I need to explain something about the Marble King.

I used to do a lot of drawing when I was a kid, and I wasn't nearly as good as Johnny. During the Christmas of my eighth year, Johnny and I watched *Rudolph the Red-Nosed Reindeer* on television and afterward decided that we had to draw our own elves. Mine was okay, but Johnny's was spectacular. I told him over and over how good it was. He looked at my picture and saw my elf with its bushy beard and eyebrows and weird, curly-pointed ears, and said, "Hey, y'know, I'll bet—" Then he proceeded to fix it; not too much, just enough to make it look realer than it did. He smiled as he turned the drawing around and said, "I say we call him the Marble King."

"How come?"

"I dunno—he kinda looks like he'd be good at marbles, don't you think?"

"Sure."

"And only you an' me'll know about him. Okay?"

"Our secret."

"Yeah!"

When I was opening my presents that Christmas, there was one from Johnny. I remember as I opened it that I hoped he didn't spend too much money on it, then I pulled it out of the box.

Johnny had carved a three-dimensional replica of the Marble King in balsa wood, then painted it in the same colors I'd used in my drawing. He looked so alive I almost expected him to jump off the stand and dance a jig. I wasn't only glad that Johnny Sawyer was my friend, at that moment I was *proud* to have him as a friend.

On Saturday nearly two weeks after the dart business, Johnny came over to the house and we built some models together at the kitchen table while my mom read the paper and made sure that we didn't get too messy.

We had a couple of Aurora monster model kits. Johnny toiled over the Godzilla he'd gotten for his birthday a couple weeks before while I had the Wolfman. I always worked faster than Johnny, who seemed to take forever to finish his models. I could do one in a couple of sittings; with Johnny, a model might take him a week or two; he liked to sand down the edges, apply the glue with a toothpick so none of it would spill over when the halves were put together, and then he'd paint only one side and wait *forever* for it to dry before he'd turn it over and paint the other side. I suppose this made me grumpy because his models always looked better than mine when they were finished. Plus he always beat me at marbles *and,* whenever we had to do an art project at school, he always got the best grade because he could really draw good and whittle anything you could think of if you gave him the wood. Most of the guys thought he was kind of a sissy because he enjoyed doing that stuff, and sometimes when I was with them and Johnny wasn't around, I made fun of him for it, too, but the truth was I wished I could do what Johnny could do.

"Hey, did Doug invite you to his birthday party?" I asked.

Johnny shook his head.

"Well, he told me that I could bring a guest, so how about you come with me?"

"Boy, that'll be great!" he squealed. "I ain't been to nobody else's birthday party in a long time."

For a second I felt kind of sad because, outside of

Johnny's mom, dad, two sisters, and his older brother, I was the only person who'd gone to his birthday party, and once again I felt bad about what had happened with the darts and what I'd said, but I still didn't apologize.

"I'll bet Doug's mom'll make chocolate cake," I said. "That's a good flavor for a birthday cake."

"I *love* chocolate! But I won't be able to eat too much of it."

"Why?"

" 'Cause the doctor told my mom that I'm too fat and that's why I feel sick and tired a lot. He told her that chocolate and candy and stuff like that will make me sick if I eat too much."

"Well, you and me, we'll just have one piece, okay?"

"Okay!"

Mom rolled her eyes and called us a couple of nuts.

The Marble King told me his real name: Alvïs.

"It means 'Knowing in the Arts,' and was passed on to me from m'father, and his father afore 'im, and his father afore, and his father afore, back in the Old Place, m'home, called Tallowcross—which means, 'Sanctuary for the Outcast.'

"Listen, boy, so ye'll know why your covey-days need be ending sooner than ye'd prefer."

(For the sake of clarity, I have decided not to relate this tale in the same flowery prose as Alvïs told it to me; it's hard enough to believe without the drenching downpour of words, phrases, and idioms the likes of *mizzle, half-a-grunter, snickert,* and *skull-thatcher*.)

Here goes:

Once, when the Universe and its planets were new, the gods looked down upon the Earth and decided they were bored with the activities of Man, so they created a hidden, secret place no humans could see. And for their amusement, the gods created a race of beings to inhabit this place.

One of the gods proposed they make this new race small; smaller, even than some of the animals—the boar and sea-cow and deer would tower o'er them.

And so the race of beings—the Stillevolk*—was created. They have been known by many names—dwarves, imps,* *elves, kobolds, masariols, leprechauns, cluricaunes, wich-leins, boggarts, redcaps, jacks-in-the-green, and thousands more. They were outcasts from the beginning, and so, in their native tongue, named their home Tallowcross.*

As an added cruelty, the gods made certain to afflict each of the Stillevolk *with some deformity of the body; arms too short, legs too twisted, eyesight too blurry, and— in the case of marblesmyth named Yokelthwaite— humped backs.*

Then one of the gods—it was never known which— showed them mercy after a time. Since all of the Stillevolk *were male, and therefore had no way to procreate the species, she gave unto them the gift of Life-Art: though they could not couple with women of their race, they could nonetheless keep their lineage strong: through paint-ing, sculpting, or carving in wood, stone, or marble, each could create one being who would be given full, animate life, and those creations could go on to create one other like themselves, and those creations one other, and those one other. . . .*

I suppose every neighborhood has its Home of the Well-To-Do, and in my old neighborhood it was the Gil-ligan house. Doug's mom and dad both worked for the government and made lots of money—they were always talking about things like *stock figures* and *bond maturi-ties* and *portfolios* and *investments* and *rollovers* and *profits for the quarter* and there wasn't a thing in their house that wasn't expensive. Theirs was the only house where I had to take off my shoes (but not my socks) in order to come inside because the carpet was so expen-sive. It made me nervous to be in there on account ev-erything was so *nice* and I was always afraid I'd break something or make it dirty. Doug had two older sisters and two older brothers and all of them had really neat clothes that I guess cost a lot of money. Doug was okay most of the time, even though he was mostly a spoiled little snot, and we got along on account of him liking to build models.

For his birthday I dug into my Frankenstein bank and got out enough to buy Doug a nice model paint kit, which he really liked. I'd gotten to the party early, figuring that Johnny would meet me there, and we'd already started in on the cake when Johnny knocked on the front door. He looked nice in his freshly washed jeans and dress shirt (as far as I knew, the only one he owned), plus he'd borrowed a tie from his dad and worn that as well (even though the knot looked like something you'd see on a noose in one of those old Westerns where the posse hangs a bad guy).

Doug went over and—not opening the screen door so Johnny could come in—said, "You can't come in unless you got a present."

"I'm sorry I'm late," said Johnny, "but I had to finish my chores."

"You can't come in unless you got a present!" Doug hissed. I knew he was lying, that he just didn't want Johnny in his house, because a whole bunch of kids had come to the party and not all of them had brought presents.

"But I don't get my allowance for another week!" said Johnny. "It ain't much, but I been saving it up, and next week I'll have enough to get you a present and I'll give it to you, then, okay?"

"No!" Doug slammed the door and everybody else laughed. I was getting kind of mad. I knew that Johnny's dad was laid off from the plant and they didn't have much money coming in, so it really wasn't fair of Doug.

I should have said something, but—like with the darts—I didn't.

About half an hour later there was a knock on the door and this time when Doug answered Johnny was shaking a box wrapped in aluminum foil that had an old, torn ribbon on it.

"Here's your present!" he said.

Doug opened the screendoor and yanked it out of Johnny's hands. "It better be a good one."

He let Johnny come in and sit next to me while he opened it. I could see that it was a monster model kit and that the plastic wrap had been torn off. That wasn't good. Models that had plastic off were usually missing pieces and you had to have all the pieces if it was going to look right when you were done.

Doug pulled off the rest of the foil.

It was Aurora Godzilla model that Johnny had started last Saturday. Doug opened it and saw that some of the pieces had already been painted and glued together. He got real mad and threw it at Johnny and told him to get out.

"But I thought you'd like it!" pleaded Johnny. "I ain't so good at them kind of models and thought you'd like finishing it." (I knew that part was a lie, because Johnny was better than anyone when it came to models.)

Doug screamed so loud his face got all red. "I meant you had to bring me a present that was brand new!"

"But I don't get my allowance for another—" But Doug's two older brothers came in and threw Johnny out the door. Doug crammed the Godzilla model in the trash and then the rest of the kids all laughed as they made fun of Johnny. I told Doug I had to go to the bathroom, but what I really did was sneak out the back door. I felt sick and decided that Doug Gilligan wasn't going to be my friend anymore. I went over to Johnny's house and invited him to come over and stay all night that Friday and he said maybe, but I can't be sure because he was still crying real hard, and when I got home I went up in my room and cried too because I figured Johnny was feeling lonely and ugly and fat and dirty and I didn't want him to feel that way but didn't know what I could do to make him feel better.

Though the explanation varies among the Stillevolk, *Alvïs told me that Yokelthwaite—from whom he was directly descended—and many others were somehow able to escape Tallowcross and find their way out to mingle with Humanity, where some humans accepted and befriended them. A few—Yokelthwaite included—even fell in love with human women and were stunned to find that love returned in equal measure; thus did the* Stillevolk *come to know the beauty of physical love, and no longer needed to rely upon their Life-Art to continue their race. Still, their size and appearance ensured that the* Stillevolk *would never truly be part of Humanity, so they, along with those women who'd wed them, journeyed to a secret isle where they live to this day, watching through the Mists of Dreaming as their children, and* their *children, and*

*their children's children's children, became more a part
of humanity, growing to normal height and looking no
different from other human beings. What few of these
descendants realized, though, was that in every generation
there was born to each clan one in whom the Life-Art
was strong. These Gifted Ones had very special, very delicate souls, souls that needed protecting.*

*Johnny Sawyer was such a Gifted One, descended from
Alvïs, who was descended from the marblesmyth
Yokelthwaite.*

*When Alvïs saw through the Mists of Dreaming what
was happening to Johnny, he knew that something had
to be done, and so he left his wife on the secret isle,
vowing he'd not return until he'd accomplished what he'd
come here to do.*

It wasn't until much later that I realized what it was
about Johnny that drew me to him: He wore the expression of a child who was watching a really good game
and was waiting for someone—*anyone*—to ask him to
join in the fun.

I am glad that I was one of the few people who invited
him to come join in. I like to think it cancels out some
of my other life-sins.

*Alvïs removed the magical marble from his pocket once
again. "D'ye know what this is, boy?"*

"No."

"In time, then; in time."

Johnny was big. And fat. But I always suspected that
if someone pushed him too far, that fatness would prove
a major disadvantage to them.

I didn't truly realize how much of a friend I had in
that fat little boy until I was walking back from Turner's
Corner Market with a bottle of milk a few days after
the infamous birthday party. I was about a block from
my house when Doug and a bunch of friends (plus his
two older brothers) came out of an alley and surrounded me.

"You left my party," snarled Doug.

"You were mean to Johnny."

"So? That fatso ain't no fun. He ain't even that funny to look at no more. How come you like him better than me?"

"I just do, that's all!" Ah, the fury in those words: Portrait of a Defiant Dipshit About to Have Knots Tied in his Spine.

Doug got madder than hell. He looked at his two brothers and they grabbed my arms, twisting them up behind my back. It hurt like nothing else. I dropped the milk bottle and it shattered all over the sidewalk. I was scared half out of my mind and was afraid I was going to be sick.

"You ate my cake and then you left my party!"

"So? I gave you a present—and it was a *new* one."

"Yeah, but you left because you like Fatso better'n me."

It was then I noticed the greasy-looking brown paper bag in Doug's hand.

"Open your mouth," he said.

I clenched my mouth closed tight. One of Doug's friends pulled a long hunting knife out from under his shirt.

"Open your mouth or you'll be sorry!" The boy with the knife cut open one of my pant legs, slicing part of my thigh. One of Doug's brothers grabbed a handful of my hair, pulled my head back, and hit me in the throat with his knuckles. I gagged because I couldn't breathe and opened my mouth for a second.

That's all it took.

Doug reached in the bag and pulled out the filthiest-looking rat I'd ever seen. It was half-crushed, bloody, and—the worst part of all—still alive, if just barely.

"You're gonna eat this!"

"D-Doug, *p-p-please?*" I whimpered, my throat throbbing and the air struggling to get into my lungs.

Before I could get my mouth closed again Doug's other brother grabbed my jaws and wrenched my mouth open even wider, and Doug shoved the rat into my mouth. Someone pushed down on the top of my head and I felt my teeth sink down and through part of the rat's crushed back. I felt something thick and sick-making spill over onto my tongue and down my throat, burning.

And then the rat, in its final moments of life, cornered and in its death throes, rallied what little strength remained to tear its claws into the side of my tongue and bite down hard with its teeth on the tip. I actually *felt* part of my tongue rip away as the rat thrashed and cried out. I was certain that I was going to die.

Then I saw Johnny.

He exploded through the circle of boys, wielding a large club of some sort in his hands, swinging it back and forth. I saw the boys scatter—except for Doug and his brothers, who let me drop to the ground, half a crushed, dying rat hanging from my mouth. I heard Doug scream and was able to see one of his brothers running away, followed a second later by the other one.

Johnny fell on him like a curse from heaven. I heard fists pounding into flesh and—I thought—a bone breaking. Then it was just darkness and whimpering and scuffling footsteps until one of them ran away, and the next thing I knew there was Johnny leaning over me, asking, "Are you all right?" over and over again as he pulled the now-dead rat from my mouth—which by now was so filled with blood I couldn't talk. It would be nearly a year before I was able to talk clearly again, and then only sporadically, and another three before I'd lost enough self-consciousness about the way my voice sounded so I could have a conversation longer than two minutes.

I was in the hospital when I woke up. It felt like someone had stuffed about a ton of cotton and bandages in my mouth. Mom and Dad were there in the room; so were Mr. and Mrs. Sawyer and Doug's parents, as well as Johnny and Doug. Doug sat over in the corner, pieces of heavy tape across his nose, both of his eyes black, and his arm in a sling.

"I done that to him," whispered Johnny in my ear. "Nobody pounds on my best buddy!"

Then the doctor came in and told everyone except my parents that they had to leave. He told Doug's parents that they needed to go down to the finance office to fill out some forms. After they were gone, my mom sat down and told me that the doctors had had to remove about a quarter of my tongue altogether—some on the side, some near the front where the rat had bitten a chunk off; then Dad came over and, along with the doctor, explained to me that the rat had been diseased and that I had been infected with the same disease when it'd bitten me, and I was going to have to get a bunch of shots in order to stop from getting sicker (the word "rabies" was never actually spoken), and that the first shot had to be given to me right now.

"It's going to hurt a little," the doctor said. "But you're a tough little guy, you can take it."

I remember that the needle looked the size of a rocket, and that it didn't hurt so much going in, it was when they pulled it *out* that the pain hit; I wouldn't have been surprised to see my *skeleton* being pulled out by that needle.

It was a Sunday night a week or so after I'd finished my last series of shots. I wasn't feeling well (the soreness, though not nearly as intense, still persisted) and so had gone to bed early. Tomorrow would be my first day back at school since the shots began and I wanted to be ready.

I was awakened around 10 p.m. by Alvïs, who came crashing down next to my bed in a panic.

"Wake up, boy! Don yer boots and coat and get yerself out 'n on your way! Do it now!"

I lifted my head, still groggy, and angry that the dream had come back to bother my sleep once again. "Huh? Wha—?"

"Johnny's in trouble, ye simpleton! Ye got to help'm and soonest, I say, else it'll be a most terrible of terrible things!"

I could see the panic in his eyes and hear the fear in his voice. I'd watched enough old horror movies to know that there are some dreams you just don't ignore, and I figured this was one of them, so—without a word of explanation to my startled parents—I dressed quickly, ran down the stairs, and bolted out the front door, running for all I was worth down the hill—*not* toward Johnny's house, but Doug Gilligan's. I knew without Alvïs having to say so that whatever was going to happen would happen there.

I took a shortcut that emptied into the Gilligans' backyard. I saw that the lights were on in the garage and could hear Doug and a bunch of other boys laughing and trying hard not to be heard.

I crept over to one of the side windows and climbed up on one of the trash cans, straining my neck as I looked into the semidarkened garage. A couple of candles were burning, allowing me to see what was going on—though not as clearly as I would have liked.

I almost cried out in terror.

A large circle of boys stood in the center of the garage floor, surrounding Johnny as they'd surrounded me on Rat Day. I don't know how Doug had managed to get Johnny to come over, what lie he told or bribe of food he offered, but he *had* gotten him over to the garage, and everyone—including Doug's two older brothers—had ganged up on Johnny and tied his hands behind his back and then tied his feet together and stood him up on a sawhorse then put a noose around his neck and tied the other end to one of the thick overhead beams, and I was so scared I couldn't move because Doug was standing there with a baseball bat in his hands while Johnny was crying so hard he couldn't talk or cry out or nothing, and I knew this was about what Johnny had done on Rat Day, that they were getting even with him, and I'd all but decided to go to the front door and tell Mr. Gilligan what was going on when Doug drew back his arms and swung out and knocked the sawhorse out from under Johnny and the rope pulled tight and I was *so sure* I heard something snap and that was it, that was All She Wrote, I outright panicked because Johnny was hanging there, red-faced and shuddering, trying to thrash, and I saw him mess in his pants and I screamed as loud as I could as I jumped down and grabbed the trash can and threw it over my head into the window, shattering the glass and causing one of the boys inside to open the garage door—

—I didn't give him the chance to shut me out, I ran full-force into him, knocking him back into a tool rack that collapsed against his weight, and then I grabbed the boy who'd cut open my pant leg and hit him in the face as hard as I could, two or three times, until blood came out of his nose, all the time screaming at him to give me his knife give it to me *GIVEITTOMEEEEE*! And he finally did, but by now Doug and his older brothers were on me, trying to get me down on the floor, but I was so scared I guess I went a little crazy because I bit one brother's arm and stuck the other one in his hand with the tip of the knife, then I got away and grabbed a big hammer and hurled it through another window, and now I could hear Doug's mom and dad outside on their front porch yelling, *"What the hell is going on in there Jesus look at the windows bygod I'll teach that boy a lesson he'll never forget,"* but then somebody hit me in the middle of my back with a crowbar and I fell to my knees, dropping the knife that I was going to use to cut the rope, and as I looked over at him I saw that Johnny wasn't moving anymore, or making any sounds, or nothing, and his face had started to turn sort of bluish-white color and I didn't know if he was alive or dead or—

—a small, misshapen figure, bushy-bearded and pointy-eared, dropped down from the rafters and tore into the rest of the boys like some kind of monster from the Friday Night Chillers on Channel 10; bones were broken, noses were split, lips bloodied, eyes blackened—

—and Johnny wasn't moving, I didn't even think he was breathing *ohgod*!—

—"Run, boy!" shouted the Marble King. "Get ye away from this place as swiftly as you can fly!"—

—I tried to say something about Johnny, but by this time Mr. Gilligan was in the garage and screaming, running toward Johnny and grabbing his legs, lifting him up so the rope wasn't so tight and shouting at one of the older boys to pick up that goddamned knife over there and cut this rope *RIGHT NOW*—

—I struggled to my feet and looked at Johnny's discolored, still face, and I whispered, *"I'm sorry about the darts,"* but I don't think he heard me—

—then I ran. Fast and hard, tears blinding me, fear choking my breath, until I dropped down onto a small green hill near Chris Brothers Funeral Home.

"Catch yer breath, boy, ye'll be needing it."

The Marble King stood over me, hands on hips, one foot impatiently tapping.

"I . . . I d-don't know what . . . is he . . . *ohgodGodGOD* . . . Johnny, they, they—"

"I know what they did, boy. I was there, d'ya recall?"

"Uh-huh."

Alvïs showed me the marble once more. "Have ye figured out yet what this be?"

"Is it . . . is it some part of Johnny?"

"Aye! This be the soul of your friend, and if ever I intend to return to m'home isle, 'tis my duty to find a covey such as yerself who will take the burden of its care from out m'hand.

"Be you that covey, boy? Is your love for your friend such that you will be the keeper and protector of his soul until such time as ye both are given back to the dirt?"

My chest hurt, my tongue (what there was left of it) was bleeding again, I could barely see, I was terrified almost out of my mind and feeling like a stinking, lousy coward for having run away and not saved my friend and I didn't want anything more to do with the Marble King or what he did to my dreams or his *stupid, stupid, stupid questions*! "I don't . . . I don't know," I choked, then coughed until I vomited in the grass.

Grabbing my hair and pulling up my head when I finished puking, the Marble King looked me straight in the eyes and said, "D'ya love him, boy? When he crosses your thoughts, d'ya feel toward him as y'might a brother, had ye one?"

"Yeah . . . uh-huh."

"Then is it such a frightful burden, this? To shield your friend who ye'd call brother if'n you could?"

"He's my *best* friend!"

"Then take it, boy, take possession of yer friend's soul and care for it as ye would a newborn babe; with love and tenderness, defending it against any who would do it harm."

Alvïs placed the marble in my hand, and I knew it was all true, because I suddenly felt Johnny with me, as if he were standing right there next to me. I knew, at that moment, that whatever this thing called "childhood" was, well . . . mine had just come to its end. But still there was magic, still there was wonder.

"You'd best be getting to your task, boy," said the Marble King. "He'll be needing you soon, and forever."

I closed my fist around Johnny's soul and nodded my head, smiling and weeping at the same time. "I will. I promise."

" 'Tis a sacred thing, that promise. And know this: I'll be popping around from time to time to make sure you keep it."

And with that, starlight sparking from the heels of his jackboots, he wobbled/ran toward a patch of thick, rolling mist, gave me one last *ye-be-watching-yerself* glance over his humped shoulder, then passed through the veil and was gone.

I could hear Dave laughing at me from the far end of the counter as I resigned myself to the fact that there was no way in hell I was going to be able to finish my "Gut-Buster" burger, so Dave—grinning to beat the band—put it in a doggie bag for me. "Got yourself lunch for the next couple days here."

"Those things'll kill you, you eat enough of them."

Laughing, he slapped hands to his wondrous belly and said, "But, dang, you'll kick off with a good meal in you, that's for sure."

I paid my tab, collected my leftovers, and—instead of heading back out to my car—started toward the aluminum swinging doors of the kitchen, giving Dave a look to make sure it was all right. He winked and gestured for me to go on.

Once inside the kitchen I stood at the far end of the prep area and said to the cook, "That's one helluva burger, the 'Gut-Buster.' "

"Th-th-thanks."

"You ready to go home? Cathy's gonna worry if we're too late."

Johnny pulled off his paper chef's hat and laughed. "B-b-boy, that wife of yours!" (Which came out as *Boy-tha'whyffudyers*. It takes a while to learn to understand his speech.)

"Yeah, well," I said, "she sure treats you nice."

"Th-th-that's 'cause I help her with the housecleaning. You don't, not s-s-so m-much."

"Guess I'm lazy."

"Sure are." He rubbed his neck and winced a little.

"It hurts today?" I asked.

"J-j-just a little." There are people, like those retro-Grunge teens, who make fun of Johnny's short, almost stumpy neck. The doctors weren't able to repair the damage to certain broken sections of his neck bone (a piece of which was crushed beyond repair) and so had to remove part of it, and what remained mended well enough but the surgery, coupled with oxygen having been cut off from his brain for nearly four minutes, left Johnny permanently brain-damaged. In his mind, he'll always be nine. But that matters neither to Cathy nor to me. We see only the pureness and decency of a truly good human being; all else is folly.

Johnny lives in the small guest cottage in back of our house. Whenever he doesn't come over to spend the evening with us—two nights a week—he's back there carving away on his wood blocks, making puppies for the neighborhood children, sometimes kittens, a lot of toys, and—especially around Halloween—the "realest, scariest" monster masks you've ever seen (people swear that the masks actually become animated at times). Everyone loves him. After nearly four decades of being on this Earth, that's how it should be.

I have kept my promise to Alvïs; I have cared for Johnny and his soul as well as I can. His every moment is full and rich, he's never lonely and is only alone when he wishes to be, and I will defend him against harm—be it physical or emotional—with everything I have. He is my friend, my brother, and I love him dearly.

"I wanna get h-home," said Johnny. "I'm workin' on a Easter present f-f-for Cathy."

"Really? What is it?"

"A secret. You'll s-see. I p-p-p-promised her that th-the Easter Bunny'd leave something in her basket."

"There's no such thing as the Easter Bunny."

By now we were out the door and getting into the car.

"So you don't believe in the Easter B-B-B-Bunny?"

"No."

He looked back at the diner and grinned. "Well, that's *your* problem."

We laughed loudly as we headed for home, and I can't say for certain but I think I saw a small figure scurrying across the diner's rooftop, starlight sparking from the heels of its jackboots, long beard flapping against the wind before it leaped from the edge of the building and vanished back to that place of wonder and magic that all outcasts dream of in lonely hours before their friend comes to break the solitude.

But I could be wrong.

And if you don't believe a word of this story, well, that's your problem.

THE CÉILIDH
by Connie Hirsch

Connie Hirsch has written many excellent stories for various anthologies, including *100 Vicious Little Vampire Stories, The Shimmering Door,* and *Fantastic Alice.* she lives in Massachusetts.

By the eighteenth hour of Thanet Watt's labor, the midwife knew her patient was beyond her art, and so she sent her apprentice panting out of Dunburn and up into the green hills, to ask for Auld Annie to lend her hands. The wisewoman came back straightaway, her gray hair flying loose from under her lace cap, and quickly diagnosed the problem. "You'll be having twins," she told Thanet, "and soon, if I have aught to do with it. I'll just get the first wee bairn turned a bit, and we'll have him out."

Auld Annie showed she deserved her reputation for having more courage than five strong men, for she went to her delicate work with a will and a sureness that allayed her patient's fear, relaxing her enough to deliver first Ian and then Geoffrey, squalling red infants that the wisewoman slapped and then handed on to their grateful mother. Auld Annie would accept no coin for her service, but instead discreetly collected the caul that wrapped young Geoffrey. If she felt the inspiration of any oracular pronouncements, she kept them silent in front of the twins' good Protestant parents.

Auld Annie went home with the caul, and tanned it in the water in the hollow of an oak tree that had been blasted apart by God's good lightning, then packed it up with fresh herbs in a scrap of fine linen, and hid it away in a rafter in her attic. "You never know when you'll have a day of need" was one of her favorite sayings.

Now, the Watts never knew about the caul, and more the better, for twins are three times as much work as a single baby, and they might have spoiled them, or gone in fear, had they been expecting strangeness from their twins. In the fullness of time, the tiny babies grew into sturdy young boys, and the boys grew up to be tall young men, so big their mother could scarcely credit the thought that once she could hold each one in her cupped palms.

Geoffrey and Ian attended dame school, preferring to sit side by side on benches of succeeding size. Their teachers tried to separate them, but the boys always conspired to behave worse apart than together, and most of the transitory young women who took their turns teaching were wise enough to take the path of ease with the Dunburn Twins.

In looks they were quite alike, with medium brown hair and blue eyes, and fair faces neither too long or short. They smiled easily, and were quick with a joke to share, or hands to offer should the need arise. They were a surprise to their dour parents, for such openness is not much found round Dunburn, but being twins and thus prodigies, it was acceptable, barely.

The twins could always be found when there was a wedding or a céilidh. They'd stomp, whirl, and prance their way through the sets, with such style that any girl was shown off to the best advantage, and rival swains could not feel much jealousy, for the lads were quick to switch partners and show no particular favor to any two lasses.

Stout lads such as these were put to work early on their parents' farm, setting aside their wages to save for their own farmstead. The twins planned to go in on a fine piece of ground near Dunburn, for they could not but pull the plow together, they said, like oxen under a yoke. If they had been a team, Ian would have been the nigh ox, leading his slightly bigger, slightly more thoughtful brother in and out of trouble.

It happened in the twins' nineteenth year that they drove some of their father's steers to market over the hills to Kilgallie on Midsummer's Day, planning to stay late for the céilidh on the village green that night.

But the day dawned gloomy, and the wind picked up even as they switched their cattle along, and a fine drizzle had set in by noon. By sundown (what could be seen of it) sheets of rain were blowing through the cracks in the inn's windows, and the Dunburn Twins gave up thought of dancing, and worried about their journey home. They were loath to spend good coin on a night in the inn's loft, when for but a wet two-hour walk they could be home in their cheap beds, but they lingered late and were on the verge of spending the dear money anyhow, when the rain let up, and winds chased the clouds away to reveal a bright full moon.

So the twins set out later than they should, with the lunar light to guide them along the road under the dripping trees. Older, wiser men might have been more cautious on such a night, but the boys were jolly, and walked along singing a raucous song that echoed back from the hills.

By the time they'd reached the old stretch of road that had been built by the Romans, the clouds had regrouped, and the drizzle recommenced, and soon the Dunburn Twins were wet, and cold, and silent. Thus it was when they espied a light not far off in the hills, and the faint strains of music.

They stopped under an oak tree, shaking the water off their jackets, and rubbing the moisture off their faces. "Do you hear that, Geoff?" said Ian, the older and bolder of the two. "I cannot recall no houses along this stretch."

"Aye," said his brother. "But that does not mean there is no house. On such a night as this, it would stand out as not in the daylight. Do you think we should go see?"

His twin answered in the affirmative, so through the catching underbrush they pushed, it slapping wetly at their faces and arms. But they were strong and young, and they bulled their way across the valley and up the hill, losing sight of that tempting light but never out of hearing of the music of three pipers, and the rhythmic tread of dancing feet on a wooden floor, which guided them sufficiently so that when they saw the light again they were right on top of it.

From out of the hillside it came, halfway up the rocky face, with a little scree of gravel and roots leading to it, as though the whole hill were some cleverly immense building and the doorway to it placed high. The light was glorious yellow, so thick that it sprang out from the opening like a golden waterfall on air and trees and rocks. It was a warm light, welcoming, but so bright you could not see into it.

Now, never before had the twins seen such a thing, and most likely no one from their town, nor even their county as well. You might think that they would have hesitated more, but the music was so beautiful, and the light so, too, that the wonder of it coming from a cave hardly checked their curiosity. It was Ian who led the way up the hill, his feet threatening to slip on the wet rocks, and Geoff right behind him, grasping at the roots, and cutting his palm on a sharp rock just as he reached the opening. The pain brought him to a halt, to curse and examine the wound. He was left behind by his entranced twin as he wrapped his hand with his pocket handkerchief.

Just a moment it was, but when Geoffrey Watt stepped up to the cave, his twin was gone. It had a narrow opening, slim enough that a fat man could not have squeezed past the rock of it. Inside, he could see dancing shapes in the light, and the music was loud and raucous, so in he went.

Geoff found himself on a wooden dance floor, laid in a cave where the stalactites were like pillars supporting the roof, or perhaps it was that a building had been carved to resemble a cave. The supports were made of limestone, smooth and pale, showing darker veins, lost in shadows as they ascended beyond the level of the lamps that attached to them. The hall was vast, more than a football field long, with many lamplit passages.

A céilidh was in progress upon the floor, wild and kicking, as couples and formations of four and eight pranced together in a figure and split apart again, following some grand scheme that Geoff's dazzled mind could not compass. The musicians played on a little stand at the far end, blowing full into their pipes with effortless strength that never let up.

Most of the dancers were richly dressed, though here and there plainer folk could be seen in their homespun wool and linen, moving among their betters with gay abandon. The dancers were all beautiful and young, fair and thin-featured. More people came and went from the side passages, some to watch and some to join. On the far side, Geoff thought he glimpsed Ian, walking with a fair maid, and so he tried to hurry around the dance floor, avoiding the whirling couples that swung out as though to intercept him, their hands reaching out to invite him in. But the lad only smiled and held up his bandaged hand.

Long before he reached the other side, a young woman dressed in fine blue silks, who looked no older than his own nineteen years, came up to him. "Welcome, stranger," she said in a lilt. The jeweled combs wrapped up in her straw-yellow hair twinkled in the lamplight. Her eyes were large and green as new grass, and she weaved before him, in time with the pipers. "Would you join our dance?"

Almost Geoff found his feet picking up to follow the beat, but his hand throbbed angrily, and the discomfort made him remember himself. "I am looking for my brother," he said. "Have you seen him? I do not want to dance."

The pale maid seemed not fazed by his declaration. She smiled sweetly, disclosing even, white teeth. "Would you take aught to sup then, something to drink?"

Geoff found himself so hungry, so thirsty that his knees almost would not support him. Had it been only hours since he and his twin had lingered in the Kilgallie inn? It might have been a year or more, to judge by his starvation, like a sponge that has been squeezed of its water once and twice. "Please, fair one," he heard himself say.

"I am the White Mare," said the maid. She reached up and touched Geoff's face with her cold hand, and the young man didn't even mark the strangeness of such a name. The chill of her fingers seemed to seep up his arm and neck into his mind. "Follow me to the feast," she said, sliding her fingers down his sleeve to his hand, and pulling him along.

They walked through halls and halls, all lit with cold yellow lamps, over floors of white marble and black granite, up stairs and down ramps, past doors made of iron and wood and stone, past empty ballrooms and grand rooms where fantastic furniture loomed in the shadows, till Geoff's sense of direction had spun into flinders, till at last they came to a long dining room where couples sat at a great table piled high with all manner of food and drink, and fed each other tender tidbits.

The White Mare showed Geoff up to an empty couch, laid out for two. All around them the couples continued to eat, sitting twined on couches, all dressed in finery, all oblivious. Geoff took the seat the White Mare indicated, then she slid next to him so that her cold, cold thigh rubbed against his, and her cold arm brushed his as she reached for bread on the table before them. "Eat, my man," she said, holding a fine white crust before his mouth, "eat and feed me in my turn." Her face was close to his, and Geoff thought it was the loveliest visage he had ever seen, might ever see in his entire life.

With trembling hand he reached out, to guide the food to his mouth, but when he touched her slender white hand with his bandaged palm, the cold struck right through to his wound, so painful he shuddered and drew back. "Truly," he said, "truly, all I want is my brother." Strangely, his incredible hunger and thirst were gone.

The White Mare seemed not ruffled by his request. "Come," she said, sliding off the couch in her fine blue silks. "Come with me then, my man, and I shall bring you to what you desire." She led the way out of the dining hall, the couples as oblivious as before, and Geoff followed her again.

The halls seemed more primitive now, the bones and sinews of the earth showing through the artifice previously displayed. Sometimes the floor was smooth rock, worn as if by the flow of waters, sometimes dirt crunched under their feet. Geoff followed the White Mare up long winding stairs, mesmerized by the play of light on her dress, the way it molded around her swaying hips; then, without noticing how it came to be, he was following her through a moonlit grove, into a bower hung with veils and flowers. "Love me, my man," the White Mare said, loosening the combs that held her hair, so that her tresses fell down upon her shoulders and her breast, and unfastening her dress so that it fell in blue waves about her feet.

The sight of the White Mare's fine pale body aroused such lust in Geoffrey as he had never felt in his entire life. He couldn't help but cross the rose petal-dappled floor, and embrace her tightly, feverishly as though the heat that poured off him must be quenched by the ice of her pliant body.

But the White Mare's body was cold, numbing Geoffrey's arms and body, driving delicious needles of ice into his lips where he kissed her face. He loved it, loved her, had all but surrendered himself to her, when the bandage slipped on his wounded hand, and the icy pain shocked him back to sanity.

With an inarticulate cry, Geoffrey scrambled away from her, and the last glimpse he saw of the White Mare was her calm beautiful face, regarding him without expression, without reproach. He stumbled, half-blind with pain and half-blind with panic, out of the bower and through nightmare corridors that he never could quite remember again, until he burst into the open air, away from the strange halls where she had led him, out into a cold, snowy hillside, falling down a scree of loose rocks and roots toward a road. And there he came to rest, until the penetrating cold shook his body to wakefulness.

Only then did Geoffrey remember that his brother Ian was somewhere still inside the hill, and forced himself to his feet. He wore only the light clothes appropriate for mild summer weather, but where he stood now, it was full winter, with a thin crust of snow on the ground, and the branches all bare, and the stars twinkling harshly. There was no light from the hillside now, no enchanting music to lead him back to the céilidh, and though he cried his brother's name, there was no answer.

Geoffrey called until he was hoarse, and his hand and feet were numb, and his body had passed beyond shivering into a peculiar warmth. He knew in his heart that he might die from the cold, but so far gone was he that all he could do was stumble to his knees and then lie by the roadbed, and if a late carriage had not happened by, and seen him by the light of its lanterns, he would have indeed passed there and then, and there would be no more of this story.

But the carriage did come by, and the Christian kindness of its inhabitants saw him wrapped in blankets and taken back to the very Kilgallie inn that he and his twin had left, it seemed, only hours before. The folk there recognized him, and who wouldn't, since the twins that had disappeared the summer before had been the talk of the county. Even as the innkeeper's wife put a nearly insensate Geoff into a bath of warm salt water, they dispatched one of the stableboys over to Dunburn, to tell his parents that one of their missing sons had shown up, and by the time Geoff woke up in a large clean bed, his parents were by his side to spoon gruel to his lips, and listen to his disjointed tale of what had happened to him.

"Elf-taken" the good people of Dunburn muttered when they thought the Presbyterian minister was not close by to hear. It was the position of the Church Fathers that such people as the Fair Folk did not exist, but the common people knew better. Grandmothers reminded themselves to tell grandchildren circumspectly veiled tales of elf-abduction so that they should be duly warned.

So it was that the county discussed the nine-day's wonder of Geoffrey Watt's return, and got back to its regular business. Geoff himself began a slow recovery. Aside from minor frostbite, there were no obvious physical effects from his ordeal, yet he did not have his former energy. For days he was so weak he could hardly lift a cup to his mouth, and he slept almost constantly. When he was awake, he found himself staring off into corners, straining to hear beautiful music playing in the distance. When he ate, the food tasted bland, and his parent's home, the houses in his village, all looked small and gray and similar. Nearly all life had fled the world, he felt, and when his mother cajoled him into sitting in a chair in the dooryard, in the spring sun, the slender heat of it did not warm him. As winter passed, it was remarked by the neighbors that his brown hair was showing early silver, and lines of care were etching his young face. It was not too much to say that he had aged ten years since he was found wandering.

Auld Annie, the wise woman who had delivered the Dunburn Twins twenty years gone, had spent the winter season visiting her daughters down in the mild South, so when she came back to her cottage she did not hear of Geoffrey Watt's return until spring was well along. "Well," she said, when told, "time for me to find what has been put by," a pronouncement that completely baffled her visitor. The old dame clambered up to her rafters and rooted through two decades' worth of accumulation, until she found the little linen bag she'd sewn for the caul that had birthed Ian and Geoffrey Watt. The bright blue ribbon was faded, and some mouse had taken a nibble at it, but the caul was still in one piece. "Good," was all Auld Annie said at this, and she brought the little bag down, and put it up on the shelf above her hearth, because it still wasn't the time of need.

As spring grew toward summer, Geoff had a bit more strength. He could stay on his feet long enough to help with the simpler chores around the house and farm— nothing appropriate for a man, but enough to salve his conscience. So, too, could he make the walk into town, and sit in the tavern cajoling too many drinks from sympathetic friends. It helped to quiet the silent, murmuring music he could almost hear, and make him forget his guilt at having forgotten his twin.

It was the day before Midsummer's Eve that Geoffrey stayed late with his friends once again, and went stumbling home in a state of inebriation. He made a wrong turn on the road, on his way back to the farm, and didn't notice until he was some miles along. To correct, he went down another path, and another, and eventually, he found himself crossing in front of Auld Annie's trim little cottage in the twilight, with the old lady herself sitting out front on her best wicker rocker. "Come in, and have a chat, Geoffrey Watt," she said. "You owe me that at least, for I am the one who brought you into the world."

This, as you can imagine, stopped Geoff dead in his

tracks. "You may well wish you could repent of the deed," he answered. "For you brought two of us into the world, and the other is no longer in it."

"No longer in it, but not dead," snapped Auld Annie. "What would you give, Geoffrey Watt, to have your twin back, hearty and whole?"

"My soul!" Geoff said anguished, "My very soul! I have no need for it any more, since I turned my back on my brother!"

Auld Annie sat back in her chair, her eyes glinting. "No need for so high a price," she said mildly. " 'Tis true enough that you lost your way when you left your brother behind; but for that you can make amends, if you've bravery and determination enough."

Geoff entered through her front gate, and knelt down on the ground before her chair. "Then tell me, good lady, what I should do," he said, "to deliver my brother from this evil?"

Auld Annie shook her head. "First, do not call it evil," she said. "The Fair Folk are neither evil nor good; they just are. A good heart and a strong will prevail against them sooner than great anger and a strong arm. So put anger out of your heart, and blame yourself not overmuch for your failure. Not many would have broken free of the Fair Folks' glamour, you know."

Geoff looked thoughtful, for indeed he had never considered his own escape to be to his credit. "What must I do?" he said.

"You must go back to the wild hills," she said. "And when a door opens in the hillside, you must enter there as before. The Fair Folk will not stop you—they have no power to do so, only to lead you astray with temptations and illusions. I have prepared two things for you."

She pulled them out of her apron. "First, this cross I have made for you, plaited from rowan withies." It was a small thing, not even as wide across as his palm. Auld Annie held it out in her knobby old woman's fingers, as though she passed him Communion bread. "Keep it in your pocket, and hold onto it whenever the Fair Folk tempt you," she said. "Your faith is the only armor you can wear in their realm."

Geoff took it, and put it in his pocket, tracing its

whirls and twirls with his fingertips. "And the other that I gift you with," Auld Annie said, holding out a little bag on a string, "is the caul that you and your brother were born in. Keep this around your neck, and it will tell you when your brother is near. When you see him, lay your hands on him, and lead him straight away from the hill. If you are out before the dawn, the spell will be broken."

Forthwith Geoff left her side and went back to his parents' house, his remaining drunkenness drying up as he went. He thought of telling them about his plan, and decided against it. Better two whole sons than one broken one, he reasoned. He spent the day wandering the country around their farm, the haunts that he and his twin had played in as children. Ian's absence had been like a missing tooth in his mouth, a missing step in his staircase. He never would be able to put his life right again if he could not fulfill his obligation to his brother.

At twilight Geoffrey slipped away from the farm. He did it often enough, to go down to the tavern, so it would not be remarked unless his parents happened to remember what day it was. He took the rowan cross in his pocket, and the caul in its bag around his neck, and he set out to walk slowly on the Roman road to Kilgallie, listening intently for sounds in the night that should not be there.

It was a moonless night with bright stars, so there were no travelers save for Geoff. Sensible folk kept themselves in on such a night and clapped up their shutters tight, if they had any sense, so he was sure what he had found when he saw a light gleaming from out a nearby hillside, and faraway, familiar music tinkling beautifully over the distance.

The crack in the hillside was much as it had been before. It awoke seductive memories that Geoff had tried to murder, how bright the colors had been, how delicious the smells, how pleasant the music. The whirling céilidh, full of rhythm and beauty, faces and bodies flashing past him—he grasped the rowan cross in his pocket and took a deep breath, and squeezed through the tight passage into the elven ballroom.

As before, the dancers held out their grasping hands

as they passed by in their unceasing gavotte. The tread of their stamping feet seemed to echo his heartbeat, to lead the rhythm of his body and breath. The musicians played their endless tune, and the loiterers still lingered in the shadows. He stared at the bright crowd, searching for his brother, without success.

Geoff found himself not surprised when the crowd parted to let the White Mare come to his side. She, too, was dressed as before, in her blue gown, with her pale hair caught up with combs. "Welcome, my man," she said. Her voice was a tune that had haunted his dreams. "Would you join our dance?"

"I have come to take my brother home," Geoffrey answered. The White Mare's grass-green eyes did not so much as blink, so he repeated himself. "Take me to my brother," he said. "I want nothing more of you, Lady."

"As you will, my man," she answered languidly. "Follow me, then."

As she turned to leave, Geoffrey caught hold of her wrist. Her flesh was as cold as he remembered, numbing his hand, but he held on. "Take me to my brother," he said. "I want no ballroom, I want no dining hall, I want no bower or bed. Take me to him straight away, and no tricks."

"No tricks, my man," the White Mare echoed in her passionless voice. She ran her free hand down her arm to clasp his hand, gently tugged him after her, as calm as a full moon sailing the starry sky. She led him through corridors and stairs and rooms, but Geoff kept his eyes focused on his feet and his hand on the rowan cross in his pocket. "Ian," he whispered to himself. "Brother."

More music made him look up. They had arrived at another ballroom, identical to the first, but instead of the motley crowd there were dozens of couples, all identical, moving in a great pattern dance. Every woman of them looked like the White Mare; every man of them looked like Ian Watt; and all the couples were reflected again and again in the dark mirrors that lined the walls.

"Your brother, my man," said the White Mare, dropping his hand. Geoff looked over at her words, to catch the slightest hint of malice flavoring her serene façade. "Come dance with me, my man," she said. She held out her pale hands, their fingers long and beautiful. "Lead me in the pattern—"

Geoffrey Watt was mightily tempted, but he squeezed the rowan cross inside his pocket until it flexed. "I want my brother," he said, choking out the words slowly and precisely. As the dancers formed their squares, marched in their rows to the music, he slipped out onto the floor, stepping aside from time to time to avoid collisions. Now he could see that despite their first impression, each dancer was slightly different from the next one: a wider cheekbone here, a darker eye color there. His true brother—the one he had seen practically every hour of every day for most of his life—should be as plain to him as his own appearance in a mirror.

And there he was. Ian—if it was he—did not notice his twin, having eyes only for his partner. Geoff hesitated, though. He did not know what would happen if he chose an impostor though he did not imagine it would be good. But how could he be sure? As he pondered, he realized the bag that hung from the cord around his neck, containing the caul, was vibrating, stronger the closer he came to the suspected Ian.

A movement at his elbow made him look over. The White Mare was standing by his elbow. "Come away, my man," she said, and for a moment Geoff could have thrown away all his life to do just that—but he had become practiced in self-denial. Without a word, he walked between the rows of dancers, right up to his twin. "Come away, Ian," he said, placing his hand on his brother's shoulder. "It's time we went home."

No sooner were the words out of his mouth but the lights went out in the ballroom, and the music shrieked into silence, and the twins were all alone. "Geoff?" said Ian in the darkness. His voice was steady and real. "I thought me you were right behind. Have the dancers flitted somehow?"

His hand still on his brother's warm shoulder, Ian looked around to see a glimmer of starlight off to his right. "We're in the cave," he said. "Let us get out into the open air, brother." Clasping each other's arms, reluctant to let go, they felt their way together to the opening, as tight as it had been before, and onto the hillside, where the stars still burned in the summer night, and the lightening of dawn was on the far horizon.

All the way home, Ian berated his twin for spoiling his fun, just as he'd gotten started dancing, and with such a beauteous maid, too. He would not believe his brother's story until they came to the farm, and he could see for himself the changes wrought in a year's time—repairs to the building, calves grown up into cows and all the other evidence of time's passage. The twins' family were overjoyed, and showered love—in a restrained Presbyterian fashion—on both their prodigal son and the one who brought him back.

Auld Annie heard news of the Dunburn twins' return several days later, from a farmer passing by her house. She permitted herself the space of a smile, and got on with the rest of her daily chores.

Ian Watt was largely unaffected by his sojourn in the hillside. He swore all the days of his life that he had only just begun to dance with a willing maiden when his brother laid hands on his shoulder. As for Geoff, he was more thoughtful, and became in later years known for the strength of his wisdom. His fame for sagacity couldn't have been hurt by his appearance, for his hair went gray years earlier than Ian's. Though they were equally hale and hearty into their old age, he always looked a few years older than his twin brother.

And for every year of his life after, on Midsummer Geoff gave a party for his friends, and bade each of them stay over, so that they would not be on the roads late on that night. His céilidhs always had loud pipers and grand dancing, and never once did he take leave of the celebration to go looking at the hills for a golden light and the sound of faraway music.

KIND HUNTER
by Pati Nagle

Pati Nagle has been published in *The Magazine of Fantasy & Science Fiction*, *The Williamson Effect*, and *The Book of Swords*. She lives in Albuquerque, New Mexico.

The hunter paused near the end of the tunnel, gathering himself against emerging. He had not been to this place before, but he knew he would not like it. Already the unnatural smells and the roaring, constant cacophony were hammering at his mind. Had his quarry not been here, he would never have come.

A brush of soft warmth against his calf. "Stay close, Shade," he said softly. Golden eyes glanced up at his, flash of green in their depths. Shade didn't like it here either.

Bad place. Torril go home? queried the cat.

No.

Torril shifted the case that carried his bow and pulled his hood forward, covering his ears. This was a city of mortals; he must not be recognized. His kind rarely walked among humans now, and to be noticed would have undesirable results. A deep breath, and he started toward the light.

A musician sat at the tunnel's end strumming a guitar, soft chords hanging in the air, lonely, aching. For a moment Torril wished for his flute, but he'd left it behind when he'd taken the kind hunter's oath. He dropped the change from his train fare into the open case and walked on, not bothering to query the man's mind; humans were too busy with their own tumbling thoughts to heed gentle questions. There would be birds, maybe mice, dogs and cats he could ask. Some would have seen his quarry.

Gray skies outside, but brighter light. Torril shaded

his eyes. This was the older part of the city, built of brick and stone rather than glass and steel, still too stark for his comfort. Pavement separated his feet from the living earth, isolating him. A carved stone cross towered over the walk, a symbol abhorred by the creature he hunted. A good omen? Perhaps.

Pigeons sat atop the cross. Torril greeted them silently.

Do you know of a nightwalker hereabouts?

Nightwalker, no. Night we sleep. Food? Food?

No, I'm sorry.

Feathers whipped at the air. Torril walked on.

Cold. The gray buildings seemed to suck the life out of him. No green anywhere near them; they were trad-ers' halls full of dusty books and such. Torril pulled the lacings of his hooded coat tighter to hoard his warmth.

The coat looked enough like the current fashions of mortals for him to escape notice, though no mortal had formed it. His surviving sisters had woven the cloth and wrought it into coat, tunic, leggings. He remembered their hands in the dance of its making, dappled by green-gold sunlight, while he sat apart carving the arrows that now lay in the case with his bow. The essence of his sisters' gentle touch remained in the caress of the fabric against him. He smiled softly, sadly. Perhaps he would see them again, if all went well. Perhaps.

Humans hurried along the sidewalks, and Torril fell in among them, leaning forward to keep his face hidden and to lessen his appearance of height. Shade ghosted at his feet, stopping now and again to sniff at interesting crannies and doorways. A shopkeeper shouted unwel-come and batted the cat with a broom. Grey hackles rose. A hiss, and he darted between Torril's feet to ex-plore some friendlier spot further on.

The sun was too deeply veiled to be seen, but Torril knew he had less than a quarter-day before dark, when the hunt would begin in earnest. He would do well to find shelter before then. He glanced up at the grayness, troubled by the thought of a storm, and hurried on.

In the lace-curtained window a small, flat-faced dog sat on a cushion. Its eyes watered. It was staring at Shade.

Where are trees? Torril asked.

Downhill, the dog answered. *Cat there—careful.*

Cat's a friend. Many thanks.

The dog opened its short muzzle to bark as they passed. The window glass muted the sound. A circle of mist appeared before the dog's face, then faded.

The next cross street sloped downward and Torril turned that way, scenting grass on the cold breeze. His steps quickened. He had not seen a free growing thing since leaving home that morning, and after the rattling train ride and the noise of this man-city he craved peace. Shade scampered ahead toward a small park—a haven—at the foot of the hill, and Torril had to force himself not to run after her.

Trees, their green leaves singed with yellow, whispered welcome. Autumn was coming, and summer things would soon slumber. Torril stepped onto the grass and sighed as its aliveness tingled at him through his boots. He walked straight to an old oak and laid his hands on the rough bark, felt its sleepy strength flowing into him, closed his eyes.

Thank you.

The tree's glow washed through him slowly. He drifted as if under a sea of golden warmth, drinking in renewal, peace, life. Then through the depths a sound came to him, distorted; a cry. Reluctantly he took his hands from the trunk, stepped back, blinked his eyes open. The cry became clearer. A human child, sitting on the ground near a bench where two women chatted. Young enough to hear; Torril touched its mind gently.

Trouble?

Toy! Toy!

Torril glimpsed bright colored triangles in the infant's mind. The child stopped wailing and looked straight at him, empty-handed, hopeful.

Shade?

Here. Bushes. I smell mice.

Find this, Torril asked, sending the toy's image to the cat. With gentle urging, Shade abandoned his hunt and went to a holly bush near the human child. Rustles followed; a many-colored ball rolled out toward the child, who grabbed it tight.

"Ba!"

One of the women looked up. Torril faded close to the tree trunk, cloaking himself in rustle-green breeze.

"Ba!" cried the child, pointing at him and beating the toy with its other hand. The woman looked toward Torril and tree, saw only tree, and picked up the child.

Torril smiled to himself, turning away. So far from his own people, it was good to have helped a small one. His race bred slowly, their numbers diminishing as the mortals' increased. With every forest cleared to make way for farms or towns it grew harder for his kind to survive. His own sister—Tana, the youngest—had recently died in childbirth.

Tana. Lightning and terror; a pale face streaked with rain and tears. The memory swept all pleasure from him, cold anger filling its stead. He became aware of the man-city's towers fringing the park. With a shiver he moved on, away from the women and the child, deeper into the park toward a small cluster of trees that might shelter him until dark.

A pathway led past the little grove: willows and ash, grouped to form a pretty backdrop for a small pond. They had gone untrimmed a while, the willows dangling long trails of leaves into the water. Small shrubs at their feet offered a few last blossoms to grace the harvest season. Torril left the path and entered the tiny forest, inhaling deeply of the green smells.

Shield me? he asked.

A swell of well-being answered him. The green, growing things of the world had no words, nor clear-shaped thoughts. Feelings were their language. He had not realized how sharply he would miss them until he'd left his forest home. His hand went to the band of white cloth at his brow: the kind hunter's badge. Not until he had completed the task he'd sworn to perform would he remove it or return home. A kind hunter's oath set him apart from his people. Killing was not their way, yet killing was sometimes necessary, and he had chosen to seek this kill on behalf of his kin.

Shade burst from beneath dark, glossy leaves, a tiny mouse in his jaws. Fierce eyes glowed then vanished, gray tail twitched welcome. Torril sat on the first thin layer of fallen leaves beneath an ash, and took bread and fruit from the pouch at his waist. His sister Alia had made the bread that morning, and handed it to him in silence. No one spoke to a kind hunter; he stood outside the circle of his people, apart from his kin, until his task was finished.

The bread tasted good. The apples were still tree-crisp; he cut them into slices with the small knife he wore at his waist. A fierce little tooth, that knife. He had traded a quiverful of his best arrows to have Yoren dip it in molten silver. Its edge was not quite so keen since, but would deliver a more bitter sting to his prey.

He finished his meal, cleaned the knife, and leaned back against the ash. Around him the grove's strength glowed softly, calming him. He opened his case. Bow and quiver were ready in a few moments. He laid them across his lap, leaned his head back, and inhaled sleep with the musty dry scent of the leaves.

Darkness clung in sharp corners formed by the buildings of the street. Tall man-houses, squared-off blocks built of smaller blocks, marched in straight lines as far as Torril could see. Here and there a small tree or bush, imprisoned in a man-made pot, formed a beacon of life in the bleakness. Shade roamed near, questing for game in the shadows. Torril listened to his thoughts, ready to interpose questions before the cat made his kill.

Torril's quarry was here, that was certain. Shreds of rumor led to this dark section of the town, always the thoughts tinged with fear. Though Torril had never sighted his prey, there was no question about the creature's nature. Terror and blood by night were the trademarks of his kind, and these things echoed in the minds of the small creatures of the city, rippling outward from this district. Torril listened to their wisps of thought, some nearer, some stronger and more distant, a murmuring stream.

He chanced upon a hollow in the flow—a curious calm—and stopped to listen. No such eddy would ever occur in the life-filled forest. That was the trouble with forests. Too many layers on layers of living things. In a

man-city it was easier for a hunter to isolate his prey, to
control it, to . . .

Realization, revulsion, a moment's touch of hunger
and hate. Torril wrenched his mind free and shut away
all thoughts, reaching out a hand to steady himself, finding cold stone. The creature had sensed him, perhaps
knew now he was hunted. Torril felt the ghost-touch of
a powerful mind questing, seeking him. He sat at the
foot of a building, willing the thoughts to flow past.

A bump against his shin. Reach out a hand to stroke
warm fur. Shade mewed a query, and Torril opened his
mind enough to hear the cat.

Go now? Go home?

Not yet.

Bad thing near.

Yes.

Eyes open, the world retreated into gray-and-brown
blocks once more. Torril got to his feet, shook off dark
feelings and started on, deeper into the heart of the man-
city. Shade did not roam far ahead now, but clung to
Torril's ankles. Their way took them down narrower
streets, not as well-kept, not well-lit. Keen eyes in the
dark caught tiny movements in the shadows; Torril queried briefly, sensed a rat's fear of Shade.

Nightwalker near?

Hunts. Hunts.

A skitter and the rat was gone. Shade made no move
to follow but stayed close, eyes wide, fur fluffed and
angry. Torril slid an arrow from his quiver and set it
noiselessly against the bowstring, calling the shadows to
cloak him. Shadows of stone and brick were less accom-
modating than forest shadows; it took an effort to bend
them to his will.

Tana, he thought, seeing her weary, rain-soaked form
stumbling toward him through the woods, weeping with
joy and sorrow. For her sake he would do this, kill one
of the creatures who'd caught her, enthralled her, defiled
her. A life for a life; that was the kind hunter's oath.

Breathing too fast. Torril focused on clearing his mind,
on silence, on hearing and seeing. The pavement was
damp now; a moist night. Tang of blood on the heavy

air, fighting the city smells. Shade growled soft and low, and fell back behind Torril's feet.

The hunters turned down a street lit by strange colors—red and orange and the brilliant pinks of summer flowers—glowing unnaturally in windows and over doorways. For all their weird illumination the street was still dim. Though the night was more than half gone, mortals strolled the walks or stood in clumps at corners here, restless and sullen-looking, the lost or becoming-lost. Torril held his bow as close as he could and wrestled the shadows to conceal him, knowing he could not continue so for long. The effort was costing him some of his alertness, and it was Shade's hiss that brought his attention to two figures disappearing around a corner a short way ahead; a male—tall and dark, somewhat slender—preceding a ginger-haired female in high boots and a short skirt. They seemed clouded by shadows, a skill Torril's folk shared with the nightwalkers.

His scalp tingled. This was his quarry. How much better it would be to meet him in a forest glen instead of this dead city. But, of course, the creature knew that; it was part of the reason nightwalkers tended to live in the cities of men.

Torril saw cat-shelter behind a discarded box. He flashed the image to Shade and told him to wait there, then crossed the street alone, following the nightwalker and his victim. Down an alley, dim and still, each step that brought him closer to his quarry weighing on him.

To kill a being of high intelligence was wrong. That was the rule he'd been taught, and, in part, it was the kind hunter's justification, for the nightwalkers had no such philosophy and caused great destruction among the world's thinking races. Yet this did not ease the trouble in Torril's mind. Was he not now, in his quest to slay this creature, sunk to his own level?

Tana. She would be avenged. A life for a life, or his kind would be overrun. The blood-seekers preyed on mortals as food, and on the elven kindred—

There. In a dark doorway; the beast was toying with his prey. The ginger-haired female stood over the lean form reclined on a clutter of rubbish. A nightwalker's eyes could mesmerize his prey into performing any unnatural act. *Avoid the eyes,* Tana had whispered to him, her cold hands gripping his shoulders, rain dripping from his hair onto her cheek.

He let go his cloak of shadows and silently nocked his arrow; pure oak, sharpened and hardened in the fire of his hatred. Move aside, woman, he thought, though only to himself. The nightwalker must not hear him.

She did not move aside but leaned closer instead, straddling her companion, bending her head to his. Torril suppressed his frustration and stepped out, seeking a clear shot. The dark-haired man moaned, a sound which lit acid flames in Torril's heart.

A plish—soft boot at the edge of an unnoticed puddle—betrayed by his own inattention. Furious with himself, Torril raised his bow for one desperate shot as the woman looked up at him.

Blood on her lips! On *her* lips! Eyes of ice stabbed even as he flung himself away. The arrow clattered on the pavement behind him.

Stop!

Yes, he must stop—all would be well if he stopped—the feeling filled his whole being, yet he ran on. Away from the command, from the desire to submit, from terror; back toward the garish lights and the mortals.

Hurt? Torril hurt?

Come!

He did not pause to look for Shade. The cat was in no danger, or not near so much as Torril. As he distanced himself from the nightwalker his senses returned. Mortals stared, some called out words unclear, unimportant. The quiver bounced crazily at his hip, arrows rattling as he ran through the streets, not bothering to hide, always seeking the brighter lights that he knew his enemy would shun. The huntress would not wish to spook her herd; he would be safe among them for now.

With fire in his throat he stopped at last, leaning against comfortless stone, gasping and shaking. A clay pot at the foot of stone steps held a young tree captive; he grasped the slender trunk and drank its small life in a heartbeat, then grieved. He had never before consumed a tree's life. Bad fortune. When he returned home he would plant a sapling in its stead.

When he returned home. Easy to say, but not so simple to achieve. He must first kill the nightwalker, and the nightwalker was a female, and that changed everything.

Tana. Lend me your strength, sister.

This was not the creature who had captured Tana, tormented her, caused her death. No matter; a life for a life was the oath, and it was hard enough to hunt a nightwalker without inquiring its identity. He would kill this female because she was at hand, and because he must or be doomed himself.

"Hey! What are you doing there?"

Torril came out of his thoughts with a start, and found himself leaning against the steps with one hand around the dead tree's trunk and the other gripping his bow stone-hard. A human male in dark clothing, with badges and weapons of office adorning his person, was speaking at him angrily. Torril let go the tree and backed away, hiding his bow in shadow. The mortal took a step toward him, then Shade ran between them, purring and stropping against Torril's legs. He reached down to scratch the cat, watching the mortal from the corner of his eye. The man seemed to relax. While Shade flirted with the mortal, coaxing him to bend and pet, Torril slipped into shadow and away.

Down an alley, over a fence, back in darkness. Deep breath of freedom. He needed to replenish his energy before he could finish this hunt. He needed green, but he dared not open his mind to inquire where to find a mass of trees, for he was both hunter and hunted now.

He found his way into a neighborhood of tall houses with small gardens, separated from the street by a low wall of bricks. Torril stepped over it into a patch of sanctuary; vines just starting to flame with autumn, clumps of tame flowers, and evergreen bushes shorn to peculiar shapes. He sank to the ground, leaned against the vine-covered wall—eyes nearly closed but watchful lest the mortals behind their stone blocks should wake—and caressed leaves with either hand, drinking deeply of the garden's strength, yet not too deeply. Control; that was the difference between the nightwalkers and his people. Control and compassion. He would kill no plant, waste no life. He took only what each could spare, reaching through the soil beneath him to the roots of the neighboring gardens.

A shudder passed through him as he slowly let go the tension that gripped at his shoulders. Shade joined him with a rustle and thump, flicked his tail in greeting, and padded to a bush to explore its smells.

The nightwalker was searching for him, Torril knew. Fear prickled up his arms as he thought of facing her again. *Avoid the eyes.* Yes, but what if she chose not to mesmerize him, merely to kill? Immortals still bled; she could strike from behind, and consume his life in moments.

Pray that she does, if she catches you.

Tana had not been so lucky. Nearly a year had gone by from the time she was taken until her escape. She had been given up for lost by her kindred, and then one morning, early, in the moist of a howling rainstorm—

Torril pushed himself to his feet. No rest, not until she was avenged. His kin had spent a year in hell. He would waste no more darkness.

Street emptied into silent street. The gardens left behind, there was no more life around him, only the dark, dead eyes of the mortals' dwellings. Shade followed in silent resignation.

Ahead at a crossing, a single tree, gnarled and scant of leaves. A bird sat upon a twisted branch, and Torril dared a query.

More trees?

His answer was a raw squawk as the bird took wing. It cried again, circling, then dropped toward him. Shade's hiss came as one with his realization—too late, both—she transformed as she fell toward him, naked and horrible.

Eyes! Torril rolled aside, scraping a knee against the hard street, flinging up his bow to ward her off. He heard the wood splinter as his arm was struck painfully to the ground, the nightwalker's weight atop it. Free hand to his waist for the knife; a slash, a hiss, and the weight was gone. He staggered up, keeping his gaze away from her face, and wound up staring at pale breasts instead. Ice-tipped, yet they stirred something in him. Her body was firm, her waist slender, hips a welcoming bowl. She raised a bleeding hand to lick the cut he'd given her, and his eyes flicked to her face before he could check them, glimpsing a smile. He tore his attention away and looked at the knife in his hand; cold silver, harsh under the dim chemical lights of the mortals' city.

She's not attacking. The thought didn't comfort him. The blade in his hand began trembling. She smelled good.

The broken bow dropped to the ground. She stepped over it, bare white feet on rough pavement. He could hear her breath, she was that near.

You're a pretty one.

Her thoughts were too strong to be blocked. Torril aimed a blow with the knife and watched in horror as his hand gently yielded up the blade to his enemy instead. she turned it this way and that in the light, sending glints off the blade, then dropped it on the ground.

Look at me.

With all his being, Torril resisted. He kept his eyes on the ground, saw her place a dainty foot between his boots. Lustful imaginings flowed through his unwilling mind and aroused an urgent response from his body. He strove to move his feet, her soft hissing laughter mocking him, her hunger washing through his thoughts, tainting them. How wonderful it would feel to take her, here, now, under the black night while the stupid mortals slept in their dead houses. How delightful to become hers, to hunt no more and care no more, to live only for their mutual pleasure, days, weeks, years of it. She was beautiful, she was strong, she would bear strong children.

Not by me!

In desperation he wrenched a foot away from the pavement. He stumbled backward, nearly falling, a hand thumping into his quiver and his back coming up against something hard.

The tree. With a wordless cry he sucked its strength—all of it, years of growth, season on season of strength—and in one vicious thrust repulsed the nightwalker's mind.

His hand drew an arrow and he flung himself forward, stabbing up beneath her ribs with the slender oak shaft, feeling it crack as her shriek filled his senses, wild elation sweeping through him. Deeper, deeper he pushed the broken arrow through the blood that slickened his hand. She clung to him, howling, weakening, falling.

He let go the arrow. No more than two hand spans protruded from her body, heaving as she gasped her last breaths. He looked in her eyes then. Beautiful, dark eyes; they had no more power to control him. They accused him instead, and he knew he would remember them always. That was the price of his oath.

The life faded from her face. She no longer saw him, no longer was something to fear. Death drew a dull film over her eyes.

Torril's senses returned all at once; he felt the coldness of the predawn air in his lungs as he breathed sharp and fast, heard the dry rustle of dead leaves overhead, smelled blood. He picked up the knife, reached down and gathered the nightwalker's ginger hair in one hand, and severed it from her head with one stroke. He faced the hoary tree whose life had saved him—the tree the nightwalker had perched in to hunt him—and saw its leaves had turned paper-white. He draped the tresses over its branches; at dawn they would crumble into ash and blow away along with the nightwalker's body, leaving no trace of her existence.

He looked down at her again; a pale, broken girl, slim like an elf-maid, reminding him uncannily of Tana in her funeral-boat. He'd stood in the rain and watched the river take his sister and her child—the child Tana had killed with her own hand—the infant got on her by her nightwalker captor. Slaying it had been her last act before death claimed her, that stormy dawn.

No hint of rain now. He kicked gently at the nightwalker's body with a booted toe. He had not wanted to hunt—and had dreaded killing—one of his own kind, however distantly related. They were more alike than he'd realized, perhaps. In the end, he had enjoyed it.

Shade came out of the shadows, padded silently to within an arm's length of the nightwalker's body and sniffed the air, then hissed softly.

Bad thing. Go home now?

Torril pulled the white band from his brow and dropped it beside the pale body.

Yes.

THE GYPSIES' CURSE

by Elizabeth Ann Scarborough

Elizabeth Ann Scarborough won a Nebula award in 1989 for her novel *The Healer's War,* which was based on her experiences as an Army nurse in Vietnam. She has collaborated on three books with Anne McCaffrey, the most recent being *Space Opera.* She lives in Washington with four cats, Kitty-bits, Popsicle, Trixie and Treat.

Squatting around the campfire, their caravans sheltering them from a strong north wind, Romany's people planned their passage the next day into Aire as carefully as Choomia would lay out the cards for a rich client. Romany, who had been gifted with clear sightedness at her christening, saw fear in the eyes of even the strongest men.

This puzzled her. She was excited, herself, to be spending her fifteenth birthday in a place she had never been before. She hoped the gloom she saw in the faces of the men and the tightness in the mouths of the women would not spoil her birthday party.

"Mama," she said to Choomia, the only mother she'd ever known. "What's to worry them in Aire? It's only elves there, isn't it? That's what Misha said." Everything that Misha said had the music of truth to Romany's ears. Misha was nearly as tall as she, with dark hair curling onto his forehead and dark eyes that softened a bit when he looked at her. His voice had turned deep early and no longer squeaked like that of the other boys near her age. Misha did not make fun of her, but seemed to like her. And Misha was not promised to any other girl. Not yet.

Choomia, sitting with her back to the wheel of her caravan as she embroidered gilt thread into a practically new scarf a farmer's wife had thrown away, pursed her lips and did not look at Romany. The firelight flicked shadows on her face. She needed little light to sew. The pattern was from her mother's mother and she had been sewing it onto skirts and scarves, shawls and blankets all her life. Just as Romany was admiring this skill, Choomia pricked her finger, cursed, and sucked the blood from the prick. She set aside the sewing then, so as not to get it bloody, and gave Romany a look hard and scornful. "*Only* elves? And what is it you think elves are, daughter?"

Romany hadn't thought much about what they were. But she knew what they looked like. "They're beautiful," she said without hesitation. It was the height of them you noticed first—long bones of arm and leg making them tall and straight as lances, unlike her people. No matter how hard they worked, the folk in Romany's band let their bodies subside into whichever shape nature cared to bend them by the time they were in their twenties. But the elves were different. The teeth in their mouths were straight, never crooked or missing, and white as the snow on the mountaintops. While Romany's teeth were good enough, those of the people around her blackened and broke until they looked like headstones in a poorly kept graveyard. Even on the young ones.

Choomia made as if to fling the sewing at her. "Beautiful, is it? Have I not taught you better than that? That's not beauty, that's glamourie, girl. A two-bit wizard's trick done with fairy gold and double-edged words to blind the eye of the stupid."

"Mama," Romany said gravely, looking down at her mother. "I am not stupid, you know. And I won't argue about what I don't understand. That well you *have* taught me. But we've seen them in the towns sometimes, at least, folk I've been told are elfin, going about perfectly ordinary tasks, and they still *look* beautiful."

"What have you ever seen them do that's ordinary?" Choomia demanded. "Slop pigs? Relieve themselves?"

Romany tried to think of something. "Drunk. I've seen one drunk. And even drunk he staggered gracefullike. And when he drooled it wasn't even disgusting— sort of like this wee stream trinkling down the crevasses

in his face. And there was this lady shopping in the
market for vegetables. They looked like gold in her
hands—long, slender hands they was and moved like
swans on a still pool. And aye, I've heard them fiddle,
as good as Timoteo, only different."

"That's ordinary, is it, to you? Aye, I suppose you
know no better. But playing music and dancing, drinking
and whoring and throwing their gold about buying the
fruits of other lands, these are things they like to do.
They do nothing that they dislike, the elves. They feed
off the labor of others."

And what do we do? Romany asked herself, we traveling people, begging for the bread baked by the farmwife, taking the odd sheep or horse fed by the settled
people, charging them the gold their sweat had earned
them for fortunes that were nothing but fantasies to
scare more gold from them. But she didn't say this,
never a word. Such thoughts were treason, the sort of
thing the settled people jeered at them with and the
polis said when breaking up their caravans and shifting
them in the middle of the night in driving rain from the
only shelter they could find.

That was the sort of thing had led them to decide to
cross into Aire after all. "It's different there now. They
welcome us." Zoltan of the Loch Quay band had told
them when the bands met briefly at a crossroads. Romany's people had been traveling night and day for
nearly a week then, for always there were angry farmers
and their sons, polis, and guardsmen who would not let
them rest. Two horses died of exhaustion and Mara's
old mother.

"But Zoltan says they'll make us welcome," Romany
added this information to make Choomia tell her more.

"Make us slaves more likely, to do their dirty work,"
Choomia said bitterly.

"But Zoltan's people weren't made slaves," Romany
insisted.

The firelight flickered in Choomia's dark eyes. "Hush
now, you. That's enough of you. Well enough do we all
know why *you'd* defend these bloody *beautiful* people.
You being as you are, but I'll hear no more of it. You've
seen them fiddle, but never have you seen them behead

an old woman or tear a child from the arms of its mother as they slew all the poor babe's kin?''

"No, I never heard that, of all the tales I've heard around the campfire," Romany said stoutly. Choomia was not above a bit of exaggeration to win an argument, and Romany didn't quite believe her. "When did you see such a thing, Mama?"

Choomia shrugged. "Not I, of course. I never did. But the mother of my own mother, now, she was there, hiding under the bodies of her uncles. You have heard the stories too, child. Who do you think the men are speaking of when they tell the trickster stories against the giants or sing the victory songs of our heroes? And how do you think we come to own the road and no more when once our people roamed our own lands without interference? But I'd never expect *you* to understand, being as you are."

Better Mama should have flown at her with clenched fists than sent her to bed with that, Romany thought as she wept herself to sleep that night, the voices of her people still chattering around the fire like horses whinnying before a storm.

Usually, it was agreed that Romany's monstrousness was not spoken of, or Choomia would tear a strip off the speaker, be it man, woman or child. For Choomia herself to refer to it, even indirectly, was very mean, especially when she did it over perfectly innocent questions. It wasn't Romany's fault that she was so different—so disfigured and ugly and outsized. Her great height was the least of it. The growth on her forehead, the hair so wiry-curly that even the walnut dye it needed to make it properly black as a gypsy girl's should be didn't tame it, the juice and mud that had to go on her wormy-white skin to keep the sun from crisping her red as a cherry, these all told her how different she was. Each time they crossed a lake or a clear spot in a river, her own huge mud-colored reflection taunted her with her ugliness and difference. What would she know about beauty indeed?

In the morning they labored up the mountains and through the slit between them that formed the passage to Aire. Behind them they left the land where the sky was always gray and rumbling, the ground always muddy, the crops were stunted for lack of sunlight and where their belongings always smelled of mold.

Romany was the last through, since she made many trips back to help the other women and children climb. Bigger than most of the men as she was, she was also stronger than most, and she spent most of her long-anticipated fifteenth birthday looking at the ass-ends of horses and caravans, soaked to the skin by a new rain-storm that ran the dye on her skin and hair until it ran into her eyes and stained her dirty white blouse and skirts. But that evening, she knew, she would have new things to wear. Only her scarf and sash, christening gifts, would remain of her original outerwear. These she knew she had to wash in soaproot and dried sourfruit peelings before the festivities began.

Suddenly, as she crested the ridge of the mountain for the hundredth time that day and finally passed through the long, chilly, but blessedly dry tunnel formed by the overhang of the peaks above, the land before and below her spread out like a dancer's skirts in full twirl.

A rainbow shone above a countryside of a thousand greens, and skeins of bright birds wove sky to earth.

And the sun was warm, even so late in the day, when it began staining the sky with rose and tangerine, mir-rored in the rivers and ponds glittering within the green.

Ahead of her on the steep zigzag downward path, her people and their once flamboyantly decorated wagons, now sun and rain-faded, threaded their way to the val-ley floor.

No longer weary, Romany ran to catch up. Now *this*, for sure, was beautiful.

They made camp at the foot of the mountain as the light was dying. With the other girls, Romany ran off into the forest to gather firewood, which was plentiful. Squirrels and rabbits scampered away as she and the others approached and the night birds had begun to call. The girls were none too soon returning with the wood, and darkness was on them before they left the trees.

But as they approached the camp, a fire was already roaring in the center, and Romany knew at once that some of the people there were not her own.

She was sure of it when she saw that there were about twenty additional figures standing around, talking to her relatives. They were tall and fair, and very beautiful indeed. But unlike the elves she'd seen in the towns, these people wore clothing much like her own and that of the rest of the band, except that theirs was new, the colors brilliant and the coin and gilt thread embellishments placed a bit wrong and shining a bit too brightly.

"But, really, you don't have to camp *here*," said a beautiful woman whose bright hair was concealed with a scarf twined with flowers, and from whose dainty ears dangled large golden hoops suspending little golden bells that tinkled when she moved her head, as she did often. "I have a much better spot for you where I live. A shady glade near a clear stream, with a great deal of grass for your horses. And, if you'll come, I'll have a wonderful feast prepared for us all so you can get acquainted with everyone."

"*You* are inviting *us* to your feast, lady?" Timoteo asked. Romany had never seen him look so bewildered.

"Not "Lady" please. Call me "Rawnie." ""

For a moment, Timoteo looked even more confused. Rawnie meant Lady in the gypsy tongue. But he smiled and bowed and said, "I am Timoteo, Rawnie. And we would be honored . . ."

Choomia grabbed his arm and jerked him back to her side, then patted his forearm as if the gesture were affectionate and said, "What my husband means to say, lady, is that we would be honored except that this is our daughter's fifteenth birthday and it is a special feast, a special celebration. You understand?"'

"There will be music?" Rawnie asked.

"Assuredly," Timoteo said.

"Dancing?"

"Oh, yes."

"Good, then we'll be delighted to be *your* guests this evening and you can move your camp in the morning and be mine for a feast tomorrow. Everything you need will be provided, of course, and you can stay as long as you like."

Choomia started to protest. Outsiders were not allowed at the fifteenth birthday celebrations of young women. It wasn't proper. Or at least, Romany didn't think it was. The celebrations were held if at all possible far from the towns and farmsteads, where no one would come asking for a fortune or a potion, or to hear the violins or see the dancing.

But now Timoteo grabbed Choomia's patting hand in his own and squeezed so that Choomia gave a little gasp. "What my beloved wife means to say, Lady Rawnie, is that we are speechless with honor to have you here to celebrate Romany's birthday. Perhaps such a great lady as yourself will even have a small gift to ease her way into womanhood?"

"Perhaps," Rawnie said, her smile slight but lovely as a sliver of moon reflected in a lake. "Are you going to begin soon?"

"You have built the fire for us already, so graciously," Timoteo said. "Our feast is but poor fare for such gentility as yourselves, but . . ."

"Oh, don't worry," said a seemingly young man who wore a woman's hipscarf over his trousers. "Our Phurai Dai always manages somehow, don't you, Rawnie?"

Romany eyed him curiously. He was an odd-looking fellow, and for more reasons than that his dress was peculiar. He was shorter than most of the elves, wiry and thin rather than willowy slender, and his face had an expression that was at the same time constantly inquisitive and comical. His movements were quick and abrupt, unlike the flowing grace of the other elves, and his hair, though fair, had a reddish cast to it that glowed in the firelight. Rather like what she had seen of her own when the dye faded. Though hers always looked dingier. He saw her staring and winked at her, as if he'd told a bawdy joke only she would understand. She quickly looked away.

Timoteo released his wife's hand, and Choomia beckoned to Romany to join her at the caravan.

"You can't become a woman all dirty and smelling as you do," Choomia told her, fury Romany could not understand making her mother's voice clipped and harsh. "I won't have your new clothes stinking before you've worn them an hour. Go find a stream and wash. Here are your new clothes. Hold them away from you."

Romany dived headfirst into the caravan to find her supply of walnut hull dye for her hair and skin. The little pots she carried it in were empty,.

"I can't wash," she said. "I'm out of dye and in the dark, I won't be able to find the right trees, even if we had time to make more."

"You won't need it tonight," Choomia said, mysteriously. "This is your fifteenth birthday. You should be as you were born to be."

"But—" *But I'm ugly,* Romany thought. *You've always said I needed the dye because I'm ugly.*

"Hurry, now. Do you want to stay a girl forever? Now take these, but mind you—"

She put her hand over Romany's, "Wash out your old bandanna and hip shawl and wear them under the new. Your other christening gifts I will give you at the fire."

"Yes, Mama," Romany replied. She grabbed the pile of new clothing and ran back to the woods, to a stream she'd spotted while gathering kindling.

She washed her body, hair, and dirty clothing, trying especially hard to get the dirt out of her old scarf and hip wrap. From what she could tell in the moonlight, both of them cleaned up better than she did. The bumpy scar on her forehead was much sorer than usual and when she put her fingers to it, she found that the skin had split back and there was an inner core, very hard. It probably looked horrible. She wished it was daylight so she could see. But her scarf would conceal it anyway.

As usual, the dye did not come completely off her skin or out of her hair. She hoped she wasn't going to be streaky and blotchy for days, but Choomia was right. In the dark, it wouldn't be too noticeable, and tomorrow she could look for walnut trees and the other ingredients she needed for dyes. She put on her new scarlet skirt with Choomia's gilt roses around the hem, and her saffron colored blouse with the red ribbon and the gilt roses down the sleeves. Her old scarf dried out almost completely in a time that was so short as to seem magical, and after tying it on, she covered it completely with the black scarf Choomia had been working on the night before, now embellished around the fold with gold coins. Even when wet, her hair began frizzing into a fan down her back and she combed it with her fingers before braiding it into a single tail, a process not much easier than taming a young horse. Finally, she tucked the braid into the back of her blouse, so that nothing showed under the scarf.

Her old flowered hip wrap she knotted over her skirt and then the new one, of blue-green cloth completely worked with Choomia's golden roses. Her flowered wrap she had had since she was a baby and it was small, so nothing of it showed beneath the new blue one. She ran barefoot back to camp.

Timoteo was waiting where the firelight faltered. "About time you got here, chavi," he said, calling her by the gypsy name that meant "daughter." "We waited for you to eat the luck cake, but those other ones," he nodded toward Rawnie and her entourage, "they made food come from nowhere. Only your mother's scoldings have kept our band from joining in while you primped." His tone was jovial, however, and he touched her shoulder with tenderness and pride as he herded her back into the circle of firelight.

The luck cake was ready by then, made with nuts Romany had ground herself over the last few weeks, and filled with berries and fruits that symbolized different virtues, talents and gifts—a bit of peach for smooth skin, apple for good health, raisin for long life, cherry for a happy marriage, and so forth.

With this cake the girl becoming a woman gave gifts to her family and friends, as they had given gifts to her upon her christening. Older unmarried girls received the first pieces, followed by younger girls, then the Phurai Dai if she was present, the girl's parents, other elders, and finally the boys, one of whom usually declared himself as husband for the girl. Sometimes it was his parents who declared him. But usually he would not speak or be spoken for until the girl gave him, of all the boys, the first piece of her luck cake—usually the one marked so that she knew it had the cherry in it.

Gypsy girls married young and had many children. Romany didn't know what she thought of that. She liked children and helped with the young ones of other families, but her own parents had no other offspring. Most other girls carried a younger brother or sister on each hip and several tugging at their skirts. Romany would rather practice knife play with the boys or ride the horses grazing in the fields the band passed. Especially if Misha was watching.

She had passed out several slices of cake to the people in the crowd and was holding one, the one with the cherry, searching for Misha's face, when it was taken from her hand, and the elf with the reddish hair and the woman's hip shawl said, "Rawnie has been telling us all about traditional luck cakes." He popped it in his mouth and then looked at her as if *she* were a horse who had just performed a clever trick. "Umm, delicious, dear. I could have done without the cherry, though."

Misha, behind him, glared at Romany and turned away, stalking to where his parents stood, also glaring. Romany stared helplessly back at them and shrugged. Surely they could see it was a mistake. They didn't think she was going to marry that runty elfin show-off, did they? He didn't even know what he'd done. Choomia stuck her hands in, pulled out another piece, and showed Romany the cherry in her hand before she inserted it into the bottom of the cake. She then went over to Misha's family and gave him the cake while she chattered at his parents. But no declaration was made.

"These things happen sometime," Timoteo said to her, "Your mother and I will handle it," and covered up the awkward silence by beginning a tune on his violin.

This was the cue for Romany to dance. Tonight, she would be the only one to dance. She had not been a bad dancer when she was younger. She used to have some lovely sandals that had been given her for her christening, and her feet had been quick and clever when she wore them. She did the twirls that were like the spinning of the wagon wheels going down a fast hill, the swooping dives of the raven who was the special bird of her people, the leaps of the mountain goat from ridge to ridge, the two moves simulating the dramatic changes life could take, for the better, the worse, the speed of soaring youth, the descent to the grave. Since she had grown so very large, she could no longer wear her sandals and was no longer quite as deft-footed as the goat in the dance. Fortunately, though, her body was supple from the constant exercise and her dancing had always been more than presentable.

This night, it began well, building from the slow sinuous movements of the opening melody lines, the river of life, the slither of serpent and lizard hugging the earth, the ribbon-line progress of the caravans across the countryside. On it slid into the pulsing contortions and acrobatics of the middle measures where birth took place and life began. At last the fiddle's flying bow drove her into the frantic soaring spiral of the main body of the tune, where the melody galloped like runaway horses, and the dance depicting the pace and substance of a gypsy woman's life turned the fire's shadow into a flickering pantomimed prayer to the moon and the Mother of all.

Spinning and diving, jumping and spinning again, she grew entranced by the glitter of the golden roses at her hips, on her hem, flashing when she raised her arms. The onlookers clapped time, nearly drowning out the violin.

Timoteo slid into another tune and did not bother with the slow beginning but went right into the fast bit, and the roses sparkled in the glow of the campfire and the clapping seemed to come from her own bare feet as she pounded the time into the ground with each revolution of her body, each dip, dive, and leap. Someone—Choomia—tossed her tambourine to her and she caught it in midair, its jingle and thump amplifying the sound of her feet and the clinking together of the coins on her scarves.

She leaped the fire once, twice, and as she was about to leap again, heard a second violin joining the first, playing another, more ornamented melody line weaving all around Timoteo's music in a manner that confused her feet and had nothing to say about gypsy life. She turned to the fire and saw someone else leap across it and saw other bodies twisting in its light, dancing and whirling with abandon but no meaning.

The melody of her father's violin stopped as suddenly as if it had fallen from a cliff while the other went on for a time, unbalanced and frantic, the movements of the dancers meaningless and at times lascivious as they whirled and leaped the fire. All of these were long pale people, weaving in the shrinking circle of firelight like white shadows among the black.

The clapping stopped, except for that from slender, pallid hands. The jingle of Romany's coins and her tambourine was reflected only in the cacophonous tinkling of little bells.

"Stop!" her mother's voice commanded. "What is it that you think you're doing?"

Rawnie raised her hand and the clapping, violins, dancing, and leaping were sliced to stillness and silence. "Is there something the matter?"

"Yes, that playing and dancing. What was that about?" Choomia demanded.

"Why, my people simply wanted to join yours in celebration. You see, I've been telling them about the gypsies I knew long ago, of the dances and the music, and we've been trying a bit on our own. Don't you like it?"

"Like it? *Like* it?!" Choomia sputtered, but Timoteo cut in smoothly, remembering the proffered stream and grass, the feast and the long stay without shifting.

Gently, diplomatically, but with sadness and disappointment seeping through in the obsequious expression he assumed with outsiders, "Lady Rawnie, ordinarily we would have been pleased to have your most graceful people join ours in the music and dance, but this, you see, was my daughter's celebration—her fifteenth birthday."

"Oh, yes, and I have thought of a wonderful gift!" Rawnie said, clapping her hands like a child, so enthusiastically that her earrings swung and their bells tinkled like icicles breaking into snowmelt.

"I hope it is, Lady, for you see, her cake is given only to her family, her traveling companions . . ."

"But we will *become* your traveling companions!" One of the ladies cried happily.

"Oh, I'd love that, wouldn't you, Fenelia?" another one chattered to the lady next to her.

"Oh, yes, the romance of it! The campfires, the music, the telling of fortunes, the . . ."

"And her intended husband," Choomia added with

force. "The morsel of luck cake your friend took was supposed to have gone to Misha . . ."

"I didn't know these people were so *self*ish," the elf-runt said. "You told us, Rawnie, that they shared everything. I didn't think they'd grudge me a little piece of cake after you invited them to one of our feasts!"

"The highborn gentleman had no way of knowing, wife," Timoteo said.

"No, I didn't," the runt said indignantly. "*Elfish* is never *selfish* . . ." his friends tittered at his lame witticism, "And with what we've offered you . . ."

"Most graciously, too, good sir. I'm sure that Misha's family . . ."

"Misha's family would never allow him to marry with such ill omens as have occurred this night," his father declared, stepping into the firelight. "And my boy does not care for your daughter, not in that way. Who wants a wife who could break him in half? We're leaving this land tonight. Any who wish to come with us are welcome." And he followed the insult by spitting into the fire and stalking off to gather his wife, Misha and his unmarried siblings back to their wagon, where Misha's younger brother was already hitching the horses.

Romany saw Misha cast a backward glance toward the fire, where she stood with her own parents and Rawnie.

"Oh, dear," Rawnie said as if she'd spilled a bit of food on her lily-white bosom, "I don't quite understand what we've done wrong, I'm afraid, but I'm terribly sorry."

Timoteo began explaining it to her in a soft voice while Choomia fumed.

Romany was none too happy herself. Of all the boys she'd met, Misha was the only one who seemed to like her at all, who didn't seem overawed by her size and skill with knives and horses. He had been her only prospect, and now he wasn't. Furthermore, she felt like an idiot after what his father had said, as if thinking Misha would have her was all her idea. It didn't take high romance to make a marriage among her people—just two folk of opposite sexes who got on reasonably well. If Misha'd taken the cake the elf got, the deal would have been made, palms spat upon and hands shaken, as sure as a horse trade. But it was all ruined now.

It wasn't as if she *wanted* to get married and have brats right away. It was just that a proper gypsy woman needed a man like she needed a scarf and a tambourine. And Misha was better than most. She turned away, sadly, and saw that the Lady Rawnie was no longer listening to her father, but staring at her.

As if Timoteo were not speaking, Rawnie ignored him and took both of Romany's large, capable and callused hands in her own soft, slender ones. Her rings, *real* gold with *real* precious stones, Romany thought, not gilded pot metal and glass like Choomia's, shot stars off into the night, shaming the puny pallid ones in the sky.

"My dear, I didn't know. I am so sorry, but I promise I will do all I can to make it up to you. . . ." Her voice was more melodious than the violin music and her eyes were practically compelling Romany to say she forgave her.

Instead, Romany felt herself blushing under her splotches of dye and sputtered, "It's nothing. Didn't want a husband . . ."

To her surprise, Choomia put her arm protectively around Romany's shoulders. "That's right, darling child. My Romany is too good for those people. Excuse us, Lady Rawnie," she said, her anger having vanished as if by sleight of hand. "But where do you live? We will sleep for a while and come to your house tomorrow."

"Oh, it's the castle on the first mountaintop after you pass Glenn Bloodbath. If it's misty, sometimes it disappears, but you can ask anyone. All the locals know us. Otherwise, you'll see it easily. Can't miss it." She clapped those delicate hands once more and cried to her entourage. "Come people, our friends have to get some sleep. We'll continue the festivities at home."

"I thought you said gypsies knew how to party . . ." complained the runt with a backward glance at the rest of the feast. But they left.

When they were well gone, the women sat on one side of the fire and the men on the other. Timoteo played his violin low and in a pensive manner while listening to the talk swirling around him.

The women tried to reassure Romany, but weren't very good at it. She knew she'd never fit in. There was speculation as to what it all meant, how it could be made to fit into what they knew already. Which led to tales of their own fifteenth birthdays and all that had come to them since.

At some point, Romany dozed off, tired from her long day. When she opened her eyes again, Choomia had left the fire.

"I guess I'd better get some sleep, too," Romany said.

"What's the hurry?" Dudee, Misha's married sister, asked. "On *my* fifteenth birthday, I danced all night."

"Yes," Romany said. "But we're going to that lady's castle tomorrow and I want to wash again in the morning."

"You'll catch a chill and make yourself sick with all that washing, mark my words," said her aunt on her father's side. "Anyway, it won't be a long trip, if those fine lords and ladies will make it and still have the night to revel in."

But it *was* a long trip. A very long trip.

Romany had not had the whole night to sleep either. When she returned to the wagon, Timoteo was also there, snoring, but Choomia was laying out the cards. When Romany asked her what they said, her mother shook her head and looked grim, and rather sad.

Then she reached into her pocket and held out a small pendant that was shaped and colored like a shell but had teeth on one edge, like a comb. "You'd better have this, I suppose. It's your last christening present. You had it with you when you came to us."

"What a pretty necklace. Who gave it to me?"

"Some women you'd best hope you never meet. It's not just jewelry though. It's a comb. Maybe its magic will straighten out that kinky hair of yours."

Romany took it and slipped it around her neck and tried to exclaim over it as one was supposed to do over a present, though truthfully it wasn't nearly as impressive as the necklace of golden coins Dudee had received on *her* fifteenth birthday. Her mother was no longer paying any attention, however, and had returned her gaze to her cards.

Romany arose very early, compared to the rest of the

camp, and went back to the woods to look for the walnut trees for dye. She didn't find the trees, but in daylight her skin was so blotchy she looked as if she had been ill for some time. No good getting thrown out of the villages because they thought she had the plague. Besides, the night was warm, the stream private.

She removed her scarves and unbraided her hair, then took off her skirts and hip shawls and stepped into the pool she had used the night before. She kept on her upper clothing for the moment as the morning was still cool. She forgot to take off her new pendant too, and as she stepped into the water, took hold of the necklace, preparing to remove it and leave it on a rock. But suddenly, she found herself slipping, falling, her feet going out from under her—literally, and herself up to her neck in the pool. She tried to stand but couldn't, and smacked her tail in frustration.

Her . . . tail.

Where her feet should have been was a long, scaled fish tail, glittering like golden coins in the first light of day. Oh, no! She was even more of a monster than she'd ever thought! But never mind that. Choomia would kill her if she ruined her new blouse so soon. Slipping and sliding, she tore off her upper garments, and the pendant with them.

When they were over her head and flung safely to shore, she took a cautious look back to that awful fish tail and saw only her own usual bare legs and feet, tucked under her thighs and hips, white and red and freckled but hardly alarming.

Before anything else strange could happen, she vigorously scrubbed her skin and hair again. This time most of the dye went away, except for some tiny dark spots all over her very light skin. When she pulled her hair forward to braid the ends, she saw that it had washed out to a very bright red—redder than a fox, though not so red as, say, a rose. An orangy-coral color, really. Choomia had always told her it was ugly but privately, she rather liked it and thought it would be very nice with her new blouse and skirt if she chose to wear it loose. But then, that would mark her as different, would be one more thing besides her great lump of a body to set her apart from her people.

All the flailing around she had done earlier had tangled her hair so badly that the tangles refused to come free with just her hands. She recalled the pendant comb and waded to shore and fetched it. Instantly she was falling into the water again. She peeked down at herself. The tail was back. She set the comb on the bank, and her own feet and legs reappeared.

Funny. She should have felt something but her only indication of the change was the way the bottom of the pool shifted under her when she switched appendages. Carefully, she sat her bottom on the bank and picked up the comb. Now she had a tail dangling in the water. She thoughtfully combed her hair with the gift, and wondered why even a mermaid would give her something that would make her even more monstrous than she was already. She pulled the comb free of her hair and looked at the swirls of pearly pink and blue twining among its teeth and embellishing the scrolled design in its top. It was kind of pretty and did look exactly like something you'd imagine a mermaid having. She wondered how a mermaid had known about her when she was a baby, and known her well enough to give her such a strange gift. Ah, well, it would come in handy fording rivers, she had to admit that.

Suddenly the small, downy hairs on her arms and torso rose in gooseflesh and not from the cold. She looked around and the brush rustled. A bird, she thought, before she heard the giggle. And heard footsteps running away. She snatched up her clothes and pulled them on as quickly as possible, never minding the headcloth, or thinking to braid her hair again, she ran back to the camp.

The road to the next village was pleasant indeed, lined with fruit trees and flowers, the roadbed amazingly smooth and unrutted. There were not even many large rocks in the way to impede the wheels.

But it still took the lead caravan three full hours before it pulled abreast of the outermost house in the village. And no castle had yet appeared on the horizon.

Romany was riding inside the caravan today, instead

of riding one of the horses or walking beside it. Choomia insisted. "You'll just be upset by people talking of what happened last night and besides, until we can find more dye, you'll burn like a bonfire if you're out in the sun."

Privately, Romany thought her mother was ashamed of her. Her people would make fun of her, she was sure, over Misha running away and the elves mocking her dance. She was afraid she'd lose her temper and sweep up the trail with the first person who opened his mouth about it. So she stayed in the caravan and tried to enjoy the ride and soon succeeded.

She found it impossible to dwell on unhappy things for long, as the day was lovely and Timoteo walked beside the horses and played lively tunes on his fiddle to pick up the pace.

At last they came to the village.

"This is a queer looking place," Romany said to Choomia through the open front door of the caravan. The town's rooftops were not tiled or thatched but covered with grass on which grew gardens of flowers. A bower of roses grew around each door and each door itself was red. The windows were covered with some sort of stuff that shimmered in the light like an insect's wing, reflecting the colors of the blooms in the flowerboxes under the windows. "Pretty, though."

"Pretty is as pretty does," Choomia said.

People who were not as tall as elves, or as slender, but who had nonetheless the pointed ears and the same make on them, came to the doorways to watch the caravans pass. Some of the people were not truly fair, but had brown hair. Romany saw no children and no old people. But at least no one made to call the guards.

"Who are these folk, living here?" she asked Choomia. "They look like common villagers, but I thought you said all elves were wealthy, and isn't this their own land?"

"Got to have someone to push around, don't they?" Choomia said through the side of her mouth not occupied with one of the small cigars she smoked when traveling. "Do you mind the stories told round the fire of children disappearing? Two things about elves, daughter. They're immortal and unless they mix quite thoroughly with humankind, they can't make children, except by magic and then only briefly. And that's strange because in the stories you hear of them from the old ones, they were always at one another, no more morals than cats."

As they rolled past the shops, suddenly people ran out of the buildings and began jogging along beside the caravans. Choomia puffed on her cigar and whipped up the horses, but the nearest merchant said, "Madame, I mean you no harm. I simply wish to inquire if you've anything to sell or trade."

"You want to buy a horse? Have your fortune told?" Choomia asked.

"I was thinking more of—well, one of those lovely bandanas you ladies wear, or perhaps an authentic Gypsy tambourine."

"Madame," the man from the other side said, holding up a pair of earrings with the pretty bells such as Lady Rawnie had held. "I'll trade you these lovely earrings for your own. See how they shine? Hear how they tinkle?"

Romany's own were plain small gold hoops, unbefitting the woman she had—well, almost-become last night. "I'll trade him mine!" she said.

"You will not," Choomia said.

Timoteo was surrounded by people begging, "Master fiddler, play us a tune, please."

"Oh, yes," the women clapped their hands like children.

"Their sort do love music," Choomia said, almost softening toward them.

"I'm a poor man, and my kinfolk and I are weary from our long journey. Weary and thirsty. And very very poor."

"Bring his honor a chair!"

"Bring food!"

"Bring wine!"

The pretty people hurried to get all of these things until every gypsy standing was seated and each person in the band had a bit of cake and a cup.

"Play for us, please," one especially pretty lady in silvery mossy green pleaded.

"Have you a request, pretty lady?" Timoteo asked

with a gallantry that did not offend his wife, since such flattery sometimes gained an extra coin or two.

"Oh, yes! Play an authentic passionate fiery gypsy love song!" she said, almost on her knees in her effort to cajole Timoteo, who really needed very little encouragement.

He began playing and as he did, the lady began to mimic gypsy dancers while, behind Timoteo, a man raised a conch shell above his head.

'What you think you're doing, you?' Choomia demanded, snatching the shell and cuffing the man on the back of the head. "Gonna brain my man, were you? Take that!"

Timoteo, still playing, his eyes closed and body swaying to his own music, took three steps forward, toward the gyrating woman, now joined by several friends, also writhing, and let Choomia handle the situation.

"Madame, please, I was only making a recording of your husband's music!"

"A recording?"

"In the conch shell. Hold it to your ear."

She did and her glower turned into a smile, "Hey, it's just like my Timoteo. What is this, an elf trick? You steal his talent?"

"Goodness no, Madame. I mean to make him famous, so that his playing will be spread far and wide and last for generations."

"And how about his poor family?" she demanded. "His loving wife and young daughter? How about us? When my man plays, people throw coins—"

Or rocks, Romany thought to herself.

"How we gonna get coins every time someone hears this thing? Pretty soon people will not come to hear my man play, they will only stay home and listen to sea shells."

What she hadn't noticed, while she was arguing with the man, was that three other men were holding up conch shells too, well out of her reach.

Romany looked out the back door of the caravan. At every other wagon, scarves and earrings, necklaces and shawls, even skirts, sandals, boots and trousers, were changing hands—sometimes for elfin clothing, sometimes for coin.

But Choomia would have none of it, and clicked to her horses and drove forward, forcing the next wagon forward—it would not have dared to stand still when Choomia wished to go, even though the Whelan family was still trading clothing for all manner of other articles. They sped up rapidly enough when Rodrigo Whelan saw the look on Choomia's face and the way her horses were nose to back door with his caravan.

The others followed suit and Timoteo abandoned the dancers to swing up beside his wife. "There's a first," he said. "We've never been run out of town by admirers before."

"Pah!" Choomia said, and spat from the side of her mouth that did not hold her cigar. "How do we know we weren't cheated? If these people wanted the clothes off our back and the rings from our fingers and ears, how do we know the Rawnie wouldn't pay more?"

"She didn't say anything about it last night," Timoteo reminded her. "Maybe this was our only chance."

It seemed as if it might be when, two hours later, they still had not seen Glenn Bloodbath, the village of which Rawnie had spoken, nor her mountain, nor her castle. Choomia ordered the wagons stopped and went to each of her people to assess what they had let go of and what they had taken in trade.

"What you gonna do with that elf-dress?" she asked Misha's eldest sister, holding the tiny dress up to her own stocky frame and mincing around with it. "It'll tear first time you try to climb a mountain in it."

"I'm going to cut it up for scarves and shawls. Maybe sell them somewhere else here," Misha's sister said.

Her youngest son ran back to the wagon in time to hear her words, "You better hurry then, Mama. There's another village around the next bend, and way off, the hill with the castle on it where that lady is making us the feast."

Romany tried to sneak out the front of the caravan. This being a woman was getting tedious. She was usually the advance scout for the band, riding ahead and spying out the territory. Red hair or no red hair, she wasn't going to be cooped up any longer.

But Choomia had eyes in the back of her head and saw her. "Romany, back in the wagon." And, like everyone, Romany did as Choomia said.

"Now then, all of you, listen to me. See what you're offered, yes, but trade nothing until you see the going price—not that there's much left. Instead we play music for them, tell fortunes for them, dance for them, make up authentic Gypsy stories they can use to scare their children. And we get gold in return. Bite the coins to make sure. Elven gold has a way of changing to leaves as soon as you're well away from the giver."

Everyone knew better than to argue. Besides, their professional pride was challenged. Usually, they had trouble getting the towns to allow them to do anything within the city limits. Here were folk begging for what they had to offer. Little clay jugs were rapidly filled with water, colored with a bit of vegetable dye and tied with red or black thread, labeling them love potions or curses. Girls practiced their dance steps and those who knew a few tricks, a bit of knife throwing, sword swallowing, fire eating, and of course, fortune telling, sharpened up their skills, so to speak, and put on their finest and brightest clothing (those who still had possession of it after the trading at the last village). Their best entertainments were usually reserved for themselves, but here was a chance to show off for paying customers. And perhaps another cup of wine and a cake or two to tide them over until they could get to the feast awaiting them at the castle of the beautiful lady. The transgressions of her followers were quite forgotten in the excitement.

And so they strode into town, fiddles playing, tambourines jingling, skirts flying in a parade of dance steps, knives flashing as brightly as their professional smiles, ready to greet their audience.

Their own music was making such a din it wasn't until they'd passed the empty houses in the outermost parts of the village and come close to the square that they heard the other fiddlers, the other tambourines, the other bells, and saw the other dancers, performing before an appreciative crowd. This time the tall slender people in the motley improvised gypsy clothing and tinkling bells were not fair-haired—they had dyed their hair black, as Romany usually did, except where hers usually lay flat and dull and stringy-looking under the dye, theirs was bright and bouncing with blue and red light, belling around their heads beneath their headscarves as if it was natural.

Romany groaned to Choomia, "Oh, no, it's that lot again."

Choomia apparently had her mind on commerce, for she was slower than usual. "No, it's not," she said grimly. "Another band got here first. We never should have tarried so long in yon first village."

"It's them, I tell you. See, there's that stupid git who jumped my birthday fire—the wee puckish one who wears the hip shawl like a woman? Only he's colored his hair now."

"So he has. Well, you haven't, so keep clear of this. These ones are no competition for our folk."

And she gave a signal and her own people, who had stopped their playing, dumbfounded, to watch themselves being upstaged, began again. This time they performed with competitive loudness and vigor, the children going among the crowd and pulling at sleeves and skirts (and sometimes pockets, though these elfin folk, even the lower classes, who you'd think would need them, had an inconvenient lack of pockets, for the most part).

And the audience did come away, looking a bit confused, and a bit put out. The gypsies were more skilled, but they smelled worse, having been on the road so long, and not everyone having bathed as frequently as Romany recently had. They were dirtier, raggedier, *shorter, darker,* and suspiciously foreign-looking. Their agility and suppleness was less graceful, fluid and ethereal and more earthy, more animallike.

"That's disgusting," one woman said of Dudee's most seductive dance, and the men merely tried to look up her skirts.

"What need has elfinkind for love potions?" asked a beautiful maiden Choomia had figured would be a good mark, since the vain are always after more admiration. "With my glamourie, I can have any lad I want without your fake medicine. Besides, I've tried them all in this valley. Twice. That fiddler, though, a bit fat and a bit old, but what wondrous music he makes! It makes me think we could make beautiful music between us as well. He*llo,* Grandpapa, want to fiddle around with me, hmm?" she asked, her melodious voice fairly purring as she sidled up to Timoteo.

Choomia grabbed her hair.

Then two of the men grabbed Choomia.

Then Timoteo almost forgot himself and brained one of them with his fiddle and Romany, quite happily, threw her dagger and pinned the hair of the sluttish elf to the nearest hard surface, which happened to be the saddle of a passing horse. The horse reared and kicked and whinnied and a free-for-all began.

For just a moment Romany was disappointed. Here she had thought they might all be like the Lady Rawnie, silken and gentle acting and soft speaking. But they brawled as well as anyone, these elves.

Murder was about to happen to someone when the little leaping fellow with the hip shawl whistled through his fingers and made everyone stop. "Cut it out, all of you! You're acting as if you're two jingles short of a tambourine! We're gypsies, you know. We have certain standards of behavior to uphold! Where are your manners, your principles?" They ignored him until he finally bellowed in a tone that started out as a roar and ended as a squeak. "In the name of my mother, the Lady, I command you to cease!"

The elfin "gypsies," muttering, clumped back onto themselves, as much as such graceful creatures could be said to clump. Melted together, perhaps, was more like it. Like streams into a pond. A very reproachful and resentful pond.

Before Romany's folk could press their advantage, the fellow continued, saying, "These people are guests of the Lady and are not to be molested but given every courtesy as we escort them to the feast in their honor. Madame," he said, addressing Choomia, "I am Nicabar, son of Rawnie. If you will allow me the pleasure of your companionship for the short and pleasant remainder of your journey, it will be my honor to lead the way to my mother's estates."

"That's all very well," Choomia said huffily. "Just don't try none of your fiendish seductive elfin tricks on me, my lad, or I'll thump you good. I've heard every line there is in my time." With that, Choomia flipped her graying braid from where it had tangled under her scarf, put her nose disdainfully into the air, and clucked to the horses.

"Not *proper* gypsies at all," the elf-woman who had admired Timoteo whispered spitefully, pouting to her friends. "Proper gypsies believe that it's better to cajole an enemy than to go about sticking dagger's in people's hair and frightening the horses."

Their self-appointed protector shook his finger scoldingly at her. "That's enough of that, Dooreya," he said. Then he mounted a fine black horse covered in tinkly silver bells and rode along beside the wagon. Timoteo had climbed up beside Choomia, since the idea was to put the town behind them as quickly as possible.

"Fine horse, that" Timoteo said to his wife. "I wonder if it would like to travel with *real* gypsies, eh, my love?"

"Psst," Romany said to her father, as she would never have dreamed of speaking to her mother, "Ask that buffoon where he got his hair dye."

But before Timoteo could speak, Nicabar began firing a barrage of questions at him. "Why does your daughter hide in the wagon? Is she shamed because her lover ran away? Will you be able to make another match for her? Will she mate with the boy before or after the marriage? Is it necessary that she be a virgin?"

He asked so many things, *all* of them very personal and about matters that even one's own kinfolk didn't ask, that none of them had much time to think up good evasive lies. Timoteo answered by telling him about his courtship of Choomia and then she chimed in telling of the great amount of wealth Timoteo had had to prove he had in order to win her.

The fact that they answered different questions than he'd asked didn't seem to bother Nicabar. He listened, his pointy ears seeming to quiver with attention, while Timoteo, Choomia and soon people from every caravan in the band bragged and complained, dropped dramatic and mysterious sounding hints or simply explained about all aspects of their lives on the road.

Once Romany thought she had a chance of getting a word in and stuck her head out far enough to ask, "What did you use to dye your hair?" but Nicabar was turned away listening to Dudee's husband Giorgio, whose voice was very quiet, explain the symbols and colors painted on the sides of caravans.

The people were so busy talking they didn't seem to wonder, as she did, why it was only now that Lady Rawnie's hill and castle were appearing at the end of the road. She asked Timoteo, who shrugged, clearly annoyed that she was intruding while he was trying to listen to the conversation churning around the elf. "Magic," he said shortly. "Elves are full of it."

The castle grew rapidly larger until she could make out the spires and crenellations, the towers and the walls, all gleaming with a soft palette of blues and greens, as if the castle were made of water.

As they drew nearer to the castle, delicious smells assailed their nostrils and the sound of musical instruments and tinkling bells filled the air.

"Sounds like they've started the party without us," Timoteo said.

After a lengthy and winding climb that crested at a plateau set slightly lower than the castle, Nicabar led them to a shady spot by a singing stream. Before they had the horses unhitched, canopies blossomed among them like wildflowers, blue and green, red and yellow, and under these tables were set with golden dishes and cloths so fine that Choomia said, "It's a shame to eat off those. They're better than my best skirt. I wonder what Her Ladyship would take for them?"

Slender elf people interspersed themselves among Romany's folk, pretending to help them make camp but actually asking questions. The elf women were flirting with the men and, in truth, the gypsy men didn't discourage them.

Twilight was very deep now. "Time to build the fire," Choomia said. "Fetch wood, children."

"No," said Lady Rawnie, suddenly appearing from

under one of the canopies. "Not here. We do not burn wood in my land. But you'll have your fire all the same." And she caused one to burst to flaming life in the spot Choomia had indicated.

Romany peered around the front of the caravan.

"Get back in there," Choomia commanded.

"I *can't*," Romany insisted. "I've got to go awfully bad."

"Can't you wait until after dark?"

"*No-oo*. I've been waiting all day and what with the jouncing around . . ."

"Your pardon, madame," Nicabar said to Choomia, as oily as Timoteo sucking up to the squire in a new town. "But you should allow your daughter freedom of the camp now."

"Not until dark," Choomia said stubbornly.

"But you see, it never properly *gets* dark here, not near Rawnie's castle anyway. She likes twilight and twilight it stays."

While they were arguing, Romany slipped her shawl over her head and ducked out of the back of the caravan. She slipped behind the other wagons and horses, and stayed out of sight until she was well into the woods bordering the glade and could have a bit of privacy.

After a time she stood with a satisfied sigh and adjusted her clothing. It was then that she heard another rustling, a moss-padded footfall. She stood still. Probably it was just Choomia, coming to tell her to get back in the wagon and hide herself some more, which Romany absolutely did not intend to do.

Nicabar appeared from the brush, the leaves forming a cap over his head for just a moment. "There you are," he said. "I need to have a word with you."

"I'd think you'd have run out by now, with all the chattering you did on the way here. What do you want? To know more about the elimination processes of the female gypsy?"

"There's no need to be snotty," he said. "Not when I've come to tell you I've decided to do the right thing. Besides, you'd hardly qualify if I was studying something about female gypsies. Most of them, unless my other research is very much mistaken, lack fish tails when they bathe."

"That was *you* spying on me, was it, you sawed off excuse for an elf!"

"No need to get personal," he said, grinning and clearly not offended. "This is a very bad way to begin our engagement."

"Engagement! You're daft," she said. This fellow was not only funny looking, he was full of fancies, and she meant to take no notice of them. "What do you use to get your hair like that?"

"Black you mean?"

"Yes, and shining and all. Can't be walnut bark."

"It's not," he said. "It's uh—a tribal secret."

"Tribe? What tribe?"

"My mother's."

"That's another thing. How can Rawnie be your mother? She's an elf, and *my* mother says elves don't have children. And you don't look like the other elves."

"Well, you don't look like the other gypsies, so I suppose that makes us a good match."

"We are not any *kind* of a match," Romany said, swinging around to face him, her fists on her hips. "You took that cake out of ignorance. It didn't mean anything."

"How do you know? It meant your intended didn't think enough of you to accept the piece he was given in its place and pretend nothing had happened. Face it, big girl, you don't fit in with the people in your band as it is. In time you'll be an outcast. It's my fault to some extent, so I've decided to do the honorable thing, as any gypsy gentleman would do, and marry you."

"You are *not* a gypsy gentleman," she said.

"That's what you think. I'm more gypsy than you are."

"Oh, *really*?" she asked sarcastically, wishing she wasn't the guest of his mother so she could just put her fist in his face and be done with his nonsense.

"*Really*," he insisted in the same tone. "My father was the King of the Gypsies—a fiddler—not like your father, young and handsome."

"My father was young and handsome, too. Now he's—fatherly."

"Indeed. Well, this fellow wasn't. Yet. My mother fell in love with him when they were passing through. But he had already married a woman who couldn't bear children properly—she had a deformed, sickly child who had no brains at all. And so my mother sent me to him and his wife. They were very good people and I stayed with them until they died, at which time my mother returned to get me. While I was with them, I learned all about being a gypsy and brought our culture back to my mother's people, who, as you see, embrace it."

"Umm hmm, and how old were you when your gypsy parents died?"

"About three."

"No wonder you ask so many stupid questions and wear a shawl around your bum like a woman," she said.

But by then their conversation was drowned out by the sound of fiddle, squeeze box and tambourines, with a sort of lilting flute in the background. The gentle evening breezes carried on them delicious aromas, no less lovely than the music. Roast pheasant, nut-stuffed fishes, candied fruits and hot breads, cakes with gilt icing, all manner of wine and beverages were piled high on the tables. Romany had a hard time believing the time she had spent in the woods, even arguing with Nicabar, had been long enough for all of this to be prepared—and largely consumed. It seemed already as if the festivities had been going on for hours.

Dudee's husband had an elf-woman on his knee. Her skirts looked like rose petals and little bells tinkled against her bare midriff when she laughed. Her bodice looked like two pink painted mushroom tops tied together with a bit of vine.

The children were clustered around an elfin magician, far cleverer than any of the sword swallowers and fire eaters in their band. Those worthies were too busy impressing the elf girls with their prowess to pay any mind to the magicians. Dudee was taking flute lessons from a man with fair, wavy hair and eyes that bore a calculating look as his hands strayed away from the flute, ostensibly to teach her to breathe properly. Miri was teaching that friend of Rawnie's, Fenelia, she called herself, to dance properly. Orlende was sharing a pheasant leg with an elf man who had started at the opposite end of the same morsel. Meanwhile, the two of them each had a hand on the thigh of the other. Romany was disgusted. Nicabar caught her eye and wiggled his brows suggestively.

At last she saw Choomia and Timoteo drinking and laughing with Rawnie. As she strode toward them, the three of them had raised their glasses in a toast.

"There they are now, the happy couple!" Rawnie cried, laughing, beautifully of course.

"Mama! Papa!" Romany said to her own parents, who were also laughing as if something was funny. "Not so fast! I never said I wanted this one." She jerked her thumb at him.

"What's to say? How do you know what you want before you've got it, chavi?" Choomia said. "Believe me, many girls feel this way when they meet their husbands-to-be for the first time. And yours is from a rich family, he's clean, not too bad looking, and, uh—" she rose and pulled her daughter to her to whisper, "he'll *take* you, and frankly, having declared yourself and having been refused, you're used goods now. No other man of our people will have you. Romany, my chavi, please, I need grandchildren. Humor an old woman."

"Yes, indeed," Rawnie put in with an enticing smile, flashing pearly, gleaming, and now, it seemed to Romany, slightly sharp looking teeth. "Not only is my Nicabar a fine, obedient boy, talented, quick and intelligent, he is even willing to follow *your* tribe's custom of giving presents to the parents of the bride if they are willing to follow ours and offer in return a small dowry."

"Dowry?" the entire band said in unison. Obviously this was the first anyone had heard of it. Romany grinned now. Her family and her band would never agree to part with anything to see her married to this elflet.

Rawnie smiled again, radiating warmth and generosity. "It's very little really. Generally, according to the custom of ancient times, the christening gifts are given so that the bride will have familiar things with her when she marries. The dowry doesn't go to the husband, of course. It stays with the girl, so she has something to bring into the marriage. But we'll discuss this later," she said, as doubt remained on the faces of all of Romany's people.

She stood. Her long, low cut green gown this time was topped with a skirt of crimson flowers and green vines, and this bound with a crimson hip shawl, the whole embroidered heavily with precious stones and hemmed with golden coins that clinked tantalizingly as she moved. She did not cover her glorious golden hair, but departed from the gypsy fashion to wear a wreath of red wildflowers on the crown of her sun-gilt hair. Her golden earrings and many matching bracelets, her begemmed rings and a long necklace filled also with coins, clinked and winked in the twilit evening in a hypnotizing sort of way.

"Fenelia, spread your shawl so that Nicabar can fill it with the first gift."

Nicabar had picked up a finely ornamented amethyst jar that Romany hadn't noticed before and from it poured a small mountain of golden coins like those worn by Rawnie into the shawl.

Timoteo gasped and Choomia picked up one of the coins and bit it.

"Now the horses, Simen, if you please," Rawnie said. And fourteen prancing purebred horses, seven black stallions and seven white mares, were led before Romany's people and hobbled with their own horses. Timoteo stopped to examine the teeth of the nearest mare and was mumbling approvingly to himself.

"And a brand new wagon for the parents, so that the young people can have their old caravan . . ." Rawnie concluded. Timoteo did not even tell her of the boards he had been painting for Romany's caravan in anticipation of her fifteenth birthday and the marriage that was supposed to have followed.

"Plus, of course, some scarlet silk, some bottle-green velvet, samite white as snow, and cloth of gold and silver. The usual. With a few gems for good measure and enough of our best vintage wine to toast the couple for a year." The woman who was surely going to become Romany's mother-in-law finished and Romany was sure that had Rawnie not been so fine and ladylike, she would have spit on her hand and extended it to shake on the deal.

Romany wondered that no one insisted on checking *her* teeth.

Nicabar did rub his hands together. "That's settled, then. I will marry Romany and will roam the world with you, as the traveling man I was born to be."

"Er—not quite, my darling," Rawnie said.

And Choomia and Timoteo also shook their heads.

"Why *not*?" he demanded, and Romany thought he was about to stamp his foot.

"Because according to our custom, the bride stays with her husband's family," Choomia said. "Though perhaps in this case, Lady Rawnie . . ."

"We'll talk about it. May I see what the girl has for a dowry?" She was as businesslike now was Timoteo at a horse trade.

Romany had had enough. "Am I a slave to be bought and sold like this?" she asked. She was so angry she was sputtering, but her voice came out as demanding as Choomia's, quite unlike her usual self-effacing and rather whiny tone. "They are *my* christening gifts, *my* property and if I am worth so many horses and so much gold and wealth as all this, surely I have a say?" Before anyone could get over their surprise, she continued, pointing accusingly to Nicabar. "*He* doesn't want to marry me because he's sorry he spoiled my ceremony. He just wants to continue to play gypsy. How many ceremonies are you going to let him bollix up? And once he learns our secrets, what do you think he'll do with them but sell them off to outsiders for the attention it gets him? Or bring them back home to his mother here." She nodded in Rawnie's direction and for a moment, looking at the beautiful, slender woman, who moved herself so gracefully, whose bells tinkled so delightfully, Romany could not believe she suspected this woman of any trickery, of having anything but her best interests at heart. Indeed, Rawnie's wide green eyes seemed to register dismay at Romany's reaction.

But then Choomia spoke. Romany's tirade had given

her mother time to return to her senses and for the gold lust in her eyes to die—mostly.

"My daughter surprises you, I see, Lady Rawnie. She surprises me as well. I did not think I had taught her so well. She never seemed to listen to me. But I see that she has after all learned a few things. You have given us many beautiful and valuable gifts to take from us this poor girl. And yet you are not a stupid woman. I cannot help but ask myself why you would do such a thing?"

Rawnie beamed at Nicabar and pulled him close to her. "Why, I have many reasons. Commerce for its own sake means little to me. I have and have had more than I can ever use for all eternity. But the happiness of my son, who reveres your people, as I have come to do, this is worth all the gifts I give you. I know that your people do not normally care to have strangers among you, and so I show you the prosperity that can be yours if you accept my son for your daughter."

"Also, Mother, don't forget to tell Romany's parents of my own gypsy heritage," Nicabar put in smugly.

"You mean hair-it-age," sneered Bowle, Misha's best friend, who mourned the departure of his former playmate and did not wish to see him so easily replaced. "Weren't you blond before, you elfin peacock?"

His father struck him a casual backhanded blow across the mouth and sent him sprawling. Bowle's father didn't handle wine very well and liked gold and horses very much.

But Garridem, another croney of Misha's, took up the taunt. "If you're such a gypsy, elf, where's your earring?"

Nicabar touched his ear self-consciously. One part of Romany was a bit thrilled to see Misha's friends, if not Misha, wade into verbal battle on her behalf. There was another part of her that wasn't so happy, though. This was the part that always made her feel very much an outsider among her own people. It was the part that felt so outraged when a settled person was cheated by a false fortune or had something stolen, that she invariably snuck around behind the caravans to try to find a way to reimburse them. Sometimes it was by giving them a bit of truth as she saw it to balance a fantastic fortune.

Sometimes it was to return a purse that had been stolen. This part of her saw Nicabar's face fall and while loathing the unmanly tears that glistened in his eyes, Romany nevertheless felt that she had to do or say something before the tears made their way down his cheeks, which would cause more jeers from Misha's friends. "I don't suppose you lot would know that much about being an elf either, if you never saw one," she said to the tormentors. "You ought to be flattered a gentleman like him wants to be like us."

Nicabar wasn't very grateful to have a girl stand up for him, though. "Like who, big girl?" he asked, and jerked her braid out of the back of her blouse. "A pale-skinned, redheaded giantess whose legs turn to a fish tail when she bathes?"

That knocked the gallantry and fairness out of Romany. She went for his throat. "You don't have to tell everything you know, you!" Suddenly a cadre of armed elves stood between her and her intended spouse and mother-in-law. Gently but imperiously, Rawnie parted the guard, drawing Nicabar behind her. She didn't look repulsed at all. In fact, she looked fascinated. "Is it true what my son says?"

Romany dug into her blouse, pulled out the comb pendant and threw it at the Lady's feet. One of the guards picked it up and with a low bow handed it to his mistress. She held it by the ribbon and studied it.

"Go ahead, take it! I give it to you! Along with the rest of my worthless gifts." She pulled off her scarf and her hip shawl. "Mother, go get those sandals and the other things I was given. You want to be rid of me, go ahead, marry me off to him. But you, you squealer," she said to Nicabar, "will have neither me nor my people for your amusement. I'll slit your throat on our wedding night and run away to join them."

"Romany!" her father cried.

"But first, I want a couple of my own questions answered," Romany said, her tongue moving faster than her brain now. "For instance, do you, Father and Mother, know what you're doing? Mother told me elves were immortal, and that long ago they killed most of our people and drove us from this land so that we took to the road. How then does Lady Rawnie, who must have been alive then as she is now, come to play the gypsy and have a son who claims he was gypsy born by his mother and a man of our people she loved?"

Rawnie began to speak over her, not more loudly, but somehow or other more compellingly, addressing Timoteo. "I see now that this girl is not a proper gypsy bride, and in fact lacks even simple manners. Therefore, you may keep my gifts on condition that you allow Nicabar to travel with you and I keep the girl here to teach her how to be a proper bride to my son, since you have failed to civilize her."

"I wouldn't marry her if there were no other girls in the world," Nicabar said with sudden revulsion, pointing at Romany's face. "Look at that! I thought I saw it the other night when I saw her fish tail, but I thought surely my eyes were playing tricks on me. Where'd that come from, big girl? Don't tell me you're half unicorn as well as half fish?"

Choomia came running back from the caravan, carrying an armload of things on what looked like a wooden platter. These she tossed at Romany's feet. "Here, daughter. They're yours to do with as you like. I don't know what to do with you, I truly don't."

"I think," said Rawnie, "that it is time the five of us had a private chat," and she raised her arms.

Romany, thinking she meant to call the guards, snatched her dagger from her waist and the nearest thing she could find to shield herself with, the wooden platter Choomia had brought her gifts on. To her surprise, it wasn't a platter at all, but really *was* a shield. There were two straps in back for her arm and furthermore, though the shield was small, the straps were large enough for her hand and forearm to pass through easily.

She turned her head slightly toward Choomia. "Mother, where did this . . . ?"

But Choomia was standing with her mouth open and both hands flung into the air, as she sometimes did when telling Romany she didn't know what to do with her. Timoteo was caught in mid-shrug. And all of the other elves and gypsies were likewise frozen in motion.

Romany turned her full attention to Rawnie, who gave

her a smile in which her teeth gleamed less like pearls
and more like the blades of silver daggers. "Just in time,
my dear. Good work. I see you are indeed who I suspected you might be. Only one of the Rowan line could
wield the rowan shield and protect herself from my
magic."

Romany glanced at the front of what she had taken
to be a platter. Red paint was chipping from it but a
branch of some sort of berry-bearing tree did seem to
be carved into the crest on the front of the shield. "I've
never seen this before," she said. "Mother must have
hidden it and then forgot to give it to me. I'm sure if
you take your witchy spell off her, she'll explain it all."

The lady just stood there, with her arms folded. Nicabar stepped toward Romany. "Here, let me see that."

"No!" cried his mother, and pulled him back. "Don't
touch that or you'll be undone!"

"I only wanted to see the crest, Mother," he said.
"What's wrong with that? And why would a *girl* get it
for a christening present, and a gypsy girl at that?"

"Yes, why would I?" Romany asked, advancing on
Rawnie, who stepped back first one, then two, paces.
"Why, you're afraid of this, aren't you?"

"Why should I be? I can unfreeze my guards at any
time and have you all taken to the dungeon."

"Mother, please, you're embarrassing me!" Nicabar
protested. "These are my friends! Soon to be my
relatives!"

"I don't think so, dear. You really must get over this
gypsy phase of yours. It's getting tiresome. I only went
along with it thinking that perhaps by casting my net
over the wanderers, I would catch this band and this
false daughter of theirs."

"Why? What has she done? Is she a very great
monster?"

"Shut up, you! And you, lady, you unfreeze my parents or I'll cut you good, I swear I will."

"Oh, very well. But they're not to speak unless spoken
to," Rawnie said, and nodded toward each of them.

If Rawnie had been deceiving them, she had been deceiving her son as well.

"Mother, don't do this. For the love of my father, let

these people go. If this is to make me stay here, I will. I won't leave you, even to wander with my people. But these people must be free or die."

"Oh, do be quiet, Nicabar. I'm sick of your romanticizing. These people are nothing but the dregs of a barbaric race who thought they had a right to this land simply because they had spread their seed upon it. There was a certain primitive charm to them, true, but they had to go. My own father was the one who rooted them out and exterminated all of those who hadn't the sense to flee. Oh, I know what you're going through. I, too, once thought them noble and adventurous. I even went so far as to offer myself to one, once, when they were camped by the border. I spoiled him, giving him my best songs to play, showering him with gold, but he spurned me, saying he had a wife. *And* a mistress. A pregnant one. And there, on the log I shared with him while I poured my heart out, that lump of a woman found us and jeered at me, at *me,* saying her man wanted a fertile woman and not some dried up old elf, unable to bear him children to replace the one he'd been searching for. I did not show that I was angry. I put them under a sleeping spell and in each of their ears, whispered that I was nothing more than a recurrent dream, now gone. Only at the last, when no one knew, did I express my true feelings. I raked my fingers down his cheek and took with me a little piece of him, and upon them all I laid a doom. Then I went home. What else could I do?

"My old nurse told me that the woman was right, that when your people left, they had laid a curse on mine that though we might live forever, we could never more bear children. I'd not thought that much about it before, to tell you the truth. I hadn't wanted children, yet I saw women who had them. I asked my nurse of this and she laughed at my innocence. "Those are changelings, my Lady," she said to me. "Only changelings."

"I asked what she meant and she told me they were the children of mortals. One of us might enchant a log, say, or a tiresome goat, even a frog, and cause it by glamourie to resemble a certain child. Then we would exchange that child for the mortal child, and thus have a real child to hold until it grew to be stupid and ordinary like its parents, at which time it could be trained to become a servant."

"You took me from my real parents, then?" Nicabar said. He was not so pleased with his mother now. "Or will you claim that I am actually a log?"

"Oh, no, dear, you were a fox kit. But I was not content with the simple spell. I intended to make Jacopo be haunted with dreams of me again, the part of me he saw in you. I took the bits of his skin from under my nails, and a lock of my own hair, and by my magic fused these with the fox kit, until the whole became you. In my pool I saw that their babe was born, and I disguised myself as a gypsy using the very dye you have today, and took myself by magic to their camp. Where their squalling, puling infant lay asleep, I took it from its blanket and left you instead, my son. So you see, although you are a changeling, you really are flesh of his flesh and mine and more than worthy for any bride or any adventure you wish."

"And you're *proud* of that?" Romany asked. "It's as if you took his father by force."

"Yes. Isn't it?" she said, the silver dagger teeth showing again. "But it served him right."

"No wonder you froze our people as well as theirs!" Nicabar said, drawing himself up with righteous indignation. "You don't want them to hear that their Lady, their Phuri Dai, dishonors honorable men, steals children, and breaks her own hospitality with her invited guests!"

"And raises impudent children," she added with a lift of the brow. "Don't be silly, dear. I froze them because it pleased me to do so. I'm not ashamed of what I've done. Everyone does it. If they want to."

Romany advanced on her another step so that the Lady had to bend backward against one of the frozen guards. One more half step and Romany was touching her with the shield.

And a very strange thing happened. The moment she was touched by the rowan shield, the Lady's beauty vanished. She was still tall, but her slenderness was bony scrawniness. Her teeth were long and yellow and her green eyes clouded by a wilderness of fury, grief, cunning, and pain. And something else that might have been remorse, but it seemed so out of character that Romany discarded the notion at once.

"Release us all or I will stay here until you rot that way," Romany threatened.

"I will not. Not until you marry my son and declare your intention to live here with me. Otherwise your people can die of hunger where they stand."

Choomia's mouth was working, and she was running around waving her arms but still could not speak. Timoteo pointed to his own mouth.

"You may speak," Nicabar said.

"Keep your gifts, woman," Choomia told her. "This marriage must not take place."

"Look, the horses are nothing but rats and the gold has turned to dead leaves," Timoteo said.

"Typical elfery," Choomia said disgustedly. "Leaves for gold, rats for horses, and the proposed bridegroom not only started life as a fox, but is the girl's half brother as well."

"Don't be ridiculous!" snapped the Lady, still looking very unladylike while in contact with Romany's shield. "Do you know who this girl *is*?"

"Yes, we do," Timoteo said. "Did you know who your friend Jacopo was?"

"A good-looking man with poor taste," Rawnie spat.

"Romany, let her up, but stand near her," Timoteo said. "If she gets up to her tricks again, touch her again."

"My father was King of the Gypsies," Nicabar answered. "Mother always said so."

"He was also the King of Ablemarle, until he and his wife had a falling out over the disappearance of their daughter. He abdicated his title, left his wife the Queen, rejoined his people and remarried. In the meantime, Choomia and I, with the help of another relative of hers, reclaimed the child. Jacopo died mysteriously before we could reunite them however."

"What did you do to him?" Nicabar asked, his voice quiet. "What did you do to my father?"

"Don't you remember? He died in that fire, trying to save you and your mother when she carelessly tipped over a candle inside her wagon. You were never in any danger of course. I had you out well before he even entered the caravan. But neither of them survived. It was just as well. It was time for you to rejoin me."

"But I was just a changeling!" Nicabar said. "You told us so yourself!"

Rawnie reached out to touch his cheek but he recoiled from her. "Ah, but for one to be a true changeling, I should have had something in exchange, and their child was dead. Most of the creatures we place with them instead of children are noxious things, tiresome things, but your father, instead of being tormented by you, cared for you. Even *she* did. And she couldn't have you. Not you and him both. So I brought you home to me. After all, you may not be the child of my loins, but you are still part of me and part of him. I only want what's best for you."

"And you thought that the Crown Princess of Able-marle would do nicely, eh?" Timoteo thought.

"What?" Romany asked, almost dropping her shield. "Do you mean *me*?"

"Of course they do, you silly girl," Rawnie said. "how many other gypsy girls do you know who are as large as you are, with red hair and pale skin, and with such elaborate christening gifts? I couldn't tell at first when I saw you in all that dye, but your size was impressive. On your mother's side, you are of Frost Giant lineage, as well as some elfin blood, which is what gives you a certain beauty despite your gauche bearing and behavior. All you seemed to have inherited from your father was your black eyes and a taste for gaudy clothing and travel. When Nicabar reported to me what you looked like in your bath, I thought it must be you, but when he told me about the comb, I knew it had to be. The mermaids bragged from shore to shore of their magical christening gift to the missing princess."

"First I heard of it," Romany said, stooping to pick up the comb, which lay at Rawnie's—she could no longer think of her as any sort of a lady—feet.

"The positive proof is in the rowan shield. Ablemarle is an ally of Aire. In fact, I believe your maternal grandmother and I are distant cousins—her branch of the family left Aire before we rid the land of *these* creatures," she waved her hand dismissively at Romany's people.

"Ask them why they did not return you to your mother, knowing that your father was dead. Ask them why they didn't give you your shield at your birthday celebration, and why they were trying to marry you off without telling you who you were. Go on. *Ask* them." And she regarded Choomia and Timoteo with a haughty, triumphant glance.

Romany turned slowly to her parents, whose mouths were moving uselessly as if they had once more been forbidden to speak. As indeed they had been, unless given permission. "Mother, Father? You knew this? I thought you took me in out of kindness, because I was a monster. I thought I was ugly and that was why I had to hide myself behind dye."

"No, no, my beauty, you were never ugly. Never did we mean for you to think so. It was only that you had to be disguised as much as we could—" Timoteo said.

"To keep you safe," Choomia added. "As your father wished. Your mother had her throne and her country, but he had only you, and he feared if you lived in the palace you would be stolen again."

"But no one steals a child from us," Timoteo said. "It is a point of pride. We hid you, disguised you and kept you safe."

"I can understand that you would do that until I was old enough to look out for myself, but why try to marry me off?"

"We wanted you to choose for yourself at first and Misha, he was a nice boy."

"Hah!" Rawnie said. "They wanted you to marry one of their own to reinforce the Gypsy blood controlling the throne of Ablemarle, so that a child three quarters gypsy would succeed you to the throne."

"No, we didn't. We wanted only her happiness, her safety," Choomia protested.

"But you tried to marry me to that one," Romany said with a jerk of her head toward Nicabar.

"Well, we didn't know what his family was like at first and your father said to me, 'Ah, well, she has to marry someone.' And he showed proper respect to your people," Choomia said, but she could not look Romany in the eye when she said it. She, who could tell the most outrageous fortunes to gullible clients without blinking, could not meet the eye of her daughter. And Timoteo seemed to be staring off into space, as if he might start whistling at any moment.

"It was the money she offered, wasn't it?" Romany asked. "You knew who I was, knew my mother was longing for me, had my future entrusted to you by my father, and you were going to sell me to *her* for *him*."

"Someday you'll understand, daughter . . . Romany. It is our way that a girl be settled with a man of wealth, if possible. It is a good thing. When you're older, you'll understand and we'll laugh about this."

"Before I'm older by a single day, you'll never see me again," Romany declared. "What of this stone in my head? What is that?"

"It happened at your christening," Timoteo said. "A great crystal idol broke and a shard of it lodged in your forehead. We don't know what it means really. We made sure you kept it covered because some of your enemies knew you were marked by it. Please, my chavi, don't be angry with us. You are the only daughter we ever knew. We wanted only for—"

"I know what you wanted," she said, still angry as her entire world, a world of lies, tumbled around her and left all of her ideas about herself, her parents, her home and her way of life in senseless shards. *"You,"* she said to Rawnie, threatening her with the shield, "will travel with us to your border, and guarantee us safe passage. And then I will take Slipshod, Fath—Timoteo, and ride away from you. At least I trained him myself and know *he* will not turn into a rat."

She left them at the border, turning north, toward the Sea of Glass, beyond which, she learned, was Ablemarle. They had promised to turn south.

With her was her rowan shield, proof against magic even as strong as the Lady's, her comb, the scarves and shawls and dangles of her gypsy attire and her old sandals, which Timoteo had hastily remade to fit her, saying they had magical properties, as all her gifts did. There were so many of them, and the christening so long ago,

that both he and Choomia claimed they could not remember them all.

She camped that night in a pouring rain, building a
small fire with green wood under a sheltering rock ledge.
Whatever her gifts did, none of them seemed to keep
her warm, or dry, or fed. Her clothing was soaked and
she had no warm caravan to climb into, no hot food
cooked with the other women and girls to fill her belly.
No one chided her or teased her, no one scolded her or
comforted her. But no one lied to her either, she
thought.

She was thinking she might as well go to bed hungry
when the hairs on her arms prickled with more than the
cold and she felt herself being watched once more.
"Come out," she said.

A fox trotted out and dropped a pheasant at her feet.

"Nicabar, I presume," she said, but began plucking
the pheasant.

The fox said, in Nicabar's voice, "I told Mother I
could not bear her company any longer after learning
what she had done, and your people—the gypsies I
mean—would rather have the plague than me for company now. You, it seems, are my only other family, Sister. I chose to come with you. Mother—the Lady—
relented before I left and told me I would have the
power to shapeshift between this form and man form as
I wished. I thought appearing as a fox was less likely to
get me killed—"

"You were right."

"And besides, as a man, I'm not a good enough hunter
to capture such a fine bird. And as a fox, I no need
of a horse to travel. So what will it be?"

She looked down at the sharp face and dark eyes of
the fox, whose hair was something like her own, who
had tried so hard to learn her customs, and who, like
her, had been kept in ignorance of his true origins. Besides, she wasn't all that used to hunting. "I usually like
a leg, myself," she said, turning the spit which now contained the plucked pheasant. "What will it be for you?"

They ate silently until the food was gone and exhaustion overtook them. The fox's breathing lulled Romany
to sleep and his fur kept her hands warm that night.

ELF HELP
by John DeChancie

John DeChancie has written more than seventeen novels in the science fiction, fantasy, and horror fields, including the acclaimed Castle series, the most recent of which, *Bride of the Castle,* was published in 1994. He has also written dozens of short stories and nonfiction articles as well, appearing in such magazines as *The Magazine of Fantasy and Science Fiction, The Kenyon Review* and many anthologies. In addition to his writing, John enjoys composing and playing classical music and traveling.

Once upon a time there was a very old and very tradition-minded manufacturing concern named the Mittelberg Shoe Company, located, appropriately enough, in the town of Mittelberg, Pennsylvania, not far from Philadelphia. Gottlieb Mittelberg, born in the German principality of Hesse-Nassau and emigrating to America in his boyhood, founded the company in 1790. In the long span of years between that date and the late 1950s, the Mittelberg Shoe Company manufactured work shoes and boots for farmers, farmhands, factory workers, day laborers, and machine operators. Its share of the market was always small, but it did a steady business and manufactured a fine product.

Until foreign competition almost drove it out of business. Gerald K. Mittelberg, great-great-great grandson of Gottlieb and president of the firm until his death in 1961, was a political animal who loved to wheel and wheedle in Washington. He turned the company to manufacturing specialized footwear for highly specialized jobs—shoes for aircraft workers who walked on the delicate, burnished wings of supersonic aircraft, shoes for brave engineers who traipsed around the containment buildings of nuclear reactors (with soles that would not pick up any "fleas"—microscopic flecks of reactor core material), shoes for the tiptoeing workers who tinkered nuclear warheads together, shoes for all sorts of esoteric medical and scientific uses, and, most lucratively, exquisitely crafted nonskid, nonshedding, dust-shunning, germ-intolerant shoes (at $10,500/pair) for technicians to tread the meticulously clean rooms where space satellites, probes, and other lapidary technological wonders are assembled.

The Mittelberg shoe company did well during the '60s, '70s, and '80s, raking in hundreds of millions in defense and other contracts. But then came the 1990s, the end of the Cold War, defense cutbacks, a Democratic administration, and other calamities.

"No illegal immigrant workers! That's out!"

"Take it easy, Jerry," John Szell, VP in charge of production, told his agitated boss. "Nobody said anything about illegal immigrants."

"I take two weeks hiking in New Mexico. When I get back, I got a sweatshop," said Gerald K. Mittelberg II (son of Anton "Andy" K. Mittelberg, who had recently and tragically succumbed to Alzheimer's Disease at the age of sixty-one). "The Mittelberg Shoe Company has never stooped to running a piecemeal operation." He ran a hand over his bald pate, ironically enough, to wipe sweat. "Damn hot in here. Lower those blinds, would you, Krista?"

Jerry Mittelberg's huge desk angled out from a wall into which was cut a window with a panoramic view of the warehouse's loading dock, where a titanic eighteen-wheeler was inching backward up the steep slope of the parking lot. The factory had been built on a hill that the dray horses of yore found not uncongenial, but up which the big rigs of today grunted and complained. The eighteen-wheeler let out a blast from its diesel.

"We're running the air-conditioning on low to save electricity," said Krista Lutz, the company comptroller. Still attractive and looking surprisingly young for her age, she had started as a secretary years ago. It had been a big company event to have a woman move into Upper Management.

"We're always saving money," Mittelberg complained. "And losing money."

"Well, look, Jerry," John Szell went on, "we're always saying that with NASA and defense cutbacks, and the nuke plant freeze, we can't make enough from the high-tech footwear business, so we gotta have a new product line. Ordinary shoes for ordinary consumers. And if we're gonna offer product at a competitive price, we either have to contract out the manufacturing to foreign contractors—"

"Never!" Mittelberg said. "This is an American company, always has been, always will be. No farming out to Pacific Rim sweatshops. I won't have our shoes stitched together by ten-year-olds. We got ethics. This town was founded as a religious community, long ago. We have a tradition of charity and goodwill to uphold. Old Gottlieb would spin in his grave if we didn't."

"Right," Szell agreed. "We got an ethical problem. But we also have an economic problem. When you sell shoes at ten grand a pair, you can afford to hire American workers at competitive wages. When you're selling your shoes for forty-nine ninety-five a pair, you can't do that. But like you said, we got an ethical problem. So we let someone else worry about the ethics. So contract it all out to a U.S. firm. They hire workers who are willing to settle for something less than a competitive wage."

"I won't use illegal immigrants!"

"They won't be illegal. They're immigrants, but they all got visas and work permits. That's guaranteed."

Mittelberg sat back in his chair. "Yeah?"

"Sure. We don't have to do anything, we don't have to hire or fire, we don't have to do payroll, we don't have to pay workman's comp, health insurance, or any other benefits. All we do is open the doors of the shop at night and let 'em work."

"At night?"

"That's the way they like to work. All night, every night. All we do is let 'em in."

"That's a little strange," Jerry Mittelberg said.

"Sure, it's a little strange. But that's the way they like to work."

"I just don't know about contracting with an outside firm for something as crucial as sourcing labor," Mittelberg said uneasily.

"We've been doing it for years. Don't we use temp agencies for most of our office help?"

Jerry Mittelberg reached under his suit coat and scratched his trim waist. He liked to keep in shape. He ran or jogged every day, and spent vacations backpacking. "Well, put it that way. . . ."

"Hey, that's right," Krista Lutz said. "Never thought of that."

"Who runs this outfit?" Mittelberg asked.

"Guy by the name of Kobold."

"German?"

"Yeah, I think it's a German name."

"Well, appropriate," Mittelberg said with satisfaction, nodding.

"Sure. And here's the part you'll really like, Jerry. All the workers are German, too. Displaced East German workers."

Jerry beamed. "No kidding? Hey, that's great. That almost makes it . . . well, almost charity, fer crissake. Those people are hard up over there. We'd be giving them opportunity."

"Old Gottlieb would be pleased," John Szell said.

"He sure would! When can I meet this Kobold guy?"

"Got him waiting outside your office," Szell told his boss.

"Why didn't you say something? Go get him, by all means."

Kobold was a strange-looking sort, a short, thin man with a caricature face that put one in mind of a ventriloquist's dummy. The mouth was a bit too wide, the ears were—well, it was hard to tell about the ears, because they were partly covered by a sort of strange hat—a three-cornered affair of green felt that more or less bunched up to one side of the head. The rest of his attire was of various shades of green.

A strange-looking little man indeed.

"Gut ahfternoon, chentlemen."

Just these three words came riding on a Black-Forest-thick German accent that modulated a surprisingly strong, deep-throated voice. You'd expect squeaks from this fellow.

"Hi," Jerry Mittelberg said simply, a bit nonplussed. He recovered instantly and said, "Glad to meet you. Do sit down, Mr. . . . Kobalt?"

"Kobold."

"Kobold. Interesting name. And you're from what part of Germany?"

"The wild parts," Kobold said, smiling. (He said, *"Dee vye-elt pardtz,"* but we will dispense with distracting spelling.)

"I didn't know . . . well, I guess I did know . . ."

"Parts of Germany are pretty rugged," Krista commented.

"There still are wolves in the Schvartzwald and the Odenwald," Kobold said. "Few, and seldom seen. But they are there."

"Didn't know that," Jerry said.

"But the forest is disappearing," Kobold went on, suddenly wistful. "The oak and the beech, the larch, the birch. The pine."

"Oh, yes, I know. We give to environmental causes all the time. Don't we, Krista?"

"Absolutely."

Just then the big rig outside roared again. The effect on Kobold was remarkable. He jumped to his small feet—(my those were curious shoes—did those toes come . . . *up* a little?)—and craned his neck to look out the window. "Bah," he said with some annoyance. A bit shaken he sat down again. Noticing the curious looks he was getting, he smiled. "Noise bothers me. I am sorry. I do not like the big trucks. They come through the forest on the autobahns at night. They sound like dragons fighting. You can't sleep."

"Uh . . . yeah," Jerry said. "Sorry. Uh . . . your workers. What did they—?"

"We are shoemakers. We worked in the shoe factories. They have closed."

"Great," Jerry Mittelberg said. "I mean—sorry—that's fine that you have an experienced crew. Have they had much experience with machines?"

"We work with our hands," Kobold said.

"That's good, but our situation is going to change. We've put out a handmade high-tech product for years, but with consumer product we're going to have to mechanize the operation somewhat. In our high-tech operation, there're quality-control considerations. With the new line, though—"

"We can work faster than machines," Kobold stated flatly.

Jerry Mittelberg looked incredulous. "Yeah?"

"John Szell laughed. "Jerry, I should have set you up for this, but I couldn't resist springing it on you. We won't have to automate at all. These guys are used to storming."

"Ja," Kobold said.

"Storming?" Jerry and Krista chorused.

"Command economy practice," Szell went on. "You can't get materials for the first three weeks of the production month, so everybody sits around. Then the stuff finally comes in, and you have to storm to make quotas. Rush, rush, get out the product, all in a weekend, sometimes."

"Ja, this is how it goes, some of the time," Kobold said, nodding.

Jerry said, "But what about quality?"

"They won't be storming with us," Szell said. "But they can work like demons. They can put out product, good product, in record time."

"How do you know?"

"We had a trial run while you were in New Mexico."

Jerry's eyes slitted up. "It's a plot. My managers are plotting against me."

Everyone laughed. Jerry was a big kidder, and everyone knew he was kidding now. Actually, he hated being a business executive. He liked the money and the perks, but his real passion was hiking and backpacking and doing generally environmentally friendly things. He loved animals, especially the wild variety. He had once donated ten thousand dollars to a fund for nurturing the orphaned cubs of a puma that had been hunted down by authorities when it had killed a hiker. (He had not contributed to the orphans of the hiker.) He liked to think of himself as an enlightened, modern businessman.

He hated being thought of as a capitalist exploiter, and did everything he could to ameliorate this image.

He didn't like running a shoe company. He lived to explore old native American trails in the East and deserted canyons in the West, always on foot.

Szell deadpanned sincerity as he said, "Jerry, I didn't want to propose something so radical without absolute confidence in the plan. So I had Herr Kobold and his crew come here last week and do a dry run. What they produced was good product."

"What product? What product?" This time Jerry's concern wasn't faked. He felt a pang of guilt for having absented himself from the corporate quarterdeck so frequently over the years. *Serves me right,* he thought grimly.

"This product. The latest thing in athletic footwear. Radically new." John Szell took a cardboard box out from under his chair. From it he took a strange-looking athletic shoe and set it on Jerry's desktop. Its color was a bright forest green.

"Wow," Jerry said. "That does look radical."

Szell put the shoe's mate next to it. "It's the way it wears that you'll like. Try 'em on. They're your size."

"Really. Well . . . maybe—"

"Go ahead, Jerry. Believe me, you've never worn shoes like these. They're going to remake our company."

"Where'd they come from? Who developed them?"

"Herr Kobold, here," Szell said. "They were making them on a small scale in East Germany up to the very end. The trouble with their system wasn't that they couldn't put out quality. It was mainly productivity snafus and cost effectiveness problems that crippled 'em over there."

Jerry Mittelberg put the shoes on and laced them up. They really didn't look like much, but they felt good. They felt extremely good. He stood and walked a few paces toward the inner wall, then turned and came back. The fit was uncanny. He had the feeling that his feet were encased in the softest of cushions, cool, dry, and comfortable. More than that, he got an overwhelming sense of pedal *well-being.* These were shoes. They were shoes for walking, for walking long distances. For hiking.

He felt as though he could hike seven miles in these things, right now. Just walk out the door and light out for the horizon. Nothing could stop him. Remarkable.

"These are great," he said simply, still looking down at them. "But . . . the color?"

"Of course, we can vary the color all we want," Szell said. "That right, Herr Kobold?"

"These are green shoes," Kobold said without expression.

"Uh . . . yeah. But there'd be no problem, right?"

"The green is of the forest," Kobold said.

"The green could be a selling point," Krista said. "Green is a very in color. The environmental movement, Greenpeace, that sort of thing."

"Sure," John Szell enthused. "That's it. Krista, you may have sounded the keynote of our whole sales campaign. O'course, we'll have to take it up with the ad agency."

"We'll need a new agency," Jerry said. "A really upscale New York one. Product like this rates a blitz of an ad campaign."

"Actually, they're damned ugly shoes," Szell mused, almost in spite of himself. "Look at those funny toes."

"I think the toes are cute," Krista said.

"Still, kinda ugly, if you get right down to it. But strangely . . . I dunno . . ."

"Cute," Krista said. "I don't like the color either, but somehow—" She shrugged. "It works."

"I knew you would like them," Kobold said with a satisfied grin and an impish eye-twinkle. "Most people do. They are not fashion shoes. They are walking shoes. People should walk more. Too many machines. There are too many machines in the world."

"He's right," John Szell said. "There's the health angle. And those funny toes have to be good for something orthopedic. Remember Earth shoes? Those were orthopedic, I think."

"They hurt," Krista said, remembering. "Always made my arches ache."

"Anyway, 'orthopedic' always sounds good."

"I can't get over these *shoes*," Jerry Mittelberg said, still unable to lift his gaze from the floor.

John Szell guffawed. "Herr Kobold, I think you have a customer here."

Kobold's smile was erased by another loud snort of diesel exhaust, followed by a sharp hiss of air brakes.

"Ach!" Kobold got up, went to the window, and scowled through the antique mullioned pane. "Zere iss too mudge noisse!"

"Greenfeet" shoes were a world success. In fact, they were a world phenomenon. They caught on first in the United States, and the massive ad campaign—TV, radio, print, and World Wide Web—was merely icing on the cake, for the shoes seemed to have a sales life of their own. People bought Greenfeet and wore them. Children wore them to school and to play, grown-ups wore them to run and jog, and then began wearing them to work. Movie stars appeared on talk shows wearing designer outfits bottomed out by Greenfeet. The shoes became fashionable at all levels of society. Greenfeet went with anything people would wear. Fashion designers endorsed them. Basketball players endorsed them. Steelworkers swore by them. In cities all across the land, millions of green-shod feet padded up and down the sidewalks. Business executives wore them, secretaries adored them. Politicians and lawyers wore them. In courthouses around the land, dark-suited lawyers and judges shuffled around wearing green athletic shoes. Out the front doors of the nation's churches burst breathless wedding parties—the men in tuxes or morning coats, the women in gowns—all wearing Greenfeet, including the bride.

What people mostly did wearing Greenfeet was walk, jog, and run. The running and jogging and walking fad of past decades took on new life. Marathon foot races took on the importance of major league sports events.

Parks, trails, and forests became choked with people tramping through and over them.

Greenfeet shoes sold all over the world. You would think that a tiny manufacturing plant in Pennsylvania would have trouble keeping up with such universal demand. You would be wrong. Mittelberg Shoe Company had no trouble at all, until the day that Herr Kobold came marching into Jerry's office. Jerry had just been

commenting to John Szell that no one had ever seen
Kolbold's crew actually at work. Each night, the lights
would come on inside the deserted factory just after
dark, and would go out again just before dawn. At day-
break, the day crew would arrive to find piles of boxes
filled with Greenfeet shoes.

"It's spooky," Jerry said.

"But bottom-line effective," Szell commented.

"You never told me how you ran into this guy,"
Jerry said.

"Popped out of the woods behind my house. Just
came up to me and starting talking about the company,
how he could solve our problems."

"Just like that?"

"Just like that."

"Out of the woods," Jerry said, nodding. "Makes
sense."

Just then Jerry's office door flew open and in came
Kobold. He stalked to Jerry's desk and stopped, standing
arms akimbo, defiantly.

"No more! We will not make any more shoes!"

"Why?" Jerry Mittelberg asked.

"The woods are full of you people! You come tramping through every night! Tramp, tramp, tramp. Big feet,
all night, smashing down the undergrowth! You make
campfires, and you snore. All night!"

Jerry grinned. "You should have seen that coming.
People like to walk, take hikes. They like to walk in
woods. You like woods. You people."

Kobold scowled. "You know who we are?"

Jerry shrugged. "It didn't take long for us to catch on.
You're elves. Little people. People of the forests. You
made those shoes because you didn't like our industrial
civilization. You hate trucks, automobiles. You hated the
highways we built through your forests. You hated
everything about science and technology. They were
eroding the environment. And now you got what you
want. People go to work on foot, no matter how far
they live from where they work. Masses of people every
morning, all jogging, running, or walking. The highways
are practically deserted but for delivery trucks, the things
you hate most."

"This is true," Kobold said. "We did not think—"

"Of course you didn't think. Logical thinking is what science and technology are all about. You little guys think intuitively. But that's not always reliable. You didn't think things through. You thought that by getting people out of their automobiles, you'd turn back the clock to a pre-industrial age. And you've practically done it. All across the world, automobile companies are going out of business, and the factories that supply things the industry needs are closing. There's a worldwide depression, but nobody seems to care. That's because you magicked these shoes."

"Yes, we did," Kobold said. "You know this, too."

"Sure. Like I said, didn't take us long to catch on to what you little guys were up to. It was a plot. And we went along with it. You know why? Because I'm on your side. I've always been a big environmentalist. I like the outdoors, I love forests. I wanna save 'em, too. And if it takes a little magic, what the heck."

Kobold stamped his foot. "No more! We will not make any more shoes for you."

"I think you'd better."

"Why?"

"Because if this walking and running spell ever wears off, you're going to see industrial civilization come back with a vengeance. People are going to be tired, very, very tired. I mean, they're being forced by magic to go on foot. After the spell wears off, they'll be good and tired, and good and mad. They'll think up new ways to avoid walking. Souped-up new cars of every sort, roaring down those autobahns faster than ever. Drag races will take the place of marathons. No one will walk ever again. Science and technology have been dormant for a couple of decades. That was just a pause to rest. After Greenfeet, they'll come into full bloom again. Why, in a thousand years, the surface of the planet could be entirely paved over."

Kobold grabbed his slender throat. "Ach!"

"So, you'd better keep everyone on foot," Jerry Mittelberg said. "Keep those magic spells coming."

Kobold turned and stalked out of the office.

* * *

After Jerry's divorce, he married Krista, with whom he'd been trysting for years. They both went into semiretirement and devoted themselves to backpacking all the ancient Native American trails of North America.

They were just coming down the last leg of the Oregon Trail, about a hundred miles south of Portland, hiking down the western slope of the Cascades. The Pacific was in sight, and the scent of pine and fir was perfume-heavy. Their Greenfeet shoes, never tiring, carried them along as a stiff breeze would two sailboats.

"Did you know they were elves, right off the bat?" Jerry asked.

"Sure. Kobold is a German word for elf. Did you?"

"Sure. My grandfather used to tell me stories about them. About how you couldn't trust them, how they were always playing tricks on humans. But we got the best of them. The environment is saved. Nature has returned. And the human race is saved in the process."

"But the elves are mighty ticked off about it."

"They got no choice. And the best thing about it is that I didn't do it out of greed. I could have liquidated the company and retired comfortably."

"Not as comfortably as you did," Krista said.

"No, I admit it. Being one of the richest men in the world isn't at all bad. I'm worth more than Bill Gates and Donald Trump put together now. But that doesn't matter. I did it for the environment, for the Earth. Out of public-spirited selflessness. I'm proud of that."

"I'm proud of you, too," Krista said, trying to peck his cheek on the fly. She didn't make it. "Slow up!"

"Can't," Jerry said. "This new model is even better than the old one. You don't want to slow down for anything."

"Yeah. but I'm tired, sort of," Krista said.

"I'm not. Got to get to the shore."

"Why?"

"I don't know. Just gotta get there, to the very end of the trail."

They came down from the slopes and proceeded inexorably toward the water. The sun was bright, the sky cloudless. It was a spectacularly beautiful day on the Oregon coast. Ahead lay a rocky shore, bright with churning surf, its cool northern Pacific waters inviting. The smell of the sea mingled with the pine and the fir, and the effect was exhilarating. Jerry couldn't wait to get to the water.

He noticed lots of other hikers coming out of the woods. Hundreds . . . he looked again. Thousands. Thousands of people had been out walking this day, and they were all walking toward the sea.

"What do you make of this?" Krista asked, a little breathless. She wasn't in as good shape as Jerry.

"People gotta walk," Jerry said over his shoulder. "Come on, keep up."

"I'm trying."

They passed a line of shops that edged a two-lane coast highway and crossed the pavement, not bothering to look in either direction, for there hadn't been any traffic on it for more than a year. They hit sand and continued strolling along.

"Ah, smell that ocean!" Jerry drew in deep draughts of sea air. He felt absolutely wonderful. A tremendous sense of well-being, of completeness, of *naturalness* suffused his soul.

"This is the world we lost," Jerry said. "We have the natural world back. We'll never lose it again. And we have the elves to thank for it."

His Greenfeet hit the water, and he continued walking. Soon he was into the surf to his crotch. But he kept his stride. Behind him, Krista splashed to catch up. Up the shore a little way, other people were wading into the surf as well.

"Jerry, wait! This is the end, there's no more trail. This is it. Why can't we stop walking?"

"Can't," he said, feeling just a little strange as he splashed on into the sea. Then the stunning realization hit him full force.

He knew he wasn't going to stop.

WITH HIS OWN WINGS
by Bruce Holland Rogers

Bruce Holland Rogers is no stranger to anthologies, having appeared in *Feline and Famous, Danger in D.C.,* and *Cat Crimes Takes a Vacation.* When he not plotting feline felonies, he's writing excellent fantasy stories for such collections as *Enchanted Forests* and *Monster Brigade 3000.* He lives in Eugene, Oregon.

Once upon a time, in a valley where the trees towered like cities, there lived a man called Richard, a woman called Marnie, and their son, whom they had named Daniel. They lived in a little house with a roof that sagged and paint that peeled, near a logging road where the timber trucks rumbled by too fast, churning plumes of dust in the summer and scattering sprays of mud in winter. Wild blackberry vines overran the porch, and starlings nested noisily and messily in the gaps beneath the eaves. Anyone who turned from the road and drove along the tire ruts to the house might have thought the family poor.

But they were not poor. Richard was a code wizard who spent his mornings in the glow of his computer monitor, animating three-dimensional device-independent objects that he built up from two-dimensional images. FedEx trucks delivered his assignments and checks. Behind the house were clusters of satellite dishes that Richard used to upload and download the spells of his craft.

There was more to their wealth than big checks and satellite dishes. Richard's riches were in that certain smile of Marnie's, in the work that absorbed him, and in the hours he spent teaching Daniel to read. Marnie's riches were in Richard's low laugh, in Daniel's eagerness for fairy tales, in her peach and apple and cherry trees, her roses and rhododendrons, in the wild blackberry vines that long ago made the garden fences into a sweet and thorny wall. Daniel had his mother's stories, his father's books, and a bicycle for riding across the meadows. And birds.

Thanks to Daniel, they were all three rich in birds. Even before he could read, Daniel had studied the pictures in the old field guide in Richard's office. Richard had read him the names of birds Daniel had seen in the meadows and pine woods, and Daniel had let the birds themselves teach him their songs. Before he was five, he had taught his mother that even though robins and tanagers sang the same notes, they didn't do it in the same way. Robins sang as if they had something important to tell you: *"Pit-ik pit-erik pit-ik! Pit-ik pit-erik pit-ik!"* But tanagers weren't sure what they wanted to say: *"Pit-erik? Pit-erik? Pit-ik?"*

Before Daniel had come into the world, Richard and Marnie had noticed crows, magpies, and sparrows in the garden, and not much else. It was Daniel's attention that gave names and colors to the lazuli bunting, the yellow warbler, the rufous-sided towhee. It was Daniel who taught them to see how unalike the sparrows were from the mountain chickadee, or even how different the song sparrows were from the fox sparrows. He taught them to look for tricolored blackbirds croaking from the cattails where the redwings sang. And it was Daniel who showed his parents that if you walked across a meadow early in the day, the orange and blue barn swallows would spin tight circles around you, dining on the insects you had startled from the dewy grass.

At the far end of the meadow, Daniel would spread his arms like wings and whirl.

He could whistle the easy song of the chickadee or the lark's rapid fugue. But what astonished his parents was the harder songs, the sounds that no boy should be able to make. As Richard and Marnie, holding his hands, walked Daniel toward the river one evening, the boy opened his mouth and out came a bright rasping that sounded just exactly like a scrub jay.

Marnie laughed. Richard said, "Wow!" And together

they lifted Daniel from his feet so he could fly between his parents for a pace or two.

Of the stories Marnie told him, Daniel's favorite was about the origin of elves. It was a story that went like this:

In the beginning of the world, God dropped in on Adam and Eve. They greeted him with respect and showed him all around their house. Eve showed her children to God, and He praised them. "But have you no other children?" asked the Almighty. And Eve lied. She said that these were all the children she had, when the truth was that she hadn't finished washing some of her sons and daughters and was ashamed to let God see them as they were. But God knew the truth, and he said to Eve, "What you have hidden from me shall be hidden from your own eyes." So it was that some of Eve's children became invisible to her and are still invisible to us now, unless they wish to be seen. But those other children of Adam and Eve live alongside us in the meadows and the hills, among the stones and wild rivers. What seem boulders to us are their houses. What seem tangled forests to us are their farms.

"The *trees* are their houses," Daniel told Marnie once, "not boulders." He looked around the garden, then pointed at the great grandfather cherry tree. Ancient lower branches spanned the ground like bridges before they grew upwards. The tree was wider than it was tall. "*That* one is a castle."

"And who lives there?"

"The king elf! And the queen. And the prince. They talk to the birds and they watch me play. They watch you in the garden."

"Can you see them?"

"*I* can," Daniel said. "They're *dirty*. But they make things grow."

"Like what things?"

"All kinds of things. Roses. Rhodies. Everything! Just ask them, Mom!"

One day, Daniel's eyes were on the sky as he rode his bicycle. The crows were calling down to him, and he strained so hard to hear what they were saying that he pedaled right onto the road where the timber trucks drove by too fast. Just like that, he was dead.

At first his parents grieved as any parents might grieve for any son. Marnie looked at the grass around her garden, and she was angry. How dare it keep growing. Didn't it know the world was dead? Richard stared at the unopened packages that came from his clients. Why had he ever thought that images were interesting to shape? They were only empty echoes of a world that was itself empty.

As the days passed, they did not cease to mourn. They found no comfort in one another, saw no solace in each other's eyes. Indeed, the time came when Richard and Marnie looked at each other and saw no one at all. There was no one there to see. "Three take away one leaves zero," said the emptiness that once was Richard.

And the emptiness that once was Marnie said, "If he's gone, then nothing else can be."

So it was that they turned their backs on one another and each began to weave a spell. Richard began to weave at his computer, and Marnie in her garden. And as they wove, a silence fell over the house and garden both. No birds sang. The blackberry brambles twined their way across the road. The air between the house and the world began to shimmer. When the FedEx trucks came with packages, the drivers could not find the tire ruts that turned from the main road.

Richard wove with numbers, with computer words, with photographs of Daniel and images of birds. He wove a world of light and digitized bird song, a world visible only through the screen. In that world he searched for the Daniel beneath the image, Daniel who was a boy, a creature of songs and feathers, the original of an image scanned and vectored and rotated, morphed and masked and animated. All through the nights, he searched the images for Daniel, who would fill the empty world again.

Marnie wove with words and soil and leaves. "Where?" she said. "Where?" In her silent garden, she broke the ground with a spading fork and sifted through the clumps. She parted the stiff foliage of the rhododendrons, searching the shadows. From time to time she turned toward the cherry tree, feeling the eyes of the elves upon her and asked, "Where is he?" so they might show her which stem or leaf it was that hid her son from her. And day by day, as the elves invisibly guided her hand, their world became visible to her. The garden began to bear Daniel's shape—his face was a shadow in the plum tree, his hand was in the twisting of a daylily root. All through the days Marnie worked, sleeping in the nights. All through the days, she searched for traces of Daniel, who could make her whole again.

As they worked, the shells around their emptiness became more and more brittle. Richard still worked through the nights, and then through the days, and he never entered the garden. Marnie gardened every day, and then into the nights, and she never entered the house. Each forgot the other. The blackberry brambles grew higher and higher around the house. The air became thick with silence.

At last the days and nights grew gray, each becoming like the other. Neither sun nor stars showed between the blackberries that began to lace a canopy over the garden.

And still they worked.

In the house, light began to tumble from the screen that could not contain it. Daniel's image stepped into the world of the house, and he embraced his father. Richard cried out for joy.

In the garden, Marnie harvested the shapes and shadows of Daniel. To the daylily root of his hand, she added the apple branch of his arm. She brought these to the shadow of his face in the plum tree, added the spine that grew out of the Shasta rose. "Show me!" she said to the elves. And her fingers moved against stem and thorn, twined leaf and root to shadow, until at last Daniel's green shade stepped whole into the world of the garden, and he embraced his mother. Marnie wept happy tears.

The light in the house grew bright, and brighter still. The edge of the garden glowed with it.

The green shadows of the garden deepened, and stretched toward the house.

At the window, light and darkness wavered like a flag of black and brilliance. Richard's eye was drawn to it at the same time that Marnie glanced up. For the first time in an age, they met each other's eyes.

He is dying, Marnie thought, for there were deep shadows under her husband's eyes and he was pale as paper. Looking into his arms, Marnie saw what was killing him. What glittered around her husband was nothing but a game of images and sound effects. "That's not Daniel!" she cried. "That's only memory and light!"

She is nearly dead, Richard thought, for his wife was skin on bones and smeared with dirt. And for what? For shadows? The bundle she held in her arms was rose stems tied to dirty taproots and hung with spider web. "That's not Daniel!" he called out to her. "That's only hope and thorns!"

With those words, the light in the house winked out and the shadows in the garden faded. Richard stood alone for a moment, looking at the hands that had held his Daniel. Marnie wept.

The air was still and silent. The light inside and out was gray.

Richard opened the door. He opened his mouth, but there could not yet be words between them. He went to her and held her.

"He's gone," Marnie said.

Richard held her closer.

"He's gone," Richard said.

Together they returned to the dark house to sleep without dreaming, without memory, without hope.

Slowly, silently while they slept, the roof of blackberry vines began to unwind. Thorny tendrils grew back upon themselves. Bit by bit, the thorny ceiling opened, shrank back.

The wind that had been absent lifted the curtains. One by one, the insects that had been silent began to sing. The gray sky opened into blue.

Richard and Marnie woke to one thought, one absence.

They washed their faces. For the first time in a long time, they remembered to eat. And then they went out into the light of the garden, then into the meadow. They walked across the wet morning grass. Barn swallows, blue backs shining in the sun, spun tight circles around them.

Later, as they walked back toward the house, a scrub jay flew over their heads and landed in the great grandfather cherry tree. It sang with a bright rasping that sounded just exactly like a scrub jay.

THE UNBETRAYABLE REPLY

by Peter Crowther

Since the World and British Fantasy Award-nominated *Narrow Houses* (1992), Peter Crowther has edited or coedited eight further anthologies, continued to produce reviews and interviews for a variety of publications on both sides of the Atlantic, sold some 50 of his own short stores, and completed *Escardy Gap*, a collaborative novel with James Lovegrove published in September 1996. A solo novel, a short story collection, more anthologies and *Escardy Gap II* are all currently under way.

The trouble with discarded conversations was you could never find them when you needed them.

Skrodge stared around the room. He didn't simply *look*, he *stared*. He peered at nooks and crannies, even time-glanced forward and backward in case the words he sought had somehow been temporally displaced—but he took great care not to dwell on the mischievous shades of future possibilities. He shook his thick-maned head—almost dislodging his steep but somewhat crumpled conical hat—and lifted his right leg from the floor, taking hold of the thigh in his hands to suspend the weight. Then, with a furrowed brow and eyes closed in concentration, he passed wind with all his might, hoping against all reasonable hope that he might not follow through. Not again.

The air (and the noise) mercifully ceased, and Skrodge was more able to turn his full attention to the quest. He had always enjoyed a quest, particularly in his younger days, shlepping across the world in one direction, only to shlepp all the way back again scant days later—and with little but a spell-filled book and the occasional rune-etched artifact to guide and protect him.

The acknowledged King of the Elf Kingdoms—but now more old man than maker of magics—Skrodge's searches were few and inconsequential. But not so this one, he mused to himself. This one was important. He could feel it in his bones, and even in those of the many subjects which he had implanted over the years to minimize the onslaught of age. He dragged his arm-worn, wing-backed chair across the dusty floor and positioned it carefully. For a moment, he watched the constantly moving figures carved into the scrolled wood. The figures moved slowly and blindly, negotiating the thick handiwork of spiders where once they had traveled faster and unhampered, beneath long runs of hessian and the finest silk. Skrodge climbed upon the once-proud throne of his reign and stretched toward the rafters.

Where to start?

He reached up and curled his long, sticklike fingers around a small cocoon of fluff which he tugged at gently until it pulled away from the beam. Remaining on the chair, his face alight with anticipation, Skrodge picked at the fur ball, undoing the long, gossamer strands of conversation-dust. He concentrated so as not to break the threads and thus muddle the words. As he worked, the tiny, elongated arm of one of the imprisoned sprites curled away from the chair back and touched his leg before withdrawing. Skrodge kicked his leg against the wood, barking his shin. He muttered gloomily and continued.

After several minutes of careful picking he created a small split out of which, with a soft *phtttt!*, a wadge of dialogue flew into the air, traveling around the ceiling like a trapped bird. It wasn't the one he sought.

"How many years until never, Lamb?" he heard his long-ago voice ask. "Too many to worry, oh, King," came the warbled reply. "Why does time concern you so?" it added. "Oh," his own voice said, sounding tired and paradoxically older than it did now, "it does not worry me. I inquire only that it may pass." The sounds faded into the rafters like liquor haze and were gone, echoing faintly as the old wood gobbled them up greedily.

He dusted his hands together and heard the chittering

clash of mutterances and teeth-clack, and then looked around the room at the other minuscule balls. He set his face in grim determination and droned a few words, a simple flattering, and waited until his arm had fully extended. Then he reached out and brushed his pliant fingers around the dust and grime and cobwebs and watched them fall and split open, tumbling long-forgotten words into the late afternoon.

"The sea shouts loudest in the autumn—"

"When do we count the sometime blessings of—"

"There's a man on the beach, look, over—"

Skrodge's room was suddenly afire with talk, not one conversation but many, all of the conversations that had taken place within the four walls since the last cleaning, long, long ago. The words and phrases fell freely, wafting and dopp1ering around the room, a hubbub of questions and answers and opinions and fears and suppositions. Skrodge stood silently still on his throne, concentrating on the many voices—most of them his own—as, one by one, the voices grew fainter, and fainter, and fainter still, until, like a plague of fluttering balloons spewing air onto the winds, they faded away completely.

Nothing. The words he wanted had not been there.

The King of Elves pushed back the sleeves of his cardigan and tutted, shaking his head. Getting down from the chair he thought how good it had been to hear Lamb's voice again after so many years.

"It was good to hear you again, Lamb," he said to the carcass hanging from the window top. The carcass grinned its rictus grin and turned slowly in a sea breeze which drifted through the open window. The words drifted up above his head and collided gently with one of the ceiling rafters, immediately pulling dust to them and folding themselves into a tiny cocoon which adhered itself to a small patch of splintered grain.

The mark on the wall was slightly larger again, he noted as he shifted the chair back to its formal position. It had spread around the latest of his penciled outlines and now looked for all the world like a long stain of spat bilberry juice, narrow at the top, wider in the middle, and trailing off to a spindly, shaky taper. He felt a mixture of curiosity and apprehension. He had spoken of something to do with this he was certain, and not so very long ago. But what had he said? And to whom?

He looked around the clutter of furniture, letting his eyes wash over the old-woman skin of dear Assidora, the Elf Queen, hanging over the hearth . . . letting them drink in the pleasing patches of death-light around the old couch where his wife had breathed her last, and the rickety three-legged chair and matching table where he had scribed most of his books of spells and incantations. Looking around the room he caught sight, out of his eye corners, of the dust-protected one-sided conversation he had just had with Lamb as it detached itself from the ceiling and drifted to the polished worktop beneath, where it landed with a dull *plip*.

Skrodge frowned. He walked over to the worktop and lifted the ball from where it lay, turning it in his hands . . . gently, so that he would not free the words so soon after they had been cocooned. The ball seemed secure enough and surely sufficiently adherent to stay on the ceiling. He looked up and saw the unmistakable browny-yellow ring of a watermark above him and the faintest sheen of grease emanating from its center. Could that be it? Could the conversation he sought also have fallen from its place amid the rafters? He looked back at the worktop. There were no other conversation balls to be seen.

At first Skrodge felt thwarted, but just as he was about to sit down on the floor to meditate, he noticed that if he looked a certain way at the worktop, he could discern a circular mark which was noticeably cleaner than the worktop that surrounded it. He bent down and considered the mark from an even sharper angle. There it was, plain to see. Something had resided in that spot . . . something he had removed only recently and which, even now, possibly contained the information he sought. Skrodge concentrated on the circular mark and suddenly his eyes widened. He had it!

Spinning around, Skrodge marched across the room, ignoring the bulbous stain that shimmered on the wall— and which, had he but stopped to consider it, had grown appreciably larger even in the few minutes since his last check—to the uneven shelves that lined the sides of the doorway. Without hesitating, he lifted an old, cracked pot from a clutter of parchments and bone fragments. Holding the pot before him, he blew a mighty breath and sent a myriad tiny dust motes careering through the doorway and into the sea air outside. Then, carefully averting his eyes, and hoping against all hope, he held the object to his chest with his left hand and inserted his right into the fluted opening of its neck.

His carefully searching fingers found two soft shapes inside the pot. He lifted them out, allowing them to roll gently into the palm of his hand, and replaced the pot on the shelf. Then, leaning against the racking he had constructed for sticks and other makeshift supports, he placed one of the balls on the window ledge while he began to undo the other. After a minute or so, the loosened strands twanged abruptly, and a flurry of words sprang into the air, narrowly missing the ends of his whiskers, skittered around his towering hat, and darted to the ceiling where they ricocheted, amid a small shower of sparkling dust, and quickly gathered themselves into their original sequence.

"Then what is the holder of all answers?"

The voice was that of Skrodge, some few months ago. The question, he now remembered, had occurred toward the end of a conversation between him and a sea-elf who had washed up on the rocks with a broken fin. Skrodge had repaired the fin and, by means of several beakers of strong mead laced with a few leaves of gungic weed, restored the elf's good humor.

"Chimneys, spires and treetops," came the reply, delivered in a brittle chimelike voice, "for only they can see both what is to come and what has been."

Quickly spent, the words effervesced in a spray against the rafters and were gone. Skrodge scratched his beard, adjusted his hat, and reached for the other ball.

"What is the strongest element in the universe?"

The words were, again, his own. This was a meditative monologue, spoken on one storm-tossed night when the winds had swirled and the seas had raged, and Skrodge had by necessity cloaked his escarpment in a thin veil of tranquility that it might survive the elements at play.

"Is it," his voice went on, "the wind that blows down

the forests and sends the fragile houses scurrying along the ground? Or is it the water that rises up in huge columns, flattening all before it without mercy? Or, mayhap, is it the fire that rages in one or another part of the land, waiting to erupt in a cleansing conflagration and remove all that ever stood before? Still yet, might it be the earth itself, its unimaginable bulk shifting and tearing, without thought or design, to swallow up all that exists?"

There was a short silence, a hissing of air from within the ball, and then, "No, it is none of these. The strongest element of all is a simple one: it is belief. For without that, no other power could exist."

With a sharp squeak, like a duck's fart, the ball imploded and the freed words rough-and-tumbled along the rafters and out of the open window. Skrodge followed them with his eyes, saw the shimmering words, mere ghosts of old thoughts, skim the air currents and pop like soap bubbles.

In the distance, far along the uneven and craggy promontory that connected his escarpment to the far-off mainland, Skrodge could see a turbulence.

The way to the mainland was long and twisted, winding its way through numerous spells and keepsakes until it reached the shoreline. But though Skrodge could see the vaguest of outlines which denoted the world of mankind, he knew that, from the other direction, his own small world was protected from unfriendly eyes. However, he noted now with the faintest first sign of concern, the turbulence he had identified was directly above the promontory and some way out from the shore.

How strange.

Skrodge shuffled over to a tallboy of drawers from which a multitude of funnels and clothes scraps halftumbled. He thrust his bony hands into the third drawer and felt among the bric-a-brac until his hands found what he was looking for and he pulled it out into the light. An eyeglass.

Holding the eyeglass close to his chest, Skrodge walked to the door. As he passed the wall on which the stain throbbed darkly, he closed his eyes. It was much bigger now . . . and was it his imagination or did it actually seem to be moving as if with a life of its own?

Once outside, Skrodge lifted the eyeglass to his right eye and looked through it. It took him a few minutes to get his bearings, but soon he was able to discern that section of the promontory, all those miles away, above which the storm raged. The sight of it took him back, shook him where he stood, and he pulled his head away from the instrument as though he had been stung by a sea wasp. He shook his head and blinked his eyes quickly in rapid succession.

He had seen clouds roiling in the sky, from which sprang great lengths of orange light. In the sea around the promontory, he had seen huge waves, capped with gray foam, lashing the already crumbling edges of the path. But worst of all, he had seen something else. Something on the path itself. Something coming toward him.

He looked again.

Now he could see it plainly. It was a figure . . . a blurred, dark shape which shimmered as he watched.

Skrodge fumbled with the rusty mechanism on the side of the eyeglass in an attempt to make the image larger, but it was no use. He lowered the glass and stared out over the ocean, thrusting his face into the wind and feeling his whiskers blow with its force. As he stared, he noted with dismay that the turbulence now seemed more distinct to the naked eye than it had only minutes earlier. He turned around and strode back to his hut.

As he replaced the eyeglass in the drawer, he looked across at the wall. That the shape was larger now was unarguable. But, worse than that, it was now visibly moving, shifting, and swirling within itself. As he kept looking at it, Skrodge saw that the shape resembled that of a person and that the movements looked for all the world like the act of walking.

There could be no mistake. The shape on the wall was exactly that of the distant figure making its way toward the escarpment. And as the figure got nearer, the shape got bigger. Already it had covered most of its original wall and spilled off at either side and onto ceiling and floor.

Skrodge ran back outside and clapped his hands

loudly, calling above the sound of the wind, "Hear me, all you who live with me in harmony. I, Skrodge, the King of Elves and all things magic, call you to me for a favor. A piece of information. Nothing more. Hear me and come to me. Come now."

And Skrodge made the appropriate divining signs in the air and then sank to his knees in the sandy soil in front of his hut where the land narrowed to begin its journey across the swirling waters of the ocean.

Soon, they were all about him, all the creatures of the escarpment. There were griffins and centaurs and even a unicorn or two. Small, scurrying things on a multitude of legs, large things on thick pairs of trunk-legs and even a single, lofty creature perched upon a single foot which telescoped and sprang the animal into the air as a means of propulsion.

Skrodge gathered them around himself, stroking manes and rubbing fur, whispering phrases of beauty and encouragement to settle their nervousness. And when they were quiet and attentive, Skrodge asked them if they knew anything about the distant figure. They did not.

The old elf dispersed them then and called together all the flying things that coursed and swooped above his escarpment, asking them the same question.

Amid a flurrying of wings and a rain of feathers of all shapes and sizes—making the scene resemble one huge pillowfight in which all of the weapons had suddenly been rendered unusable—the birds and bats listened attentively, the silence being interrupted only by the occasional *plop* and *thrrrrp!* from one or another airborne backside. But the meeting had been in vain. They did not know either.

And thus it was, leaning above the swirling waters, cupping his wizened hands to his mouth, Skrodge issued a further Royal Elfly Ordinance to all the things that lived in the sea. As he waited for them to appear, he looked to the horizon and saw that the turbulence had spread so that it covered the skyline. Way off still, he could now see the figure clearly.

Within a few minutes, Skrodge was repeating his question to a host of finny friends, including mermaids—not one of which ceased preening herself during the interrogation—and even old King Neptune himself. None of them knew anything about the approaching figure.

"But it is getting nearer, my brother," Neptune mused from his position on the rock. "And it seems colder, too," he added.

Skrodge nodded, following the Sea-King's gaze, and pulled his cardigan tighter about his frail frame.

Neptune turned to him and, just for a minute, the old man's eyes seemed far off . . . as though they were looking past Skrodge. Then they refocused and Neptune smiled, though it was a smile not without an element of sadness. "I think it's time to go, old man," he said. "Our time is almost done." And, with a loud splash, Neptune rolled off the edge and into the water, disappearing immediately beneath the waves.

In a final attempt to glean information, Skrodge called forth the dead.

As always, they were with him immediately, wraithlike, opaque, and translucent; they skittered about his body like wind-blown scarves. Patiently, Skrodge asked them the question. But the answer was the same.

When the last of the animals and the birds and the fish-things and even the discorporeal had gone, leaving the old elf completely alone, Skrodge shuffled to the edge of his land and hunkered his feet beneath his bottom. He pulled his cardigan down around his ankles and waited.

He no longer looked at his hut. The last time he had looked at it, following Neptune's departure into the waves, the stain had filled the hut's inside with a cold darkness and, even then, the constantly undulating shape had been edging its way from the hut doorway across the land itself.

He waited in this way for several hours, facing into the steadily rising wind and holding his hat in place with his hand.

At last, the storm and the figure that marked it had speeded up considerably. Now Skrodge could see clearly, though the winds had grown in intensity and a stinging rain drove across the land and into his face. When it reached the end of the promontory, it stopped. Skrodge rose wearily to his feet and walked to meet it.

They were in the eye of the storm, a relative calmness around which everything changed and turned and crumbled.

The figure remained stationary as Skrodge made his way toward it. It was a man, of that there could be no doubt. All around him the dust flew in flurries, and the rain squalled in huge, wet sheets.

On his head, the man wore some form of protective headdress, like an upturned large-rimmed, black bowl. Nestled on the bridge of his nose was a contraption containing two circular pieces of glass wound around with a wire which stretched to and around his ears. In each of the ears was a shiny object from which some kind of tube extended and disappeared around the back of the ear itself.

Skrodge said nothing, only stared.

The stranger also stared.

On his feet were polished black slippers, each with a thick sole and an even thicker heel section. In the blowing wind, Skrodge could see that, beneath the strange, dark leggings—each one bearing a sharp creases right down the center—the stranger wore some kind of additional covering that seemed to go even into the footwear.

Above the leggings, the stranger wore a tunic. The tunic was dark, presumably to match the leggings, and fastened together by one of three buttons. Above the top button, the tunic cut away to the outer edges of the collarbones, thus exposing the chest area to the elements. The chest was protected, however, by another garment, a plain cloth of pure whiteness boasting an additional collar from which hung a piece of patterned cloth apparently suspended from the stranger's neck.

In one hand, the stranger carried what looked at first like some kind of weapon. It seemed to be made of cloth, but Skrodge saw on closer examination that there was some kind of instrument concealed beneath the folds of material, pointed at one end—the end which rested on the ground—and curved into a handle at the other.

In the other hand, the stranger held a multicolored

bag bearing some kind of runic inscription. Skrodge read it aloud, his voice faltering in the wind: "NIKE." Beneath the word was a strange flourish, like a signing-off.

"Nike?" said Skrodge again. The word seemed foreign, and this to a man who was a past master of all languages and arcane scriptures. Clearly it had to be the man's name. Without waiting for confirmation, Skrodge responded by slapping his left hand on his bony chest and saying, in as deep a voice as he could muster, "Skrodge!"

The stranger nodded and rested the bag on the ground between them. Then he crouched down and pulled open a metal fastening composed of many small teeth. Pulling back the sides of the bag, the stranger reached inside and pulled out a clump of white hair.

Skrodge frowned.

"The beard of Santa Claus, King of Children," the stranger said. He thrust the hair back into the bag and lifted out a small fork, broken at one end. "The trident of Satan, King of the Underworld," he said.

The fork went back into the bag to be replaced by a small pouch which swung on a speckled green cord. The stranger pulled the cord and emptied a few coins into his hand. "The gold from the very rainbow's end."

And so it went on, the two of them crouched at the end of the promontory: the oddly attired stranger (whose name might or might not be Nike) and the old elf named Skrodge. Behind one lay the vast panoply of mankind; behind the other, a simple hut.

The objects were withdrawn from and returned to the bag without any explanation save for a simple description. Among them were a pair of vampire's teeth on a cord; the shards of the vial which had once contained the waters of the fountain of youth; a tuft comprising the strands from the last flying carpet; a five-leafed clover; a pair of tiny buckled shoes once owned by the King of the Leprechauns; and, finally, the tiny, jewel-encrusted brassiere of Phelaine, Queen of Fairyland . . . the small strap on which, Skrodge noted uneasily, had been broken, the clasp buckled and bent.

As the last one went back into the bag, the stranger restored the teeth and rose to his feet.

"Who are you?" Skrodge asked.

The stranger shrugged. "I have many names. Call me 'Civilization.' Call me 'Reason.' Call me 'Doubt.' "

"But not 'Nike'?" Skrodge inquired.

"No," came the reply, "not 'Nike.' But call me anything you like; a name is not important."

Skrodge looked back at his hut and saw that the darkness had blotted it out so that he could hardly see it. He looked up into the sky and saw that the storm had now extended beyond and around them, and was already far away out from Skrodge's escarpment and up the sky path, behind the hut, which led to the eternal light.

Looking back, Skrodge said, "I think I will call you 'Stain.' "

The stranger shrugged again. "It is as good as anything," he said without any trace of emotion.

"What do you want of me?"

"Your hat."

"My hat? Why do you want my hat?"

"It's symbolic."

Skrodge frowned. "It's a hat," he said, correcting the stranger. "*My* hat."

"To you, it's a hat. Now. Once it was a crown," the stranger said as he reached out and removed Skrodge's conical hat. "To me, it's a symbol." For a moment he regarded the hat with an expression which was at once part sneer and part sympathy, fingering the moons and stars and the many faded runic symbols with a perfectly manicured hand. Then he crouched down and, undoing the bag once more, pushed the crumpled hat inside.

Suddenly, the Lord of the Elf Kingdoms felt old. He sat down on the ground with a thud, thrusting out a hand to steady himself. A sharp pain hit the hand and Skrodge pulled it back and rubbed it. When he looked at it, he saw that the hand was black. As he rubbed the blackness, one of the fingers cracked and splintered. He took hold of the finger gently and saw it crumble, watched the dust settle on the tattered fringe of his long cardigan and then blow away in the wind. There was no pain.

Skrodge looked at the place where he had rested the

hand just in time to see its outline on the ground filling up with darkness like an imprint in the sand fills with the oncoming tide. The stain now stretched from where the hut had been—for there was no longer any trace of his former dwelling—to within a few inches of where he now sat. As he watched the stain edge closer to his cardigan, Skrodge asked, "And what is this . . . this creeping darkness which gobbles all before it?"

"Progress," the stranger said. "A new reign."

And, lifting his bag, the stranger stepped over the Elf King and walked through the gathering darkness to the first stair that led up into the sky. The stair which King Skrodge had protected these many long years.

"Where do you go now?" Skrodge called into the wind.

The man stopped, one foot on the first stair, and turned, shifting the bag bearing his name from hand to hand. Already the storm had traveled up way ahead of him.

"I go to the final court, to stand before the last of the old thrones," he said softly and, Skrodge thought, not without sympathy. Not without some small element of regret.

Skrodge shifted himself and grimaced at the effort. "What . . . what is it that you seek from him?"

The man shrugged. "Whatever he holds most dear. I'll know when I see it." He frowned and, just for a second, made as though to lift his hand in . . . what? A symbol of recognition? Of fealty? Or simply one of leaving? But the hand dropped quickly and grasped the hem of his dark leggings. Turning to the stairs, the man said, "Sleep well, King of Wonder."

The stranger began to climb.

As the darkness spread into his right leg and deep inside his right buttock, Skrodge droned a short incantation. Then, reaching with his good hand into his cardigan pocket, he threw a handful of dust into the air. The last thing he saw was the strands of the conversation he had just had with the stranger gathering themselves into a cocoon and dancing off against the wind, back along the promontory to the world beyond.

"Believe!" cried Skrodge, though the word was lost in the storm.

Soon the darkness had spread across the entire escarpment and, even above the distantly rumbling thunder, a new sound could be heard from the direction of the now empty stairway.

It sounded for all the world like the knocking of great knees.

MORTAL THINGS

by Esther Friesner

Esther Friesner's latest novel is *Child of the Eagle*. She has written more than twenty novels and coedited two fantasy collections. Other fiction of hers appears in *Excalibur, The Book of Kings,* and has made numerous appearances in *Fantasy and Science Fiction* and other prose magazines. She lives in Madison, Connecticut.

All in the garden was grim and cold. The old woman plucked the edges of her cloak closer around her with fingers knob-jointed and red, their skin cracked and chapped with winter's chill. The lonesome stone cross rose high on the little slope where the garden's fallow beds climbed to meet the forest. It was a beacon of silver more than stone, and her tired eyes answered its summons with the mute submission of a beaten dog.

There was no wind. In the sky, the stars stabbed through the purple dark, piercing and icy as a woman's sudden, curt refusal of her lover. Smudges of blue hugged the tranquil humps and hollows of the banked snow, until the old woman's passing churned the solemn whiteness to a tangle of shadows. Her cape cut a plow's furrow all the way up the hillside until she came at last to rest her wizened cheek against the rough indifference of carven rock. The warmth of her sigh set a darkening patch of dampness against the cleanly cut granite, a moist breath of life that froze at once to ice's deathly sheen.

"Widdershins," she muttered. "Old Nancy told me that it must be widdershins 'round the cross to call up such as he. Gibberish, but still it's all I have to use in the last ditch. Perhaps all I need do is what he told me, but it won't hurt to tie a double knot. Old Nancy claims she knows *their* ways well. Firsthand, poor daft creature, though if she remembers even that much it's a wonder. And I'm even more daft for taking her counsel, yet I *must* be sure. Now which way—?" She lifted her weary face to the moon, which shone in full glory clear of the pine trees. A pause, a grumble over a mind that would not yield its wit as quickly as it had been wont to do, and then a choice made, a direction taken, and slow, majestic steps that still recalled the grace of a courtly dancing measure to trace a path three times around the silent cross on the hill.

She brought her lone procession to a halt only three steps past the place where she had begun it and glanced backward over one shoulder at the wreath of trodden snow her booted feet had left behind. The rich velvet of her cloak caressed a cheek that had known still more tender caresses in its time. A scent of sweet herbs still clung to the heavy fabric, gift of a son's devotion.

"Devotion . . . But love?" She shook her head. In the years when men had sworn that they were captive in her golden curls, she had valued the word as lightly as laughter, easily come by, easily dismissed, easily called back to her again with a snap of the fingers or a flutter of her smoke-lashed eyes.

And now? She turned her shoulders to the cross and let her bare head tilt back until it touched the stone. She could feel the chill of it hard against her skin in the spot where the golden curls had grayed and thinned and fallen away into an ever widening space of naked scalp, prickling with tiny bumps like a plucked chicken's skin. Colorless lashes rimmed eyes gone from the blue of mountain lakes to the milky gray of ash-scummed ditch water. "Love," she repeated, without bitterness, without hope, and she touched the ring.

It was very small and very plain, carved of a green stone speckled brown like a toad's back. She wore it on the littlest finger of her left hand just as she had always worn it for sixty years. Her marriage band had vanished soon after her husband's death—tucked away with all her lost happiness was the tale she told her son—but this circlet never left her finger. To others' eyes it seemed to be a smooth hoop of stone, but only she knew that there was a tiny dimple, a faint indentation hidden by the curve of the next finger over. Though her fingers were thin and other rings might turn upon them at will, this one never moved from its place unless she was the one to give it a deliberate turn. Now she twisted the ring to bring this dint into the moon's sight, filling the shallow cup with diamond light, then raised it to her lips and drank the dregs of the moon.

This done, she called his name into the dark.

No branches rustled to herald his coming from the forest way. No snow, frozen to a sparkling crust by winter's harsh enchantment, crunched underfoot to warn her of his coming from the garden. He was simply there, a presence at once sudden and eternal. His tall, slender shape made all things around him shiver into place, proclaiming that it was not *he* who had suddenly become visible, but they. The world's shabbiness intruding on his beauty was the shock, not that an old mortal woman had performed certain rites and let his name fall from her withered lips.

"Ruth?" His name from her lips teetered on the brink of sacrilege, as if one poured the sweet and precious blood of saints from a stoat's skull, but her name on his was heart music, a foul thing made fair by magic. He raised a hand, paler even than the moon's maiden light, and took a step toward her as if he meant to stroke her hair.

"Stay where you are!" The shrillness, the vehemence of her voice scraped the night air between them bleeding raw. She bowed her head, cupped hands over a face whose silken skin had turned to oak bark and flint, and sobbed into her fingers, "Don't touch me."

"But why?" His plea crept over her skin, waking old dreams. She knew that if she lifted her head she would be compelled to look into his eyes, and then she would be lost forever, drowned in seas of green where golden mermaids swam and sang. Oh, sweet green seas without a shore, and nights of love without an end, and breath that fell over her bared breasts as gently as a tumble of apple blossom!

Her hands dropped from her face. She parted the edges of her cloak and gazed down. Her breasts hung slack and low, two drained wineskins where once—once—

"Because I have grown old," she said, and her voice broke into a thousand tears.

He let her weep. He did not try to cover over the sounds of her sorrow with hearty chatter, as her husband used to do, or to implore her to suppress her tears, which was her son's way. She cried, and when the tears had softened to long, shuddery breaths, she stopped of her own accord. Only then did she lift up her eyes, only then did he speak.

"Old?" His brows like the feathery antennae of moths knit together hard in perplexity. "Is this some new law of your kind, Ruth, a thing like betrothal and marriage and honor and all the rest you taught me the other night? Can it stain me through your touch? Will it steal anything from me or mine?"

"No," she replied, trying not to stare at him so greedily, for his elfin grace was a feast for eyes left starved by earthly things. "It has no power over you, my dearest, and all power over me."

"Then why—?"

"I am afraid that you still keep the other Ruth before your eyes, beloved, and that if you touch me, it will be her death."

"What other Ruth can there be?" Faun's ears pricked forward, and perplexity shone in eyes like willow leaves.

"A young Ruth, sweet lord of Faerie. A Ruth who came to life in your embrace and died within the compass of her eighteenth year. A Ruth to whom you offered up a kingdom, and who fled from it like the foolish child she was, for all that she was a settled matron with an infant in her care."

"Oh, yes!" The elf looked for all the world like a schoolboy who has only in the nick of time recalled the answer to the question which his schoolmaster has posed him. "Your little son. I saw him sleeping in his cradle and was so vexed with the answer you'd given me, for his sake, that I ordered my sister to spend full half what was left of the night, matting up his hair. See!" And he drew up a wisp of silver chain from which a crystal raindrop dangled, a knotted lock of baby's hair imprisoned in its depths. "I claimed this as my trophy."

"So that you could also claim a victory, whether it was yours to claim or not?" The old woman chuckled. "You've lingered in our mortal shadows too long, my dearest one; you grow too much like men." She shook her head. "I was occupied almost all the next day, picking out the elflocks from my baby's silky hair and desiring the proper curses to hurl after you for leaving me that task as a parting gift. And now my baby is a man whose hair is no more than a fringe of snowcloud gray above the ears, and *his* sons, too, spend hours before the looking glass, watching their foreheads climb."

She laughed over that, and he laughed with her until she realized that the two sounds heard together was the trill of birdsong trapped by the wheeze of an ancient pipe organ's leaky bellows. The shame of it killed her mirth cold.

"Ruth?" He stepped toward her, long feet sheathed in delicate brown slippers, sprinklings of amber glowing against leather tanned softer than a kitten's ear. "If you will not laugh with me or let me touch you, will you let me go?"

"Let you go . . . Oh no, my love, not yet, not yet. I haven't come out at this time of night, in weather that sinks steel teeth into my old bones, merely for one last sight of your pretty face. For that, I have my dreams."

"Then why have you summoned me?"

"Shall I tell you straight out, or will it please you to guess? We once could play at guessing games for hours, you and I, when my husband was away at Court and all the servants were busy snoring in their beds. Do you remember?"

The elf inclined his head and smiled, a slow, sweet smile that was the sun's own self emerging from behind the moon's black shadow. "We played at forfeits. For every riddle I set you that you could not answer, you paid me with a kiss; for every riddle you set me that I could not answer, I paid you with a gem."

"I filled your wicked mouth with my kisses, but when I opened up my jewel box next day to count *my* winnings, all I found were acorns and chestnuts and burrs."

her eyes twinkled. "So you see, I got the better of the bargain. Our cook could *make* something of chestnuts." Against her better judgment she began to laugh again, but there was a flash of blue silk beneath the moon as the elf's arm shot across her sight, strong fingers taking her hand captive in his own.

"We are past games, Ruth. Answer me," he said, eyes no longer warm, alien seas, but colder than snakes, colder than stones.

Ruth looked down, seeing once more his flesh against her own. This time it was only one hand lying across the other. Once it had been her pleasure to survey the languid tangle of their legs when they lay together after love. Silver and gold, silver and gold, all hers to gloat over like any common miser in his countinghouse.

"Gold to ash," she murmured, her eyes wandering over the gnarled and liver-spotted and almost bloodless ruin clasped in the glowing splendor of the elf's hand. Then she raised her voice and said, "I've summoned you because you left me with that power when I sent you away." She pulled her hand free of his grasp and drew the stone ring from her finger. "I've drunk moonlight from it to call you to me only for this: To ask one favor of your deathless grace and give you back your ring again."

"What favor?" His face was closed and guarded with mistrust. The ghost of an old night, long in the grave of vanished years, rose up to let them both recall this same garden, this same trysting place, a badly frightened young woman whose monthly blood had ceased to flow despite the fact that her wedded husband had not crossed her bedroom threshold for over a six month, and at her feet a creature less and more than human made desperate as any mortal man by love. He had pressed that very ring into her hand, forced it onto her finger, laid a spell of binding over stone and flesh, making it his pledge to grant her any boon she might desire, any time she chose to ask it, even to the scouring of her womb.

But she had not asked that. She had only run away.

"Bring her back to me," she said. She spoke it all in a rush, driving the words from her lips like a stampede of wild horses. "Let me see her, hold her, know her once, this once, if only for a little, only a little—!"

He turned his face from hers. "She is dead," he said. "You of all should know this. You birthed her and looped a white ribbon around her neck and stole the breath from her body as easily as if she'd been a kitten you meant to drown."

Ruth shook her head violently, a stubborn look blazing in her eyes. "You lie, my lovely lord of Faerie. All elves suck falseness from their mother's breasts, but you are their king in this as in all things."

The green eyes narrowed. "Have a care, lady. You presume."

"On what? On your good temper? Do you know nothing of mortals? I have not many years left me in this world, if I have any at all. Death stands beneath my window and sometimes flings a handful of pebbles at the pane to hurry me along to our tryst. I feel them lodging in my joints and in my guts, all those small, burning, aching pebbles. You can kill me if you like; I don't fear dying."

"Then do you still fear your god so much as once you claimed you did?" he challenged her. "You told me of the torments hell reserves for adulterers in words so vivid, so terrible that for once I rejoiced in my lack of an immortal soul. But your hell punishes liars, too, my love, and if you claim you did not kill our child, you lie."

"I meant to kill her." The old woman bowed her head. "That shame I can never deny. After I sent you away that night, I called upon my God daily, imploring His mercy, begging Him to keep my husband gone until my time of confinement might come and go. God was merciful, as is His wont with the worst of sinners. Sometimes I wonder whether He leads us to the lip of the abyss in order to enjoy a greater pleasure when He deigns to snatch us back from our doom."

"So you *did* kill her," the elf lord insisted, ignoring all the woman's talk of gods and mercy. Beautiful, ageless as a stone, he cared nothing for the mortal currency of souls. "So I was told, but still I did not want to believe that you ever could—"

The old woman shook her head. "I didn't," she main-tained. "Whoever brought you such news was deceived. Before my belly grew big enough to catch the servants' eyes, I took myself off on a journey of my own, supposedly to visit a distant connection in the north, in the shadow of the border. I left behind me a trumpery tale of women's woes, too trivial for my husband to examine closely even if he had come back from Court while I was gone. How fortunate I was that he did not! And with me I took a jewel, a gem, a priceless treasure, my handmaiden, Nancy Blye."

She sighed and leaned one shoulder against the cold stone cross. "Poor Nancy. All she has become is my doing. She was such a bonny girl, so bright, so cunning! Loyal as a dog, too, a skilled midwife, and greedy for my gold. I knew she would obey me to the letter in all things save one: She would not kill the child."

"Why not, for the proper price?" the elf asked. "Was she afraid for her soul's sake?" He twisted a sneer into his speech.

Ruth paid his sarcasm no mind. "Not for the sake of any mortal thing, but for fear of you and your kind. I'd told her the infant would be born half-elfin. She claimed to have had truck with the Good Folk—*her* name for your kindred, none of mine—many times before. Knowledge bred awe, awe bred fear. She would not risk drawing down your vengeance for all the gold I might give her. And so, when the child was pushed out of my womb at last and I lay spent from my labor, she snatched up the infant and fled with it into the forest."

"The forest?" the elf repeated, wondering over this new knowledge. "Where—?"

"Beyond the wild wind's back, for all that anyone here ever knew. But in truth, you know the spot well: the wood where we two first met, my dearest, that May eve when I went out riding late because the devil was whispering in the shadows and because I was too young for sense. There is a cottage there, by the path that skirts the ruined convent's garden. None go there but desperate women. It is Nancy's place now, poor soul, poor elf-shot soul. . . ."

A haze lay over the snow, the blue breath of winter made visible in mist that lapped itself around the ankles

of elf and woman. It wreathed frost flowers up the shaft
of the stone cross and rimmed the moon's mocking face
with swansdown.

"I never knew your Nancy," the elf lord said, his face
keen as a hunting cat's. "I never laid arrow to bow to
bring her down. If you want to distract me with these
accusations out of your own guilt for what was between
us, find another fool."

"Oh!" Ruth's eyes widened with pain and pity. Almost without the body's will behind them, her hands
flew up to cradle her lover's face in a soft, papery clasp.
"Dear heart, I never said that it was your doing, the
dark touch that turned a pretty, singing girl into a crone
between sunset and sunrise! All I know of the matter is
this: That I labored hard to birth an infant girl; that I
fell into exhaustion before I could cut off her cries and
her life with the pretty, silken ribbon; that when I roused
myself to face the deed, there was nothing in the cradle
and no Nancy in the cottage; that I staggered from the
bed, calling my handmaid's name until sleep took me a
second time; that when I next woke, there was a dead
child in my arms, a little white ribbon tied too tightly
round its throat, and Nancy stretched out on the floor
beside the bed, white-haired, gape-mouthed, her limbs
curled in like a burned spider's, and babbling."

"Prettily woven, prettily told." The elf lord's mouth
was thin and grim. "No fault can fall on you with such
a tale to guard your back. Why practice it on me? Take
it to your black priest and let him make you clean of
the crime."

"You cold-eyed thing!" Despite the agony it shot
through her hip, the old woman stamped her foot in
rage, fists clenched tight. "Is there nothing between your
ears but sand? If you walked this world for twice ten
thousand years, you could not begin to imagine how it
pains my heart to see you now, as tall and fair and shining as the night we met, and me so eaten up by age.
And yet I summoned you. Trust in my words, my vain,
my beloved lord: I did not do so lightly, or merely to
bait you with lies. I want only one thing from you, and
then begone. I want my daughter back again."

He stood there gazing into her face for the time it

would take a water bubble to rise to the surface of a pond and break. The ice that encased his eyes began to thin, to melt away entirely until there was only the old tenderness left. "Forgive me," he said. "Forgive me for my words as I pray you will forgive me for this: I cannot give you the boon you ask. Whatever befell the child your handmaid stole away, I know nothing of it."

"Now you are the liar, my lord," Ruth replied evenly. "You are because you must be. All the evidence shouts it to your face. If you did not steal our babe from Nancy's arms in the dark woodland, if you did not strike her down to snatch the child away, then whose hand placed that poor, strangled creature in my arms? If not you, then it was one of your minions acting on your word. I saw that small corpse well, too well. I was the one who gave it decent burial, weak as I was. It was nothing human. All brown and wizened, an ancient mannikin, an infant mummy, it was no babe of my birthing."

"A changeling." The elf spoke with conviction. "Some goblin's brat, from what you say. But still I swear to you, it was as much a stranger to me as our child. I know nothing of this." His eyes met hers full on. No lies lived in them. "Nothing at all."

"Nothing . . ." The word seemed reluctant to leave her mouth. She leaned heavily against the cross and her legs weakened under her. The velvet cape made a soft, hissing sound as she slid down to huddle in the snow. "Then there is no hope. None. If even you have never seen her . . . Oh, Nancy! Only you might be the one to tell us both what became of that unlucky child, and you never will. You never can." And she wept out her heart's misery.

When she raised her face from her hands, he was gone, her lover of so long ago, and there was the pale hint of false dawn stealing through the trees.

"And what did I expect?" she muttered to herself, slowly getting to her feet, climbing a stairway of pain. "What should he care, when all's said, for a mortal slip of his planting, for any mortal thing?"

She thought of old Nancy, more than half out of her scanty wits most times, and how the stricken hag would sing the old ballads of the Fair Folk to pass the hours.

She sang of how beautiful they were, and how carelessly cruel. A pretty girl was no more to the lords of Faerie than a summer's blossom, easily plucked, briefly admired, casually cast aside. Ruth sighed and gazed at her hand where the speckled green stone ring still nestled between crabbed fingers. She touched it once, lightly, with a fingertip. It shriveled up brown, crackled into a smear of dust, and blew away.

"This, too, then, he takes from me at last," she said, and turned her footsteps back to the great manor house.

All the morning she kept to her bed, more in a series of dozes and catnaps than in true sleep, after the manner of the old. She got no good rest from it and awoke haggard, out of sorts. Her servants knew the edge of her tongue that day, and even her son—sole heir and almighty lord of the great house and the grounds ever since his father's passing, the man on whose charity she now depended—had reason to cringe under the bite of her words.

That night she did not rest. She walked long galleries where moonlight danced away before her plodding feet, her crooked shadow. She did not dare to sleep, she did not want to dream. It was a dream that had planted in her heart that impossible longing for her lost child, a dream in which she lay upon her deathbed and saw a fair vision bending over her. It was her own face, soft with youth once more, yet different. There was a wild slant to the eyes, a greater delicacy to the bones beneath the skin. In that dream she knew that her daughter had come back to give her peace before she shut her eyes one last time against the beauty of the world.

"No, no," she muttered to herself, hands knotted in the collar of her nightrobe. "I will not sleep again. Let death take me waking, I will not sleep. I could not bear the pain were that vision to find me again. Oh, my baby! God forgive me for your begetting! God grant me Hell for wishing your death. I will accept His darkest judgment on my soul if only He will in mercy grant me one last sight of your sweet, living face." Thus she prayed, prayers that any priest would dread to hear.

But she tired in body long before her spirit flagged. In the night-steeped hall where her late husband's portrait still kept a proprietary eye over all his earthly holdings, she slumped into a high-backed chair and fell into slumber.

Ruth . . . Her name swam through the shadows of dream to touch her ear with a breath that smelled of honey. *Ruth, I have returned. The pledge will stand redeemed. Ruth, awake to me.*

She opened her eyes, or dreamed she did. In the high-ceiled hall the elf lord stood, his limbs shimmering with cloth-of-silver. He was not alone. A lady stood beside him, a lady of his own immortal breed and kin, gorgeously appareled. Her hair was a tumble of autumn leaves and her eyes were hard, green spears of springtime grass surprised by frost. The elf lord held out one hand to this miracle of frozen loveliness and she rested her fingertips on his proffered palm as if she gave reluctant charity to a leper.

"Is this—is this she?" Ruth's lips trembled. There was nothing of her blood in this proud, cold being at all, none she could see. "Is this my—our child?"

The pale, alluring face of the lady tightened with disdain, and it was the elf lord who answered, "No."

"Then who—? Why have you brought—?"

"My bride," he said, turning his face away from them both. "My wife. My queen."

"But never his love." The lady's voice broke forth so suddenly that elf lord and mortal woman both jumped in their skins at the sound. "That he reserved for you." Her eyes traveled up and down the old woman's face and form, piercing to the bone. Under that long, scornful stare Ruth forgot to breathe. *"You,"* the lady repeated, and then she laughed her contempt aloud.

The harsh sound roused her lord to anger. He glared at her, then with gentleness turned to Ruth and said, "Here is our stealer of infants. Here is the one who kept secret watch on us—on you—from the first, who followed you even after you sent me away. Here is she who spied on our every meeting, but could not see what it was drew me to your arms."

"What was there to see?" the lady replied haughtily. "A willing whore is a common sight."

"So it is, my lady, in your mirror," the elf lord countered. "Your person for my kingdom, now *there* was a fee! But your love?"

"I gave you pleasure and delight," the lady spat. "Why did you require more? What do such as we care for love? It is a mortal thing, a spangle to catch the light and blind their eyes so that for a little while they are too dazzled to see their waiting deaths."

"My lady—" Ruth hesitated. Never had she seen so much hate pent up in so dainty a shell. She dreaded to risk kindling the elf queen's rage—no mater that her lover might protect her from it—and yet she felt compelled to speak. She had told the elf lord truly when she'd said she did not fear death. "My lady, were you indeed the one who stole my daughter from poor Nancy's arms?"

"*Your* daughter?" The lady seemed to grow taller as she looked down her nose at the old woman. "She is of his blood as well, and all that is his must by rights be mine."

"Ah." The light of understanding came over Ruth's face. "So that is why you speak as if you despise love, yet you begrudge that your lord found love with me. Nothing but pride of ownership, nothing but greed for your rights of property, nothing more than—" She was about to say *Nothing more than how my husband held me,* but prudence stilled her tongue.

She got up from the high-backed chair and with all care for her fragile bones she lowered herself to her knees before the shining lady. Her lover gave a short cry of startlement and tried to prevent her, but she waved his intervention aside. She joined her hands in a suppliant's pose and lifted her rheumy eyes to that clear, green gaze so steeped in hate. "My lady, I ask your pardon for my sins against your marriage bed. I would offer you my life if I thought it would appease you, but we both know that is no great offering now. So I ask you—I implore you in the name of your bright beauty— gave me back what you have taken from me. Only for a little while, give it back, that treasure I don't deserve to hold."

"Ruth, there is no need for this," the elf lord protested, trying to help her to her feet. She shrugged aside his efforts and remained stubbornly on her knees while he pleaded: "She has no choice. When I left you last night, it was to solve this mystery, and by my powers I have done it. I have found out her hiding place and discovered her crime. She stands under my orders to submit to your word. You have only to say what you desire of her and she must obey."

The old woman shook her head in denial. "There is every need. You have done wrong to take her choices from her, my beloved. Even if we have not offended against her heart, we have offended against her pride, and she holds that pride dearer than any heart. It is not just or right that I command her obedience when I should beg her forgiveness."

This time when the elf queen laughed, there was a vagrant note of warmth in the sound. "Well said, woman. And as for the boon you would have of me, well asked and willingly granted." She jerked away from her lord's touch and clasped Ruth's gnarled and wrinkled paw in both her slim, white hands, urging her to rise. "Come and have your child back again."

They left the sleeping house, those three, by paths that never knew wall or door. Outside the snow still lay in thick furrings over the earth, the winter wind still worried the bare tree limbs with iron teeth, but the old woman felt neither wind nor snow nor cold. A shining warmth encased her as she walked between those two tall, proud figures. They left the manor house and its gardens, skirted the forest, crossed fallow fields, and all with as little effort as if their steps merely spanned the width of Ruth's lonesome bedchamber. The tireless pace of the elfinfolk was to be expected, but Ruth marveled at how she too remained unwearied. His gift to her or his queen's? Old Nancy's ballads sang of how elves made bad enemies; Ruth could have added a verse to tell of how they also made unsettling friends.

At length, their path ended at the side of a great mound in the middle of a flat expanse of land. The elf lord spoke a word and the hillside opened into a golden light. A squat creature came scampering out, brown as new-turned earth, with tiny red eyes like holly berries. The goblin scuttled over the snow on three limbs, a well-

wrapped bundle in its other arm, and threw itself against
the elf queen's skirts like a too-eager hound.

The elf queen bent down to take up the little bundle
and held it out to Ruth, all smiles. Her look of gracious,
condescending charity flickered out when the old woman
backed away as if she had been offered a serpent in
swaddling clothes.

"No," Ruth moaned, wringing her hands. "Oh, gentle
heaven, no."

"What is this?" the elf queen demanded, a scowl
sharpening her beauty. "What is the matter with you,
woman? You asked for your child back. I have brought
her to you. Take her!" She tried to thrust the bundle
into Ruth's arms, but the old woman shrank from it and
covered her face, sobbing.

"My love, what ails you?" the elf lord gently asked,
slipping one arm around her heaving shoulders. "See,
my queen has kept her word: Our child is here! Why
won't you take her? Isn't this what you desired? Wasn't
it for this you called upon my pledge?" His finger traced
the dark smear above her knuckle where she had once
worn the speckled green stone ring.

"Time, time, time," the old woman groaned. "Nancy's
songs do say the truth, how time passes in your realm,
my lord. Our hours here in the mortal world fly, yours
drift. Our days are your moments, our centuries are your
days. Oh, can't you see? My babe who was stolen off to
Elfhame is a baby still, with all of life awaiting her and
I—I wait only for death."

"Is that all that troubles you?" The elf lord kissed her
cheek. "Then come, my dearest; let it be as it might
have been for us, if you had never run away. I offered
you the life of Elfhame then; I offer it anew. Come with
us and live your remaining days as centuries. What keeps
you here anymore? Your son is a grown man; he doesn't
need you. Come with us and care for one who does.
Come and raise our daughter."

"As what? Her mother? A fine mother, a cradle
crone! I am too old to take an infant's care. And when
she is old enough to know, what will she think of me?
My age and ugliness will frighten her. She is half mortal,
but why should she see so soon the end mortality brings?

Let her be innocent of that hard knowledge for as long as may be."

"Is this how my generosity is received?" the elf queen demanded peevishly. She turned on her lord. "Was it for this that I allowed you to humble me, to drag me before your mortal mistress? If she will not accept the child, then let us give it to the goblins."

"My lady, a moment. Let me reason with her, please, I beg of—"

The elf lord's words were ignored. His queen's anger would not be pent. With a toss of her head she stalked toward the golden gateway in the hillside and cried, "Take her!" And she tossed the swaddled bundle into the light.

The old woman heard a tiny wisp of wailing rise up from the bundle as it left the elf queen's arms, she saw a small, pink hand wave helplessly in the air, and suddenly she was running. Her mind screamed out that it was hopeless, that age had fettered her limbs, that she was slow, that a legion of the elf queen's goblin minions would lay hands on that little life before she could cross half the distance between herself and the hillside. But her heart outshouted her reason. She ran, arms outstretched, eyes fixed on what the elf queen had thrown away as heedlessly as if it were a withered bunch of flowers. Somewhere in that headlong race she felt her toe catch against the edge of a stone. She fell forward, a cry of despair tearing her throat.

The grass broke her fall, the tender grass of an unending summer. Her head filled with the scent of a thousand flowers, a dizzyingly sweet perfume, and warm breezes stroked her skin. All of this was wondrous, all of this meant nothing. All that mattered was the bundle that now filled her arms, the laughing face of the baby that looked up at her with eyes almost her own.

Very cautiously she crept to her feet, sheltering the gurgling infant against her chest. She could not take her eyes from the small face, and when the baby nuzzled at her bosom she was only a little astonished to feel her breasts ache with milk. She opened her nightrobe and let the child suckle, velvety cheek pressed to skin no longer wrinkled, breasts no longer slack. A curl of her golden hair fell forward and the baby grasped it tightly in a fist too small to hold anything but a heart.

She did not even hear the sound of the hillside sliding shut behind her, though it was a sound loud enough to rouse the master of the manor house and bring him running into his gardens. He was standing by the stone cross, staring off into the frozen darkness, when the servants came rushing out to tell him that his mother was gone.

He looked down at the crumpled velvet cape at the foot of the cross. His own large tracks had all but erased the smaller set of prints that had been there before, yet still he could tell that hers had been the only feet to come this way since snowfall. They came this far; they did not go back. He knew this was impossible—she had gone into this garden the other night and assuredly she had come home again.

Yes, impossible. He was a man of business, of common sense, of reason. He did not believe in wasting time over impossibilities. He knelt to pick up the discarded cape, his gift of duty if not of love. Violets fell from the velvet folds, starred the snow, and the red tears of anemones.

And in a poor cottage by a ruined convent's garden, an old woman who for years had known nothing of reason heard a knocking at her door. The sound roused her from fitful sleep. She cast aside the ragged bedclothes and made her way across a floor dusty from neglected sweepings, cluttered and unclean with all the small detritus that her feeble mind overlooked to clear away.

She opened the door to a bright-eyed girl with a baby at her breast. The vision leaned across the doorsill to press a kiss on the old woman's cheek and cry, "Oh, Nancy!" with a wanderer's joy at finding her way home once more.

"Who—who are you?" For once the sheltering clouds of madness parted, leaving Nancy's eyes naked to pure dread. She cupped the wrinkled cheek the girl had kissed as if it were a wound. "What do you want from me?"

The girl touched the old woman's tangled hair and drew out the small, black sliver of flint that only her eyes could see nested there and that no mortal comb could ever dislodge. The elf-bolt burned itself white in her palm; she blew the ashes away with the breath of her laughter. The old woman stared, reason coming back into her eyes, and recognition with it:

"R—Ruth?" She looked down at her own aged hand, then at the girl's smooth skin, and wondered whether she were not still mad. Other questions bubbled to her lips, but each and every one blew away before she could utter it. She turned from the cottage doorway to see her home transformed, all the clutter changed to cleanliness and comfort by a scouring spring breeze that blew with magic's lingering breath from the golden girl's mere presence.

She looked back at her callers, still lingering beyond the doorsill, and her restored mind cast aside all doubts and questions of possibility. She knew only what she saw before her now.

She planted her hands on her hips and with a sigh of feigned impatience said: "Well, if you're bound to wait on *my* invitation, you might as well come in."

With a burst of joyous laughter, Ruth and her child crossed the threshold of their only true home. Faithful Nancy took the infant from her mother's arms. "Of course you didn't *think* to bring a cradle," she chided. And as the door closed after them, she began to sing the infant one of the old songs, a ballad of the Fair Folk—beautiful and cold, unchanged by age or time, armored in magic, and all their power scattered like the petals of a flower by so small a mortal thing as love.

MY LORD TEASER
by Richard Parks

Richard Parks lives in Mississippi, works with computers, and writes. He firmly believes that his stories, which have appeared in *Robert Bloch's Psychos, 100 Wicked Little Witch Stories,* and *Wizard Fantastic,* are much more interesting than he is. Humor him.

Every man deals with pain in his own way. Some groan, some swear, some opt for stoic silence even when a little tactical complaint might bring relief. John of Devonleigh, called "Running Jack" by friend and foe alike, tended to philosophize. After a night in a bed that had nothing to do with sleep, and carrying a head that felt two stone too heavy—not to mention the size of a ripe melon—he had ample reason.

The only trouble with "the night before" is the morning after.

It was a minor paradox as such went, but this was as much mystery as Jack could handle just then. He came to a clear running stream just inside a grove near the forest of Dunby and there he didn't so much dismount as slide off his mount like a sack of loose grain. Reynard, the big dun gelding, drank gratefully from the stream without dwelling too much on the imponderables. Jack splashed his face with the cool sweet water and did little else.

Jack found a quiet pool where a boulder diverted the faster water to the side, and there he studied his reflection. It had been a while since Jack had taken notice of himself; time being the slippery thief it was, he was a little relieved to note that he was still a relatively young man. The black of his hair was untouched by gray as yet, and his dark eyes were still clear and bright. There were fine lines near his eyes and mouth that spoke of diminishing time, but not loudly. Not yet.

Still time to make a life for myself.

The question was: Did it really matter now? Jack considered this, and came to the answer he always reached, because it was the only one there was.

"Reynard, they're going to catch me sooner or later."

Reynard cropped grass near the bank. If the horse thought of it at all—unlikely—he wouldn't have needed to ask who "they" were. They were legion: the brother of Jack's former knight and Reynard's former master, now deceased, too many inn and tavern keepers to count, the fathers and brothers of a dozen or more village girls, and, for purposes varying from matrimony to mayhem, the village girls.

Jack never meant to complicate his life so much; indeed, he was working hard to avoid complications before the disaster at Charcross. Now he was forced to live life moment by moment, because the moment was all he could count on. Jack didn't like to think about it. He decided to soak his aching head instead; it seemed a more profitable way to spend the time. When he finally emerged from the water again he heard a horse whinny.

"Reynard . . . ?"

Not Reynard. Too far away. Jack crept to the edge of the trees. A man rode down the road Jack had come, a large man wearing armor, followed by two mounted squires and a small pack train. He rode with his helm hanging from his saddle, but Jack didn't need to see the man's face to know who he was.

As far as Jack was concerned, he was Death.

"Sir Kevin Grosvenor," whispered Jack to Reynard. "Now it ends."

He looked around. The grove was small, and the path led right through it; there was no place to hide. There was a chance he could reach the forest proper before Sir Kevin, but there was no point. He was traveling lighter than his pursuers but Reynard was too spent from the previous evening's flight to go far.

Jack considered; Sir Kevin hadn't spotted him yet, but that wouldn't matter in a few moments. He might manage to surprise them, but it was three to one and Jack knew he was no match for the burly knight even if they had been equally armored.

"I suppose," he said, "it's time to show the honor that Sir Kevin claims I do not possess. Do you think the contradiction will give him the slightest pause, Reynard?" The big dun snorted and Jack was forced to agree. "I didn't think so."

Jack loosened his sword in its scabbard and started to mount.

"You chose death, then."

The woman sat on a stone by the stream. She hadn't been there a moment before, Jack was sure of it. It took him a moment before he was sure of something else—he knew her. The long dark hair and dimpled smile was very familiar from the tiring—but blissful—prior evening.

"Edyth? How did you get here?"

"Aren't you pleased to see me, Jack?" she asked.

Actually he was indeed pleased, though Jack had never expected to see her again. When they had met the previous evening in the Houndsfoot Tavern, it was Edyth who had sought *him* out. Likewise, there was nothing in her manner or conversation in the time they'd spent together that led him to think that she expected more from him than his company for that little time. She had been quite unexpected that way, as in others. Jack, in turn, surprised himself to think that he might have been quite content to spend a good portion of his life—perhaps all of it—delving her mysteries, if that had been at all possible.

Jack glanced back at the road; Sir Kevin was coming uncomfortably close. "Certainly, but your timing could be better."

She laughed then. It was probably not quite loud enough for Sir Kevin to hear over the clink and flap of his accoutrements, but almost. "I think my timing is perfect as it is. You are about to die," she said.

Jack blinked. "So it seems, though I never thought you would savor the idea. I thought you were somewhat fond of me."

"I am quite fond of you, and there's my meaning,"

she said. "I offer you this choice: Face that angry man
out there, and die. Or come with me, and live."

"Come where?"

"With me," she repeated. "It's not necessary that you
understand, only that you choose. Know that I do have
the power to save your life, but I wouldn't dawdle, if I
were you."

Jack glanced back at the road. "That's no choice at
all. Lead on."

There was a white palfrey, fully caparisoned, standing
beside the woman. Jack was sure *it* hadn't been there a
moment before, either, but in a moment Edyth was
mounted and reining her horse toward the far end of
the grove. Jack climbed back on Reynard and trotted
after her.

"We can't reach the forest before Sir Kevin sees us;
I'd already considered that," Jack said as he caught up.

"He's not as close as you think," she said.

Jack glanced back, and got an even bigger surprise.
By Our Lady . . .

There was nothing behind them but trees, as far and
as wide as Jack could see: no sign of the road, no sign
of Sir Kevin, though both, as Jack was certain, were only
a few yards away a moment before. As far as Jack could
tell, they were out of the grove and into the main forest
now, though in truth the trees seemed both thicker and
larger than he'd expected.

"What just happened, Edyth?"

The woman just smiled at him, and Jack realized dully
that she had changed, too. The hair and the smile had
not changed, but her face was more angular than he
remembered, her frame, slighter. There was also something different about the eyes, something . . . older.

"Edyth, who are you?"

She smiled at him. "You may call me Lady Devoted.
I am the humble servant of my mistress, the Queen of
the *Sidhe*."

Jack reined in. "Not another step," he said, "until I
know what this is about."

The woman's horse stopped, too, though she gave no
command that Jack could see. The palfrey turned slowly,
elegantly, like a dancer. When the woman he had known

as Edyth faced him again she looked even more different. He could still see Edyth there, in this stranger's face, but it was no village maid who sat before him. She wore a gown of fine green brocade; gold spurs were strapped to the heels of her soft leather boots. Edyth had been pretty; this woman was not containable in such a pitiful word, or indeed any other Jack knew.

"I am Lady Devoted, as I told you. I just saved your life."

Jack nodded. "Yes. Why?"

She studied him in a way that was a little disconcerting. "Most men would assume it had something to do with our idyll of last night, and my affection for you. Why are you not making that assumption?"

"I am, in that I do believe it has something to do with the previous evening. But what? There's the question. You're not what you seemed, Lady, and thus it follows that our time together was not what it seemed, and so I must ask: Why did you seek me out?"

She smiled approval. "You're a clever man, Jack, and not as blinded by pride as some. That will help. I sought you out to test you, to make certain you were the man I thought you. Nor was I disappointed. I think you will do nicely."

"For what?"

"For the Queen of the *Sidhe's* lover."

Running Jack was beginning to wonder if, perhaps, Sir Grosvenor was the lesser of the two threats confronting him now. They had been riding for a while, and though Sir Kevin was still out of sight, the edge of the forest, dimly visible ahead, had not gotten any closer.

"How much farther, Lady?"

"A little or a lot. It varies."

That wasn't very helpful. Jack pictured himself riding for an eternity through this dark forest which, Jack was pretty certain, was *not* Dunby Wood. The company was pleasant enough, but the situation did seem uncomfortably short of options.

"Lady, if I ask a question, will you tell me the truth?"

"Anything you ask in my lady's name, I will answer so," she replied. "But, since you don't really know Her

Majesty's given name and I've no inclination to reveal it, that doesn't help you much."

"No," said Jack.

She smiled then. "However, you are free to ask as man to woman—for such I am, whatever else I may be—and you may believe what you will. Isn't that how you mortals normally conduct business?"

Jack had to admit it was. "Very well, then: You said you were testing me last night. What was the test? That I could lie with a woman?"

She laughed then. "By the Glamour, no. The meanest lout in that tavern could have managed that, even the few whose tastes don't run to women. I wasn't looking for ability," she said, then added, "or skill, come to that. Though you were . . . passable."

"You are too kind," Jack said, a little wounded.

She shook her head, and she wasn't smiling. "No, Jack. I am not kind. If you don't believe anything else I tell you, believe that. I chose you for our advantage, not yours. Leaving you to that large angry man back there . . ." she glanced back down the path, "might have been kinder. A sword in the head or heart isn't the worst thing that can happen to a person. What you face now is a sort of war, Jack, and we of the *Sidhe* have been at it a very long time. You're in more danger than you can possibly know."

"You said I was to be the queen's lover!"

She nodded. "It's the same thing."

It was as if Lady Devoted had been waiting for something, Jack thought, and he'd just given it to her. The forest around them grew even thicker for a moment, as if they were riding in night. Then there was a definite lightening of the path ahead. Another few minutes' riding and they crossed the border.

It was the most beautiful country Jack had ever seen.

He looked around with a rising sense of futility, trying to imagine a time, if any, when he would look back on the moment he was now in. What would he tell himself? What images, sounds or emotions filtered through imperfect memory could recapture what he saw, what he

heard, what he felt right now? Could there actually be
a truth so strong or a lie so golden to be a match for it?

"I couldn't even imagine a place like this."

"What do you see?" Lady Devoted asked.

"What . . . ?" The question sounded ludicrous, but
one look at his companion told him she was deadly seri-
ous. There was almost—no other word quite fit—a *hunger* in her expression as she waited for his answer.

"I see a stream with water clear as glass. I see a palace
with turrets shining like finest marble, whiter than snow
and taller than any mountain I have ever seen. I see folk
of such quality that the meanest among them puts the
finest mortal king on his throne to shame. I see such
that, if I were to see much more, I would burst into
flame like the Greek maiden who saw Zeus in his Glory
and could not contain it."

She nodded, and her eyes closed as if she savored each
word like some rare and delicate pastry. "Thank you."

"I don't understand," he said. "What do you see?"

"The same," she admitted. "And ever the same, for
millennia past counting. Look at the finest emerald in
creation long enough and sooner or later a dung heap
will become the most fascinating change of pace." She
sighed. "But to see, for a moment, with new eyes . . .
that was a gift, and so I thanked you. Simple courtesy,
and manners. Understand that proper behavior is life
and death here."

"I would consider the debt paid if you would teach
me," he said.

"As much as can be done for you, I will. Pray it's
enough."

There was so much that was new and strange to Jack,
but a few things seemed to stand out. For instance, all
the grand palaces and castles he saw upon crossing the
border were still there, but no one seemed to be using
them. No matter where he and Lady Devoted rode, none
of the fine buildings ever seemed to get any closer. So
when Lady Devoted brought him a change of clothing,
he bathed in a cold-water stream, shaved using a bronze
mirror hung on a tree. A gilt bucket appeared with oats
beside the stream for Reynard, who didn't seem inclined

to question farther than his stomach. Jack was different. When Lady Devoted reappeared, Jack finally had to remark upon it.

"You are not deceived; the buildings are but aspects of the Glamour."

"You mean they're not real?"

"They're real enough, but they're not what you think they are. They suit their purpose by doing what they were envisioned to do."

"And what is that?"

"To attest to the glory of my mistress and her kingdom. Aren't they fine?"

"Yes, but what good are they if no one can use them?"

She looked at him as if he were a dull-witted child. "What good is a human palace? It's a testament to the wealth and power of the crown, but as a place to live? Most are somewhat lacking. These are different. They never age or need repair; they do not gather dust and they do not wall us off from the natural world. Which, as you said yourself, is a splendid place indeed."

"Yes, but what about rain? Or winter chill?"

Lady Devoted smiled then. "Sometimes I think you forget where you are. We are the Changeless, Jack. The Not Born of Eve. What are such things to us? What is a palace but something to admire, as you would a mountain or a fine horse? All the same."

Jack shrugged. "My expectations rule me, My Lady, and they are poor masters at best. So. What happens now?"

"Now we go to see my mistress. What 'happens' remains to be seen."

"Lady Devoted, you did not tell me she had a husband!"

Jack kept his voice down to a harsh whisper, but barely. Lady Devoted seemed more amused than chagrined. "I didn't tell you that earth should be under you and sky above, either. Some things you take for granted."

They stood at the edge of a clearing: Jack in his borrowed finery, Lady Devoted in a new gown that was as delicate as a garment of moonbeams and cobwebs, and about as substantial. It had been difficult to take his eyes off her when she directed him to look at the approaching company. Now it wasn't difficult at all. Jack's mouth had dropped open at the sight.

The lords and ladies of the *Sidhe* walked hand in hand, their entrance a pavanne to hidden music. At the head of the column walked a lady of indescribable beauty, a creature not so much perfect of form as something beyond the notion of form, and the ethereal fashions of beauty. *She* was beauty, and whatever came closest to her in even the palest imitation would be beauty, too. Her hair was whiter than snow, her eyes the faint blue of glaciers. She was at once ancient as earth and new as springtime. Jack lost his heart to her at once. He really had no choice.

It was several long moments before Jack was able to even notice the lord at her side, and then for a moment he had all of Jack's faltering attention. In some ways the lord of the *Sidhe* reminded Jack of Sir Kevin. Besides the comparisons of size and strength, there was the same sense of *implacability* about him. He looked otherwise human except for two fine horns springing from his brow like those of a yearling buck. He wore a fine tunic of silvered thread; his hose was sky blue. He carried a fine longsword in his right hand as he held his lady's with his left hand. The blade was hidden in its scabbard and wrapped in a fine jeweled belt, but Jack had no doubt there was nothing of delicacy and show in the blade. The fairie lord, for his part, looked as if he knew how to use it, had used it, and would again at the slightest provocation.

"Who is that?" Jack had asked.

"My Lady's consort, of course. The king of this realm."

After she seemed certain that Jack's outburst was over, she took him by the hand and led him out into the open, before the dancers and the magnificent couple who led them.

"Keep silent unless directly addressed, and try to follow as I direct."

Jack felt every single glance as they company turned

their eyes on him. No one spoke, but the hidden music ended, and so did the dance. All stood watching them approach. Every instinct in Jack's soul told him to break Lady Devoted's grip if he could and flee to whatever safe haven he could find. His wits told him differently: that Lady Devoted's delicate grip was more than he thought, and there were no safe places for him there. He remembered Lady Devoted's words, kept silent, and tried to follow her lead.

The Queen of the *Sidhe* was the first to speak, in a voice that was the source of all music as far as Jack could tell.

"You have returned to us, Lady Devoted, and you bring company! Most welcome. Who is our guest?"

Lady Devoted bowed low, and Jack copied her. "Your Majesties, may I present Lord Teaser."

Lord . . . ?

In his surprise Jack almost spoke then, but managed to prevent it. The gaze from the massed company seemed even more intense now, if such a thing was possible, and the last thing he wanted was to draw more attention than he could help. If anything, he wanted to make himself very small and hide someplace inconspicuous, such as behind the nearest rock. But then, he reasoned, he would not be able to hear that voice again, nor see that wonderful face.

The queen extended one perfect gloved hand. Jack had presence of mind enough to glance at his companion before he accepted it, but brushing the delicate lace with his lips made him a bit light-headed. He caught a scent of something undefinable, but fascinating. When the queen withdrew her hand, it was all Jack could do to let it go. Indeed, he wasn't sure if he'd have been able to release her hand, had not the King of Fairie caught his eye. The *Sidhe* lord nodded once, and Jack found himself bowing again. When he straightened up, the king's eyes were still on him.

"You must join us at the feast this evening," said the queen. It was a polite enough request, but Jack realized he would have fought armies to be anywhere she wanted him to be, do anything she wanted him to do. In a moment the music began again and, two by two, the dancers passed by. As the royal couple pavanned away from him, Jack heard the king speak to his Lady.

"And thus it begins?"

At least that's what it sounded like; the queen made no answer that he could hear. One thing Jack did know for certain—the king's horns were definitely larger now than they were just a few moments before.

"You're not eating," Lady Devoted said.

The feast was laid out on three tables, the head table and two others turned at right angles to it. Jack and Lady Devoted sat opposite each other at the head of the rightmost table, close but not too close to the royal couple seated at the center of the head table.

Lady Devoted had risen and gone to speak to her mistress on several occasions as if summoned, though Jack heard nothing. After the last time she acted as if something had been settled, and deigned to enjoy the feast herself. There was a great deal to enjoy: venison, turbot, compotes of great delicacy and the most delicious scents. Jack's mouth was practically watering, but all he allowed himself was a little wine. A very little, well mixed with water. Jack wanted his wits about him.

"I dare not," he said.

"That old story about eating the food of fairyland and being trapped forever?" She smiled. "Would that really be such a terrible thing?"

"Being trapped anywhere is a terrible thing," he said. "And though your perspective is far vaster than mine, I can see the same thought in you."

Lady Devoted denied nothing, admitted nothing. She merely looked thoughtful. "Why does Sir Kevin seek your death? What did you do to him?"

Jack allowed himself another sip of wine. "I lived."

"That's all?"

"Even simple things have roots past counting. Specifically, I lived and his brother died. At Charcross."

"Charcross . . ." Lady Devoted frowned briefly. "I remember hearing something of that. A border skirmish between two barons, was it not? Hardly more than a trifle."

"Normally, yes. One lord claims a serf's croft is on *his*

fief, another disputes. Sometimes they fight, more often it's a brave show and bluster, a little gold changes hands and all is agreed. Unfortunately, there was already bad blood between the Grosvenors and Percys going back some years. They were just looking for an excuse."

"What happened?"

"They fought," Jack said simply. "I was squire to Sir François, Kevin's brother. During the melee his banner was torn. Another bloody trifle, but he sent me back to Grosvenor Castle to get a new one. I think the fool *still* thought it was some grand show. He was wrong. By the time I returned it was over; Sir François was dead on the field. I don't think old Percy himself meant it to go as far as that."

"Fools, to squander such wealth," was all Lady Devoted said.

Jack shrugged. "Wealth was squandered, and that's the truth. The Percy family paid a heavy fine to Sir Kevin and the king took a larger one. I wasn't so lucky. Sir Kevin couldn't believe his brother had been so foolish. Easier to believe I had betrayed Sir François and fled."

"That wasn't what I meant, Jack. I meant *wealth*. What does one value more than the thing one does not possess? There's not a fay at this table who wouldn't pay more gold than the world has seen for a moment with such depth of feeling, and humans waste it on nothing." She shook her head in disgust.

Jack didn't understand at first, then he looked around him. He remembered what Lady Devoted had told him about seeing this kingdom with new eyes, and he tried now to see the company around him with a different perspective. He tried to see the fays as Lady Devoted must, one who had beheld the same tableau for ages past counting. For several long moments he could not get past the jeweled flash, the colors, the Glamour. Then he noticed something he had not noticed before.

What's wrong with their eyes?

The fays were laughing, but not with their eyes. They were flirting, but the broad smiles and coy expressions were only on their faces. What spoke of joy and life at their feasting and merriment spoke only on the surface.

Jack tried to understand what was in their eyes, instead of all the things that *should* have been there. All he could sort out of it was boredom, weariness, a kind of hopeless *sameness* that did not change whatever fair face he looked at.

"Is everyone here really so weary of existence?"

"It's not as simple as that, but I get your meaning. And the answer is 'no.' For instance, at the head table just now."

Jack looked where Lady Devoted was looking. The queen and her king were in a discussion that was quite animated, even—if Jack could believe such a thing were possible now—heated. There was a definite reddish cast to the king's features, and the queen's fine mouth was set in a hard firm line. For a moment the king looked directly at Jack, and their eyes met briefly. Then the king was smiling at something a courtier had said, the queen had risen from her place, and Jack was trying to remember how to breathe. He had seen something in the king's eyes and no mistake, and it certainly wasn't boredom. Jack shivered.

"Prepare yourself," Lady Devoted said.

"For what?"

"For the first skirmish. This is a war, remember?"

Jack didn't know what to say, nor did he really get a chance. He sensed rather than saw someone behind him, and he rose from his chair to find the Queen of Fairie standing behind him, smiling radiantly as the hidden music began again.

"My Lord Teaser, will you consent to dance with me?"

The dance was no stately pavanne this time; it was more like a *braisle* but not quite as energetic. There was time to talk. The Queen of Fairie seemed perfect in every way, and her conversation was no exception. Jack couldn't remember the last time his wit had been so clearly matched, except perhaps with Lady Devoted. She asked him riddles, and he felt fortunate to get one or two of the lot. She asked him to speak of himself, which was never very hard.

Soon others joined them in the moonlit glade that was

their feast hall and ballroom. The dance could have lasted for minutes, hours, or days; Jack didn't know or care. Almost the only thing that mattered was that the queen did not find him foolish, or clumsy, or slow-witted, or any of the things Jack felt he most certainly was in her presence. The "almost" came to mind whenever Jack happened to notice the king, standing with a group of his pale knights, looking at him. The king's hand had crept closer and closer to the pommel of his dagger until it rested there, and Jack was pretty sure he never took his eyes off him the entire time he danced with the man's Lady.

Finally it was Lady Devoted who interrupted. She appeared at the queen's side and made a graceful curtsey. "Your Majesty, the hour grows long. Perhaps our guest is fatigued."

Jack almost protested, despite the Fairie King's darkening mood, but a glance from Lady Devoted stopped him. He merely bowed low and took the queen's hand as she offered it, and again brushed the glove with his lips before Lady Devoted and several other attendants escorted the queen away.

Just before she left, Lady Devoted whispered in his ear in parting. "You will be afraid soon, Jack. Try not to show it."

She was gone before Jack had a chance to ask what she meant. Another moment and he didn't have to. The King of Fairie was at his elbow, smiling a smile like burning ice. "My knights and I are going on a hunt. Will you attend? I think you'll enjoy the sport, Lord Teaser."

Jack barely managed to keep his teeth from chattering. "If you insist, Your Majesty."

The chasm of his smile grew even wider. "Oh, I certainly do."

Jack had heard enough stories about the Wild Hunt to wonder if he himself—or his soul—might be the quarry, but the hunt was nothing so straightforward. They hunted no creature that Jack had ever seen, or imagined. It could have been a unicorn, or a pegasus, or something more snakelike than cloven-footed. Indeed, it seemed to be all those things, at one time or another.

The fays rode long-legged creatures with red eyes that might, at first glance, pass for horses. They carried barbed spears and blew curling horns that made the country echo with their blasts. Reynard gave a good enough account of himself as he carried his master over thickets and through thick woodland, now in sight of the quarry or other hunters, now in a forest so dark and still that Jack and his mount could well have been the only living creatures for leagues.

In time Jack noticed that, one by one, the other hunters turned back. Soon it was only Jack and the king. Jack wanted to turn back himself, but a small quiet voice inside told him that this was a very bad idea.

Jack caught up with the king at the crest of a wooded hill. He arrived just in time to see the rump of their prey—if indeed it was a rump—disappear into a narrow valley before them. He started after it, but the king did not. Jack drew rein beside the fairie lord.

"What manner of creature did we hunt, My Lord?"

"The same thing we always hunt, and have for a very long time," said the king. "Which is to say: I don't know."

Jack blinked. "Surely you could have caught up to it before now, whatever it is."

The king smiled grimly. "Then what would we hunt?" The smile went away. "I know why you are here, My Lord Teaser."

Jack studied the far rise as if it were the most interesting piece of earth he had ever seen. "Then you are most certainly wiser than I," Jack said.

"Look at me, Mortal."

Jack did as he was told, and immediately wondered if he had ever truly seen the fay king before that moment. The face was much the same as Jack remembered, though the horns had now sprouted into what was becoming an impressive set of antlers. No yearling now, but an almost-grown stag. Jack could almost hear the trumpeting of the fall rut as the king let out one gusty breath on the chill air, and watched it drift away like smoke.

"I am the king of no common domain, My Lord Teaser. I command folk the least of whom could make any mortal power quake in its boots. What I rule, I rule. What I claim as mine, is mine. Lady Devoted brought you as a guest, and such you are, but there is more to it as I think you know. Do not presume that guest protection means safe passage in all things. That would be a mistake."

Jack looked at the king's eyes. Time still nestled there, heavy as it did for all the fays, but there was something else, something that was not in the least bit weary. And it was getting stronger by the moment.

"I would not presume," Jack said, bowing slightly.

"You do," the king said, "and you will. It is always thus."

Then, as if he had been no more than the mist of breath he left behind, the Fairie King was gone.

Jack could not sleep.

He was weary beyond telling, but that seemed to work against him. Worse, when sleep did briefly touch him, his dreams were full of the face and image of the Fairie Queen; it was at once a sweet image and a nightmare, a font of reverence, desire, and fear. Sleep and the burden of her, imagined, was like a weight he could not hold for long. He came to himself again in his green bower, full awake.

At least, he *thought* he was awake.

So why did he still hear her laughter? Jack rose from his shadowed bed, dressed quickly. He slipped through the thicket; after years of running it was almost second nature. He emerged from the trees into the open meadow that had been their feast and revel hall, now a darkened expanse vaulted over with stars.

Jack wandered around. The tables were gone now; in the darkness Jack couldn't even find definite sign that they had *ever* been there.

Is this the dream now, or was the dream before?

For all Jack could tell, he had fallen asleep in the forest by the stream, and all that had happened since— the narrow escape from Sir Kevin, the transformation of Edyth, the visit to the Fairie realm—was just the imaginings of a guilty brain.

Jack knew better. He knew that someone was waiting

for him, someone very close. Nor was he wrong. She
stepped out of the trees across the meadow from where
he himself had emerged, and stood there, just outside
the dark wood. The Fairie Queen, veiled in gossamer
and crowned in starlight. She smiled at him, and his
knees shook. She held out her hand to him, and it was
not an invitation.

"Come."

Jack started toward her. He really didn't have any
choice. He was just a little past midway when he heard
a new voice.

"So. It happens."

The speaker sounded like Death itself given mouth
and tongue to speak. Even so, it took every ounce of
will that Jack possessed to turn his head far enough to
see who spoke.

The Fairie King stood at the far side of the meadow.
Jack almost didn't recognize him; he had a full set of
antlers like a rutting stag, and, if anything, his ears had
grown larger and more pointed. His eyes were as red
as an animal's reflected in torchlight, but there was no
torchlight. The king held two great white hounds at
leash, and they strained toward Jack, snarling.

Jack turned back, saw the Fairie Queen disappear into
the woods. Jack felt his life in the balance, but when he
ran it was toward the Fairie Queen, and not away from
anything. He sensed rather than saw when the king released the hounds. Not that it mattered; he couldn't run
any faster than he already was.

He got a glimpse of a figure in white, just ahead, and
ran toward it. It was the Fairie Queen, waiting for him.

"Your Majesty, the hounds—"

"I know. Seek the Fairie Queen, Jack. It's your only
chance."

He stared at her. "But you . . . ?"

She wasn't the Fairie Queen. Another moment and
she had changed enough that he could see who she was,
though by then he had already figured it out.

"Lady Devoted, you have just deceived and betrayed
me. Why should I trust you?"

"Because you're not the only one at risk here."

In a moment she changed again, and it was no woman

at all, but a gray doe standing before him, looking at him with familiar eyes. She raised one dainty hoof, indicated the way he should run. "I'll distract the hounds; the rest is up to you. Go!"

Jack heard the baying hounds, closer now. "What shall I tell her?"

"Nothing. She'll either save you, or she won't."

Jack heard a thrashing in the undergrowth and he turned and fled the way Lady Devoted had said. For a moment the hounds were so close he was certain he felt their hot breath at his back, then the sounds faded, their baying grew fainter as the fairie hounds followed new prey. Jack kept running.

Something else pursued Jack then. Something that ran like a human and yet was not much like a human at all. This time he did feel hot breath behind him, and a harsh, sensuous whisper at his ear.

"What shall we hunt now, Lord Teaser?"

Jack saved his breath for running. Now the Fairie King was more stag than man, now something like a will-o-wisp, now something very much like the beast they had hunted together earlier that evening. Always changing, but at heart the same, and all focused on him. Jack's foot caught on a log and he almost fell, but managed to catch himself on a sapling just long enough get his feet under him again.

Pointed tines raked his left shoulder and Jack almost fell from the blow. He staggered on. The second blow caught him in the thigh, and he stumbled.

"Now it ends."

Jack's motion carried him through one last thicket, into an open space diffused with white light. He sprawled headlong before a pair of dainty feet. He looked up, gasping, into the radiant face of the Fairie Queen.

"My Lord Teaser, to what do I owe the pleasure?"

She spoke the words, but she wasn't looking at him at all. The Fairie King stood just inside the bower, his chest heaving, his eyes glowing bright.

"He's mine," the king said. "You were together. I saw it. If you love him, he must die!"

The Fairie Queen did look at Jack now. She smiled

at him, but only for a moment. All her attention from then on was for the king alone. "I do not, My Lord."

Jack heard the words, and he heard the truth in them. He wanted to die. He thought, perhaps, if he stood up just then the Fairie King would grant his wish. He started to rise, when he felt a hand on his shoulder, restraining him.

"Follow me, if you want to live," Lady Devoted whispered. Jack didn't see where she had come from; he was pretty certain she had not been present a moment before.

"I don't want to live," Jack said. "She doesn't love me."

"She never did, and never would. Look."

Jack did look. He saw the king meet his queen halfway and, if anything was lacking in their embrace, it was not passion.

"Come."

Jack still wanted to die, but it was clear that the Fairie King had things on his mind besides murder now. Jack allowed himself to be hustled away, half running, half crawling, by Lady Devoted. Jack was pretty sure that neither the king nor the queen even bothered to notice.

Lady Devoted led Jack to where Reynard was settled for the night. The gelding took his rousting stoically enough. Lady Devoted stood by as Jack saddled and bridled him. He finally noticed the bandage on Lady Devoted's arm.

"You're hurt."

"I said you weren't the only one at risk. War, remember? No matter. We heal quickly. Far faster than you will, I fancy." She sighed. "We did use you ill, didn't we, Jack?"

" 'My Lord Teaser.' I should have guessed."

She shrugged. "Perhaps. The word has many meanings."

"One of which is to refer to the farm stallion that, though he is not allowed to mate, is the one who raises the passion of the mares."

"Or in this case, both stallion *and* mare." Lady Devoted shrugged. "A little novelty, a little jealousy . . . a little *reminder,* if you will, and the two Powers of our realm remain committed and in balance. When marriages last for millennia, and every day has the curse of immortal *sameness,* sometimes even love needs help. And they do love each other, Jack. Despite the occasional indiscretion."

"But I love her, too," Jack said softly. He stopped to loosen the saddle girth, which, in his anger, he had tightened a little too much. Reynard whinnied his gratitude. Jack sighed. "Well, it wasn't a very kind thing you did, but you did warn me. I'll take my leave now, if there's no objection."

"Sir Kevin is out there," Lady Devoted pointed out.

Jack almost smiled. "There was a time when that would have terrified me."

"So you still want to die?"

Jack thought about it for a moment, then sighed. "No. But with the Fairie King within and Sir Kevin without, how can I live?"

"Let me ride with you a bit. Perhaps I can think of an answer."

When they reached the border, the King and Queen of Fairie were waiting for them.

"One last betrayal, Lady Devoted?" Jack asked.

"As I am not in your service, I can hardly betray you," she said primly. "But, like so much here, this is not what it seems. Dismount."

Jack, seeing no other option, did as he was told. Lady Devoted walked beside him as they approached the royal couple. The king's expression would have done a statue proud, but the queen smiled at him. Jack thought of being out of sight of that smile for as long as he lived and remembered that he didn't want to live very long at all.

The queen turned to Lady Devoted, looking somewhat petulant. "Must I?"

"You did promise me, Your Majesty. And it is such a little thing."

The queen did not look happy, but she nodded. "Very well." she turned to Jack. "A parting gift, Lord Teaser."

The queen changed. It was like the first time Jack had

seen transformation in Lady Devoted, only the queen did not change into a different person. She was still the queen. She was still lovely past all understanding.

She was not however, perfection.

Jack saw the age in her eyes. He saw the faint tracings of veins under skin so delicate it seemed worn smooth, like stone. Jack realized that he was seeing her as she really was, and the goddess that he had loved because he had no choice was now only what she was and no more. The spell was broken. Jack's soul was his own again. He kissed the hand she offered and bowed low.

Now the king reached out and took her hand from him, holding it close. "That was my queen's gift. Mine is that I will not finish the hunt I began last night."

The queen smiled almost shyly. "My Lord, you already have. Or have you forgotten already?"

He smiled, too. "That," he said, "I have not."

Without another word the royal couple turned away, walking together off into the forest where they were joined by other members of their entourage. As they disappeared Jack heard one final time the soft chords of the hidden music.

"The king's anger seems to have passed. Could I remain here?" Jack asked.

"Certainly," Lady Devoted said. "And the next time you see Her Majesty, the Glamour will be in place and you will be hers again. She will make you love her and you will go to her, and sooner or later the king will catch you. In fact, I'd help him."

Jack wondered if that was a trace of jealousy in Lady Devoted's eyes. Jack sighed. "I'm a fool."

She smiled then. "I know. It's part of why I chose you."

"What was the other part? You never did answer me."

"Because you like women, Jack," she said frankly, "and that's rarer than you think. It was never conquest with you, no matter what the number. I knew you would look on my mistress and love her. Any man would desire her, but desire is fleeting and, in the fullness of time, meaningless." Lady Devoted smiled again, and it was the smile of a cat—all teeth. "But love? That's very dif-

ferent. Love is a proper threat. One that would rouse
the queen to ardor and the king to defend his rights.
That was what my test at the inn was all about. Now
let's be gone."

They reached the edge of the woods in no time at all.
Jack looked out into the sunshine, which seemed almost
impossibly bright compared to the twilight of fairie.

"You've received gifts from my Lord and Lady," Lady
Devoted said. "But I have a gift for you, too, Lord
Teaser. It waits for you beyond these woods. You will
know it when you find it. I hope you will use it wisely."

"Will I see you again?" he asked.

She smiled a bit sadly. "Do you want to?"

Jack thought about it. "Yes."

"Then the answer is no. You will never see me again.
And that's kinder than you can possibly imagine."

She raised a hand in farewell, and then Lady Devoted
was gone. Jack looked about for a bit, though he knew
he would not see her.

Sir Kevin be damned.

He rode out into the sunlight. There was no sign of
Sir Kevin either. It was a beautiful day. Running Jack
pointed Reynard back down the road he had come two
days before, but otherwise let Reynard set the pace.
There was no hurry.

No hurry at all, as it happened.

It wasn't until he reached Grosvenor Castle that he
discovered Lady Devoted's gift. The current Master of
Grosvenor was away, but the affable cook was more
than happy to tell of Sir Kevin.

"He's dead, young man. Killed on Crusade nearly fifteen years ago. He took the Cross five years after he'd
given up the search for the man called Running Jack.
He was never the same, after. Just between us two, I
think he sought his death in the Holy Land."

Jack was too human not to feel a great relief, even
with the slight regret that came with it. Sir Kevin had
deserved better but then, Jack reminded himself, so
had he.

Jack was surprised to find gold in his saddle pouch
when he got around to opening it later, but he knew the

gold was a mere token. The real gift was *time*. The King of the *Sidhe* may have spared Jack's life, but it was Lady Devoted who had really given his life back to him.

To truly honor this gift, I need to make the best use of it.

So he did. Jack used the gold to buy himself an inn, since he knew most of the tricks of avoiding payment and could prevent them. In time he found another woman to his liking and married, and had a family. He made mistakes enough, over the years, but unlike before they were mostly new ones. Which, Jack decided, was about as much wisdom as he could hope for.

As the years went by, Jack found his memory of the glorious Fairie Queen starting to fade. It was Lady Devoted's face that remained with him, her that he remembered best. If there was any meaning to that beyond a trick of memory, he never knew; but to Jack's everlasting relief and regret the Lady Devoted remained true to the only promise she ever made to him—he never saw her again.

Attention:

DAW Collectors

Many readers of DAW Books have written requesting information on early titles and book numbers to assist in the collection of DAW editions since the first of our titles appeared in April 1972.

We have prepared a list of all DAW titles, giving their authors, titles, reissue information, sequence numbers, original and current order numbers, and ISBN numbers.

If you would like a copy of this list, please write to the address below and enclose a check or money order for two dollars or the equivalent amount in stamps to cover the handling and postage costs. Never send cash through the mail.

DAW Books, Inc.
Dept. C
375 Hudson Street
New York, NY 10014-3658

Science Fiction Anthologies

☐ **FUTURE NET**   UE2723—$5.99
Martin H. Greenberg & Larry Segriff, editors

From a chat room romance gone awry . . . to an alien monitoring the Net as an
advance scout for interstellar invasion . . . to a grief-stricken man given the
chance to access life after death . . . here are sixteen original tales that you
must read before you venture online again, stories from such top visionaries as
Gregory Benford, Josepha Sherman, Mickey Zucker Reichert, Daniel Ransom,
Jody Lynn Nye, and Jane Lindskold.

☐ **FUTURE EARTHS: UNDER SOUTH AMERICAN SKIES**
Mike Resnick & Gardner Dozois, editors   UE2581—$4.99

From a plane crash that lands its passengers in a survival situation completely
alien to anything they've ever experienced, to a close encounter of the insect
kind, to a woman who has journeyed unimaginably far from home—here are
stories from the rich culture of South America, with its mysteriously vanished
ancient civilizations and magnificent artifacts, its modern-day contrasts between
sophisticated city dwellers and impoverished villagers.

☐ **SPACE OPERA**   UE2714—$5.99
Anne McCaffrey & Elizabeth Anne Scarborough, Editors

Welcome to an interstellar concert beyond your wildest imagining, as you rocket
to distant worlds in twenty original tales powered by the music of the galaxies
written by such modern-day maestros as Gene Wolfe, Peter Beagle, Anne
McCaffrey, Alan Dean Foster, Marion Zimmer Bradley, Elizabeth Ann Scarborough, and Charles de Lint.

☐ **SHERLOCK HOLMES IN ORBIT**   UE2636—$5.50
Mike Resnick & Martin H. Greenberg, editors
Authorized by Dame Jean Conan Doyle

Not even time can defeat the master sleuth in this intriguing anthology about
the most famous detective in the annals of literature. From confrontations with
Fu Manchu and Moriarty, to a commission Holmes undertakes for a vampire,
here are 26 new stories all of which remain true to the spirit and personality of
Sir Arthur Conan Doyle's most enduring creation.

Don't Miss These Exciting DAW Anthologies

FANTASY ANTHOLOGIES

☐ **ALIEN PREGNANT BY ELVIS**   UE2610—$4.99
   Esther M. Friesner & Martin H. Greenberg, editors

Imagination-grabbing tales that could have come straight out of the supermarket
tabloid headlines. It's all the "news" that's not fit to print!

☐ **ANCIENT ENCHANTRESSES**   UE2677—$5.50
   Kathleen M. Massie-Ferch, Martin H. Greenberg, & Richard Gilliam, editors

Here are timeless works about those most fascinating and dangerous women—
Ancient Enchantresses.

☐ **CASTLE FANTASTIC**   UE2686—$5.99
   John DeChancie & Martin H. Greenberg, editors

Fifteen of fantasy's finest lead us on some of the most unforgettable of castle
adventures.

☐ **HEAVEN SENT**   UE2656—$5.50
   Peter Crowther, editor

Enjoy eighteen unforgettable encounters with those guardians of the mortal
realm—the angels.

☐ **WARRIOR ENCHANTRESSES**   UE2690—$5.50
   Kathleen M. Massie-Ferch & Martin H. Greenberg, editors

Some of fantasy's top writers present stories of women gifted—for good or ill—
with powers of both sword and spell.

☐ **WEIRD TALES FROM SHAKESPEARE**   UE2605—$4.99
   Katharine Kerr & Martin H. Greenberg, editors

Consider this the alternate Shakespeare, and explore both the life and works of
the Bard himself.

IRENE RADFORD

THE DRAGON NIMBUS HISTORY